THE HANGING
OF
POLLY PRUITT

by

Nick Light

Light Partners Publishing

1 3 5 7 9 10 8 6 4 2

Copyright © Nicholas David Light 2021
Illustration copyright © Wil Harvey 2021

The moral right of Nicholas (Nick) Light to
be identified as the Author of this work has been asserted by him in
accordance with the Copyright, Designs, and Patents Act 1988

ISBN 978-1-5272-9506-3

3

For Sally and Anna
with love

…more than 50,000 convicted felons were forcibly shipped across the ocean and…played a significant role in performing needed work in colonial America…

Bound With An Iron Chain: Anthony Vaver

Prologue

Polly Pruitt, costermonger to Cheapside's poor, picks up her heavy basket and secures the cutting straps across her shoulders. It is dawn. The low sun, breaking across the fields of Islington, is still cold. Polly has exhausted her precious, meagre cache of coins buying leeks, cabbages, potatoes, carrots and a few speckled, shrivelled apples from the village farmers and now she must trudge back to the City and begin her trade for the day.

Polly thinks she is twelve or maybe thirteen, though her age is not a subject that occupies much space in her mind. She has never had a birthday party; in fact, she does not know the day nor date of her birth. She is small, though no smaller than any other twelve- or thirteen-year-old girl from a poor home in the labyrinth of Cheapside, but she is strong and, as she sees herself, brave, so it is with determination and spirit that she navigates the streets of her native town. She ignores the catcalls and whistles, smiling to herself as she goes, for she is happy to know the city boys think she is worth a whistle, though, having no brothers, she knows little about them and wants to know less.

Her mother, who loved Polly extravagantly, was affectionately calling her second daughter a hoyden by the time she was seven, but Mary Pruitt was killed by her ninth baby, a boy Polly's father failed to name. The innominate child went to the grave with his Ma and Polly grew up untended and loved only by Laura, her elder sister, in a house of bitter, half-starved, riotous daughters ruled by an abusive drunk. It was living under the violent reign of Joseph Pruitt, without the protection of her mother, that knocked the hoyden out of Polly,

8

but she has escaped now, escaped these last two years, to live with her aunt Susan and, though she may not be the boisterous, noisy, sometimes fractious little girl she was, she is, once again, a creature filled with the vital spark of life and, under her quiet aunt's stoical guidance, she has built back her self-confidence.

So now, she walks the ways of the City, knowing it so well she hardly notices its colourations anymore. All of London's character is mere background staging to Polly as she makes her way to her customers, hoping she will sell her whole basketful this slowly warming, mid-autumn morning. Polly Pruitt, London girl, born, bred, and fully educated in street lore.

She has heard the new King is a German, though Polly hardly knows what that means. What she does know is he is not from London and he is called George. The gossip on the street is that he is to be crowned at the Abbey in Westminster town. She wonders as she walks, avoiding the piles of horse dung and deeper puddles from the overnight rain if there will be a parade or procession as some are saying. Will she be able to look upon this god-like being?

Word is the King has only been in the City a week, delayed after Queen Anne died by the contrary weather of the late summer, so maybe even he doesn't know yet about processions or parades or cavalcades. In truth, Polly doesn't really care. There's not much she knows about the Quality, only that they don't buy her stock or cross her path much, only that they don't live in her narrow part of Cheapside, only that they do not want for money and food like she and aunt Susan so often do.

There's a shout from behind her and she turns at the sound of her name. It's one of the shit-pickers filling his bucket with horse manure. She knows the boy and doesn't like him, though she knows he likes her. He whistles through gapped teeth and barks a vulgar compliment on her newly emerging womanly shape. Polly puts on her best pout, flicks her long black hair off her face, and walks on as tall and straight as she can.

She has not gone twenty steps when she spies a small leather purse lying half-buried in a pile of horse shit. Pulling it out and hurrying into a sunless alley, she finds five coins inside, a farthing, a penny, a sixpence, and two shillings. Throwing the soiled purse down, she pockets the coins, but senses she is being watched. She looks around. Standing at the entrance to the alley is a girl she thinks of as a friend, Agnes, who is a little older than her.

"What'cha got there, Poll?" asks Agnes.

"Nothing."

"Come on, Poll, I saw ya pick summat up."

"Just some old thing."

They walk on together and Polly is aware of Agnes's eyes on her. She does not look at the girl, so she does not see the gleam in her eyes. Polly takes her treasure home and hides it. She has plans for the money. Every day she gives her aunt all her takings to help towards paying the rent and feeding them. Now she has some money to spend on herself and she means to keep it, though she makes a silent promise to buy her aunt a pretty posy.

The money stays hidden, time passes and May Fair has come. Polly is with her friend Agnes and means to spend some of her fortune today. The streets are choked with people. Every hawker, tinker, broadsheet seller, pieman, balladeer, juggler, and entertainer is out and the atmosphere is tense with excitement. As the girls stroll, arm in arm, Polly spots an older boy, Agnes's brother, John. She knows him a little, though, being older, he does not mix with the younger street kids. He grins as he approaches and holds something up. It sparkles in the weak sunlight.

"Here y'are, chick," he says and laughs.

Agnes squeals with delight and takes the present. It is a bracelet of coloured glass beads. Agnes slips it on her wrist and Polly instantly covets it. Seeing her friend looking at it, Agnes asks Polly if she would like to try it on. Once it is on her wrist, Polly knows she has to have it. It is the only fine thing she has ever worn.

"I'll give you tuppence for it…"

"Tuppence!" shouts John and laughs again. "You'll need more'n that, chick. But hark, there's more where that comes from. I might be able to get'cha one."

Agnes, seeing how much her friend likes the bauble and, hurtfully, not trusting that she will not run off with it, has already taken the bracelet back and Polly's wrist feels naked without it.

"Do you think you could, John?"

"Might," says the boy with a sneer, "but I've a mind you ain't got the money."

"I have too," says Polly with conviction.

"Show us yer coin then, chick."

Polly digs in her pocket and proudly presents the handful of coins. With a grunt, John grabs the money as Agnes barges Polly sideways into the street, almost under the wheels of a passing carriage. By the time she gets back to her feet, they are gone; she has not even cried out for help. Her hands are covered in the muck of the street and her only good dress is stained and disheveled. She stands for a long time

11

staring in the direction they ran. All of London, it seems, surrounds her, closing in like the ranks of an advancing army; the teeming humanity, the sounds, the smells, the sights and marvels of the street entertainers, but she is dead to it all.

At last, she wipes her wet cheeks dry, smearing dirt on her face. She moves to sit on a milestone and spends the next hour watching the world go by her. Nothing has changed, she tells herself, it's the same old London, the same old sights, sounds and smells, the same deceitful boys. She had money for a while and now it is gone. It ain't the end of the world, she thinks, but I am Polly Pruitt and I will never be cheated again. I am Polly Pruitt and I will not ever let a man take me in again. I am Polly Pruitt and I will *do well*.

Who knows, she might be right…anything can happen in London.

Chapter 1

In Which We Meet Mr. Louis Silston and Miss Abigail Eleanor
Charlotte Colliton

I am pretty. I knew it years ago from the attentions of the wolfish
boys when I was on London's streets and, though I am no dasher, I
am no one's fool neither. George told me he liked my looks enough
times before he was thrown on the street without so much as a by-
your-leave for answering back Mrs. Colliton, the beef-head. I see
myself in the mistress's looking glass most evenings when I lay out
her bedclothes, though I linger not long on that image for my aunt
Susan taught me to be modest in the eyes of our Lord. And I see Mr.
Louis looking at me when he thinks I don't notice. I swear I don't
like that one. He thinks he's God's gift to women because his daddy's
a nob, but I think him sharp-faced and too hungry. I pity my poor
mistress.

'Tis six years since I came to this house. I knew not a jot about
how the Quality lived 'til my aunt Susan's daughter, Liza, a scullery
maid in this house, got me a job here as maid-of-all-work. Thirteen I
was then and did my hard labour on my knees many a day 'til I'd
earned the household's trust. So, when Miss Abigail came of an age
and needed a maid of her own, 'twas me that got the job and my life
has been good since, saving the day my aunt wrote to tell of my sister
Laura's death. Fell from a window, she said. More like thrown from a
window by my Pa in a drunken snit. He ever was an evil man. So, I
have lost the one person in this world who loved me and looked out

for me, though I have Miss Abigail now and she treats me well and, I think, I am her friend.

There's only two years between us, but we couldn't be more different. She's never known anything, but the family estate here in Surrey. Had her own maid, her own horse, a whole bedchamber all to herself, and almost anything she might wish for. I was born in Pissing Lane not far north from Old Man Thames, at Blackfriars. When I think of my poor mother, dead before her time and my drunken brute of a dad, it's like it was another life. Leaving home and living with aunt Susan was the saving of me, though I can't say the same about my six sisters. But she's seen me right, has my mistress. Mr. Colliton thinks his daughter should have learning so Abigail's had her own tutor for years, poor pale Mr. Owen, and she's taught me my letters and numbers and passed on the learning she's got from her lessons. She never liked my 'London jabber', as she styled it, so she's taught me how to speak and write the King's English, is what she says.

It's deep winter and February has come, colder than January, and I am lighting Miss Abigail's fire in the dark every morning. Sir Crisp Silston and his son Louis are in the house. If the master gets his way, Mr. Louis will be my mistress's intended and I do not feel right about that. There is something in that man's eyes that takes me back to my father, gives me the shivers.

I've done for my mistress and seen her to bed, finished my little chores for tomorrow morning and my work should be done, but Mary is sick and in her bed so I have to finish my day doing for her. I am in Mr. Louis's room banking his fire when I hear a voice behind me. I never heard the door open, so I jump and catch my hand on the fire irons, which rattle enough to rouse a corpse.

"Miss Abigail's maid, is it not?" says he. His voice is soft.

I stand and give him a little bob. When I look up, I see a smile on his face. He is a handsome cove, that I have to admit, but this smile is playing at his lips and has left his eyes quite out of the game.

"Yes, sir," says I.

In one step he is facing me, staring at me so that I lower my gaze to the floorboards.

"Your hand is bleeding," says he.

"'Tis nothing, sir," I tell him. He steps closer and takes my fingers, gentle like. He gets out a kerchief.

"No, sir, do not stain it," says I, but he's already laid it on my hand and sopped the blood. There is something new in his eyes as if my blood has lit a fire in him. Inside me, my belly twitches and flicks.

"Well now, what a pretty little thing you are. I had not noticed."

Liar. I've seen him notice enough times.

"Tell me your name, Miss Abigail's maid," says he. His voice has changed, no longer light.

"Polly Pruitt, sir."

I did not think to be scared by this arrogant man, but the flutter in my belly has turned awful heavy. Now his face changes, like a sudden summer storm a'coming. He pulls my hand, rough like, to his mouth and sucks at my wound. His eyes narrow and his cheeks crease up in a leer then he grabs me by my shoulders, turns me, and pushes me to the wall, pressing against me.

"Well, my little chick," his brandy breath on my face. "I know what you want. I've seen you watching me when you think your mistress ain't looking."

"No, sir!" says I, not too loud for I know better than to make a fuss, but I'm not having him frighten me.

I turn my head and bring my hands to his chest to try and push him away. He is strong and presses harder and pushes a hand between my legs.

"No!"

It's a sort of grunt that escapes my lips. I'm still pushing, but it does no good.

"Oh, don't play coy with me, girl. I know you sluts all want a man of quality."

I struggle, try and kick out, but he grabs my wrist and forces my arm up my back. The pain is horrible and I think to lose my supper. He brings his mouth to my ear and whispers.

"Not a sound, bitch, or you'll never work in service again. I will ruin you."

He pulls me around and throws me to the floor. I scramble, trying to rise. He kicks me in the belly and knocks the breath out of me. While I gasp for air, he stands over me and unbuttons his breeches.

"I say again, Polly Pruitt, not a sound or, I swear, you will be on the streets begging for the rest of your miserable life."

It only lasts a few quick minutes, but it hurts me so. His hand is pressed hard over my mouth to stop my cries. I keep my eyes closed, trying to think of anything but what is happening to me. The pain as he presses into me is too strong though, so my poor head is filled with his body and his face and his hands upon me and him pushing into me and his foul, hot breath on my cheek.

When it is done and he stands to right his clothing and I am throbbing in my most private place, it is the humiliation that I feel, the loss of my rights over myself in such violent circumstances that makes me weep. I know I will never be the same. When he is dressed, he leans over me and curses me, vile words the like of which I ain't heard since being with my father.

"Don't forget my words, draggle-tail. One word from me in any ear and you will never work again. The streets will be your home. Now, get out and be happy you've known a gentleman, for it is the only time you ever will, I'll wager."

I stumble to the door and think to myself, here is another man I will hate until my dying day and I know, in my heart, I can never tell anyone, not even my poor mistress.

*

It is a cold March night and I am laying out mistress's nightclothes when she bursts into the room like a wild thing. I can tell she must have run the full length of the stairs and hall for she is all red in the face and panting like the master's horse after a gallop. She runs across the bedchamber, near knocking me out of the way, and throws herself full on her bed, burying her face in the nightdress I have just laid there and beating her fists against the coverlet in rage.

I stand still, knowing Abigail well enough now not to do anything to make this tantrum worse. She is fair and kind when happy, but fierce and difficult when riled. I hold my peace and, though we can be close betimes, I have found myself on the wrong end of her scoldings. After a minute or more, she rolls over, growls at the canopy, and sits up.

"Oh, it is impossible, just impossible!" she cries.

Her voice is strangled with her rage, but I see sadness as well as anger in her face. It's like I'm not there, or I may as well not be, but I'm well used to that. I wait, take a step backwards, and join my hands in front of me. Now she looks direct at me.

"He will not be moved, Poll!" says she. "He won't be moved!"

"Who, mistress?" I ask in my best and quietest voice.

"My father, of course, fool!"

"Is this about Mr. Louis, mistress?"

"Yes, yes, it's about *Mister* Louis."

She looks up at me and I see the rage again, the rage and the hurt. But then, just as she looks away, for a moment, I see the little girl in her, the desperate, worried, frightened little girl and it breaks my heart. I want to take her in my arms, hold her close, kiss her lovely cheek for I know what Mr. Louis is. I waited long enough after that night for my blood to come in, waited in terror that I would be found with child and thrown out. Waited, too, to see if that devil had given me a dose of the flapdragon, but of that, too, I seem free thanks be to Christ. So now, I look at her sweet face, all sadness, and fury and it nips me deep.

She's calmer now, but still, she strides to the window and glares out over the gardens. I'd never known gardens afore I came here. In my time in this great house, I've learned about the little hedges in their neat squares, rose beds, lawns, and bushes, clipped and tended. From where I stand, I can see Billings, the under-gardener, busy on

18

his knees at the corner of a run of hedging. Albert Billings has been my teacher when it comes to gardens.

Now Abigail marches back and slumps down on the chair in front of her night table. Such a beautiful chair; French she says it is.

"I will not marry Louis Silston, Polly, I will not. Just because Sir Crisp is father's oldest friend, I don't see why I must marry his odious son. I'm seventeen, for heaven's sake, and I want to choose my own husband. Don't you think that only right?"

"Of course, mistress," says I.

On the night table, she has her tortoiseshell hairbrush and hand mirror, basin, jug, powder, rouge, hairpins in a pretty ceramic bowl. She's picked up her hairbrush and she's turning it over and over, staring at it.

I look at her back, shoulders rising and falling as she gets her breath and calms herself, and I think how lucky I am to have a mistress I love. I look at her long golden hair and, all over again, can't believe she's her Ma and Pa's daughter. Mr. and Mrs. Colliton, very grand they are, are both dark of hair, as are the mistress's two older brothers, Arthur and Charles. I'm woke from my dreaming when the mistress bangs her hairbrush on the night table and stands up. She stamps her foot hard. It is not over yet, I see.

"It's just so unfair. I wish to see something of the world before I am married off and settled in boring seclusion. I have heard my father speak of the exploits of the Company and it all sounds so exciting; India, the Orient, plying the world's oceans. Some days I wish I had been born a boy."

"I wouldn't want to be born a man, miss," says I, low and mean, like. "They can be cruel and hard and I would not want to think of myself like that."

I want so much to tell her what Silston has done to me in this very house, yet I hold my tongue for I am not ready to share my shame and maybe never will be.

"Oh, but many are good and kind, Polly. You only have to look at my brothers to know that and, although Papa can be severe, he has a soft heart. But Louis Silston, I suspect he is not kind, he is so arrogant. Oh, Polly, what can I do?"

She throws herself back on the bed, lying staring at the canopy. I have to smile; I am so fond of her. She can be flighty, but she's got spirit and intelligence and she's been good to me. She tells me I'm her friend and, when she is low, she hugs me close and I love that. She is so soft and smells so good. I know her mother would surely disapprove if only she knew what secrets her daughter tells me.

"If Charlie were here, I could talk to him," says she. "I cannot speak to mother; she is father's dupe, a mouse. She would only repeat what he says and father is implacable. When I marry, Polly, I wish to choose the man myself and he will be like Charlie or Arthur, a good man, a Christian man who will respect me and be a friend, not just a husband. And I want to wait, Poll, I want to live before I marry, see something of the world. Why I never even saw London in my life! But father will not be moved. It is as if he's had enough of me and wishes me gone."

"Oh, I'm sure not, mistress," says I.

I am close to the bed now and take her hand in mine. It is dry and warm, soft as a baby's cheek.

"If only you knew, Polly. I am the family nuisance. Arthur is father's favourite; 'such a good marriage' he says, pleased that Arthur has Elizabeth's money. And already they have given father a grandson to continue the Colliton name. They are the golden couple. And Charles is a captain already in the Horse Guards. If only he were here, Charlie would understand."

"Will Mr. Charles be home soon, mistress?" I ask her, for I like Charles and can see how he might help his sister, for he seems truly fond of her. A well-favoured buck, he is, full of life, always smiling, with a mischievous gleam in his eye.

"His regiment is away somewhere, I know not. Anyway, I need him now. What should I do? I cannot marry Louis Silston. He is a boor and a prig and I hate him!"

Chapter 2

In Which William Staples is Ambushed And Mr. James Corbett
Attorney at Law Holds Out the Hand of Friendship

William Staples had been on the road for several days. Today, a fine,
crisp day for walking, he had made good miles and he had enjoyed
the sights along the way and the encounters with locals in the villages
he passed through. The early spring had been kind to him. Since
leaving his home village of Harsham in Buckinghamshire the weather
had been fine and clear; cold at night, though not frosty, and warm
during the days.

The sun was making her slow way down toward the horizon
splashing the sky with paint box colours. The leafless trees to the
west were silhouetted against the darkening sky, the lush fields of
cabbages and other winter greens on either side of the road gradually
sank into shadow. Will noticed the air was laced with a smell he did
not recognize; a smoky, reeking stink. An old woman he had met
three hours earlier had told him the city was only eleven miles away
and that he would smell it before he saw it. He had not believed her.
Now, however, his nostrils twitching, he wondered if she had been
telling the truth and he felt a thrill of excitement. Tomorrow he
would be in London.

Apart from the crone, Will had met few people that afternoon,
but now, ahead, two dark shapes appeared out of the dimness of the
fading daylight and gathering evening mist. In the distance Will could
see flickering lights, fires silhouetting the shapes. The young man had

known good cheer and charity from many people on his walk to London, but these two put a cold hand around his heart.

He slowed down, feeling in his bag for the stout cudgel that, until now, he had not needed. One of the shapes, slowly congealing into the harder-edged form of a man, raised his hand. In greeting? A warning? A threat? Will stopped. Night was coming and the air had quickly become cold. He shivered as the two men approached. His heartbeats clipped up a step. He thought to call out, but his voice caught in his throat. Who would he call to his aid? He was alone.

They came on until he could see them clearly. They were moving apart as they came closer and that alone convinced him that these were footpads. People he had met along the way had warned him about such road agents. He knew, in his heart, that they meant to have his bag and few coins. He also knew that, if he fought them, they might kill him. He had been told that these road agents had been known to murder for less than he was carrying. He pulled the club from his bag and let his arm drop, feeling its comforting weight in his hand.

They were close now. The one on Will's right was as tall as he, nearly six feet, gangling, with big hands and feet, a mess of dark hair and a patchy beard. Will could see no weapon. The second, moving out to Will's left was squat and square, broad shoulders atop a fat gut, heavy arms, and hairy hands. He had a leering grin on his filthy face and his lank hair almost hid his small, animal eyes that glittered in the last light of the day.

Will felt a strange mix of emotions. His heart had him ready for battle, beating like a drum, but he didn't feel any fear. It had been like that for years. Regular beatings from his father when he was drunk had driven the fear of violence from him at a young age, toughened him up. He dropped his bag to the ground and took off his hat, letting it fall on top of the canvas pack that contained all his worldly belongings. He gripped the club like his father had taught him, hard and strong. *I have come so far,* he told himself, *walking day after day from my home. I ain't giving up what's mine, even if these two brigands take my life. I'll make them pay dearly for what they mean to steal.*

Lanky was circling slowly. He came no nearer, but he kept his eyes fixed on Will. His mate, ambling and bear-like, made a low noise, a grunt as he came to a stop four steps from Will. Lanky stopped too and Will raised the cudgel, his head swiveling from right to left, left to right. No one spoke. Lanky broke into a grin and slipped a bony hand inside his long greasy coat. When it reappeared, it was gripping a long-bladed knife. Will glanced to his left. Bear-man was holding a shaft of dark wood, ebony, the carpenter in Will surmised, but then he shook the thought away. *What does it matter what wood they use to kill me?*

Every sinew and muscle in his body was braced, ready. He crouched lower. He had already decided he would spring at the first man to move, swipe at his head, and hope to lay him low with one quick smack. He thought of his father, crushed in the sawpit; such a useless death. He vowed silently that his own death would not be without retribution. Someone else would be coming to the after-world with him.

Bear-man laughed, a low gurgling noise that sounded more like a death rattle than a chuckle. Will's eyes were still flicking from one man to the other. Bear-man stamped his foot and laughed again. Will thought the fellow was about to speak, but he kept his silence. Will smacked his cudgel against the palm of his hand.

Time had stopped. Bear-man was edging forward. Will glanced back at Lanky and he too was closing on him. Both thieves were moving slowly as if in a dream, both with their eyes fixed on Will's trusty staff. He swung it about his head. It made a sound like the wind rustling the leaves in Baggot's Wood, behind the old cottage where he had spent his first twenty years. He calmed his breathing. He was ready.

Lanky stopped, stood up straight, and tilted his head at an alien noise. Will heard it too, a sound from behind him. The gangly man looked at his partner and nodded. With a harsh cry and a long stride, he stepped into Will. He heard another grunt from Bear-man, but swung his staff at Lanky's head as the man lashed out with his knife. Lanky faltered, but was too slow. The tip of Will's staff caught his cheek with the dull crunch of breaking bone. Will started to turn to the other, but was stunned by a heavy blow that landed on his shoulders. He half-turned as Bear-man brought his club round for another blow. Pain shot up through his neck to his head, but he managed to stagger away and the weapon flashed harmlessly past his face. He thrust his staff viciously at Bear-man who jumped backwards.

Will risked a look at Lanky. The thief was on one knee, his left hand swaddling his face, his right holding the knife outwards. Will heard a grunt and turned just in time to dodge a heavy blow from Bear man's cudgel. The footpad staggered with the force of the swing. Will stepped forward and, with all his strength, thrust his club into the man's face. He felt bone splinter and blood gushed from

Bear man's nose. The fellow roared and spun away, his free hand to his face.

Lanky, his cheekbone shattered, was back on his feet and filled with rage. He had moved behind Will and now he swung his dagger in a wide arc at the young carpenter. Will was turning when his jacket sleeve took the brunt of the thrust. The blade slashed through the loose fabric at his wrist, missing his skin by a hair's breadth. With a hiss of fury, Lanky withdrew the blade and raised it to finish Will when there came a cry.

"Hold hard!"

He heard footsteps and looked to see Bear-man running away. Lanky was growling, a guttural, animal sound, and looking at something behind Will. With a curse, the man spun around and, following his mate, stumbled away into the night. Will was panting from his exertions, but, even so, he could hear, as the sounds of the fleeing thieves receded, another's breathing behind him. He lifted his club to head height and turned slowly to see a man astride a black horse, a pistol in his hand.

Will could not see the rider's face. Dark habit, dark cloak pulled up high, dark cocked hat, black horse, and all half-hidden by the encroaching darkness. He could see the pistol though, some part of its structure glinting in what light was left, and it was still pointing at him. Will had heard stories of highwaymen, how they were more treacherous, more violent, quicker to take a life even than footpads.

All was silent. The adrenalin thrill of Will's encounter with the two thugs was subsiding, but he was determined not to speak first. He waited, watching the man, watching the gun. He stood his ground, holding his club high. The horse twitched, stepped forward and then back again. It was as if a spell had been broken.

"Come, lad," said the horseman. His voice was cultured and low. He chuckled and lowered his gun. "I mean you no harm. I am not like those two rogues."

Will kept his silence and didn't move.

"Oh, come along, fellow."

The horseman slid his pistol into its leather holster and swung his leg over the saddle, sliding nimbly to the ground. Slipping the reins over his arm he took a step towards Will, his right hand extended in friendship.

"James Corbett, lawyer in chambers at Lincoln's Inn, London. And you are?"

Now that Will could see the rider properly, he found that he liked the man's face. There was a smile on his lips and his eyes. Will thought they looked friendly eyes, crinkled at the edges with humour. He lowered the cudgel and put it in his sack so that he could shake hands.

"Thank you, sir," he said, "for chasing off those thieves."

"You're welcome, young sir, but you have yet to declare yourself. Your name?"

"I am William Staples, sir."

"Well, William Staples, you are going to London, I suppose?"

"Yes, sir."

"You and thousands of others, it seems. Well, now…tell me your story while we walk."

"My story, sir?"

"Where you're from, lad; mother, father, your history. Spare me nothing."

Will started his story with the night in the depths of the winter of 1699 when his mother, Amy had given birth to him while his father, Jasper lay dead drunk on the floor of the village pub. Amy, he said, had brought him up for more than village life. She had taught him to read and write, to think for himself, to be curious, critical. He had not been an especially adept student, he said chuckling, but he was eager and hardworking and enjoyed reading the bible with his mother every evening.

"I was still a sprat, sir," said Will as they walked on together, "when I started to wonder why my mother, the youngest sister of the local squire, had married my useless father. I guess it must have been love, though I never saw how."

At fourteen, he had been apprenticed to the carpenter Walter Riddlecote, his father's employer. He had been learning his trade for barely a year when his beloved mother died in the winter of 1714. Father and son had lived on together in mutual hatred for another two years until Jasper himself succumbed in a ridiculous accident; crushed by a massive tree trunk at the bottom of the sawpit when he had been too inebriated to dodge the weighty butt as it slipped and fell. The senseless death had been an ongoing source of shame to the young man, but he had felt a sense of relief and freedom since the day Jasper was buried in the pauper's plot at the churchyard.

"After my dad died, I continued my apprenticeship with Mr. Riddelcote, but, before three years were out, I knew I had to leave Harsham and make my own way in the world. And so, here I am, sir."

"A sad history," said Corbett when Will fell silent. "I am full sorry for your mother's death, lad. I can see it hurt you deeply. But come now let's speak of happier things. You go to London and make your fortune, eh?"

"I don't know about fortune, sir, but I'd be glad of honest work."

"And you're a carpenter, eh? Any good?"

Will grinned, relaxing at last. He was good and he knew it. Old Walter had told him so enough times. The old carpenter would tell anyone that "the boy's as sharp as me best chisel. Thank the good Christ he takes after his Ma and not his good-for-nothing Pa."

"Yes, sir. I'd say so."

"You'd say so?" Corbett laughed. "Well, I like a man who knows his worth, William Staples. Look, I am riding back to Lincoln's Inn tonight, why don't we travel together? Much safer that way, don't you think?"

"I ain't afeared, Mr. Corbett."

He laughed again, his head cocked back.

"No, I can see that, William, though I would tell you, sir, that though courage is a fine thing, a little fear keeps a man on his mettle, especially in a city like London."

"I learned to kill my fear long ago, sir," muttered Will.

Will looked again into the stranger's eyes. Walter Riddlecote used to tell him that the eyes will always tell you if a man is good or bad. He thought he could see that this man was good and, so agreed to the lawyer's suggestion. Mr. Corbett strapped Will's bag to his saddle and they continued on together, on through the gathering darkness.

It was not long before they came to the fires that Will had seen in the distance. Someone had set piles of rubbish to burn. The smoke combined with the mist to make a thick smog, which stung their noses and clawed at the backs of their throats. Minutes later they had passed the fires, coughing to clear the smoke from their lungs. Their noses were still twitching from the smoke when Will's keen senses recognised a new smell; the stench of rot and mould mixed with the sickly-sweet stink of pigs. Mr. Corbett told him, with another laugh, that he must "sniff some very fine odours before you come to London town."

They walked on in silence for perhaps an hour until Will spotted a long, low cottage and beside it, a brick kiln, its smoke rising into the night sky. A deadly weariness suddenly overcame him and he knew he could not walk another step that night. He thanked his new friend for his kind help.

"I will rest here the night, sir, if the brickyard owner will let me sleep by the warmth of his kiln."

The lawyer shook his hand and wished him well before mounting his horse.

"You are close now, Will Staples," he said. "You will walk through the villages of Hammersmith and Kensington and across the fields of Hyde Park and, be prepared, you must needs pay the toll to enter the town of Westminster and again London herself. Do you have coin?"

"Aye, sir, thankee," said Will briskly. He was proud of the savings he had made and carried in his bag along with his few tools, clothes, and trusty staff.

"Well then, good for you. Come to my chambers, lad. Find me at Lincoln's Inn, ask for lawyer Corbett, I am well-known to most in that place, and I will give you the name and address of a carpenter, a good man known to me for some years. It may be that he has need of an apprentice or, if not, he may know of another carpenter who can offer work."

Will was struck once again by the kindness of this stranger and thanked the lawyer profusely. He watched as man and horse disappeared into the night, waiting until he could no longer see them, and then he walked to the cottage to beg the favour of a warm night's sleep.

Chapter 3

In Which Polly Eavesdrops and Abigail Makes a Plan

Louis Silston was the youngest of five children. Three of his four sisters had doted on him from the day he was born. His oldest sister, Hermione, had been different. Whether through jealousy at his instant position as their mother's favourite or through some sixth sense that the boy was inherently a bad lot she had never taken to him as her younger sisters had.

They had babied the boy until he was in his early teens, by which time Hermione had been married off. Once her more critical influence had been removed from the house, Louis had flourished as the centre of attention. He had been the bane of his tutor's life; avoiding lessons, insolent, refusing to do any work on his own, playing pranks on the poor man.

In 1711, when Louis was seventeen, Sir Crisp arranged a commission in the Dragoons for Louis was, if nothing else, a good horseman. His father had seen the writing on the wall. Louis was already dissolute, spoiled, and lazy. If he was to be saved, Sir Crisp had thought, then the army was the place to do it. Louis left the cossetted environment of home and found himself in the harsh, judgmental arena of Queen Anne's army. Far from wallowing in self-pity or shrivelling in the man's world of Her Majesty's Royal Dragoons, Louis had quickly taken to army life. The raucous fun of the officer's mess, the weaponry, the gorgeous dress uniform, the fine horses, all of these appealed to his personal sense of self-worth and natural arrogance.

He also made a good friend in Reynolds Garland, who, in character if not in looks, was almost a carbon copy of Louis; hard, arrogant, self-opinionated, and greedy. He did not come from the same money as Louis, but Reynolds was nothing if not ambitious. The two gambled at cards at the Crown & Rolls, Chancery Lane, and, a favourite haunt, The Queen's Arms, St Paul's Churchyard. They drank coffee, wine, and sack at the best coffee houses in Covent Garden and Charing Cross where they hatched their plans for the future. When Reynolds disclosed his idea to take his small inheritance and invest in land in Virginia and become a tobacco planter, Louis's excitement was palpable.

"By, God, brother, I would go with you if I did not owe my father my time. You know well fine how my father despises me. Nothing I do is good enough for him, but I will stake you, friend, and buy from you a share in the adventure."

And so, the two friends sealed their pact to get Reynolds to Virginia and build an empire of land and tobacco production in the colony.

Louis left the army in the summer of 1715, disappointed later in the year to have missed the battle at Preston, when the Jacobites rose up. His friend, Garland had left the service two years earlier with his bequest and Louis investment to purchase his plantation in the American colonies. It had been a difficult parting for the two friends, but Louis had pledged to visit in the future to see how his investment was faring and to enjoy Garland's company once again. By the time he left the dragoons, Louis was a hardened version of his boyhood self. His hubris was granite and his self-importance was adamant.

Aged twenty-two, after a year of indolence, his father found a place for Louis in his business. Sir Crisp Silston had inherited his title, the family home in Bedfordshire, and massive debts from his profligate father. The family estate returned a good profit, but it was not enough to staunch the financial wounds of his degenerate father. Unlike Louis's grandfather, Sir Crisp was a good businessman and had seen, early on, the opportunity afforded by the incipient trade in human cargo between the west coast of Africa and the British Caribbean. Taking a loan, he had invested in his first ship in the time of Charles II. By 1700, not only had he left any debt far behind, but he owned two more slave ships and a large estate in Jamaica that produced a healthy percentage of the sugar imported into England.

So it was that, in 1716, Louis began to learn the dark and labyrinthine details of the slave and sugar trades. As with the dragoons, the young man took to the business as if born to it. He may have done well, such was his aptitude and quickness to learn, but, even though Garland was long gone, he had other dissolute friends to drag him away from the business and turn his head towards his true passions of gambling and drinking.

On a bright spring morning, four years after joining the business and six months after Sir Crisp had started his campaign to marry his son to his friend Vicimeous's daughter, Louis, and his father were sitting in the grand drawing room of the Colliton's house in Surrey. They had been settled there after arriving from London, earlier than expected for a weekend stay. The Colliton's house steward had made apologies for his master and mistress. Mr. Colliton, he said, was still out on estate business, expected home imminently and Mrs. Colliton was abed suffering a crippling headache. The steward saw his guests comfortably seated and supplied with glasses of Madeira before giving a bow and leaving to notify Miss Abigail.

Once the door was closed, Sir Crisp turned on his son. The trip from London, having been bumpy and more than usually uncomfortable as the jarvey strove to navigate the winter-battered roads and lanes, had put the old man in a foul mood. Now he returned to the diatribe he had had to postpone on arriving at the Colliton's house.

"I tell you, boy, I will no longer suffer your lassitude and insolence. The gambling is bad enough, but I could stomach that if you'd only apply yourself to the business. Christ's blood, man, you have the knowledge, you have the ability, why can't you see the opportunity before you. When I am dead, you'll be on your own. I fear to think how you will destroy all I have built. Why, I am minded to put you on a ship, send you to Jamaica, and have you labour on the estate there. Maybe that would bring you to your senses!"

Louis Silston, his face serious, took a sip from his glass and nodded.

"I would not shy from that challenge, father, and once I have served my time in Jamaica, I could travel on to Virginia to see what Reynolds Garland has done with my money…"

"Our money, boy!"

"…but do you not think," Louis continued, ignoring his father's interjection, "we should apply ourselves at this moment to the wooing of Miss Abigail? Surely, that is our priority?"

"Do not preach to me, sir, about priorities. A fine thing from a man whose own priorities seem to be losing money at the cards and getting drunk. As to checking on your investment with Garland, 'tis the first right thing you have said since we left London. Garland has a lot of your money, family money I would remind you, in his trust."

"As to trust father, I would put my life in Reynolds' hands and, I remind you, sir, his letters glow with success in the tobacco." Louis, who had perfected the playing of his father over many years, could see that the old man's anger was abating. One more act of mollification should do it. "You're right, sir, I should make the voyage and I will, you have my word. As to your own priorities, father, should we return to the task at hand?"

"Yes, yes, very good," spluttered Sir Crisp, defused and deflated. "Let us turn our thoughts to Abigail."

*

The house is quiet. The only sound I hear is the rumble of talk from the room next door. I am in the parlour, where a bright fire is blazing. I love this little room. The saloon, dining room, and library smell of old things, but this parlour smells of clean linen and soap, good polish, and the comforting fire. I would be happy to be here, but for Silston being back to stay, though I have not seen him yet. I waited and worried a long while after what he did to me, and each day felt like a week. The hurt he gave my poor body went soon enough, but I was in constant fear and had to deceive my mistress, pretending nothing was wrong, and that hurt me too. I do believe I will be waking at night from sorrowful and horrid dreams for the rest of my days.

I am laying out my mistress's shawl across the back of a chair in case she should become cold during the evening. I recognize Louis

Silston's voice and my hackles rise, but I cannot help myself; I creep to the part-open door between the two rooms and put my ear to the crack.

"You must get this right," his father is saying.

The old fool's growl is so quiet I have to press to the door and strain to hear.

"Abigail comes with Colliton's money behind her and we cannot afford to have another…mistake."

"Father, I…" says Mr. Louis.

"Enough Louis, enough of your empty promises. I know what young men are, but you must put your wolfish ways behind you. The business with Clarice Farquarson…"

"Was an error of judgment, father, no more. Nothing like that will ever happen again."

"It will not, sir, because, and I am serious in this, if it does, you will no longer be my son. For God's good sake, man, Richard Farquarson is one of my oldest friends! How could you? It is only because of Richard's loyalty to me that word of your reprehensible mistreatment of his daughter has not been spread through all of society. Worse than the possible social opprobrium, you put our business at risk, sir, and that is intolerable. No sir, it will certainly not happen again and you will proceed with care and the utmost gentlemanly behavior in your courtship of Abigail."

The front door bangs and I jump out of my skin. Mr. Colliton has returned. I cross the parlour quickly and slip into the corridor from the main hallway, curtseying to the master as he strides past. Hurrying to the back stairs, I cannot get Louis Silston's words out of my head, "…nothing like that will ever happen again."

I know what he likes, the hateful man, and so I can guess what Miss Farquarson may have suffered at his hands. I hurry up the back stairs; my mistress will be waiting for me to help her dress. Then something I have kept locked in a private room at the back of my mind comes pouring like the contents of a pisspot. I try to push it away, but it brings me to a stop on the stairs.

I am a child again maybe eight years old, sleeping on the lumpy straw-stuffed pallet I share with my little sisters. There is something wrong with my belly and the strange feeling wakes me. I am thick with sleep and it takes a few moments to understand. There is a cold weight lying on my middle. I don't scare easy, but my imagination is racing away with thoughts of animals or vile crawling things. My heart's bumping inside me like the landlord's lackey hammering on our door. I hear a small sound and lift my head to look. There's my Pa's greasy, grey head. What's he up to? His forehead is lying against the bed. He must be kneeling on the floor. I understand it is his dirty paw on me.

His hand closes up so his fist lies on my skin. I don't understand, so I keep still, still as the dead. It's like his hand has a life of its own. His body has not moved yet the fingers open and close, rising and flattening on my belly and moving side to side so's I can feel his hard skin rubbing me. I'm thinking, maybe he does love me after all, maybe he's come to tell me so, tell me sorry for all the beatings. I raise my head and shoulders off the pallet and watch him like maybe he might look at me and smile.

Then he scares me again for he is making small noises, groans, as his hand circles and circles. I'm just getting brave enough to say something when his hand moves down on to that part of me that is only for me, the part that must be kept hidden, mother used to say. Suddenly, everything is wrong and I am so frightened. With a grunt he's looking at me, his nasty little eyes staring into mine. His face looks grey for there is no candle only what light comes through the slack muslin at the cracked pane. It's like those grey-blue eyes of his are trying to see inside of me and now I know it is not love he has come for because all I can see in his face is contempt and hatred and it's as if he's putting guilt on me like this is my fault.

He comes close and I can smell his breath, sour with beer and tobacco and the stink of puke. I want to move, get away but I can't. His eyes hold me as his fingers slide lower, between my legs and he smiles, and I see violence in that smile. I am crying. As he pulls his face away something crashes into him, sends him falling to the floor. His hand is gone and I sit up, try to see. I pull my scrap of old nightdress tighter around me and my little sisters start to wake. Sarah cries out and rolls over, opens her eyes. All I can see on the floor is a mess of legs and arms. Pa's grunting and cursing, terrible words that scar the very air. Then Laura's head appears, my brave, brave big sister has saved me. But now Pa's grabbing Laura, dragging her up, punching her in the face.

I shut my eyes and shake my head and I am back on the servant's stairs. I must go on, mistress is waiting. As I climb, I hear my sister's voice; "he done it to me, Poll. I wasn't having him doing it to you." I rub my face and try not to see the bruises and split lip spoiling Laura's lovely face. No, I will not see those pictures again. I am strong, I am my own woman, I know men and their ways and I will not let them win over me. I got away from my Pa, I suffered and withstood Louis Silston, I will be my own maker, no man will have a hand in who I am. If Silston's words had not brought back those terrible memories I may have kept my silence but now I am determined that my mistress should know.

Abigail is sitting before her looking glass, brushing her long hair when I come into her bedchamber. Her natural prettiness is gone in her anger.

"Where've you been?" she cries. "They want me down there already. Papa is still away and mother is unwell. I have to face the two of them alone, Polly. It is horrid and unjust."

"It's all right, mistress," says I, and I stand behind her, taking the brush from her hand, seeing her poor bitten nails, and I start brushing her hair. "Your father is home, so there's no hurry, but we must get you dressed. Here, let me help you."

As she stands, I summon my courage.

"Mistress, I have heard something…I am not sure I should say."

She turns her head and her face has lit up with a smile. She is all mischief again now that there might be a secret or some gossip.

"Oh, what is it, Poll? Is it something wicked? Come, you must tell me."

So, I do, I tell her just what I heard in the parlour, that is enough, and her face goes pale with anger.

"This is too much, Polly. I knew he was not right for me, but this…"

"What will you do, mistress?" says I.

She lets out a small sound, a sob or sigh, turns, throws her arms around me, and pulls me close. I take a breath of her scent and it is so fine and warm. I don't think my mistress would admit that I am much more than her maid, but a friend's what I am. If her mother saw us now she would be shocked and I'd be out of a job, of that I am sure. I cannot know what Abigail feels when we embrace in this way, but what is in me is so strong, it scares me a little, yet it excites me too.

She pushes herself away, bows her head, and stays quiet and still. I'm glad now I never told her what Silston did to me for it seems that my mistress is crushed just by the thought of what Mr. Louis might have done to the Farquarson girl. I think, maybe, she is going to cry, but I am wrong.

"Come, Poll. Dress me while I think. There is no hurry now and I would like to keep *mister* Silston waiting a little longer."

All the while I work, she is quiet, staring away into the distance. The dress she has chosen is dark green silk. The needlework is wonderful, each stitch a minute, exact miracle. Its hem is even and straight, the lace so white and perfect it could make me cry. I have seen many fancy dresses since I came into service, but none as perfect as this; it is my favourite. Sometimes, when I feel the softness and weight of it, smell the rich silk, I think I might kill someone just to be able to wear it for a day.

"There, mistress," says I, stepping back to look at her. "You are a picture."

She ducks her head and pauses. When she looks up again her eyes are afire. She grins, a mask of pure energy. She takes my hand she looks, all a'glitter, into my eyes.

"We will run away, Polly."

I am almost shocked to silence by this, but I manage a few words.

"Now, mistress?"

She giggles. She pulls me close again, throws her head back, and laughs out loud. The Collitons are very religious and believe that seriousness and cleanliness are next to godliness, (I have heard the missus say as much many times). In this house, laughter is to be suspected. Often my mistress and I have had to wait for the privacy of her bedchamber or the garden to laugh together. Now I hold her tight and join in her giggles.

"No, silly," says she when we have stopped. "If we run away from here, they will find us soon enough as everyone here knows the family, but father has said that our new London house will be ready to receive us soon. We will be going there for the summer, so he says. We will need to plan and make ourselves ready, but we will go, Polly, when we are fully prepared, we will run away in London and make them all pay."

Chapter 4

In Which William Seeks Out Mr. Corbett and Finds Himself
With a Job

The next morning soon after cockerel crow and after gratefully receiving the kindness of a simple breakfast from the brick maker, Will began his final day's walk to the city. As he set out, he could smell something foul and, with every step, the stink became stronger. Soon the cause became clear. He found himself walking past house-high mountains of rotting rubbish, each bleeding an oily liquor into vile ditches. Further on, pigs were rooting wild in ruined fields around filthy, makeshift hovels that had been thrown up by people living on the fringes of the capital. Their inhabitants threw him suspicious looks so that he hurried by, determined not to be cowed or disheartened by these unexpected, miserable sights.

He passed by gravel pits outside the village of Kensington where, despite its smoking chimneys, the air was fresher. He walked on past fields to the north and south of the road, which, he noticed, gradually widened. Soon he found himself in a place of meadows and trees where, in the distance, he saw a herd of deer. Weeks later he would learn that this place was St James' Park, but for now, he continued on his way until, at last, he came to the river. The Thames was a marvel to him, having never seen a body of water bigger than the small stream at Harsham; the great ships of state and commerce, the forest of masts, the small boats like water beetles plying the choppy waters and, as he turned north, there were more wonders; a palace, an abbey and more fine houses than he could count.

He had lived his twenty years in a poor cottage tied to old Riddlecote's family on a narrow lane in a small village. These London streets could not have been more different from the dirt lanes of his home. A gallimaufry of houses, taverns, shops all hodgepodge and disordered.

Everything astounded his senses. The streets were in constant motion, packed with people of every type. The air was grey with smoke from a thousand chimneys, coating the back of his throat. The roads were dense with noise: horses's hooves and coach and cart wheels against stone roads; the cries of hawkers, peddlers, and street sellers; men and women calling out for work, shouting their skills; a ballad singer on a corner; the bark and whine of feral dogs; a knife grinder's din; the babble of a thousand conversations.

For a long while, though he knew he should find a room before night fell, he leaned against a wall and watched. For Will, it was like a show or a fair, things he had heard of, yet had never seen, and he was struck dumb by the spectacle.

The road where he was standing was wide with wooden posts dug in deep all along the sides a short way from the house fronts so that those on foot could walk safely separated from the busy traffic of carts and horses. Beside the posts were runnels filled with a dark, stinking liquid, an open sewer. Leading off the street were other roads, narrow, mean-looking lanes. Many buildings around him looked newly built and of a style he had never seen; brick-walled with smooth faces, many three or more storeys, and with neat, flat fronts and clear glass in the windows. The houses down the nearest lane, though, were more haphazardly built, much older, and seemed to lean like village drunks over the narrow way.

All the streets were filthy and blemished with waste dropped by street vendors, customers, and walkers alike, and between the wooden posts were many heaps of horse manure. There was no surprise in this, at least, because Will had never seen so many horses; horses pulling carts, expensive coaches, hackney carriages, and wagons and there were many riders, wealthy-looking types in fine clothes and hats, as well as poorer travellers on ponies or old nags with sagging withers.

But what assailed him most in all this panoply of sensations was the stink of London, which was tremendous, an amalgamated stench of smoke, shit, rotting waste, untended animals, and filthy people. At length, Will moved on thinking to leave the smell behind, but quickly he learned that, as he walked, the smell walked with him. There was no escape: in courtyards, the smell of stale piss and over-boiled vegetables; the rank odour of a tannery, the sharp catch of lye in his nose; the corpse of a dog in gutter, the sickly-sweet smell of death.

He stopped and bought a mouthful from a pie-man in the street and, while he chewed, asked an old woman where in London he might find a place to sleep for the night.

"Oh, you ain't in London, son. This is Westminster town."

Will was dumbfounded. So many people, so much noise, such smells and he was not yet in the City. Taking his instructions from the woman, he walked on until he saw the arch of Temple Bar. The old lady had told him to look out for heads on spikes over the arch, but, though there were spikes, there were no traitors's heads to be seen that day.

He paid his toll to pass through the Bar and when he emerged on the other side he was amazed once again. There came, along the narrow way between the houses and the wooden posts, a finely decorated box on poles being carried by a man at the front and a second man at the back. Both were wearing good quality clothing and fine wigs. There was a window in the box and inside Will caught a glimpse of a man clothed in the most splendid coat and with the highest wig he had ever seen.

This was all strange enough, but beside the box walked a man with black skin. He had hair the like of which Will had never come across, a mat of black wool, oiled and shining, and his nose was broad and flat and his lips full. His eyes were the darkest brown. His clothes, like those of the man inside the box, were wonderful; a suit of dark blue, the jacket edged with scarlet and gold, and buckled shoes. He carried a walking cane with a gold head. Will had never seen such a man and thought, for a crazed instant, he must be made of oiled ebony. So lustrous was his skin that he wanted to touch it, but before he had time to think, they were gone, through the Bar and on into Westminster.

The day was starting to come to an end as he trudged on, his tired eyes wide with wonder. At Blackfriars he stopped to admire the many vessels moored or moving on the river; great sea-bound ships, lighters, skiffs, coasters, and wherries all bobbing at anchor or scudding across the shining surface of the Thames. On the other side of the river, he saw ramshackle houses and warehouses, and, further on, he caught his first sighting of London Bridge with its central drawbridge breaking the line of higgledy-piggledy buildings balanced like toys upon it.

He was bemused and exhausted; yet still, he walked, though more slowly now, and he found that London City was as loud and stinking and crowded as Westminster. As the last day of his journey drew to a close, his ears ringing with a Bedlam of sounds, his eyes stinging with the smoke, his mouth tasting sour, he spent a few pennies on a room and a meal in a big bustling inn and finally, late in the evening, found the succour of sleep.

*

The next morning, launched again into the bustling city, he made his way to Lincoln's Inn. Following the directions of several passers-by, he found it at the heart of the close, crowded city. It was a large, open square flanked on three sides by great buildings four storeys high. A tall monument stood at the centre of the park-like space. All around, men in black robes were coming and going or standing in groups looking, to Will's country eyes, like coveys of crows. On the open side of the square was a garden, in the form of a second square, grand and green and bordered by trees on all sides.

As he had been instructed by the lawyer, he asked for Mr. Corbett, but the first man he spoke to ignored him, walking on at a fast pace as if to escape the insult of Will's approach and his audacity at daring to address him. The second man he asked, fortunately, was kinder. This fellow did not wear a robe; his garb was humbler. With a wink, he led Will to a door, opened it, and pointed up the stairs. On the first floor Will found a scrawny clerk sitting at a high desk poring over a thick document with a quill in his hand. His face was so pale and sickly it might have been freshly whitewashed and his neck was so thin it put Will in mind of a chicken's gizzard. This was a man who rarely saw the sun. His long hair was dirty and ill-kempt, tied at the back of his head; his clothes were like those of the man who had shown Will the way. The room was bare, but for the desk and a long shelf filled with ledgers, and it smelt of something Will could not place. The clerk looked up from his work, frowned, and squinted through his thick eyeglasses.

"Yes?" he grunted, wasting no more than the one word.

Will asked for Mr. Corbett and began to explain his story when the clerk cut him off.

"Mr. Corbett is a busy man. He has no time for guttersnipes."

Will's mother had taught him to be a proud man, so he raised his voice to complain, trying to make the man understand that Mr. Corbett had made him a promise. Behind the man at the desk was a door, left slightly open, and from the room beyond came a familiar voice:

"What is all this uncomely commotion, Gunnard?"

"'Tis nothing, sir. A saucy boy with an unlikely story…"

Will interrupted and call out to the lawyer.

"It's William Staples, sir."

"Now, that's enough, boy!" shouted the clerk.

Glowering, he stepped down from his desk. At the same moment, Corbett appeared in the doorway. He had a broad smile on his face.

"You'll have to forgive my clerk, young William. He tries his best to protect me from the wicked world, don't you Gunnard?'

The clerk, realising his error, slid back without a word into his high seat with a quick tug of his forelock.

"Welcome to my chambers," said Mr. Corbett. "Come through, William, come through."

The lawyer's room was like no other place Will had ever seen. There was a desk and behind it, a hard-looking chair, but everywhere there was paper; piles of it on the desk, piles of it on the floor, piles of it on a small cabinet in the corner. Around the walls, there were shelves piled, every one, with books and books and more books. Corbett caught sight of the look on Will's face and laughed.

"Yes, Will, it is a mess, but within this chaos, I assure you, there is wisdom and justice. Now, I do believe you have come about my carpenter friend."

Picking through the confusion of documents on his desk, Corbett eventually found what he was looking for and handed Will a piece of paper with a name and address.

"Can you read, Will?"

With a grin, the young man read out the name and address.

"Good lad, your father taught you well."

"My mother, sir," Will corrected him.

"Your mother, well, that is a fine thing, William, a boy taught the King's letters by his good mother."

"Yes, sir."

"Now, give me your hand and promise me two things. Seek out Samuel Royston, a Freeman of this City of London, a fine carpenter and a fair man whose family I have helped in the law in recent times, and tell him I have sent you for work."

He shook Will's hand, looking him square in the eye.

"And the second thing that I must promise, sir?" asked Will before he let go of the lawyer's hand.

"The second promise, Will, is that, should you be in trouble, you must come back to me. Gunnard will not try to bite you the next time!"

Will happily made his promise and left Mr. Corbett and his haughty clerk. By the next week, he was apprenticed to Mr. Sam Royston of Cheapside.

Chapter 5

In Which Will Shows His Skills and Meets a New Friend

Will's new master was a good, kind man, a man of God, and a man of great talent when it came to wood and the tools of the carpenter's trade. He was a generous man with a fine family; his warm and cheerful wife named Betsy, and two hearty boys, Aaron and Ezra. The couple and their sons had welcomed Will into their home and given him a small room in which to sleep. Sam even paid out for clothing and shoes for his new apprentice, saying he could not have a man in his home with only one suit of clothes.

The Royston house was of three storeys and Will's room was on the attic floor. It had a low ceiling, which, tall as he was, begged him to bash his brains out every time he walked in the door or stood up from the bed. Will shared the attic floor with a Mr. Flint, an old bachelor gent, who rented the other room. Betsy and Sam had their room on the first floor, next to their sons' room, which the boys shared with their grandmother, Mother Royston, who had her bed behind a thick curtain that divided the space.

Everyone ate in the kitchen, which was large and had a solid, beautifully made table – the work of Mr. Royston's father, who had started the carpentry business and had died earlier that year – a bread oven, and a fine, wide fireplace for cooking. The yard was narrow and led straight to the workshop and store all on one floor with a stock of wood kept at the north end and the workshop, benches, and tools at the south.

All was kept clean and neat in the house and workshop, for the Roystons were good Christians and adhered to the belief that a tidy home leads to a tidy mind, which "brings a man closer to God" Sam told Will early on. Sam's yard and workshop had the heavy smell of wood: the fresh perfume of pine and larch, the lighter gummy odour of oak and beech, the exotic reek of mahogany and teak. Inside the house, it smelt of boiled beef, bacon, freshly made bread, and sweaty little boys. Will was so happy in his new home that he thought even the aroma of Sam and Betsy's house and family to be good and fine.

At first, master Royston had Will show his skills on small jobs; selecting woods, sawing and adzing, shaving, preparing, making joints, dowels, but soon the young man was able to show Sam that he could manage more complicated work and so he found himself completing more challenging tasks. Will was Sam's first apprentice. It had been the death of his father that had led him to need extra hands. Sam told Will they would learn together, the new master and the new apprentice.

Will's first task working on his own was to make a door for the Royston's house. The scullery door out the back of the kitchen had warped over years of use and no longer closed properly. Besty told Will that the previous winter it had let in some killing draughts from the backyard. Sam allowed Will to select the wood for the work himself, so he chose some aged oak planking and set about the construction. Though he kept his opinions to himself, the new apprentice thought the work easy enough, but he prided himself on making as good a job as he was able.

When he was finished, he used his fine chisels, chosen from the package of tools he had brought with him from home, to carve an apple blossom and a bee in the head of the door, just at eye level. He hung the door straight and true – there would be no draughts from his door – and the job was done.

"Thou hast the hands for the work, Will Staples and the thinking mind of a man made to be a good carpenter," was Sam's generous comment.

Soon Will was working with Sam, both in his well-equipped and spacious workshop and out on jobs of work for customers of various kinds. By early summer the pair were at work on a commission in the house of a merchant gentleman, Mr. Richard Wallace who lived in a grand house in Westminster. Wallace was a robust man of later years with a large red face and loud manner, who told Will on his first day of work that, when it came to replacing and extending the panelling of his large and impressive home, he had not hesitated to take up the recommendations of fellow merchants to appoint Mr. Sam Royston to do the work.

That first morning they had taken a wherry on the incoming tide to better manage their load of prepared timber. For Will, it was his first trip on the great river and he marvelled all the way at the sights, sounds, and smells. Sam and the wherryman, a surly fellow whose tongue, as Sam told Betsy later, "was pleased to pronounce the most foul of words", pointed out to Will the extrordinary variety of boats and ships, from ocean-going vessels moored in the middle of the river to lighters, barges, coasters, skiffs, ketches and the smaller boats like their wherry. There were also fishermen, Mr. Royston said, pointing some out, catching lamprey, bleak and shad for the London markets.

As they walked with the carter from the dock Sam explained that Mr. Wallace was one of many Scotsmen of means who had migrated south and settled in Westminster, the Strand, and other places favoured by the Quality. Some had come with money; some had made their fortunes in the City before buying their great houses.

"After the rebellion of '15," said Sam, "we didn't trust them, so many Scotch heads were there on pikes at Temple Bar, but now 'tis calm and no one minds them anymore. And Mr. Wallace is an honourable man, so I am told."

When they arrived at the house Will got his wish to learn more about men with black skin for they were greeted with quiet charm and welcome by Wallace's manservant, Jenkin Smith, a man whose face and hands were the colour of aged and varnished mahogany. The eager apprentice had seen a few other black men and women since his arrival in London, especially at the docks of Blackfriars, where mizzen and main masts poked up thickly behind the squat chimneys of river-side houses, reminding Will of a thicket of birch in Baggot's Wood back home.

Standing in the doorway behind Sam, waiting while introductions were made and instructions given for where the carter should unload their timber, Will thought, as he had that first day at Temple Bar, that Mr. Smith's skin was rare and beautiful. Before meeting Jenkin Smith, Will had never spoken a word to any of the people of colour he had seen in the city. He had wondered how they spoke, if they understood English, how their voices sounded. He quickly learned that Jenkin Smith was a man much the same as his master and himself and a kindly one at that, a man who took great pains to make sure the two artisans were well provided for, bringing them small beer every day at noon with a bowl of hearty broth, a generous chunk of freshly baked bread and fresh curled butter. His voice was rich and deep and pleasing to Will's ear, though he did have an unusual accent. To the young apprentice it sounded unique; nothing like the lilt and rolled r's of Mr. Wallace's speech or what Sam called the "twangy gabbling" of the common London folk.

Over shared midday meals, Will found himself both captivated and appalled by Jenkin Smith's stories of Africa and slavery. Smith's first tale had reminded Will of a sermon given in the tiny chapel in Harsham years before when the parson had taught the Christian belief that the employment of African slaves in the new English territories in the Americas was God's will and a respectable part of English commerce. Jenkin Smith, it seemed to Will, vehemently gave the lie to that view speaking of slavery as the Devil's work. On their way home, at the end of a long third day of work, the carpenters had discussed Smith's stories.

"I am confused, master," Will had said, "because I count Mr. Smith a good man and, so the way he speaks of slavery I cannot, in all good conscience, think it to be a good thing. How then, can so many of the Quality, good Christians all, have grown rich on this trade."

"Aye, lad," Sam had replied. "'Tis a puzzle all right, but we must believe it to be God's will."

The next day, when Sam was discussing with Mr. Wallace the next stage of their work, Will sat with Jenkin Smith in the small scullery, where the manservant had a chair and table for his comfort. Will listened in horrified silence to Smith's story of his capture as a young man in West Africa and his terrifying voyage to the West Indies.

"How you did not die, Jenkin on that terrible voyage, I do not know."

"I was strong and young when they caught me, Will," said the man-servant, "and determined, whatever my fate in the place they were taking me, to survive. It was that determination that has seen me through.

"I found myself a slave on a cane plantation belonging to Mr. Wallace's brother on the island of Jamaica and worked for years in the fields. Terrible hard labour, Will, under the whips and the sun, but I showed myself a good worker and learned your language quick, see? Day-by-day I showed myself a worthy and loyal servant until the day, by my reckoning, twenty years after I arrived there, I was taken into the house to be an 'inside servant'. 'Twas there I met our patron, Mr. Wallace, who was visiting his brother on the island. Strange though it was to his older brother, we struck up a friendship. Four months later, when it came time for Mr. Wallace to sail back to England, he persuaded his brother to let him buy me, though, once again I had to endure the passage to London in the hold of the ship as the captain would not hear of a black man having cabin space.

"When we come here to London, Mr. Wallace made me a freeman and invited me to stay as his manservant and companion. By my reckoning, I am in my fifty-eighth year and I been happy and at peace these last seventeen years."

Will's imagination was a soup of horror and wonder, but also of respect for the black man he now counted a friend. He promised himself, as he cut to length a plank of planed oak that he would never complain of the hardship of his place in the world again.

Chapter 6

In Which Abigail and Polly Run Away, Have a Narrow Escape and
Feel the Bite of Disappointment

Vicimeous Colliton's father had risen to become an East India
Company nabob, amassing a fortune during the latter part of the
1600s. This great wealth of money, artefacts, and company shares
were all passed to his eldest son, Vicimeous, when his father returned
to England from India, bringing with him a fatal bout of typhoid.
Vicimeous Colliton showed great acumen in the making of money,
growing his father's fortune before, late in life, marrying a Durham
coal-mining heiress. Now the family was one of the richest in the
land.

Colliton had been impressed that the likes of Lord Cadogan and
Lord Cowper had purchased houses on Hanover Square, the Earl of
Scarborough's much-talked-about building project on the fields to the
north of the city. Designed to attract only the wealthiest of the
Quality, Colliton had recognized both the social cachet a house there
would bring, as well as the promise of rising value. Colliton had put
in a bid for one of the later houses to be built and paid for the
property in cash.

The house had been completed and the plan was to spend the
summer there, showing it off to friends, family, and men of political
clout whilst enjoying the social whirl of London and allowing Abigail
closer proximity to Louis Silston. The family arrived from Surrey in a
fleet of coaches and spent all of their first three days in Hanover
Square settling into the new building, walking its corridors and

rooms, and getting to know some of the other new residents on their street.

Mrs. Colliton had presided over the first dinner in the new house at which she, her husband, and Abigail had been joined by Charles and Arthur, his wife and their child. The next day the family would be joined by Louis Silston and his father for a celebration of Vicimeous' coup in buying the property.

Polly had been kept busy unpacking Abigail's trunk and bags, hanging, pressing and primping all her clothes, laying out her shoes and hats, organizing and reorganizing her bedchamber whilst her mistress dithered about where to put everything and, all the while, waiting to hear when the two young women would carry through Abigail's plan to run away.

*

For weeks the mistress has been plotting her 'great gesture', as she would have it. Great lunacy, I call it, but I am ready. I have tried by my lights to teach her the London way of speaking, for she will have us masquerade as seamstresses, but she has no ear for the tongue of my home and we have agreed I will do the talking should we be stopped or challenged.

As soon as she heard that Silston would be in the house on the morrow, she says to me, Poll, tonight we will go. So, now it's gone midnight, the house is settled and I am creeping to her room with a bundle of my own clothes. I've got her a long skirt of cheap wool, my oldest blouse, and a cotton bonnet, but she won't wear my ugly, square-toed shoes, so she has on an old pair of her own. She looks a sight with her golden hair down over her shoulders and my blouse that's too big for her frame, mite that she is, yet she is determined and as excited as a kid in the street that's found a florin.

I wake her, gentle like, and help her dress. She gives me a hug and I can feel her grin against my cheek.

"Off we go, Poll," she whispers and we slip out of her room and down the stairs.

We creep round through the kitchen and out the back door and it all feels too easy. Right nervous, I am, that we'll be caught, but we come round, without being seen, to the main street and walk away into the night.

There are no streetlights here, but 'tis not quite full dark and so we walk by the smear of light from the little chip of moon. The air is warm still, for which I give thanks as we have no coats. We hurry round the first corner and Abigail weaves her arm through the crook of mine and pulls me so close our bodies touch and we hop and skip until we walk in step. She gives a small laugh, covers her mouth with her hand like a kid caught out in a lie, and throws her head back, a grin on her lips. I can feel her excitement, almost like a buzzing bee, but my insides are knotted with fear. My mistress has never understood what I stand to lose from her 'wonderful adventure'.

"Oh, Poll, I mean, Peg," says she, stopping and looking at me, "we have done it. Now I am Lizzie and you are my little dressmaker friend."

She hugs me close again and whispers in my ear. "We shall show them, Poll, we shall show them."

For the tiniest moment, that hug, the closeness of her dear body, blows away my fear like the autumn wind stripping the trees of their leaves. Ever have I worried about my mistress's plan, but now, our bodies locked together, I feel such pleasure as I cannot describe. It fades on the instant, though, as I think about Mrs. Colliton discovering her daughter gone.

"Come, mistress…" says I.

"Lizzie! You must call me Lizzie, *Peg!*"

"I'm sorry, Lizzie, but we must keep moving. Once we have found Tottenham Court Road, it will be a long walk to Chancery Lane and my aunt's house. I fear..."

She laughs again and squeezes me.

"Be still, Poll, oh! I mean, Peg. I will get it right, I will. Do not fear, I pray; let us enjoy ourselves. We are free!"

I do not know this part of London so, all spring, my mistress has had me asking questions, clever little questions that none would suspect, of cook and the footmen and Rawlings, the butler, about this new house and in what part of the city it lies. Now I lead on and we walk at a clip, arm in arm. When we are on Tottenham Court Road, I will easily find my way to my aunt Susan's. To my shame, I have not written her in a year, but I know her to be a kind and quiet woman who will give us shelter. I believe she will forgive my laziness when she sees her niece at her door.

We walk in silence for a long time along wide streets lit at times with the new 'globular lights', as they are called. I feel in my bones we are nearing Holborn when I descry a light in the dark distance. It blinks at us and goes out. I know it to be a watchman with his lantern. He's seen us and masked the light. Now I'm getting a'feared again, but we have to keep moving, can't stop here. He swings back the cover and we can see how close he has come.

"Night watchman," I whisper.

Now the bits inside my belly are all clenched up like a fist. What mistress does not understand is that, if we are discovered 'tis me that will pay. Oh, mistress will be scolded and probably put to her room for a week, but I will be gone, out on the streets. I have feared all along that, even though we might succeed in making Mr. Colliton see that Abigail must not marry Louis Silston, 't'will be Polly Pruitt will be blamed and punished.

The lamp and its owner are getting close now. He's holding it out in front, sending its light to us, trying to see our faces, I have no doubt.

"Say nothing," I whisper, meaning 'let me do the talking'.

"Ho!" he cries, sounding hoarse in drink. "Whass this then?"

"Drunk," I hiss at Abigail to warn her to be silent. "Two dressmakers, sir," says I, loud enough, "going home after working late on a special order."

"Special order, eh?" His voice is deep and his words messy with the drink.

He stops before us, barring our way. He is a big fellow, that I can see, but he keeps himself in shadow, holding the lamp's window so that it points at us. Knowing what he's wanting, I walk close to him so he can see my face.

"Let's see the other," says he.

My mistress comes forward to stand by me and lowers her hood. Her hair flows over her shoulders. No one save me and her mother has ever seen her like this and it gives me a shiver, for, this close, even with the light in my face, I can see the watchman's dirty smile.

"Well now, two beauties!" he growls like the dog he is. He sways to the side, almost falling and the lantern swings hard.

"S'all right," he mutters, straightening himself. "So, where you goin', eh?"

"Just by Drury Lane, your lordship."

I hope my voice is one a man might like, but my poor heart is beating like a caged bird's wings and it is hard to think right.

"Come closer, my pretty. Let's see your 'ands."

I hold up my hands for him to see them. He grabs the right one and turns it over, inspecting my palm like he might tell my fortune. I pull my hand away.

"An' the other," he grunts.

I put my hand on Abigail's arm. Her hands are soft and white. He must not see them.

"Let us go, sir," says I in my meekest voice, just like the Bible tells. "We are so late and must be home."

"F'I let you home, what do I get in return?"

"Let us know your name, sir, and we'll do a little job for you for nothing," I mutter.

The laugh he gives out is like the gurgle of filthy water draining from a sink, but I step nearer again. He lets the lamp turn just enough that we can see him clear. His face is round with fat and his eyes are set wide apart. One is looking at me and the other is ogling Abigail, 'tis the strangest thing. There are warts on the side of his nose and his hair is thick with dirt. He's reaching out to grab me.

"Let's take a sniff of the goods, eh?"

I'm not going down under this wretch like I did under Silston, so I hitch my skirts and crack the edge of my shoe against his shinbone and scrape it down to his ankle. He staggers backwards with a yelp and drops the lamp. I don't have to say anything to my mistress for she is already running. I see she is going to run all the way down the street, in full view of the blackguard, so I catch her and turn her down a lane.

I can hear the watchman yelling behind us and know he will be chasing for his pride if nought else, so I lead my mistress down one lane, then round a corner, along a broad road, into another lane, then another, heading all the time, I hope and pray, to Holborn. Soon his shouts fade. We are both tired, but I tell Abigail we must continue running. I think she must be a'feared and hope she will want to go home and sneak back in the house, but I see her face is all smiles and her eyes glow with excitement.

It feels like hours of roaming stinking back streets and alleys, keeping our skirts off the filthy ground, and avoiding the horse shit, but at last, we come to Holborn. From there it is an easy walk to Chancery Lane and into the warren I know so well. Abigail has taken my hand and I keep looking at my mistress. Her little nose is screwed up against the stink and her face is full of disgust for the rotting things, dead dogs, and what I know to be the meanest, dirtiest houses she has ever seen. I feel I know what's in her mind; she's looking at these places and thinking to herself, 'this is where my maid comes from, these houses fit only for rats'.

Now I come to a stop and take a long look around. I lead Abigail to the end of the lane and we turn right into a broader way. There is aunt's house, crooked and narrow and held up between two larger places like a drunk between friends. I lead my mistress to the door and gaze up at its two floors; it is just as I remember. Built in the old style with timbers and plaster, the upper floor heaves out over the street like a fat woman's bosom. It looks poor like aunt has let it go. There are broken windowpanes and the door is cracked.

"This is it, I'm sure," I whisper, "but it…"

"What, Polly?" My mistress sounds frightened. The watchman has knocked the proud peahen out of her, I suppose.

"It is…aunt Susan is a proud woman, mistress, something must have happened. This is her house, but not as it was."

I have to knock on the door many times before we hear a voice from inside. A scrawny old woman in a dirty nightcap and tattered nightdress opens the door. She leans heavily on a stick and eyes us from under a knotted brow. Her voice is harsh with anger.

"Who's making all this fuss at this time of the night? Come on, speak up quick afore ye feel the bite of me cane!"

I look at my mistress and know not what to say. This woman is not my aunt.

Chapter 7

In Which Will Meets Polly and Falls in Love With Peg

Will was awoken by shouting in the street outside his attic window. He roused himself and sat for a minute on the side of his cot, rubbing his eyes. There was a fractured gleam of light from outside, the shine of a shy waxing moon. He swung his legs back onto the cot, deciding to ignore the harsh words and shouts from outside when there came a scream.

At once, he was out of bed and flying to the door. His master and family might still be asleep, though he suspected they would have been woken, but there was no movement in the house. It was his job to help protect the household. He ran down the stairs to the front door. His eyes passed over the old blunderbuss that Sam kept propped in the front window behind heavy bars to deter any who might think to break in. Its ancient mechanism was broken so he left it and swung open the front door.

Outside in the street were three figures. A fourth was hovering inside the door of the neighbour's crooked house; old Mrs. Gribbon, her walking cane gripped tightly in the claw of her hand. Her good-for-nothing son, Fuller, had his hands on a young woman who was wriggling and kicking out at him, her long, fair hair whipping about. Another girl was standing watching with her mouth open.

The night was warm, but Will felt a chill creep down his spine. Fuller Gribbon had a boy's appearance; soft turned-up nose, large eyes, wide face made with too much fat beneath his hairless skin. He was not as tall as Will, but he was wider, heavier, with the set of a

65

young bullock. With his facial fat, he looked like a grotesque overgrown baby, but Sam had warned Will early on that Fuller Gribbon was a dangerous man. Will hesitated. The black-haired girl watching the affray noticed him and jumped in surprise. Then she stepped to him and put her small hand on his arm. Her eyes were wide and she looked frightened.

"Oh, please, sir," she cried, "you must save us!"

Will could feel the warmth of her hand through the thin fabric of his nightshirt, but he was conflicted; he wanted to protect his master and his family from the clamour, but he was unsure how to proceed.

"Please!" the girl shouted at him.

He had to shake himself as if from sleep. Fuller Gribbon was still shouting abuse and obscenities into the blonde girl's face.

"Come now, Mr. Gribbon," Will started.

Gribbon released the grip he had on the girl and turned on Will. His face was contorted with fury.

"What's it to you, pig-boy?" he barked. He liked his name for Will, a soubriquet he had landed on when he discovered the young carpenter came from the country.

"Nothing, Fuller, nothing to me," said Will stepping between him and the young women.

"*Mr. Gribbon* to you, pig-boy!" he snarled, pushing his face close to Will's.

"Please, sir." The girl Gribbon had been abusing seemed stunned.

"Comin' bargin' into our house, wakin' my poor old Ma."

"'Twas an honest mistake, sir," said the black-haired girl.

She took Will's arm and half-turned him so that he could see her properly in the half-light.

"This was my aunt's house, sir," she said, looking with sincere appeal into Will's eyes. He had no idea what to say to her and felt himself blushing.

"I did not know she was gone."

"Cock-and-bull story," growled Gribbon. "Me and my Ma been here years."

From behind them came a new voice: "What is this dreadful ranting, breaking an honest man's sleep?"

Samuel Royston stood on his doorstep in his nightgown and nightcap. Everyone, except for the blond girl, spoke at once and it took Sam some minutes to calm them all. He was able to confirm that the dark girl's aunt Susan had, indeed, lived in the house before the Gribbons, so that, at last, Fuller, still not fully satisfied with the explanation of the dark-haired girl, retired with his mother into their hovel.

"Oh, thank you, sir, thank you." The dark-haired girl addressed Sam directly. "I am Peg and this is my good friend, Lizzie, and we are dressmakers who have lost our lodgings. We visited Lizzie's ma's, but she ain't got the room to help us out so we came to this place to see my aunt Susan and beg a bed for the night. Last I heard, aunt Susan still lived here. I thought I knew the way, sir, but we got lost and now it's so late."

"Yes, thou art right, this is the same house," said Sam, his voice quiet and kindly, "but thine aunt Susan was a sick woman when we took up our lease here. I am sorry to tell thee she died this one year hence and the Gribbons have been in that house since."

"Oh, sir," said the girl called Peg, her lovely face squeezed up in grief, "what will we do?"

Will did not want to give up his comfortable bed, but he saw only one way to resolve the situation and get back to his rest.

"They can have my room, master," he said.

"And you, Will, where will thee lie?"

"Out back, sir."

"In the workshop?"

"Aye," replied Will, with a sheepish grin. "There's space enough and I have slept on worse than your clean floor."

Will knew how clean the workshop floor was because it was he who swept the sawdust and turnings every evening when they closed up the shop.

"Mm," hummed Sam, turning back to the girl, "and if we do this for thee, what will thou do next?"

"Oh, sir, if you would do such a kindness, we would seek out another one of my family to stay with until we are fixed up, sir."

Sam took only a moment to think before he nodded his agreement. So, it was settled. Will followed the others into the house, shutting and barring the door behind him. In the street, still half in the warm clutches of sleep, Will had only seen two young girls. In the light of Betsy's kitchen, now fully awake, his heart swooped while something tightened in his belly and groin when he looked at Peg's face. A subtle, thrilling shiver passed through him. He had known girls, Martha and Daisy and Kate, in the village, but he had never felt like this before. He saw the curve of her cheek, the point of her chin, the thick, lustrous, black hair, the slight uplift at the corners of her startling green eyes, the set of her mouth in a constant smile, the plane of her pale forehead, the enchanting labyrinth of her ears and he was hypnotized.

At length, after Sam had laid down the house rules, he listened to their footsteps as his master led the young women up to his room and stood a moment in wonder before making his way silently to the workshop and settling himself on the floor. He had never felt this way before; a strange, delighted mix of tension and excitement roiling in his chest and gut. For the longest time, he lay staring up at the cobwebbed spars of the workshop roof while in his mind all he could see was Peg's lovely face. Up until this moment in his life, there had been nothing he had wanted to know about other than the art and craft of carpentry and the woods, the tools, and the skill of the hands, but now he had a burning desire to find out everything he possibly could about the beautiful Peg.

*

The next day was a Saturday. Sam and Will spent a long ten hours at Mr. Wallace's residence continuing their work on the parlour. Despite Jenkin Smith's amusing stories and Sam's occasional chatter, Will could only think of Peg. All through the day, he counted the ways she has captured his heart; her pretty face and eyes that lit up at even the smallest pleasures; the way she cared for her shy friend, Lizzie; her smile, slight, but rich with a wealth of warmth; her voice, a magical sound; her laugh like little bells bringing joy to a room. He decided that, when his labours were done for the day, he would take the young women walking by the river as they had happily confessed at breakfast that Lizzie knew little of the Thames.

He decided he would make it his business to spend as much time with them as possible. All day he looked forward with excitement to the evening stroll by the river and then, tomorrow, after chapel, he would take them to the Inns of Court, the King's palace, and Mr. Wren's great church of St Paul's, where, in his view, there was the finest woodwork to be seen in London. He pledged to himself to take them anywhere that kept him in Peg's company for as long as possible. Will had met more people since arriving in the city than he had in the whole of his life before leaving Harsham and he had seen plenty of girls, but when he had looked at Peg for the first time it had felt as if he had never seen a pretty girl before. Untutored in the skills of courtship, ignorant of the ways of young women, it had seemed to him that the air around her sparkled with some 'heathen magic', as he told himself. In her presence, his strong body turned to milk-softened bread and it felt as if someone was holding him by the throat so that his head became dizzy and his legs weak. He hoped, with all his might, that Sam and Betsy's good Christian charity meant that he could look forward, perhaps, to many days in the company of the girl he already thought of as 'my Peg'.

*

Sunday dawned grey and cool. Will joined Sam, Betsy, their two rowdy boys, and the two young women to break bread. After a lengthy thanks to the Lord for His bounty, Betsy asked Peg about her aunt and the girl broke into a dazzling smile. Her friend Lizzie sat silently watching how everyone used their cutlery, how they chose and applied condiments, how they ate, before assiduously copying them. Nobody noticed her, though, as the whole family and Will were swept up in Peg's story.

She was all smiles and talk of her days as a girl when she lived with her aunt. She told how she had left home to be apprenticed to her aunt, to learn the trade of a weaver of silk ribbons. She said nothing of how her aunt could not get enough work to support them both, leading to her becoming a street hawker selling fruit and vegetables. And she said nothing about going into service. Instead, she regaled them with carefully edited tales of her life in London and wove soft lies about a family she never had. She finished by saying that perhaps she and Lizzie could stay a few more days until she could locate one of these bogus relatives. Nobody seemed to notice she said nothing about her 'job' as a dressmaker.

"'Twas only a short time we knew your aunt after moving our business here," said Betsy when she had finished, "but she was a good Christian woman and the Lord wanted her by his side. We must give thanks for that."

All the time Peg spoke, while he chewed mechanically on his breakfast, tasting nothing, Will could not stop himself looking at her and admiring her perfect features. He noticed how kind she was to the shy, uncertain Lizzie and he thought that her eyes sparkled with goodness. He loved the way she automatically slipped a finger from each hand through her hair and eased it over her ears. Why, he asked himself as he chuckled at one of her colourful London stories, did Peg have this magical effect on him? What kind of sorcery could set his mind reeling and his loins stirring?

At last, Sam stood up and smiled. He raised his arms in the air and declared a holiday.

"Thou hast worked hard, Will, and earned a reward. Tomorrow that devil John Hill and his gang of ruffians are to be hanged and the whole of London will be at the Tyburn Fair. Take the day as a holiday and show these two fine young women how the Lord's vengeance is carried out."

By this stroke of luck, Will, dazed at his good fortune, found himself blessed to be able to look forward to two days in Peg's company. After church, he led Peg and Lizzie down Chancery Lane. The sun was already hot and in the labyrinthine lanes the humid air was black with flies breaking from their feasting on horse dung and dead animals. The swarms waved and flowed like dark veils of some unspeakable fabric, which parted like curtains drawn back as they walked. Having eyes only for 'his Peg' he did not notice Lizzie shuddering at the sight of them.

They came to the Strand and immediately the young women, talking over each other in their excitement and marching arm in arm, gave themselves up to the delights of the London shops. For the next four hours, as they made their way slowly along Fleet Street, up Ludgate Hill and on to Cheapside, they had to stop and pore over every last vendor: apothecaries, milliners, cobblers, tailors, sellers of exotic spices and herbs, and, especially, mercers's shops where the girls wondered at the abundant, colourful textiles. They laughed at Will's ignorance and tried to teach him the names, to him all so foreign, of all the fabrics: velvets, paduasoys, tabbys, damasks, silks, satins, and sarsnets. Though he did not know the words, he found himself charmed by them for, in his mind, like his timber raw materials, these were the stuff of the dressmaker's trade. No wonder, he thought, Peg and Lizzie were so delighted.

The women giggled and laughed, pointing out as many rude and vulgar things as those that were refined or comely. They held each other's arms, walked with a swish of their skirts, and chattered interminably about clothing and shoes. They were charming company; Will's face began to ache from grinning and when Peg smiled at him, he felt the sky was brighter, the smell of horse shit stronger, the din of the city louder, its shapes sharper, its colours more brilliant.

It was late when he finally persuaded them to go with him to what he called, 'Mr. Wren's great church'. They spent an hour before the start of benediction enjoying its extraordinary space, sounds, smells, and, on Will's insistence, woodwork. He was very pleased that, when he explained the work that went into the wood-carving and elegant joinery, Peg asked questions and looked him in the eye.

At last, they walked slowly home. As they made their way, tired and happy, back along the Strand, the evening girls were taking their places along the walls, fluffing their skirts and scouting every passing male with sullen, knowing eyes. Naïfs, Will and Abigail hardly noticed the women, but Polly, recognizing what they were and knowing their ancient trade, avoided their gaze, worried she might be known to one of them.

They wandered through the still-thronging streets and lanes to Sam and Betsy's. After a supper of bread, cheese, and small beer, they said their goodnights and he laid himself down for a second night on a rough pallet on the workshop floor. Lying, open-eyed, and still excited, he knew that he already loved Peg, for, apart from the beauty that he felt sure every other man could see, she was bright and quick to laugh, intelligent and soft of tongue in equal measure.

It was no surprise to Will that he felt this way. His mother, towards the end, had quietly and patiently explained to him that she had fallen in love with his father 'in an instant'. She was, he had known at the time, trying to excuse herself for landing Will with a brutal father. Jasper Staples had been a fine, tall young man then, she had told him, unsullied by drink and bitter jealousies. Falling in love with the wrong man had blighted his mother's life, but Will knew that his choice was right and all he felt was luck. As he rolled on his side and tried for sleep, his heart was again full of that warm, astounding feeling he had never before known.

Chapter 8

In Which Will and His Two New Friends Attend a Hanging and a
Terrible Thing Happens

Abigail can be quite the poet. This morning, when we woke early, she said to me that "the door of the sky has cracked open to let in a shy dawn", bless her. We have shared a bed for nights in this carpenter's house and to feel her body so close is a wonder and a miracle. I have hardly been able to sleep for wanting to hold her and kiss her, God forgive me. And now I will spend another day with my love once again as equals. It is more than I could have dreamt of only three days ago.

We broke our fast heartily with Mr. Royston's family, feasting on eggs and Betsy's wholesome bread and home-cured bacon. Ezra begged his betters to let him go with us to see his first execution, but Betsy was sure and firm that it was not a sight for children. So, after cheerful farewells, we left with the carpenter's boy to walk to Tyburn.

With my mistress by my side, I can enjoy the warm sun on my face and the streets and narrow ways filled with excitement and fun. There are so many people going the same way as us, there will be such a crowd at this hanging. The apprentice, all grins and silliness, leads us through the merry crowds. I've seen how that young cove looks at me. When he talks to his master, he is serious and his sharp face looks like a man's. When he looks at me, his face goes all soft, the fool, and he smiles more. He becomes the boy he is, not the man he wants his master to see.

Abigail has seen it too and she is getting great joy from teasing me. For all I love her, she is vain and I warrant she has never noticed my looks. But she is so high-born, she is too proud to be jealous of the carpenter's attention. Instead, I can tell it pleases her that I have an admirer.

"That boy has eyes for you, Peg," she whispers.

"Oh, no mistress," says I.

"Lizzie, Peg, Lizzie," she hisses at me, "and do not argue, for I know an admiring glance when I see one. He looks at you as if you were a hoard of gold."

I see what she means. I admit he's not a bad looking fellow, with his blond hair, straight nose, and stubbled chin. He is tall and is blessed with a good straight back and he has been kind to us, 'tis true. But he is like a big puppy, eager to please, his tail always wagging and that irks me the while. And he is a man and men can turn, this I know. All this I keep to myself; there is no need for my mistress to know my thoughts so I tut and roll my eyes at Abigail.

She grins and slips her arm through mine. She is enjoying herself. She told me when we woke this morrow that she's pleased she has been able to stay hidden from her parents for two days, but it's my guess that what goes unsaid is what she doesn't like. I know she cannot enjoy sharing a bed with her maid and eating what she will think is poor fare. And I can tell when she dresses, that the wearing of my old clothes is almost too much for her to bear.

I have been thinking much on what comes next. It is my belief that when she hatched her plan, my mistress did not think through what would happen if we did run away. She sat still as a rock this morning when I brushed her hair and I could almost read her mind. I do believe she was thinking of the search that must be going on for her and perhaps she may even have realized the pain her mother and father may be feeling, or at least, their anger. I have a deep gut-fear that when we return home, someone would be seeking a scapegoat.

There is a shout that brings me to my senses. A drover is breaking through the crowds, coming on with a flock of aggressive-looking geese. Will moves aside and looks back at me with a silly grin. We step back, Abigail and I, into a narrow alley and I look in her face as she squints in disgust at the fellow and his gaggle. I see there a new resolve. I do believe we will be going back to Hanover Square tomorrow.

*

Will was frustrated. He had no idea that there would be so many people on the streets or that the crowds would be so loud and happy, talking and laughing, shouting vulgar jokes and phrases about the condemned men. They had already been delayed by a herd of sheep on Chancery Lane before making their way past Lincoln's Inn Fields. Will wondered if Mr. Corbett would be at the hanging. Did lawyers attend executions?

Once the drover and his geese were out of their way, they moved on, bobbing like so much flotsam on the current of Londoners who made their noisy way to the place of execution. They passed street sellers, pamphleteers, puppeteers, tinkers with their paraphernalia, and balladeers singing new-written songs about the hanging of John Hill and selling the printed lyric sheets, the ink hardly dry.

After an hour, they found themselves arriving in a surging throng at Tyburn village. The place was already packed. The stands set up by the villagers were filling quickly, but Will, Abigail, and Polly decided not to pay for a seat, as Sam Royston had warned them that the stands had been known to become so crowded with eager onlookers that, on more than one occasion in the past, they had collapsed.

Tyburn Tree, a grim scaffold, was visible in the distance. Ropes were already strung from its beams and the three could see men pulling on them to test their strength. They found themselves somewhere to sit on the grass a good distance from the scaffold as, Sam had told them, the crush up close to the Hanging Tree could be unbearable.

There were jugglers and stilt walkers, a half-man with no legs on a little cart wearing fingerless leather gloves, disabled uniformed soldiers on crutches, mothers with children and babies, old men and women, groups of young men, mostly apprentices, ranging around, laughing and making a nuisance, whole families and small groups of older men wearing finer clothes, some with the high white wigs of the latest fashion. There were groups of poorer looking men of the middling sort, sporting aging perukes, some in cocked hats, their once quality clothes now shabby and threadbare, playing dice and cards, smoking their clay pipes and laughing loudly.

Near the scaffold were two coaches filled with wealthy folk, each with their coachman sitting on top. The bright brocade and silks of their clothes could be seen through the coach windows. The smell of unwashed bodies, animals, and their excrement was tremendous, but Will hardly noticed so inured was he to the stench of London streets.

Polly also seemed unmoved by the smells and sights around, but Abigail's small button nose was permanently wrinkled.

They made themselves comfortable on some scrubby grass and Will lit his pipe, drawing in the rich smoke and letting it drift away, as he watched the two young women beside him. He thought how lucky he was, to have met a girl as lovely as Peg. He thought never to meet her like again and vowed to himself to keep her close. One day, he knew, he would need to marry, and, at that moment, watching her animated face and captivating smile, he knew that it was Peg who would be his wife.

Wending their way through the throng were hawkers and vendors selling food and drink, trinkets and other fancies, pamphlets of religious tracts, or political rantings. The sellers wandered with their trays on straps around their necks or stood next to the barrows or baskets containing their wares. Will spotted a pie-man heading towards them and selected meat pies from the man's tray, proudly paying for all three himself.

The atmosphere was of a fair or celebration; there was much laughter and some shabby-looking girls were dancing to the fiddle of a stringy young man. The dance tune was almost drowned out by the sounds of voices, children shouting and crying, babies wailing and the barking of the ever-present feral dogs of London weaving in and out of the crowd.

A great cheer went up as the open cart bearing the condemned men hove into sight. The four convicts were standing and waving to the crowd, one of them laughing and exchanging jibes and banter with the throng. The other three looked more serious, but still, they waved.

"Full of Maister Blacker's courage," said a man close to the three friends.

He was wearing a dirty army uniform; his face was filthy, his hair matted and dusty. The left sleeve of the worn and faded livery was empty and pinned across his chest.

When Will raised an eyebrow, the man continued.

"They alvays stops for 'em at the Bowl Inn, Ben Blacker's place. They give 'em a few ounces of liquor; makes 'em brave, ready for the rope."

People were trying to follow the cart, as it wound its way slowly through the multitude to the gibbet, but the mass of people was so great that they had to give up and watch it as it processed on to the four men's end.

"That's John Hill," said the man, leering, "the one laughing and shouting his infernal Godless gospel. They say he has no fear in his body, that one."

It took a long time for the cart to rumble its way through the packed crowds. At last, it came to stop under the gibbet and the four nooses were laid over the men's heads and tightened on their necks. Polly edged closer to Will and touched his hand. A thrill coursed through his body. He glanced at her and she was smiling shyly at him. Lizzie stood close to her friend her face turned to the gibbet.

"'Tis all right," said Will quietly, taking and squeezing Polly's hand, "I'll take care of you."

"Here ve are ven," muttered the man, his face falling dark and serious, "they'll be dancin' the Tyburn jig now."

Will and the two girls craned to see over the crowd, but Polly seemed tense and kept casting her eyes around the crowd as if she wanted to look anywhere but at the scaffold. Will kept a tight hold of her hand, a feeling of euphoria filling him up. There came a shout and he looked up to see the cart being moved away, but the cry had not come from the gibbet. Breaking through the crowds, running towards them, were two men and a woman. One of the men was holding something close to his body, the other had a knife in his hand. Will sensed the danger and pulled Polly close. The men barreled towards them, knocking people over, raising shouts and yells.

The crowd around them surged like a living animal. All three were buffeted and Will staggered to keep his balance, never letting go of Polly's arm. Before he could react, the runners were upon them. The man with the knife collided with Abigail before she could step out of his path. The other fellow ploughed into Will and Polly. Will was knocked off his feet while the fugitive tumbled to the ground with Polly.

Behind them the crowd had parted like the Red Sea and more men, shouting for help, crying to anyone to "stop the thieves", were racing forward. The thief threw a terrified glance at the approaching posse, thrust something into Polly's hand, and leaped to his feet.

Will had hit the dusty ground with a thump that knocked the breath from him. A dull pain shot through his chest and he rolled to one side, pushing himself up onto all fours. Raising his head, he saw Abigail close beside him. She was screaming and holding on to the man with the knife. Their bodies writhed and swung to and fro like trees in a wind. The man was grunting. The cries of the pursuers were at hand.

Before he could get to his feet Will saw the knife blade flash and disappear into Abigail's body. The girl let out an awful inhuman groan and her body crumpled towards the ground. A foot flew out from somewhere and connected with Will's head, sending a bolt of pain crashing behind his eyes. He collapsed back to the ground and knew no more.

Chapter 9

In Which Will Awakens to Find Himself in a Living Nightmare

When he came to his senses, Will found himself on the ground. There was a swirling ache in his head, he was so dizzy it was hard to focus his vision and he felt sick. A man in a tattered army uniform was kneeling beside him. He seemed familiar, but Will was struggling to remember where he was and what he had been doing.

"All right, young friend?" asked the old soldier.

Will shook his head and wiped his hand over his face.

"Meriwether Johnson," said the raggedy man with a lop-sided grin. "Late of his majesty's wictorious army."

"Will Staples," Will muttered groggily.

"Well, master Staples, you vas knocked down," said Meriwether in his rich cockney accent. "Cut-purses, boy. Stole some grand man's pocket-vatch and vas running."

Now it came to Will, through a fog of nausea and pain, images of a man with something held close to his chest and a desperate-looking man with the knife. The knife; now he saw it, stabbing into Lizzie.

"My friends!" he croaked as he tried to get up.

"No, no, lad, you stay still now. You took a devil of a knock."

"I need to find my friends," gasped Will, putting his hand to his head, trying, impotently, to defuse the pain.

"What friends was that, lad?"

"The girls, Peg and Lizzie. I saw a knife!"

"Ah, you vas vith that young 'un vas gutted, ver ye, lad?"

Gutted. At the word, Will's heart lurched. He gagged and fought to keep the contents of his stomach. He closed his eyes

"Is she dead?" he asked, not wanting to hear the answer.

"Aye, lad, the young chick's gone to God."

The horrors of Hell burst from the ground beneath him and flew up inside him, racing through his limbs and guts, hurrying up through his chest and pouring out of his mouth as a strangled cry. Lizzie dead? He shook his head again as if the mere movement might prove the lie to Meriwether's story. The dizziness wrapped its rough fingers around him and he fell back to the ground. He lay there moaning, his eyes wet with tears.

"They took her lad, she's gone," said Meriwether Johnson.

As if a light was switched on in his mind, Will remembered the whole day. The breakfast, the thronged London streets, the cart, the nooses, and Meriwether Johnson, "late of his majesty's wictorious army". It was all clear to him and, as that clarity came he felt another great shock and his scalp prickled all over. He sat up and reached out to the old soldier, latching onto his good arm.

"The other girl," he barked, "where is she."

Meriwether looked confused.

"The girl who was with the one who …" it was hard even to say the word, "the one who died?"

Old Meriwether shook his grizzled head as if baffled.

"Well, what of the man, the fellow who stabbed Lizzie?"

"Got away," said Meriwether, "both of 'em, Godless pair, lost in the crowd, but they caught the girl."

"What girl?" Will asked as he started to get to his feet.

"The thief, the girl, her as 'ad the pocket-vatch in 'er 'and."

"But, wait," said Will, confused again. He rubbed his face for this made no sense. He was clear what he had seen. "'Twas the man who held the watch."

"Nay, lad," Meriwether replied with a shake of his head. "It vas that young girl; 'ad it in her 'and, she did. She screamed blue murder ven they caught hold of her. Run up, they did, like God's justice, and grabbed her. Howling like an animal, she vas, and them slapping her across the face to let her know she vas caught good and proper."

With a cold, hard knot in his belly, Will asked Meriwether what the girl looked like and he described Peg. Will's heart skipped and then began to beat against his chest like a hammer on good strong timber.

"No, no, that's…" He started.

In despair he turned full circle, seeing again the running men, the knife, the precious thing clutched to the chest, and, with horrible certainty, he understood what had happened. The thief, knowing he would be caught, put the watch in Peg's hand, his pretty Peg, and it was her the crowd seized.

"Where is she?" he asked Meriwether, his voice cracking. "Where did they take her?"

"Ah, she'll be in Newgate. Down in the Hold, son, the vurst place in the vurld, so they say."

The pain in Will's head surged again, dizziness and darkness took him. He slumped back to the ground and lay there for some time. At last, when the pounding in his chest had slowed, he sat up again. There were the gallows in the distance. Four bodies hanging, slowly twisting and turning, yet he hardly saw them, his heart was so heavy. He knew what he had to do. The heat of his shock had subsided; now he felt a cold clarity of purpose, a determination coloured by frustrated anger.

He must find Peg. He had only known the girl for two days, yet a fire had been lit within him. He knew, with a religious fever that he must do right by her and declare her innocence. He thought of Lizzie too. Should he find out what had happened to her body and arrange a Christian burial for her, he wondered. The thought of the pauper's pit for that young, laughing girl, was horrible. But it must be Peg first, of that he was sure.

He was a witness and would present himself to the authorities. He had seen the woman and the two men; the fellow who had pushed the watch into Peg's hand, the flash of the knife that had killed Lizzie; he must bear witness to what he knew, that the crowd had mistaken Peg for the woman who had been with the cut-purses. There, on that sunny, lethal day, sitting on the dusty ground, he pledged to find Peg, speak up for her freedom and tell her of the depth of feelings he had for her.

Meriwether stayed with Will until he was able to walk and saw him on his way. Will thanked him for his kindness and put two pennies in his beggar's bowl before he went. It was a long walk to Cheapside, but the crowds had gone and the way was easier. He had seen Newgate many times since he started working for Sam. It sat like a great stone monster, squat beside the road between Cheapside and Holborn. He had heard tales of its stony depths, its stinking holds, and lightless dungeons and his mind quailed at the thought of Peg in that foul place.

It took so long to get to the prison that he was almost in tears with desperation, but at last, he stood before it, a massive, stone fortress with enormous gates of oak and huge hinges and locks. Though there were people and traffic on the street outside the fortress, few looked up at its forbidding walls and notorious arch. Undaunted, Will banged his fist against the great doors until one was swung open just enough so that he could see a dirty, lined face topped with lank hair.

"What the devil d'ya think you're doing?"

"I'm looking for a girl, brought in…" Will started.

"Name?"

"Oh…Peg, she's called Peg. She's a young girl, black hair…"

"Only one Peg 'ere and she's as old as Methuselah."

"She must be here; I was told they brought her from the hanging."

"You a relative?"

"No, but…"

"You her lawyer?"

"No," Will snapped angrily, "I'm…"

"Then you can just fuck off, can't you, 'less you wanna do a personal inspection of the Hold, and once yer in, lad, you ain't comin' out."

With a soft thud, the gate swung shut and Will was left standing like a fool on a fool's errand. He began hammering again, but after lashing his hands against the unyielding oak for so long that both his fists were bruised and aching, he turned away, frantic and miserable. It was his fault, he knew that; the girls had been in his charge, he was the man, he was supposed to protect them and look how he had failed. He pushed all thoughts of guilt and culpability away and tried to concentrate on who he could turn to for help. It seemed obvious when he thought clearly at last; his master, Sam, was a Freeman of the City. Surely, he could help.

A breeze whipped down the long street ahead, raising summer dust and discarded broadsheets. Will, his head bowed, hurried back towards Cheapside wondering if he would ever see his Peg again.

Chapter 10

In Which Sam Agrees to Help Will Find Peg in Newgate Prison

Sam Royston was a good man, but he was also a God-fearing member of his local Baptist community, a freeman of London and a Mason to boot and when he heard Will's sorry tale, his first thought was not, as Will had hoped, to save Peg, but, instead, it was to protect his own good name.

He had let two young women stay in his house, with his apprentice lying not yards away from where they slept, and now one was dead in a brawl at Tyburn Tree and, so Will seemed to think, the other accused of a felony and locked up in Newgate Prison. If this news got out to his fellow members of the congregation and his Masonic peers, his name would be besmirched and his reputation damaged.

Betsy was more sympathetic to Wills' predicament, but she saw the sense of her husband's adamant stance. Will had worked hard in the months he had been in Sam's employ; indeed, he was a fine young apprentice with many skills already mastered, but neither Sam nor Betsy was prepared to let him get involved in a dirty little case of robbery and murder.

For two days Will laboured in Sam's workshop, making the carcass of what would become a fine sideboard, once Sam had added his own expert finishes, and all the time he worked, he tried, as Sam had asked him, to put Peg out of his mind. At the end of the second day, when he was cleaning his tools, he could stand it no more.

"Sam," he said as his master removed his work smock, "I beg you, master, to help me. I have tried to forget Peg, but I cannot. I do not want to blacken your name, sir, for I know how hard you work and how high in regard you are held, but I cannot leave that poor girl who I know to be innocent of any crime."

"Any crime, Will?" said Sam as he hung up his smock and brushed off his shirtfront. "Few of us are innocent of any crime, lad."

"I know, sir, and I am a sinner myself, I know that, but I also know that girl did no harm and stole nothing that day."

"Yet, as thou hast told me, thou were knocked senseless."

"I was, sir, but I know what I saw before I fell and I know that cut-purse, thinking he was about to be caught, pushed that time-piece into Peg's hand."

Sam sighed and wiped his brow. He studied his apprentice for a long time, while Will stood regarding his master, the chisel he had been oiling in his hand. Then the older man bowed his head and spoke softly.

"All right, Will. This I will do for thee. I will go to Newgate Prison. I have some standing in this parish and I will use that standing to gain an audience with the chaplain. But and this is my final word, if this comes to naught, thou must agree to never speak of this again. Do I have thy word?"

"You do, master, and I give it freely. Thank you, Sam, thank you."

*

The next morning crawled by. Will tried to concentrate on his work, tried to put all thoughts of Peg, and Sam's visit to Newgate, out of his mind, but it was hopeless. Twice he hit his thumb with a hammer; once he even had to return to a joint to mend his poor work, something that would normally dent his pride, but which, today, he hardly noticed.

Shortly after noon, he heard voices in the yard. It was his master returned. Will dropped his work and ran out of the workshop. Sam and Betsy were standing just outside the kitchen door. As he ran up, they stopped their chatter.

"Did you see her?" asked Will, his face alight with hope and barely suppressed excitement.

"Nay, lad, I did not see her, and thou must prepare thyself for bad news," said Sam, reaching out and placing a calloused hand on his young apprentice's shoulder.

"You did not …?"

"She is not there, Will."

"But, she must …"

"Hush, boy, listen. I spoke with the Reverend Archibald, the prison's chaplain. I told him thy story and how the girl Peg was not guilty of the crime she was accused of. He told me that the only Peg in Newgate Prison is an old woman, not right in her mind, who has been there years and helps out with the women prisoners."

"But …"

"Hush, lad. Let me finish. He told me that there are many young girls, Lord save us and save their souls, locked up in that terrible place and many, if not most, are cut-purses or common thieves. Three alone were brought on the day of the hanging, caught stealing amongst the crowds, but none, Will, was named Peg. She is not there, lad, and now, to thy promise, thou must forget her and ask God to save her soul, where 'ere she may be."

Chapter 11

In Which We Enter Newgate Prison and Polly Goes to Trial

I am in hell and my heart is shattered. If it t'were glass, it would be scattered over these hard stones, lost in the filthy straw that soaks up our piss and vomit. My love, my beautiful Abigail, is gone. I could not save her. Her silly, childish idea of making her parents pay for betrothing her to Silston has killed her and I did nothing to stop it. I have cried, oh, my dear Christ, how I have cried and the women here think me a Bedlamite, as some among them truly are, but I think I am not mad, unless madness with grief is a kind of lunacy, and if it is, then so be it, I am mad. Oh, Abigail; how senseless your death, how wasteful.

I know not how long I have been in this hard place. The crying stopped and the emptiness followed and I might have surrendered to it had it not been for my anger, which grew quickly in the soil of my loss and now fills my head like a wild plant. Once the fury took me, I started to think clear. I looked around me and saw that Newgate is the most terrible place. The women say it is the worst prison in England and I believe it, though I know most of my fellow prisoners must be liars, else, why would they be here? This is a place designed to be like Hell for those destined to go to Hell and, though it lacks the fiery furnaces of that dread underworld place, it has all other sorrows, tortures, and pain known to man.

Of course, it is designed by men, this place, as are the degradations they put upon us and 'twas a man who sent me here when he pushed that pocket-watch on me, and men who grabbed me, slapped me, and spat on me, and men who dragged me here and men who keep me here. Wharton and Quince our warders are called and they control this place. Biddy Spicer is the one we see each day, the one who brings the slop they call food and calls us names and blasphemes. Wharton and Quince I only saw the once, when they brought me here first; the one fat and greasy, the other tall with broad shoulders, arms and hands like thick, branching trees.

When I first came to Newgate, that sunny day that feels like years ago, 'twas Quince and Spicer who took me down into the depths of the prison to a foul, stinking, underground hole with no daylight. So deep in the bowels of the place is this hole that it felt it should be hot, being so close to Hell, but it was damp and bone cold.

Quince lowered me through a hatch into the cave-like place. There was an open sewer running down its middle, no beds, only foul straw mats on the stone floor and stink enough to kill a weak soul. There were chains and hooks on the walls and a man, crumpled on the wet floor, had his hands held in shackles above his head. Only later did I discover the name of that horrible place; the Stone Hold. I sat against a wall, damp and slimy to the touch. It was worse than I could ever have imagined, yet it took hours for me to see the place for what it was so bound up was I in my grieving for Abigail.

Sure I am that I would have died there in the Hold had I not held on to what I had with Abigail, forced pictures of my life with her into my aching head: brushing her sweet hair; laughing about her mother's silliness; dressing her in her gorgeous clothes; enjoying her teaching me to write and talk properly; walking with her in the gardens. Then, just those last few days before she went away forever – God, I would think in disbelief, was it only a day or two ago? – sleeping with her at the carpenter's house, giggling like geese at the mercers's shops in the Strand, walking arm-in-arm with her round St Paul's church with that silly boy, Will. These things I would hold to my heart, but when the pictures disappeared, when my mind was taken by despair, then the light went out.

How long ago was that? I do not know, but the women who share my quarters tell me I was raving and crying when Biddy Spicer brought me up from the Hold. This new Hell is a bigger room, all stone walls, heavy wood door with a spyhole cut through and bars across it, rough wood floor and dirty straw underfoot, but we have pallets, lice-ridden though they are, and most of us get a few hours' sleep each night, though the moaners and groaners never seem to need to sleep, noisy bitches that they are. There are thirteen of us and I could not count even twenty teeth among most of them; only me and Sophia have the teeth God gave us. Sophia doesn't look or talk like the others. They all wear rags and some have no shoes, they all stink and they all are filthy, both in body and in language. If I had a heart left, I might feel sorry for some of them, especially the younger ones, but the heart has been ripped from me.

Sophia is different. She is tall and, even here, bears herself with pride and a rough elegance. Her clothes are not fine like Abigail's, but they are good and well-made. Like me, she uses a splash of the little drinking water we get to keep her face and hands clean, though neither of us can do anything about what is hidden under our dresses. We stink just like the others and we have as many nits in our hair as them, but Sophia speaks well, though she has an accent, Yorkshire, she says, and tells me she has her letters and numbers. She will not tell me why she is here, but she has been kind, in her way.

This morning Biddy Spicer put her foul mouth to the peep-hole in the door and told me I am to go to court. Our cell is lit by the smallest of windows, barred and set high so that we can only see the sky. Today it is dreary up there and I hope this is not a foretelling of my fate.

They come for me and take me out into the grey light of the yard. There are four prisoners and two warders waiting, all men, and, as they shackle me, I get the jeers and sniping words I have become well used to. Biddy Spicer gives me the gift of some of her well-turned blasphemy and forecasts my dismal future, but none of this can diminish my joy, for I can see the whole sky and care not that I cannot see the sun. I feel the caress of a hot breeze on my face and I can hear, even before the warders start to move us, the wonderful sounds of life from the streets outside. I can smell London's summer stink, I can even smell the river and, for these few precious minutes, I have bound myself to a promise I made this morning; whatever the weather, whatever the insults, whatever the surprises, I will enjoy every short moment out of Newgate's dungeons.

The great doors swing open and the warders move us forward. We shuffle in our arm and leg irons out onto the street and make our way across to the Bailey. It is but a step yet, a woman starved of life, I hungrily devour the packed streets and the precious stink of London for it is the smell of freedom. Compared to the foul humours of the prison even these pungent smells seemed fresh in my nostrils. I look in every face that passes, ignoring their accusing stares and cat-calls, for I am looking at free people with no thought that they each might be but a single step or misstep away from the cell and its dreadful terrors and dishonour. They are all innocent of the dark knowledge I have of Newgate and, in a strange way, that ignorance and their easy freedom gives me strength.

As the doors of the courts come into sight, I know I must bring my mind back to my fix and what I will say to the judge. Each time I have pleaded my innocence I have been met with harsh laughter and disbelief. I have learned that all thieves cry "innocent" when they are caught, so my pleas have fallen on deaf ears, but I have always held that I know nothing of Abigail's murder and I will not be swayed from that. When I told my story, how the watch was pushed into my hand, they told me straight that many witnesses said different.

As to what I should do or say in court, my cell mates have been like a swarm of fat flies that have found some prime shit to feed on and have been full of good 'advice' about how to carry myself, though I asked none of them for it. Only one woman has been silent on this matter and that is Sophia. I have found her to be an intelligent, thoughtful woman, and I like that she is private and gives little away about herself. I was curious, so, one night, when the cell was filled with the snores and dog-breath of my sleeping cell-mates and seeing that Sophia, like me, was far from sleep, I asked her for her thoughts. At first, she tried hard not to give me her opinion, but I pressed her, suddenly realising that, of all the people I now had in the world, this one woman's words would mean much to me. Quietly and with her face set so that I could not read it, she said I should plead guilty. At first, I fought against the idea, it was too unfair. I have my faults and know them well, but I have always been a good girl, as my aunt Susan raised me to be. To admit to a crime I did not commit would be to dishonor my aunt and myself. Worse, it would mean letting men win over me again and, after what Pa and Silston had done to me, I had vowed never to allow that again.

My aunt was a strong woman. Never did she bow down to anyone, not the sharpers nor the Quality, nor the cheats and thieves and soft-tongued tricksters. I saw how aunt kept her pride in herself and her work and managed without a man's help or money. She showed me that I could make my own way in the world. And when they told me I was to be maid to Abigail I knew it was only my due, for I had worked hard, been loyal, and never put a step wrong. Now I see it is my pride that stops me from declaring I am guilty of something I never did. 'T'will be so hard to admit to being some cheap cut-purse.

Then there is poor Abigail, dead and in the ground, lost to her family; I cannot bring myself to think how her mother will be grieving, it is too painful. I know in my heart her brothers and her father will be searching for her or word of her. I cannot guess what will happen today, but whatever the judge asks me, I shall be resolute in my ignorance of the girl killed at the Tyburn Fair for I know well that, if the Collitons discover I have been brought to court, whatever the truth, the maid will be blamed. And though I may regret it and fear it, I have to be Polly Pruitt today, for, in my shock and grief, 't'was my own name I foolishly gave when they took me at Tyburn, so I will stand up and answer for myself. In my long days in Newgate, I have prayed to my loving Jesu that they will not know the name of the girl stabbed at the Fair nor anything about the blond-haired boy. I shall not be the one to tell of them and my good Christ be pleased, they will not guess the truth.

Now, as I shuffle in chains towards the court building, I think on Sophia's words, how she argued that a judge will be harder on those who plead their innocence in the face of many witnesses who tell a different story and I think on the punishments she whispered about. She said they could hang me. I shudder as we are led into the Old Bailey through a back door, for the forgotten people, the people already dead and the people filled with false hope. I fear no one comes out of this place untouched by the heavy hand of the Law.

The courtroom is all dusty and dowdy save for the judge, shiny in his silks, and it is all men, black-gowned the lot of them, many looking up at me as I climb to the dock, men in their power and glory, all full of their own importance, none of them with a thought for me, I'll warrant, all out for blood. There is a crone in the gallery holding court with a group of men and women, talking loud until the judge silences her with a harsh word and a harsher look. And then it is me, on my own, in that place of men, hoping for mercy.

Chapter 12

In Which Will Falls on Hard Times and Turns to Lawyer
Corbett For Help

Will lay on his bed, twisting and turning, unable to find sleep, unable to put Peg from his mind. That day, the day that his master condemned his Peg to rot in Newgate, was the worst of his life. All day, he had felt like a ghost, having no part in the real world, but hovering somewhere between pain and bewilderment.

He would have sworn he lay awake all night, but, come morning, he awoke and found that his mind was made up. He knew he would not be able to work for thinking of the innocent girl locked up. His mind was filled with imagined spaces, deep, dark spaces, cold and unyielding, harsh and echoing, and in each, Peg was lying bruised and abused on a filthy floor. He had never been inside a prison, let alone Newgate, but he had heard his fill of stories since arriving in London. So, he could not work, but he also knew that he could not let his master down. His only course was to leave Sam. That way his master would be able, in good conscience, to find a new apprentice, and Will would be free to discover what had become of Peg.

When Will told Sam of his decision, the older man's pale blue eyes flared wide and bored through his apprentice like well-sharpened gimlets. Without a word, he hurled the piece of wood he held in his hand at Will's head. The apprentice ducked and it crashed harmlessly against the wall, but that was not the end of it. The carpenter ranted like a crazed street preacher, calling his protégé a "stupid boy" and "taken over by senseless and ungodly longings".

"Thou hast let me down, boy, let me down bad," he rasped, struggling to control his temper.

It was a side of Sam that Will had never seen; his master had always exhibited such equanimity, balance, and poise in everything he did. It was a shock to Will, but it did not shake his conviction that he was doing the right thing.

"'Tis the Devil's work thou wilt be doing, Will, don't you see that?" He sighed, wiped his hand across his face, and stepped forward, grasping Will's arm. "If thou woulds't leave this house and try to interfere with justice, well, thou wilt be in danger of being beyond the law thyself, don't you see that? Is thy future worth the risk? Art thou willing to lose everything for a whim that thou art too young to see is not, cannot be real love?"

Will said nothing, but shook his head and looked away from his master's piercing eyes. Sam sighed again, let go of Will's arm, and walked to his bench. Turning, he began again, his voice now as measured as it ever was in the past.

"I've word that there's to be a fine new building of houses up in Harley Fields in Marybone, lad. 'Tis said there will be streets of grand houses with work a'plenty. A man like me, with a little capital, can buy a plot and curry my own men, build my own houses, perhaps make my fortune, and thou could be part of that, Will. I would value thee as a partner. What say you, son, isn't that a future to grab and hold to your breast?"

For a moment, Will could not speak. It broke his heart that this good man liked and valued him so highly he would make such an offer, but he shook his head. His love of Peg, for him, was mightier than all the money in London.

Sam spoke of the opportunity in Marylebone for a few more minutes, but the heart had gone out of his argument and he saw that he was not going to persuade Will from his intended track. At last, he shook his apprentice's hand, told him there was a place for him in his house if ever he needed it, and wished God to go with him. Will packed his precious tools and his meager belongings into the same bag he had carried all the way from Harsham, said his goodbyes to Betsy and the children – a much harder task than he ever imagined – and left the house without looking back.

*

It did not take him long to find a place to sleep. He had little money saved and knew it might take longer to find Peg than he would have cared to admit to Sam, so he settled for a room in one of the rookeries not far from Newgate. He thought the house must date to well before the Great Fire for it was of the timber and plaster construction beloved of the Tudors; three storeys of misaligned, badly executed work. On its various sloping, buckled floors there lived cockney, Irish and Dutch families as well as single men and women from near and far, all in a condition that Sam would have christened 'tatterdemalion', the poorest of the poor. It was a maze of broken windows, rotting spars, starving people who lazed all day, stank, and spent their energies fighting and shouting at each other.

Will's room was no better than a large cupboard, having no furnishings other than the stinking pallet, inherited from the previous occupant, set on the filthy floor. At first, he had tried to keep the place in order, but as time went by and his luck did not change, he sank so low that he hardly noticed the rat shit and worse that surrounded his bed. By the end of the second week, he could scratch his dirty fingers through his hair, and gather a wedge of lice under his uncut nails. By the end of his fourth week of searching his clothes were grimy and greasy, his hair was thickly matted and, though he had no mirror, he knew his face to be filthy. His clay pipe lay discarded on the floor for he had long ago run out of tobacco. Small luxuries like a smoke and a flagon of small beer had become hazy memories.

He spent his days wandering the streets around Newgate, questioning all that came and went from the prison, often being snubbed or merely harvesting hard words and the occasional kick. It wore him down, day after day in wind and rain and sun. Harder to bear was the recognition of the utter indifference to Peg's plight in the faces of all he spoke to. At night, he lay in his hovel staring at the cracked, cobwebbed, and rot-ridden beams above his head. Spiders had long ago colonized the feculent chamber and their once palely delicate structures now hung from the timbers, walls, and the one small, dust-covered window like ruined and ripped lace. There was a fist-sized hole at the base of one wall through which Will could hear his neighbour's terrible cough, hacking all day and night. Once he would have cared that the poor wretch might die; now he had been brought so low he cared neither for the man nor his life.

After five weeks of fruitless, futile searching Will was left destitute. His money had run out and he had no better prospect of finding Peg than when he had set out on his crusade. He had not eaten for days. His stomach ached with a twisting agony, his head pounded, his mouth harboured the vilest of tastes and his shit was a festering yellow liquor. He could go to the workhouse where he would be fed, but they would make him work there and he would have no time to seek out word of Peg. Desperate to eat, he went to the Thames one morning before the sun rose, to wait with other members of the dispossessed and derelict for work as a snuffle hunter, lugging great bags and barrels off the lighters that served the great ships. At the end of his first day, half dead from exhaustion and hunger, he exchanged the three pennies he had got for his trouble for two pies and a small mug of beer. He had never felt so full of food in his life.

For a week he searched every other day and worked on the docks the others, spending every penny on food and drink. For weeks he had hardly slept, eaten badly or not at all, often been deprived of good water or small beer to drink. His obsession had become his abiding passion; this and his weakened physical state had corrupted him from the inside so that he had become hardly capable of thinking straight or making a decision of any kind. So it was that he found himself begging with what, in a small preserved part of his hunger-warped brain, he thought of as 'the worst of them'; the sick, the lame, the scrofulous, the insane, crippled soldiers from the war, children, old men, and broken women, with nowhere to go and nobody to love them.

One overcast, warm summer's day, he was sitting propped against the wall of Newgate, just by the arch. His mind was wandering as it so often did these days when he became aware of an argument erupting outside the Old Bailey. The street, as always, was filled with the clatter, chatter, and jangle of London life, but the voices of the two men at odds with each other rose above the din. Roused from his self-pitying stupor, Will looked up and watched as the men, lawyers in their gowns, walked away from the law courts shouting, gesticulating, and remonstrating with each other. As they disappeared into the crowds a clarity came to his mind that he had not felt for days. He got to his feet, found a costermonger and bought an apple with one of the half-pennies he had in his pocket, and started out towards Lincoln's Inn Field.

Mr. Corbett was not in his rooms when Will arrived there, but the clerk, Gunnard, was in his usual seat, scratching away at his papers with a soiled quill. He grudgingly allowed Will to sit and wait. He had a very long wait, for Corbett had a full day of court sessions and meetings, but at last, the lawyer returned. Will had expected or, at least, hoped that Corbett would be pleased to see him, but he was cool and seemed tired, his dark-featured face lined and drawn. He gazed at the young carpenter with a hardly-disguised expression of contempt and it occurred to Will how he must look in his rags, with his straggly hair and filthy face; a very different young man from the one the lawyer had last seen. However, despite his evident fatigue, Corbett led Will to his inner chamber and bade him "be seated and tell me your tale". When Will had finished Corbett was silent. He stared at Will long and hard and, when he spoke, his tone was cold.

"So, William Staples, you have given up your apprenticeship to go on this wild goose chase?"

"Well, sir, I had hoped you would agree that a decent man could not stand by idly when he knows an innocent girl to be falsely imprisoned."

"Yet, good Mr. Royston took time to go to Newgate and investigate on your behalf. Did you think you would do better than your master? Did you believe he had lied to you?"

"No, sir, no!" Will protested. "No, I was truly grateful for my master's help, believe me, sir. It's just …"

"You think you can do better."

"No, Mr. Corbett, I swear, not that. I could not continue to labour in my master's workshop producing work I knew to be beneath his high standards all because my mind was burning up with rage at the unfairness …"

"And so, you want my help and influence, eh? Well, sir, I am no pettifogger, but a barrister at the King's bar. I am a busy man."

"Please, Mr. Corbett, I beg you. I am like to die if I do not find her. I suffer waking dreams of horror at what she might…"

The lawyer raised his hand to stop Will's pleas and sighed heavily. He shook his head and fingered the several case files that lay before him while he thought.

"All right, Will," he said, at last. He sat quietly for a while his eyes closed. "As I say, I am a busy man and have no time for this, but I will do my best to find out what has become of your Peg."

Will's heart soared when he heard Corbett use the familiar diminutive of his name.

"Oh, thank you, sir, thank you! I cannot tell you…"

"Yes, yes, save your thanks for when I find her, if I find her." Corbett felt in his weskit pocket and produced a shilling. "Now take yourself off, get a meal and a good bath so that you don't stink my office out when you return in two days when, I hope, I might have some news for you."

It took several minutes for the lawyer to persuade Will to swallow his pride and accept the coin as a gift and not, as the young carpenter at first insisted, a loan, but Corbett was in a hurry to get home himself so the interview ended with him pushing Will from the room and stuffing the shilling into his hand as he left.

"Two days, Will, two days," he said as he closed the door.

Chapter 13

In Which Will Meets Kate of the Court, Discovers Peg's Fate and
Hatches a Desperate Plan

Those two days dragged by so slowly that it felt, to Will, like a month
before he could present himself back in Mr. Corbett's chambers. He
had spent the time humping bales and boxes at the docks and had
paid for a bath at the local hammam and eaten a little on the strength
of his earnings. Corbett's gift he kept hidden away as he had a
suspicion that he might need it in what was to come at the courts.
There had been no thought of spending that shilling on new clothes,
but he had taken the trouble to rinse out his shirt and brushed the
worst of the dirt from his jacket, trousers, and well-worn boots.

As soon as Gunnard allowed him into Corbett's office, he could
tell from the look on the lawyer's face that his news was not good.
Even before Corbett began to speak, as he was ushered into a chair,
Will's heart fell. It was as if someone had placed a heavy stone inside
his chest. His mouth dried instantly and sweat prickled his scalp and
brow.

"I have not found her, Will, I am sorry. I spoke to Willard, the
clerk who keeps the court's records, and there is no Peg on his lists
from the days and weeks after the hanging. I talked to the chaplain at
Newgate and he confirmed what Sam Royston discovered; there is no
Peg there save the old crone he told you about."

Corbett continued to elaborate on his investigations, but, for a
few red-mist moments, such a rage rose in Will's breast that he heard
nothing. He wanted to scream like a child; it was so unfair! Was God

deliberately keeping him from finding a way to Peg? Corbett, still standing beside Will, put his hand on his shoulder.

"I believe there is only one way to explain this riddle, William," he said quietly. "Your girl must have given a false name to the watchmen when she was taken. If she was tried under that name, it would explain why there is no record of her."

"Then," he whispered, desperate now, "what can I do?"

The lawyer shook his head and muttered something under his breath.

"I can no longer help you, lad," he started, "but, there is one thing you might try. There is a character, a crone named Kate Withers, they call her Kate of the Court for she is there every day. It is her delight to see others tried and sentenced and they say she never misses a day nor forgets a case. Try Kate of the Court, Will, she may be your only chance."

*

The next day, Will dragged himself early from his reeking pit and, following Mr. Corbett's instructions, made his way to the Old Bailey. For a while, uncertain, nervous, he lingered in the shadow of Newgate where it cast its darkness from across the street. At length, he stepped through the gate, across the narrow courtyard, and into the court. It did not take him long to find Kate Withers, for she was well known in that place, as Corbett had said. She was seated in the public gallery. Her clothes were poor and much mended, but she was clean and sat in rapt attention as the court went about its business.

Will felt intimidated and unsure in that great place of Law with its strange smells, its dusty windows, the men in cloaks and dirty wigs, the judge up high on his oaken bench, but he reminded himself of why he had come and pushed his way along the bench to sit beside Kate of the Court. Not wishing to speak for fear of interrupting the proceedings of the court, he plucked her sleeve to get her attention. She turned her squinting gaze and looked at him as if he was a rat crawling over her mutton pie. He thought himself to be cleaner than he had been for days, yet her nose twitched at the smell of him and she moved away along the bench.

"Marm," he whispered, sliding a little closer. "I have…"

"Sshh!" She held a skinny, crooked finger to her lips and scowled at him. "Vait 'til he's done."

Will sat beside her until the judge declared the case over, found the ragged woman in the dock guilty, and sentenced her to five years hard labour.

"And no more than she deserves," muttered Kate.

"Mrs. Withers…" started Will, seizing his opportunity as the woman was led, weeping, away from the dock.

"*Miss* Vithers, if you please," the old woman threw back at him.

In her eyes, he saw a keen intelligence, yet she made a faded and forlorn sight, in her old gown and tattered bonnet.

"Miss Withers, my apologies, marm. My name is William Staples and I wondered, could help me with a case, a girl tried for robbery, some weeks ago now. I have been told you are one who knows all that goes on in this place."

Kate of the Court sat up at that; a flinty smile creased her withered and cracked lips and her eyes flashed. Will told her all he knew about the robbery and murder at the hanging of John Hill and how Peg had been falsely arrested.

"And vhat's she like this Peg?" Kate asked, leaning in to him so that he could smell her stale breath.

Will delighted in an extended and poetic description of Peg; her startling green eyes, her beauty, her long black hair, her small mouth with its rich pink lips. He tried his best to bring Peg to life in the old woman's mind. As he finished his tale she began to nod and gave him a malicious smile.

"Well, *Mister* Staples," she said. "I do know the girl, though I don't remember the name Peg, and if you have a crown in your pocket, I shall tell you all I know."

Will tried not to show his anger. He had been expecting money to be involved in the transaction, but even prepared, he could not stop the rage rising in him again at the injustice of the situation and the crone's lack of charity. He took a moment to calm himself as he faked a search of his pockets. A crown was a coin he had not seen in a long while; he could only hope and pray that Corbett's shilling would be enough.

"I have a shilling and that is all of my wealth."

Kate of the Court squinted at him and sighed. She looked away, watching as a new prisoner was led into the dock.

"Then, Vill Staples, let me see your coin."

He put the piece in her hand and she bit on it as if it were a dainty to please her sweet tooth.

"Good enough," she said with a horribly suggestive wink and told him everything she knew.

She did not remember Peg's name – "too many to put to mind every single name, boy" – but she knew of the crime on the day of the hanging, the theft and the death of a girl by stabbing, and recognized Will's description of Peg. It had been a short trial, Kate remembered, for Peg had pleaded guilty to the crime. She had been sentenced to transportation and fourteen years labouring on a plantation in the Virginian colony in America. Kate guessed that Peg would be transported sometime in the late summer and, if she survived the sea voyage – the old woman took great delight in telling Will, in graphic terms, how many died on that perilous journey – she would be sold to the highest bidder, a convict servant.

Hours later, having trudged the teeming streets, thinking, worrying, trying to make sense of what he had learned, Will lay on his vile pallet, his eyes closed, trying to sleep, though that welcoming place felt like a distant land. By turns, his mind hopped from memories to thoughts of the future and, slowly, he started to doze. In the liminal space between wakefulness and sleep, a plan came to him, a lunatic idea, but he was desperate. There would be no chance to find Peg while she was locked away, but she would be given a type of crippled freedom when she was in Virginia, he knew, and there and only there might he find her. Before he finally fell into sleep's open arms, he had resigned himself to his crazy plan. He would steal a book from a seller he had seen in Holborn and he would make sure he was caught. He would be tried, sentenced, just like Peg, and he would be transported to Virginia. There, somehow, he would find her and they would escape together.

Chapter 14

In Which Louis Silston Learns a Hard Truth

Abigail had left a short, pithy note for her parents, but it had been Polly's absence that had been noticed first, by the steward. Soon after that, when Abigail did not appear for breakfast, a search of the house had been instigated and that was when the note was found. Her father had already left for his office at the East India buildings, so her mother sent an urgent message to recall him early, as Louis Silston and his father were expected that afternoon.

Annabelle Colliton, always prone to anxiety, worried about her missing daughter from the outset, though, over tea and fancies that first afternoon, her husband and Louis Silston had tried to put her mind at rest. Abigail had been a silly little girl, all the men agreed, and no doubt would return covered in embarrassment soon enough, but when, by evening, there was still no sign, either of Abigail or her maid, Annabelle's concern, already a wildfire of rapidly proliferating anxieties, spread to her husband and Sir Crisp.

Far from worrying or becoming anxious, Louis felt slighted and cheated. He was not a man to be taken lightly, not a man to be trifled with. Around London, he was known as an arrogant, hard young buck, and he had gained this reputation amongst a set made up of arrogant, hard young men. As far as Louis was concerned Abigail was promised to him and now his possession had been taken away. His most acute concern was the effect on his reputation of any gossip about his betrothed running away from their arranged relationship.

Something had to be done to find Abigail and find her quickly. London was a dangerous place full of avaricious and desperate people willing to do anything for gain. It had been agreed that the steward be sent out to alert the watchmen and fetch Abigail's brother, Arthur. The rest of that first evening had been tense, as the family waited in vain for the return of their daughter. Annabelle sat for most of the time hunched in an elegant Queen Anne chair while Vicimeous alternately sat, stood or walked about the room. By eleven, with no sign of the girls, it was agreed that they had waited enough; something must be done. Louis argued that he knew London better than anyone else in the room and had better contacts in the military and police and so the Collitons agreed, somewhat reluctantly, that Louis would take the lead in organising a search for the girls.

A few nights later, Louis had been betting on a cockerel called Satan's Spike at Grey's Inn Cockpit. He had won well on an early bet, but was now behind, having lost on the next two birds. The air of the crowded room was filled with smoke and dust and the pit was surrounded by men, young and old, Quality and freemen, faces lit with exhilaration, mouths flapping as they goaded each other, cheered on their chosen bird or jeered at its opponent. Outside, it was raining torrentially, apocalyptically, yet Louis was unaware of anything but the fighting. As he watched, his face a livid mask of excitement, the door to the cockpit opened and a tall, heavy-set man wearing a wide-brimmed hat and a calf-length cape stepped inside. He was saturated and the brim of his dented hat was wrinkled, bowed low by the rain. Water streamed off his cape and dripped from his nose with a thin stream of snot, while his large boots glistened with a sheen of water.

For a few moments, he stood, dripping, sizing up the room. At last, he sidled up to Louis and tapped him on the shoulder.

"Bennett, how opportune," Louis shouted over the cheering, jeering crowd. "Wait you by the door and let me watch my bird…"

Bennett walked slowly to the door and turned to watch. From his position, he had a good view of his new employer. Louis's eyes were wide with excitement, a half-smile on his lips, but he did not shout or cheer, like his fellow gamblers. Instead, he stood still, one balled-up fist on the rail before him, his eyes locked on the battle below. A well-dressed man blighted with a massive belly moved to one side of Louis and clapped him on the shoulder twice, saying something in the young man's ear. He laughed, throwing back his head, missing the quick, malicious look Louis gave him.

The fat man brought his mouth close to Louis's ear again, but anything he might have said was drowned by the mighty roar that filled the gloomy room as Satan's Spike struck the killing blow. Louis raised his fist above his head and strode to retrieve his winnings. Bennett walked towards the pit to see the victor strutting confidently and crowing, ignoring its erstwhile opponent, which lay like a discarded, colourful scarf at the edge of the ring. His face still exultant, Louis led the man to the door.

Once outside in the pungent night air, they walked a short way to a rough alehouse in a nearby lane where they took their flagons of beer to a table in a dark corner. Every table was lit by a stub of tallow candle, every stool occupied by a red-faced, pocked-marked brigand-in-the-making. Louis stared silently at the man sitting opposite him. Despite his win, Louis's habitual anger was slowly rekindling; he had expected to have Abigail back with her parents by now, but this man had let him down.

He had paid good money to Bennett, a Watchman who, it was said, knew the streets of London better than any man alive and was not shy of using brute force as well as his web of connections throughout the underbelly of the city to deliver up a miscreant or missing person to whomsoever paid the most. For three days the man had been ferreting about in London's cesspools trying to find some evidence of Abigail's whereabouts, to no effect.

"It's not good enough, man," Louis hissed, leaning across the filthy table. "This is my betrothed we are seeking. I need that dowry, Bennett. My creditors are not kindly men and they expect repayment within the year. She must be found and soon!"

The Watchman, a veteran of many searches and well-versed in handling entitled and emotional clients, was unmoved. He regarded his new employer as he toyed with the handle of his beer mug. He saw before him a dark-haired, finely dressed young man, wealthy, privileged, haughty, but not soft. Louis had a scar that ran from below his right ear to his jaw line. An ex-army man himself, Bennett had noticed it when he first met Louis and knew a sword stroke when he saw one. Louis also had a coldness in his gray-blue eyes that Bennett had seen before, the same look that some of the men in his regiment had, the ones he thought of as the natural killers. No, thought Bennett, as he considered his reply, Louis Silston was not a man to underestimate.

"No, Mr. Silston," Bennett said at length, "it's ain't good enough and I'm am heartfelt sorry for that, m'lord."

"Sorry don't signify, Bennett. What are you going to do about it?" Louis's tone was full of barely suppressed rage.

"I am going to find her, m'lord. I have men out looking tonight, as I have these last two days …"

"Spending my money," Louis had barked, causing many of the grimy pub's grimier customers to look up.

It sounded good and gave Louis some satisfaction, but the truth was that the funds he was spending on the search came directly from Vicimeous Colliton.

"Yes, your worship, but coin be a great spur to those who ain't got any, better than the whip. We will find her, you can be assured of that."

"You'd better, Bennett, or I will make you suffer, by God."

*

Many interminable nights went by as Abigail's family waited for news. Her brothers made regular visits to their distraught parents at the London house and a decision was made to postpone their return to Surrey until Abigail was found.

On a wet evening some weeks later, Louis met once more with Bennett in the same miserable alehouse. Again, the two men occupied the same greasy table in the back of the small room. This time, Louis was drinking hard. Consuming the beer in this hovel was like sipping slops so he had ordered a rummer of Madame Genever, though even the gin was bad. Bennett cradled his customary mug of beer.

"Wait, wait, Bennett, let me understand you," Louis was saying. "You say this woman was killed at the hanging?"

The frown on Louis's face was one of confusion rather than one of concern. His pale eyes glinted in the weak candlelight.

"Yes, sir, knifed they say."

"But what has this to do with Abigail?"

"Well, sir, there was two of them, girls, come to the hanging to see John Hill sent to the Devil. So, Miss Abigail and her maid, I'm thinking."

"And no other girls go around London in pairs?" asked Louis sarcastically.

"Of course, sir, but what they say is the one killed in the ruckus had on fine shoes, sir, very fine. And her hair was golden, just like you said about Miss Abigail, and clean her hair was. And, pardon my saying this, sir, but they say her petticoat was lace and that's not what you see on a girl of Blackfriars or Cheapside."

"It still could have been anybody," mumbled Louis, not wishing to believe what he was hearing.

"And soft hands, sir. They say she had fine soft hands, yet she and her friend had told folks at the hanging they was dress-makers. None who makes dresses have soft hands, sir. But there's this too, sir. There was a mark on a finger where a ring had been ripped off."

"What finger? Come now, you must know?"

"Aye, sir. 'Twas the second finger of the right hand."

"God's blood! Abigail's grandmother's ring."

"And there is something more, Mr. Silston, something that ties it all up neat and proper, like."

"Continue…"

"Beggin' your pardon, Mr. Silston, sir, but I talked to me old mate Wenlock at Newgate and he told me they had a girl in some while ago. Tried and convicted of robbery at the hanging of John Hill. Sentenced to fourteen years labour in the American colony. Name of Polly Pruitt."

"The maid!"

There was a long silence in which Louis leaned back in his chair and took a large swig of his gin.

"Tried for robbery, you say?" he asked at last.

"Yes, sir."

"Not murder?"

"No, m'lord."

"This is outrageous!" Louis almost erupted out of his seat such was his fury. "This will not go unpunished," he continued in a low, vicious tone. He was silent for another minute.

"So, Abigail is dead," he said simply, his face impassive now.

"Truly sorry, your honour."

"And the maid?"

"Already at sea, master. Gone this last week."

"Damn, damn, damn!"

Both men sat in silence. Bennett looked around the tavern, sensing that they were the object now of some interest after Louis's outburst. No one caught the big man's eye, everyone returned to what they had been doing, conversations and serious drinking.

"For the moment we shall hold this information close, Bennett," Louis said quietly. "I want to tell her parents at the right time. Damn it, if only we had more."

"There might be more, sir. Seems there was a lad with 'em," said Bennett, a glint in his eye. He sensed that this need not be the end of his lucrative arrangement with Mr. Louis Silston.

"A lad?"

"Yes, m'lord. No name for him yet, but he was with the girls, laughing and eating with 'em. Close they was, so I'm told."

The Watchman leered at Silston whose eyes flashed.

"Find this 'lad', Bennett, and I will double your money and when you bring him to me, I will cut out his heart."

Chapter 15

In Which Will Discovers More Than He Wants To Know About
Newgate Prison

Will found himself in a small square, which sported, at its heart, a
grassy area flanked by twelve handsome plane trees. The houses
around the square were fine looking, not large, but broad and strong.
The street was muddy and there were piles of horse shit up and
down, but no dead dogs and no rats that he could see; a pleasant,
moneyed part of town. On one corner was a bookshop. He had no
memory of how he had got there, but he knew what he was there to
do.

It had rained early in the day and now the cobbles and narrow
pavements were slick with water glistening in the August sun. Will
had thought it a bad omen when he had awoken that morning to see
the sky filled with massing grey and purple clouds and the rain
pouring, like the tears of angels, as his mother used to say, but the
sun showed her shy face soon enough and now she shone like a bride
on her wedding day. He had chosen today because the King was to
ride through the city in his royal carriage and Londoners, he knew,
would be out in numbers uncountable to get a glimpse of the royal
person.

He remembered now, that cold feeling of bad luck in his gut as he
had hauled himself from his pallet, but he could not recall his journey
to the square. He had, evidently, made it in a dream. Now that the
crowds had sated their desire for a sighting of their German king, the
little square and the streets around it were still filled with a surging,

excited throng of people young and old, merchant and pauper, chattering, laughing and exchanging stories and lies of what they had and had not seen.

Will walked through the crowd like a fish swimming against the current. He had passed the book seller's shop eight times, stealing himself for the act, telling himself this was for Peg, that once he was caught and tried, he would soon be on a ship to the colonies and he would find her, but it was hard, much harder than he had imagined. He was not a criminal and his mother, he knew, would be disowning him if she was looking down from her seat in Heaven.

He put these thoughts from his mind and hunched his shoulders; he could wait no longer. He walked to the house of the bookseller. Outside was a table, old and crooked, and on it, lines of books stacked neatly with their spines upward. The owner was standing in the doorway, watching the crowds and smoking his pipe, a cloud of blue-grey smoke hanging in the still air around his head. Will ignored the man, picked up the book at the end of the stacked row, and turned away. In those first few seconds, when time seemed to slow, he thought his plan must have failed for there was no shout, no cry of "stop thief!" as he walked away, but then he heard a roar from the crowd and he ran.

He heard the pounding of footsteps behind him. The crowds on the street parted like summer wheat as he pushed through them. He wanted to be caught, that was essential to his plan, but now, in a cold rush, came terror; of Newgate prison, of public humiliation, of the unknown. More voices rose behind him. From the footsteps and shouts, he could hear there were many following him. People ahead of him were looking up as he barged towards them, as they too heard the shouts, but no one tried to stop him.

The blind fear of capture and the cries of the crowd chasing him like a pack of hunting dogs violently drove all thought of anything but escape from Will's mind. Forgetting his plan, he ran with the vigour of a man possessed; he sidestepped and swerved; he pushed people aside and, at the last second, dodged out in front of a hackney carriage, leaving his pursuers behind. At last, drenched in sweat and fizzing with adrenalin, he found himself in a dark lane, crouching in a recessed doorway deep in shadow, fighting to control his panting breath.

Hours later, he returned to his hovel filled with bitter self-loathing. He had failed because he was a coward; he had failed because, at the last, he had put his safety above his love for Peg. He was disgusted with himself. He felt dishonoured and, somehow, sullied. He had let himself down, but worse, he had let Peg down.

For four days, Will did not move from his lodgings except to drink at the water pump. The fourth morning dawned to find him leafing through the book he had stolen. He had snatched it at random and had had no expectations of its worth, yet he was amazed by the beauty of its binding and tooling, the delicacy of its inner papers, the glowing wonder of its illustrations. On the fifth day, hunger drove him out into the streets. He had no money. He had spent that last of his wretched pennies on a paltry breakfast the day of the robbery. All he had was the book and, though starvation had slowed his thoughts and muddled his mind, he determined, then, to sell it.

It was a dismal morning and cool, the sun hidden behind a bank of unseasonably thick, low cloud. He shivered in his rags as he wandered aimlessly along the busy byways. He could not go back to Holborn, he knew, so he must find another bookseller. If he could get a fair price, at the very least he would enjoy food for a few days. Things would be better when his belly was full, he would be able to think again, plan again.

He walked for much of the morning, becoming weaker with each hour that passed. A sort of delirium of hunger gradually overtook him as he trod his weary way until on a corner he spotted a bookshop. His one clear thought as he stepped inside was that he must get some money for the book. The proprietor was standing flanked by shelves of books, his hands flat on the counter. The hint of a smile on his face dissolved into a scowl when he saw the state of his customer's clothes. Will, his eyes half-closed, placed the exquisite text before the bookseller.

"How much for this?" he whispered.

Will caught only some of the staccato words of the bookseller, something about asking his colleague about the book's worth, and watched the man disappear behind a heavy curtain that sectioned off the front of the shop from its back room. He put both his hands heavily on the counter and closed his eyes, trying to ignore the grating ache in his guts. He must not fall over.

Will was jerked fully awake when two strong hands took his arms from behind. He opened his eyes to see, as if through a mist, the burly proprietor and a younger man holding him. The bookseller was babbling about stolen property and calling the Watchmen.

"I know this volume," he heard the man cry out, "I know where you stole it, you worthless cur."

An electric thrill of fear overlaid the pain in Will's belly, yet he allowed himself a smile. His arms still pinioned behind him, he buckled slowly forward until the side of his head rested on the counter. The word irony may not have been in his vocabulary, but he knew it when he saw it.

*

When he was brought to Newgate, Will was taken to a small, stuffy office where he was greeted by three men. They did not give their names, but he later discovered that two of them were the prison's chief warders, Quince and Wharton. The third occupant of the office that day, a small, thin man called Wenlock who lounged in a chair in a corner of the room, was one of the warder's lackeys. Few words were exchanged before Wenlock took Will down flights of stairs that became darker and danker by degrees as they descended.

When it seemed they could go no lower, Wenlock opened a hatch and lowered Will down into the Stone Hold. Without a word, he shut the hatch with a loud thud and Will was left in the resounding silence of that foul place. It was as dark as a late summer evening, though bitterly cold rather than balmy warm. In the gloom, he could make out the shapes of three people lying or sitting on the damp, straw-covered floor. On two of the walls, he saw shackles hanging from chains. There was no window and the only light seeped through the close-spaced bars in the observation slot in the hatch above his head.

The place stank of excrement and piss mingled with something worse, something that conjured the rot and putrefaction of death in Will's mind. He closed his eyes and tried to remember something bright and happy, tried to remind himself why he was there. A moment came to him, a glorious, sunny moment. He was walking with Peg and Lizzie from St Paul's to the river. Light sparkled on the muddy water like silver coins spread on its surface, appearing and disappearing. They were laughing about something and Peg turned to him, her face alive with joy, eyes sparkling like the great stream behind her. She laid her hand on his arm and squeezed for a second and then it was gone, but his heart had soared with the gulls overhead.

He heard a sound and came back to himself, back to the dreadful present. He opened his eyes. The light was gone; he was in darkness and cold again. He groped for the memory and it flickered like a guttering candle and was gone. He tried to think of other memories to warm him; walking with his father through Baggot's Wood seeking good timber to fell, learning his letters with his mother, attending school and learning of the world, meeting Peg, but his mind would not fix on any one thing.

He realised that the sound he heard was a voice. One of the shapes had risen from the floor and was approaching him. He flinched, momentarily and then, thinking better of himself, stood as tall as he could. In the shadows, he saw a pale face, thick eyebrows, and a strong jaw. The man's face was long and lean and his black hair, flowing to his shoulders, was lank. His eyes bore into Will like a beetle into soft wood; dark eyes like coals.

"Well, lad," he intoned, his voice deep and resonant, "welcome to Akerman's hotel. And what brings you to this illustrious place?"

After Will gave the man a guarded history of his crime and capture, the fellow offered his hand and said his name was John

Vertue, recently brought to the Stone Hold for fraud and theft. Though Will's experience of city people was narrow and paltry, he seemed, to the young carpenter, to be an educated man. He spoke well with only a hint of an accent that Will did not recognize and, despite the surroundings and their dire situation, had a glint in his eye and a sly grin. He told Will that if a man had money, he could pay Wharton or "that belly-gut", Quince, and be moved to better accommodation, but most had to endure the Hold before being moved to cells on a higher floor.

He wanted to know Will's history and the young carpenter faltered for a moment before speaking, wondering if he should trust the sharp-looking man. But then, almost before his thoughts were in order, he found himself telling his whole sorry tale. It was cathartic, something that Will had not expected. It was as if he had been waiting for this very moment to unburden himself to this anonymous man who he may never see again. He was a mere human who had been called upon to be an Atlas, carrying the weight of the pain and guilt of his lost love on his shoulders. When he started to explain his plan, how he had worked out how to get himself transported to Virginia, a strange look appeared on John Vertue's face.

"You think me a beef-head?" asked Will.

"No, no not at all, Will. No man is a fool who chases his dream."

He moved closer to Will and put a heavy hand on his shoulder.

"Then...?"

"Young Will, did you not think to seek to work your passage on one of the merchant vessels that sail to the colonies every week? Why a lad like you would have found work as a hand with ease. I declare, they must always want a good carpenter."

Will's stomach churned at those words and he felt faint.

"Ah," said Vertue, "I see this idea had not been part of your planning."

"I…I did not know," Will stuttered.

"Did not know you might find a way to Americee without the help of a transport ship, lad? No, that I can see from the look in your eyes and the colour of your face. Why, boy, you look like you've seen the shade of your own dear mother. And now, here you are, at the pleasure of his gracious majesty and his fawning underlings."

Over the next two days, Will came to know John Vertue and found him, against his better judgment, to be a man to his liking. He said he had been a soldier of fortune, fighting in the wars against the King of Spain, seeing the lands of France and the Low Countries before coming back to London, where he had found that his wife had run away with another man, his house had been sold, his goods stolen or pawned and his old mother dead from the palsy.

"I have always tried to be true to my name, Will," he told the younger man, "a man of virtue, but coming back from the wars to be abandoned by our glorious King, finding all I held dear lost to me, I was not about to beg on the streets with the broken and misbegotten."

Will felt his face redden at those words. In his shame, he had not confessed to John of his short time as a beggar.

"No, boy, but I should never have allowed myself to be tricked into a scheme by that rogue Henry Hamilton, a scheme so shameful and dishonest that I now find myself in this vile place with you and these other unfortunates. And Hamilton has made his escape, Will, leaving me to take the blame and punishment alone.

"That damnable devil forged an East India Company bill and I, hapless and hoodwinked, thought it genuine and a chance to get back some of my lost fortune. But they are a bad lot to try and trick out of their money and so here I am, the devil dancing in my pocket. Little did I ever think, Will, I'd be a man of no worth. I was only here a day when a fellow by the name of Wrighton turned up with an offer to use his so-called influence at St James, for a pardon. He just needed me to pay over a fee. But you can't fraud a fraudster, Will."

He laughed and continued, but Will's mind had crashed into a pit deeper and darker even than the Hold, and Vertue's words faded to a background rumble. How could he have been such a fool? As if to answer his question, when evening came their stone dungeon was filled with the low moans and cries from the newly imprisoned accused who had joined them in the Hold, a miserable clamour for succour, for lost loved ones, for lost liberty.

Chapter 16

In Which Polly Sets Out for The Virginia Colony and Will Is
Tried and Sentenced

We are in a section of a deck in the belly of this ship separated from
the men by a thick wooden wall. The boards above our heads are so
low that, when they brought us here, but for the child, Mary all had to
stoop to walk into our fine new quarters. Then they shackled to us to
benches, five on mine four on the one behind. Round my neck they
put an iron collar attached by a chain to Annie Jameson beside me,
who, for my sins, will be sharing her shining thoughts, lice, and fleas
for the voyage. Annie was likewise joined by metal to her neighbour
and so on to the end of the bench where they padlocked the chain to
the floor. Annie was a cellmate in Newgate, so at least I know her,
though she is no friend. Not that I despise her, 'tis just hard to be a
friend to any of these lost souls.

Before they brought us down here, a man in a dirty wig and
stained frock coat with a small tray hung around his neck moved
between us women gathered in the evening sun on deck. He had a
thin ledger bound in brown leather on his tray and an ink pot. Some
sort of clerk he was and he held a white and grey quill in his ink-
stained fingers.

Each woman was asked for her name, which he scribed in his
book then he reached out to pull her chin up so he could inspect her
face. Then he pushed back her lips with his dirty fingers to see her
teeth and felt the muscles of her arms. I could not help myself; I
shuddered when my turn came and the loathsome little man

manhandled me, but I swallowed my pride and stared as hard as maybe into his little bright eyes, though he hardly seemed to see me.

His work was met with cries of disgust and anger from us women, but he went on making his notes, leaving us feeling like animals at the market to be stowed below like so much cargo. But we were in the fresh air and fine it was too. The river was calm and reminded me of the broad ribbons aunt Susan used to make, though this one looked almost like metal in the low sun. We were at the Pool of London near Limehouse a sailor told us and its chimneys belched so that their smoke was like fingers reaching into the low clouds. We were below and in chains by the time the ship left the dock so we saw no more, but we heard the sailors' shouts above the slop and splash of the water that seemed right beneath our feet.

Of us nine women, the youngest is the tiny girl called Mary, who is with child, God save her, and the oldest is Mother Gantry, a toothless crone who says nothing and eyes us all with a malicious stare. One of the sailors who brought us food on the first day, told us there are forty-five convicts altogether, which means there's thirty-six men. I was surprised to hear that, for, when they marched us to the docks from Newgate, I'd have guessed there was more in the crowd of hunched and miserable manhood that shuffled before us.

When they brought us down to chain us, it dizzied me, the darkness, the low ceiling, and the smell, worse even than Newgate. The sailors laughed at our faintheartedness and told us the floor had been rinsed in Thames water and swabbed yet there was an abiding dull stink on the place.

But if I thought t'were bad at the start, it became truly horrible soon enough. What with sea-sickness, bad food, and no air, we found ourselves living in a foul brew of human shit, piss and vomit that mixed with the smell of unwashed bodies, the rank breath from mouths filled with rotten teeth, and the heavy stink of damp clothing and rotting food. By God, within days, I felt I could grab the stench by the handful. At the end of the second week, the poisonous air seemed to me to be another prisoner, locked down there with us poor women. It stalked the deck like a living thing, spicing the unmoving air with its own brand of torture.

Our journey across the sea has been a worse purgatory even than Newgate. I hated that place more than anything, but it did not buck and sway and lunge. We have been tossed in violent storms, which caused the most heart-stopping screams and howls from us as the ship was thrown around like a child's toy and seemed like to sink at any moment and we have been becalmed on still waters in a silence even more terrifying for you feel you will never, ever reach land again. The whole voyage has been like unto a terrible dream so I try as hard as I might to not think on it, to press it from my head for there is little to distract my aching mind.

And if the days have been like bad dreams, so the nights have brought the same awful nightmares that started in Newgate. In the cell, I was sure I must cry out in my sleep every night, yet no woman ever accused me of disturbing her sleep and when I asked Sophia, she told me I was always the quietest one. So, I trust the horror to be only inside me, here on the ship and back in Newgate.

The dreams are not always the same, but there is one that comes again and again. Knives flash as men with no faces lay hands on me, ripping my clothes and beating my face and body with their fists, pressing meaty hands on my breasts and between my legs and, always,

I hear a child screaming. That scream is terrifying; high, gurgling, dying. Then I look down and see Abigail; her fine clothes, her perfect golden hair, her dear face. And then I see her hands, her poor fingernails chewed down to the scut and I look again and there is a flower of brilliant red staining her lovely clothes and her face is twisted…and that is when I always wake.

Sometimes Annie Jameson will mag and gossip about her life in London, talking for hours as if her words were a river along which she could float to freedom. She ain't talking to any of us, poor woman, she has become a pure Bedlamite. Many a time have I closed my eyes and tried to ignore her and the mutterings and cries of the other women. Sometimes it works, when I can remember the good times, but I can never ignore the chafing of my collar and sores on my neck. Oh, how I hate my collar and chain, not so much for the pain they give me; no, 'tis because they weigh on me like a foretelling of my death and make me a part of someone else. I am my neighbor and she is me.

Many a day I am in a blackness that I cannot rid myself of, a bitter hatred of all around me and all I have known. Only sometimes can I raise myself up from this Stone Hold of the mind and remember my aunt Susan and my good fortune in becoming Abigail's maid. But then, when I see her face and think I can even smell her fine perfume, I remember my forbidden love for that special girl and I plunge back into melancholy.

*

For Will the trial was a haze, a half-dream of autumnal sun shining through high windows, motes of dust dancing and falling in the shafts; a rowdy audience in the public gallery and Kate of the Court up there, her beady eye on proceedings; a hook-nosed judge in his robes, a splash of colour up on his high bench; the men who seemed to wander through the court, in and out, papers in hand; the men who sat and scribbled with their quills; everywhere fine white wigs, grey wigs, old and dusty wigs and all the men wore severe black cloaks. At the door were the men and women awaiting their turn in the dock and amongst them, John Vertue.

Asked his age, Will told them twenty, which was true, though he felt much older, very old indeed and tired. Newgate had sapped him and he felt confused. He did not understand much of what was going on, but answered, when he was asked, that, yes, it was he who had robbed the bookstall. All he could think of was Peg and whether she was already on a ship bound for the mysterious distant shores of the American colonies. Would he be sent soon or would he have to wait? How would he find her when he arrived? No, he told himself, as the voices droned around him, do not ask that; there will be a way, I will find a way.

When he had made his plan, he had felt excited, but now all he felt was exhaustion and hunger, mixed with a large dose of uncertainty. The longer he had to wait before being taken to the vessel that would transport him to Virginia, the harder it would be. He became aware that someone was speaking to him, the judge, leaning forward and repeating his name.

"Yes, sir," he replied, his head bowed.

"You have been found guilty, William Staples, of robbery."

At last, thought Will, let us get to the ship now.

"You willfully and wantonly took what was not yours. You deprived an honest man of his living by stealing that book…"

Enough thought Will not looking up, let us get to the meat. His thoughts drifted away, again, to that transport across the wide Atlantic Ocean, to Peg's lovely face. Then out of the haze, out of his dream of reunion, he heard a word, a terrible word. Hanged. No! His mind raced, suddenly very awake, focused, and terrified. *It cannot be, 'twas only a book.* But it was true. For the theft of a book, William Staples was to be taken to Newgate to await that month's hanging day when he would, with others of his ilk, be transported by cart to the Tyburn Tree and there hanged by he neck until he was dead.

*

On his return to Newgate, Will was locked in the Middle Ward. His mind was still reeling from the shock of his sentence. How could this be? Peg had been accused of robbery and yet she had been transported. His mind was a cesspit of blame and terror and confusion and anger and loss. He was too bewildered to notice the improvement in his lodgings. The air of the Middle Ward was rank with the stink of the inmates and the prisoners themselves were foul, crazy, dangerous, intimidating, but the cells had wooden floors and low beds with straw and heather-packed mattresses. Will, though, was oblivious to everything after he returned from the court. At last, the door opened and Wharton pushed John Vertue into the cell. The lanky man walked to Will and stared into his eyes.

"Hanging then, lad," he said breathily. "I was at the door; heard all. I'm sorry, Will Staples, sorry for your plan and for your Peg and for your life wasted."

"And you, John?" Will asked, his voice small.

"Hanged, Will, hanged with you. We're to go west, lad, as they say in here, west to the Tree."

Will slumped onto a greasy mattress and closed his eyes. He lay there motionless for minutes until a hand on his shoulder stirred him. He looked up into John Vertue's eyes. The man raised him up and pointed to the top of the highest wall in the cell. There was a small window the size of a meat plate. Through it Will was able to see a tiny kerchief of blue sky lined with high, thin clouds of pure white. The sight brought a tear to his eye.

"God is in his heaven, Will," said John with a grim smile.

"Though not looking down on us wretches," Will replied.

He spent a restless night lying awake between short fitful bouts of dozing. When he did sleep, he dreamed of knives and nooses, running feet and heavy hands on his body. Not once in his dreaming mindscape did Peg appear. He woke to see the slow light of morning filling the small square of window, turning from black to deepest blue, to grey, to pink, then palest orange. He fell asleep at last thinking of his love and how it would never be consummated.

Later, Will was awoken by a commotion outside the cell door. He turned on his pallet to see John gazing out of the small barred opening that served as a window in the door. Standing beside John was an older man, wizened and bent who went by the name of Absalom.

"Come see the fine folk, Will," said John.

Outside the cell, in the gloom of the hallway, was a group marked out by their attire: men in long, skirted coats of brocade, velvet or silks, white wigs, and beautiful shiny square-toed shoes; women in extravagant silk gowns of many colours, hair natural, but pinned into stylish shapes. All were crowding outside an adjacent cell, murmuring, laughing, and nodding knowingly to each other.

"The Quality, here to see the Blackfriar's gang, I'll warrant," said John softly.

"See them?"

"They pay good money, Will, to come in and gaze upon the miserable visages of those condemned to hang. The Blackfriar's gang are off to Tyburn Tree on the morrow so this is the last chance for the gawkers to get their look."

Will could not see the members of the gang, locked away in their cell, but he could hear their preening voices and boastful claims, proud to have attracted such a crowd of worthies as their last audience.

"They won't be so bold tomorrow when their chains are off, hands tied and they're on the cart on their way to meet Jack noose," muttered old Absalom as he turned away and flopped onto his bed.

Will swallowed heavily knowing that it would be himself, John, and some other unfortunates who would be the object of reviled fascination in a month's time. A horrible churning started in his gut and he thought he might be sick. For the first time since he was a little lad, he felt truly, mortally afraid. He had four short weeks left to live, one month to re-live the fleeting joy of his moments with Peg and to contemplate his stupidity.

Chapter 17

In Which Will Staples Waits in Newgate For His Sentence to
Be Carried Out

Will had always been proud to be someone who rarely felt fear. The
extremes of being raised by a brutal father and loving mother had
toughened him rather than confused him, so he could count on the
fingers of one hand the times in his adult life when he had been truly
scared. The gut-deep dread of never seeing Peg again had been and
still was one of those times, but, since being condemned to the
noose, he had realised he had never before known real terror for
himself.

In the early days after sentence was passed, he lived in a waiting
Hell. Dread became a part of his very body, deep down to his core, a
new torturer, wrapping its arms around him and holding him close to
its whispered horrors. He could not eat and even found himself
gagging on water. His friend John Vertue tried to talk to him, tried to
raise him up from where he lay trembling on his pallet, but to no
avail.

Only sleep, when it reluctantly came, was a relief; he rarely dreamt,
and when he did, his nighttime mind took him journeying back to
better times when his mother's voice was always there and
sometimes, so was Peg's. In time, the trembling stopped, the constant
feeling of being constrained by terror started to dissipate and he came
to understand that it was not death he feared. He remembered vividly
his mother's dying; death was a part of life, he knew that. He also, as
he slowly recovered the better part of himself, came to the conviction

that his Maker knew him to be an honest man, driven to steal for love, so he was able, in some small way, to look forward to meeting his mother again.

As he came to his senses and started to live again, he saw that the terror that was deeper and richer than any fear Death might bring was the dread of never seeing 'his Peg' again. Since meeting the girl, he had come to understand that life only has value when you treasure something outside yourself. He began to eat again, to converse with the others in the condemned cell who shared his fate, to take solace from his growing friendship with John Vertue, and to face his doom with what strength he had left.

One week before the hanging, they were moved to the 'death cell'. This new accommodation was narrow and confined; the condemned men were crammed in like herrings in a pot. Will's one solace since they were moved was that, like the Middle Ward, this room had a window, high in one wall and barred, but wider than the slit in their last cell and through it he could gaze at the blues, greys, whites, blacks, purples, and pinks of the ever-varying English sky, the sky he had taken for granted when he was a free man. When his cellmates allowed it, he would sit looking up at that fragment of the heavens thinking about Peg and wondering what she was doing, how she was faring in her new life in the Virginia colony. He wished he could send his thoughts to her before he was taken to Tyburn so that she might know how, in life, he had loved her.

On their last Sunday, the five prisoners were led, chained together and manacled, hands and feet, to the chambers of the prison parson, known as the Ordinary. He gave them a long sermon about their wicked ways and the love that "their true Lord" had for them, if only, he had said, they would "give up their hearts and souls to Him". The men stood shivering in their chains in his room, which was bare but for a cross on the wall and, true to tradition, a black coffin lying on the floor in the corner. Everything, it felt to Will, even this man of God, conspired to bring them fear and sorrow.

Two days later, the day before their execution, it was hot, a morning when even the cold death cell was humid and warm. The five doomed men, John Vertue, John Doggett, David Evans, Robert Makepeace, and Will, sat on the floor to break their fast together and eat the meager offerings of the prison's kitchen: a thick, sticky gruel, a hunk of stale bread and a mug of small beer. Their remaining time, which had slipped by at the start of their wait as slowly as the wheat ripened in the fields of Will's old home, was now galloping towards their inevitable end.

In the cell next to them was a man called Colhoun, an Irishman with a high whining voice and heavy accent, who took ghoulish pleasure in doing anything he could to increase and intensify their discomfiture. He delighted to stand at the barred window of the door of his cell and regale them with a detailed description of every step they would take in their slow procession to the gallows.

"Take you to the condemned room, they do, boys. Take off your shackles, tie your hands. Then it's up on the cart with Sepulchre's bells chiming for your sinner's souls. The Ordinary'll be with you, lads, praying for you, though I'd say you'll all be damned, and then it's off along Holborn and St Giles, maybe a stop at The Bowl for a dram or two, maybe a few kisses blown by the young girls, maybe a few rotten cabbages flung at your sorry faces and then it's on to the Tree. Only two miles, boys, but it'll take three good hours to get through the crowds. Better have your last words ready, they'll all want to hear what you have to say afore your necks is stretched."

Chuckling, he explained how long it would take them to die once the cart was driven away, how long they would "dance in the air". He told them some of the condemned have friends or family stationed near the Tree who would jump up and hang on the legs of the dying convicts to try to send them on their eternal journey more quickly. With Colhoun's every word Will would see that picture, burned into his memory, of the men hanging from the gibbet on that hot day when, for a brief time, he was happy and with his lovely Peg. He knew there would be no one at the gallows to hang on his legs to make his dying quicker.

Over and again, Robert Makepeace cursed the Irishman and vowed to throttle him should he have half a chance to get his hands around the man's neck. Makepeace was a truly evil man. He had been convicted of murdering two people, a merchant, and his daughter, for a few guineas. He had a temper like a whiplash and Will had followed John's early exhortation to avoid provoking the man. If Colhoun had been in the same cell, he would never have taunted Makepeace, but there were two thick walls and doors between them and he would not be stopped.

John told Will to not listen, but that was impossible. Will tried to be brave, tried not to show his cellmates that his terror had returned, but, now, at the end, he thought he must go mad with the waiting. Many a time in the last few days he had wished he had been taken straight from the court and strung up there and then rather than abide the awful wait. At other times, he had been grateful for every creeping minute of life, even in that awful place. He wondered what the others saw when they looked at him: a man like themselves or a lad, eyes sunken from want of food, face thinned and paled by hardship, hair, once fair, now dark with dirt and grease, body, once hard and strong, now thin and spindly. Did they see, not the man he was, but the lost boy that he felt himself to be?

On the afternoon of Will's last full day on Earth, the atmosphere in the cell was crackling with tension, though the men hid their terror under a mantle of braying bravado. Will was different. He had spent the morning in silence, running over and over in his mind all that had happened since he met Peg and he could make no sense of it. He could not understand how he had come to this pass, to be hanged for the theft of a book when he could have worked his passage to America and might have been with his Peg again.

"How I wish I was given more time with Peg," he said to John Vertue. "God in his heaven, I was such a fool. I shall never see my poor Peg again, John, never in this life..."

"Aw, fer Christ's sake, shut up yer whinin' about your wee whore," sneered Makepeace.

Will could not help himself. The reply came, without thought but with bitter hate, like a shot from a pistol.

"What did you say?"

Makepeace's lips curled back, revealing brown and broken teeth. Will realised it was a smile; the Scotsman was smiling, something he had not seen before and he knew in his heart what it meant. Before he could reply, Makepeace spoke again and his voice was full of vitriol and disdain.

"I said, ya weak-bawed wee mannie, just shut up about yer fuckin' whore. It's just her sweet, little cunny yer missin'..."

With a roar, Will threw himself across the cell, his arms outstretched, his hands already groping for the Scotsman's neck. His face was alight in a conflagration of rage, his head full of his father's face, the faces of the roadside robbers who would have taken all he had and left him for dead, the face of the judge who had condemned him to the noose.

Makepeace, still smiling, was ready.

He side-stepped, taking the sting out of Will's furious attack, though he took a blow to the side of his head from Will's outstretched hand. His eyes widened with lunatic delight and spittle flew from his lips with the curses that bellowed from his mouth. He was a small man, but wiry and with surprising strength in his thin arms and, in an instant, he was on Will. The lad managed to get his thumb into the corner of the Scotsman's eye and gouged hard as he pushed away, but it was not enough. The murderer, silent now, was a whirlwind of flying arms, fists, and legs, beating Will about the body, crashing his forehead into the young man's nose and kicking at his shins until Will fell to the floor, where he might have been bludgeoned to death had John Vertue and David Evans not pulled the raving Makepeace off him.

While Will crawled to a corner to rub his bruises and mop the oozing blood from his nose with the filthy cuff of his jacket, his two saviours pulled the furious murderer to the far end of the tiny cell. Makepeace may have raged on for longer, roaring his disdain for Will, had the door of the cell not opened. The jailer, Wharton stood in the doorway with a hungry grin on his lean face. He glanced at Will and the two men holding Makepeace at bay. As a stony silence fell,

Makepeace threw off the hands that held him back and slumped to sit on the floor. Wharton hitched his breeches and belched.

"Havin' a party, boys?"

Nobody spoke. Suddenly, the floor of the cell had become fascinating to its occupants.

"Well," said Wharton, half turning to the two lackeys who stood behind him, "we're sorry to have missed the dancin', ain't we, boys? But that's all over now, for 'tis time to go."

Will's mind swirled in confusion and dread; it could not be time, they had one more day. He had never thought he would feel unwilling to leave Newgate, but now he squashed himself down lower to the floor and prayed that he might stay there for the rest of his miserable life. Around him, the other inmates were up in arms.

"It ain't today, Wharton! We got another day," squealed Evans.

"Shut your mouth and come with me. Doggett, Vertue, Staples up with you too."

The named prisoners exchanged glances, bewildered. Robert Makepeace squinted up from his corner and started to rise, his dark face giving nothing away.

"Not you Bobby," growled Wharton, "just still yourself."

The warder and his helpers chained the men together and led them up out of the dimness into the light. They emerged into the yard where they breathed in the air of freedom for a few precious moments. It was raining, a light pattering that felt, to Will, a wonderful blessing. Evans began to panic, kicking out and screaming about it being the wrong day.

"Shut your noise, Welsh dog," Wharton shouted as he gave Evans a swipe across the face. "'Tis not the rope today, but the court you go to; King's pardon for the lot of you. Too many hangings, they're sayin' and hands needed in the colony. Gracious King George, eh, lads?"

The jailer chuckled as he and his minions led the four men across the shining cobbles to the Old Bailey where, in a whirl, they were taken to court, paraded as a group in front of the magistrate – a grossly fat man in the largest wig Will had ever seen – and read their pardons. It was transportation to the Virginia colony for all, said the magistrate: Doggett, fourteen years, Evans fourteen years, John Vertue and Will seven years each. The young carpenter, still nursing scoured shins, a throbbing nose, and bruised ribs, was not quite able to believe what was happening.

"What of Makepeace?" asked John Vertue as they were led back across the road to Newgate.

"The rope for him tomorrow," said Wharton, matter-of-fact. "The King's mercy only goes so far, boys."

Three days later, after waiting and wondering in the relative spaciousness of the Middle Ward, the four were led, once more, out to the yard, where they were chained together with around thirty other men. Looking up at Newgate's high dark walls, Will realised that his world had shrunken to a box of stone and some fleeting memories of a lovely young girl. As he waited under a lowering autumn sky, he felt as ignorant of the world as a newborn baby. He breathed deeply of the cool air, guessing it must be September, but even that he did not know.

The gates opened and a man he had never seen before called out for them to march and, for the first time in what has felt like a second lifetime, Will set foot again on the soil of free London.

Chapter 18

In Which Polly Completes the Atlantic Crossing

I sit with my eyes open. I do not know the time nor if any of my deck-mates, as the sailors call us, are awake like me. Over time, I have grown used to the pitch and roll of the ship. Mercifully, tonight it ain't too bad, though bad enough to send me, betimes, rocking sideways into Annie Jameson. I guess my neighbor to be asleep for she is silent, thank the Lord. Most nights, I don't sleep or, at least, sleep badly as any mortal woman would, shackled and bound and never able to lie down. Sleeping sitting up is one thing I will never learn to do well.

So, I sit, in the small hours of the night, in a fit of melancholia, as is proper for this benighted time. My stomach is paining me, guts all a'wamble. In this place, hunger scrapes and claws at a body all the time, worse even than in Newgate, for the food on this ship is not fit for a rat; salt pork, hard biscuits full of horrid, tiny animals, dried peas which have to be sucked for minutes before they can be chewed and water that tastes like it's been through every sailor on the ship. My neck and collarbones are raw from the rubbing of the iron ring and my back, shoulders, and legs ache. I have learned, most times, to put these agonies in some dark corner of my mind so I feel the pain, but don't dwell on it. In the long night, though, when I am alone among these snoring, whimpering women it is hard to ignore the hurt.

To try to stop thinking about the aches, I begin a list of everything in my body that still works. I have my teeth – though I have the taste of blood in my mouth a lot these days – and my sight is good, good enough anyway to see into the darkness of this foul prison and make out the spars and braces and planks. My ears work well. If I close my eyes, I can hear every little sound; the creaking, cracking, and groaning of this vessel, the breathing of the women, the slop and woosh of the sea and, even now, in the heart of the night, the talk of sailors and, betimes, the shouts of officers. My hair is still growing, thanks be to the good Lord, though it is lank, unwashed and a city for the lice, but one day, I have to believe, it will be washed clean. I circle my fingers around my left wrist, something I do too often. It is thin and bony and when I run my hand up my arm that too is awful skinny. I think, perhaps I might starve before we reach America.

I see the faces of all I know these long nights. My supposed friend Agnes and her cheating brother, John; I never had another friend in London 'til I went to the Collitons. My good aunt Susan, God rest her, and her daughter, Liza. My lovely Abigail, whose face I find I can see now without falling into despair and crying, though I miss her something dreadful. The kind carpenter Sam and his goodwife, Betsy who looked after us when we needed help, and that moony boy, who could not stop looking at me, another useless man. He was friendly enough, but, in the end, he didn't save Abigail and he didn't save me.

The faces come and go and, at last, I think I see a thin band of light from somewhere overhead. Perhaps today captain Gillard will let us up on deck; it must be a week since we was last out in the fresh air. 'Tis supposed to be once every week. You don't know what fresh air is 'til you come up from this dungeon into the light. A miracle it is; nothing like the air in London with its stinks; this is real air and you can almost taste the salt of the sea. There's some cages up there, with animals; sheep, pigs, chicken and 'tis good to see them, though their numbers are mighty thinned now and they look as miserable as we women.

He's a strict one is Gillard, strict in running his ship and hard on disobedience or complaint from us convicts. One time, we was on deck when the sea was rough and the ship jerked around like a bucking horse and a sailor put his hand on my rear end.

"Hands off the merchandise, Mr. Abbott," roared the captain.

Merchandise, that's what he called me. Us women are like the bits I used to pick up in Islington village and sell around Cheapside, bits, and pieces to be bought and sold.

But now I can't get me mind off going up into the air. I remember the first time. None of us knew that was one of the rules, being brought up on deck, so 'twas a surprise and a good one at that. I could hardly believe the sight of the endless sea; grey-green it was, the distant line where the sky stopped and the water began, the orizon, one of the sailors said it was called, afore he was told to shut his gob. They ain't allowed to talk to the 'goods'. And the great masts, like tall London planes, and the grey, flapping sails, so big, making their own strange songs, just like the ropes. I tell myself to remember all this for it will keep me from becoming a Bedlamite down there in the dark. I didn't know then we'd come up every week, but we do, thank the Lord. That's another thing. I thank the Lord a lot more now than I did in the good times, though, when Abigail was killed, I was minded for a while there was no Lord.

For some reason, I am thinking on little Mary. The Lord wasn't looking down on any of us that day. She gave birth right there in the row behind me. I'd never heard the like of it, had to hold me hands to me ears, the screaming and wailing like she was off the hooks and ready for Bedlam, and Mother Gantry's s'outs as she tried to help the mite birth her unfortunate child. I could not help myself; I wept like a baby when we stood on deck as Captain Gillard mumbled a quick prayer before two sailors threw the bodies of Mary and her baby, all wound up in sacking, to the sea.

I am lost in these bad memories when I hear a sound from nearby. I look round and Annie Jameson is staring at me with her lunatic eyes, giving me a toothless grin.

"What?" says I, a bit short, like.

"Land," says Annie, wagging her big hands around.

"What do you mean, Annie?" says I.

"He shouted," she says. "Land, he shouted, I heard it."

So, I am here, the Virginia colony. Well, I think, I have been in Hell on land and now Hell on the sea. Nothing in this place can be as bad.

Chapter 19

In Which We Hear of Abigail's Memorial Service and Louis Silston
Learns What Happened on The Day of John Hill's Hanging

The family's private chapel was crowded, its pews crammed with the
good and the gracious of Surrey. Pastor Ewert stood at the altar
facing the congregation, intoning a prayer for Abigail's soul, whilst
her father, mother, and brothers sat in the front pew staring rigidly
forward. In the pew behind the family sat Louis Silston and his
father, Sir Crisp.

There was no body, no coffin, only a small portrait of Abigail,
commissioned by her father when she was thirteen, surrounded by
flowers and propped high enough on a table at the front of the nave
so that most of the congregation could see it.

When the final hymn had been sung and the short service was
finished the congregation filed out into a fine late-September drizzle
to where their carriages awaited. The staff of the Colliton's house,
footmen, maids, cooks, gardeners, and all the others had left the
chapel some minutes before the end of the service to walk in the rain
back to the house to make ready the feast and bank the fires.

The house, crowded with family and guests, felt alive again for the
first time since Abigail had run away, but later, when all the well-
wishers had departed, taking with them their scandalized private
thoughts about the young girl's motives for running away and getting
herself stabbed at a public hanging, the place felt bare and cold and
empty. Abigail's mother retired to her bed, where she had spent
much of the last few weeks, lost in a world of her own, aching

privately for her daughter's death. The men moved to the library. While the butler poured brandies, the men sat in silence, each nursing his own thoughts. Once the servant had departed, their conversation began.

"So, Louis, what news from your Watchman?" asked Vicimeous Colliton.

Louis placed his brandy glass on a table and stood up. He moved to the fire, with his back to it so that he was facing the older men. He linked his hands behind his back and began to speak. Since taking control of the search for both Abigail and the truth of what had happened, he had enjoyed his position of power between the two families. He reminded his captive audience of the work Bennett and his gang of searchers had completed, the leads and evidence that had led to the awful and unavoidable conclusion that Abigail had been murdered, her body lost in an unmarked grave.

"And now," Louis said, his voiced hushed to gain maximum approbation for his news, "Bennett has proof there was another involved with that black-hearted girl, Pruitt; a ruffian who was with Abigail and the maid."

"Are you sure of this, son?" asked Sir Crisp in surprise.

"Sure as I stand here, father."

"And the name of this ruffian?" asked Vicimeous, on his feet now.

"That I do not know, sir, but...but, there is more excellent news, new evidence, received yesterday in a note from Bennett."

"And this is...?"

"Well, sir, we know that the maid, this Pruitt girl, was at the hanging, for it was there she robbed someone and was captured.

Abigail had become mixed up, I would hazard, in some scheme of this Pruitt girl and the man that was with them. As you know, Pruitt has been sentenced and transported to the American colony. But now we come to the crux."

"Yes, yes, Louis," Vicimeous interrupted, "but what is this evidence that Bennett has?"

"Sir, please, I beg your patience. Bennett and I believe that the villain and Pruitt planned the whole thing and that Abigail was unwittingly drawn in. Now, we do not know the name of the ruffian, but Bennett has heard of a beggar who was at the hanging."

"A beggar? I hardly think…" Vicimeous began.

"And the significance of this, Louis?" Sir Crisp interjected, his eyebrows raised.

"The significance, father, is that this beggar, a soldier of the old Queen's campaigns, attends every public hanging and is the fount of all knowledge about the goings and comings at such spectacles. Bennett has word from one of the witnesses that this beggar was seen with a younger man at the scene of Abigail's slaughter."

Vicimeous winced and turned away. Louis continued, unabashed.

"Bennett has his men out looking for the fellow and, as soon as he is found, I intend to meet with him myself. I assure you, gentlemen, it will not be long before we discover who was the architect of Abigail's death."

*

Less than a week later, Louis found himself in a grimy London tavern sitting with Bennett and the old soldier, Meriwether Johnson. The beggar sat on a low stool. He looked very unhappy to be sandwiched between the big Watchman, who was smoking his long clay pipe and grinning smugly, and the hard-faced young gentleman he had been told wished to speak with him.

"So, Meriwether, my fine friend, tell Mr. Silston what you told me."

Meriwether Johnson looked up at Louis and forced a toothless smile.

"There be a reward, m'lord, that's right, ain't it?" he whined.

"Yes, yes, man," snapped Louis impatiently. "Just tell what you know."

Meriwether rubbed the stump of his left arm through the rags of his old uniform. He hesitated, looking sheepish until Louis slammed down a half crown on the tabletop. The old soldier nodded approval. His face hardened as he looked up at Louis.

He began his story of the day of the hanging, the robbery, the chase, and the killing of Abigail. He was not a good storyteller and many times Louis interrupted him to make him repeat something or to clarify a point, but, finally, he came to the part of his story about a handsome young fellow who was knocked unconscious.

"Wait, wait. You are saying that this fellow was with the two girls?" Louis interrupted.

"Vell now, m'lord, I never saw him vith the girls, ye see, but ven 'e came to 'is senses 'e said 'e'd been with 'em. Ven I told 'im the young 'un was murdered he keeled over, sir. White as the clouds, sir. And ven I told 'im that the other one …"

"Polly Pruitt?"

"So, I been told by My Bennett here, sir, though I don't remember that name meself. Anyways, ven I told 'im they'd taken 'er to Newgate 'e damn near died of fright right there, sir. Vailing, 'e vas and saying no, that's wrong and all. Says 'e saw the fellow vat stole the pocket vatch shoving it in the girl's 'and."

"What arrant nonsense!" Louis barked.

"S'what 'e said, m'lord."

Louis hesitated, deep in thought. The old soldier looked at the coin lying on the table and then sideways at Bennett, but the Watchman gave a slow shake of his head.

"This scoundrel was in league with Polly Pruitt, I'll wager. His evident fear at the knowledge of her being taken shows that. The two of them must have taken Abigail to the hanging with intent to rob and in the melee, the poor girl lost her life, or worse, this man friend of Pruitt's obtained her silence with the point of a knife."

"But 'e said the timepiece was put in 'er 'and," mumbled Johnson.

Louis ignored the ragged man. He stared hard into Bennett's eyes.

"You will scour the streets, Bennett, and find me word of this young devil." Without waiting for the Watchman to reply he swung his gaze back to Johnson whose eyes were once again locked on the half crown. "The boy's name, Johnson, do you have a name?"

"Vill Staples, sir, as I told Mr. Bennett here."

Bennett grinned at this and took a deep draw on his pipe.

"Well, Bennett?" asked Louis, impatient and agitated.

"My lads are out there at this very minute, your honour. 'T'won't be long afore we have him and, when we do, sir, I will place him in your hands myself."

Chapter 20

In Which Will and John Vertue Are Transferred to a Ship In the Thames

It was a fine autumn day, warm and dry. The sun shone on the busy London streets, the carriages and carts rumbled over her stony roads, the air was rife with the noise of life. Will stood outside the arch of Newgate breathing in the sweet, stinking air of free London. Despite everything he had been through, despite his hunger, the pain of missing Peg, the insults and injuries of prison, he smiled. He, who was to be hanged, could hardly believe he was seeing the wonderful filth and disorder of his city again. Soon he would be aboard a vessel sailing for the Americas.

Earlier, the convicted men and women had been gathered in two companies in the courtyard whilst the warders shackled them together, hands and feet and now they waited by the famous arch. John Vertue was strangely dejected. He stood beside Will and grumbled quietly to himself, looking always at the ground. At last, he lifted his head and held Will's eyes with his. What Will saw there was pure rage.

"They're scraping the scum off this little pond that is England, Will, and dropping it like shit on the Virginia colony, purifying their own water while they feed the colonist's greed for free labour."

Angrily he kicked out at a pile of well-dried horse dung, sending it spinning and rolling across the street. Will had never seen him so angry and could not think what to say. He was too consumed with drinking in the sights and sounds he had been kept from for so long.

It was only moments, but, for Will they were glorious minutes before they would set off, their chains clanking, their feet scuffing, through the streets towards the river.

One of the guards raised a hand, as if in greeting, and Will followed his gaze. Walking towards the arch were two Watchmen leading three new prisoners to their Newgate fate. The sight of one of the men, a squat, well-built fellow with a shock of jet-black hair and a square jaw pricked Will's memory. He had seen the man, but where? John continued to grumble beside him, but Will was consumed by something that felt like fear for those few seconds as the men passed and turned in under the arch. A cold electric jolt ran through him, twisting his guts and rattling his ribs. The cut-purse from the hanging! This was the thief who had stolen the watch, the man who had condemned Peg with a single thrust of his hand. Every good feeling at being free of the prison drained from Will's mind with the blood that drained from his face. He twisted to watch the man disappear into Newgate's maw and drew breath to shout the truth, but the cry of grief and accusation solidified like a stone in his throat, for this Will was a wiser, much older man than the hot-head who had thought that stealing a book would magically bring him to his Peg.

He felt a tug and realised that John, who had made sure to be shackled to Will, was moving. The guards must have given the order to start their journey to the river, though Will had heard nothing above the roaring of injustice in his ears. He started off, reeling at his absolute powerlessness in the face of such gross unfairness. It was as if God had slapped him across the face.

John, risking the wrath of the guards, leaned in to whisper.

"Be ready, lad, for our fellow man's derision and condemnation. All will know of our fate, for lists of names with accounts of trials and dates of transportations can be had on the streets and in the coffee houses. The crowd will be waiting, Will, to send us off to the New World with a jeer and a foul word."

Will nodded, but kept his counsel. He knew it would be days, perhaps even weeks before he could get the image of the common thief who had caused all his misery out of his head. For now, knowing he could do nothing to change the past, he tried to shake all memories from his mind and concentrate on the present moment while preserving some small hope for the future. He forced himself to gaze about him and try to enjoy his few minutes of illusory freedom on the streets he had come to love.

John's prediction turned out to be correct; the streets nearer the river were indeed lined with a ragtaggle brigade of London folk all jeering, laughing, and shouting unkind words, blasphemies, and curses, many thanking their luck that they were not among the condemned.

At last, they arrived at Blackfriars where, in better times, Will had done some work for his old master, Sam Royston. He had expected to see a ship waiting to take them aboard, but there were only a few wherries. The prisoners were unceremoniously loaded onto the small boats, many of them falling and pulling others with them, unused as they were to the movement of the vessels on the unsympathetic water. Once all were loaded, the human cargo was rowed out into the river and downstream about a mile with the outgoing tide, until they arrived at their new accommodation; a massive, decaying prison hulk. If any thought of the cut-purse had been creeping back into his mind, the sight of that once-proud vessel now brought so low was enough to set a new flock of fears flying through Will's mind.

He had thought the Stone Hold of Newgate prison was the worst place in England, but, once stowed safely in the depths of the superannuated warship, he quickly came to understand otherwise. The unmasted prison ship was anchored in the middle of the river, slowly rotting, its lower decks the temporary home of a hoard of souls without hope. After the small pleasure of seeing London's streets again, of breathing the city air, and the expectation of setting out for America, Will crashed from hope to despair. There was no way of knowing how long they may be held on the hulk, no information about when and how they might be shipped to America, no hope, even, of seeing the light of day, as it was constantly gloomy, day and night, in that dank space lit only by a few smoky oil lamps.

It was wet all the time, stank of mould, decay, and the vile bodily outpourings of the wretched human cargo that languished in its holds. The prisoners were chained at all times and there was little comfort save their louse- and flea-infested pallets, which lay in ranks on the soft, damp boards. To keep himself sane, Will fought off his brooding anxieties by talking often to John or allowing himself the stunted pleasure of reveries about Peg. Much of the time, though, he lay on his pallet, staring into the dimness, listening to the hack and retch of men coughing their lungs out and thinking he must surely die in that benighted place.

*

Josiah Bennett made his way into Newgate prison behind the short, lean figure of George Wenlock. The two men walked in silence until they came to the warders' office, a small room with an open fire and comfortable chairs as well as a small table piled high with papers. Wenlock gave a quick nod of his head to the big man with enormous hands who sat at the table.

"Mr. Wharton, sir, this is Mr. Bennett, a well-respected Watchman what needs a private word, sir."

"Private word, is it?" said Wharton with a scowl.

"If you'd be so kind, Mr. Wharton." Bennett gave a slight bow as he spoke.

"Shut the door on your way out, Wenlock" growled Wharton. "Sit, friend Bennett," he continued with a crooked smile. "What was so secret you could not speak of it at the gates?"

"My patron, a certain lord of this land, does not wish his business to be broadcast to the beggars and sluts who grace your doorstep, Mr. Wharton, nor to your lackey, so I thank thee for this indulgence."

"The business, Mr. Bennett, if you please," grunted Wharton.

"The business, sir, is this. You have in your wards a young fellow name of Staples."

"I know the name," said Wharton, his eyes lighting up as he sensed the chance for an easy crown or two.

"My patron wishes to meet this villain. It has taken me weeks to track him to this place and m'lord's patience has been sorely tested, but here we are, come at last, Mr. Wharton, to what I hope will be a generous ending for the both of us."

"Generous ending, eh? So, there is something here to the benefit of…the prison?"

Bennett smiled and pulled his pipe from his pocket. He knew the expectations at Newgate; no one got anything for nothing here. He stood up, leaned over the fire, picked up a spill, held it to the flames, and lit his pipe.

"My lord is a generous man, Mr. Wharton. I have a contribution to the prison fund in my pocket," he said settling himself back into his chair.

"Well, sir," said Wharton, his face impassive. "Let us see this contribution."

Bennett placed a crown, tarnished and old, but a crown nonetheless, on the edge of the table.

"A very small contribution, Mr. Bennett," grunted Wharton.

Bennett placed another, shinier crown on top of the first and turned to stare at Wharton, his eyes hard.

"Let us see what news you have of Staples before the contribution increases any more, shall we, sir?"

Wharton, sensing he had reached the limit of his negotiating power, leaned forward and scooped up the money, dropping it carelessly into his copious coat pocket.

"The prisoner you seek, Mr. Bennett, is not here no more."

"Not here, you say?"

"No, sir, he lies in the hulk Pemberton on the Thames waiting transport to the Virginian colony."

Bennett stood up and knocked his pipe out on the fireside.

"Then, sir, I will leave you and attend the hulk."

Wharton grinned.

"Make haste my friend, for I hear that the transport leaves on the morning tide."

With that Bennett hastened out of the office and bustled along the narrow corridor leading back out to the yard. His men waited for him at the gate. It would not take them long to get to the river.

Chapter 21

In Which Watchman Bennett Comes For Will

It was impossible to know how many days had elapsed since they had been incarcerated in the hold of the Pemberton, but, on the morning when Will, John Vertue, and the other convicts who had been brought there were led up through the innards of the rotting hulk, out into the cold sunlight, it felt like forever.

"Ho, young Will, now we really are to go west," John whispered as they boarded a wherry. "West to the colonies, west to a new life."

So spent was Will that he could not bring himself to reply nor to take any joy in his fleeting liberty. He was rowed with John and the other prisoners to Blackfriar's dock where they were unceremoniously unloaded onto the quay beside a huge, sturdy vessel. Will had seen many such ocean-going monsters at the docks here and further up the river and the sight of them had always filled him with a fizzing excitement. Today he felt nothing other than relief that there were no ogling crowds, though the docks, as usual, were crowded with sailors, stevedores, merchant's men, clerks, and factors. There were no cheers and jeers, only the clack and flap of rigging and chains, the slap of the Thames' brown waters against the ships' sea-hardened boards, the sarcastic cries of the sea-birds aloft.

"They ain't ready fer ye yet," said one of their guards. "Jes you move down the dock a bit and sit while we wait, lads."

As they shuffled along the quayside, Will caught a whiff of the delicious smells of burning tobacco and fresh varnish. The first reminded him of how much he missed his pipe, the second of his life with Sam Royston. Surprisingly, both served to lift his spirits enough that it was as if he was waking up from a long, murky, maudlin nightmare. Now he watched fascinated as the ship was loaded with supplies. The decks were busy with sailors; some shepherded barrels – salt beef and dried peas, John told him – that were being lowered on ropes into a gaping opening like a huge mouth, other men worked on the upper deck with tar buckets, a cat sat lazily on a coil of rope. Again, that pungent smell of pipe tobacco; oh, my Good Lord, Will thought, how I miss my pipe and baccy.

After a long wait, one of the wherrymen appeared and waved to the guard.

"Orright you sorry blackguards, time ter move," he shouted.

To Will's surprise, the convicts were hustled back onto the wherries which took them out to an even larger ocean-going ship anchored in the middle of the river. After scrambling up the rope netting that draped the side of the vessel, they were made to stand on the bleached deck, men to one side and the few women to the other. Will felt his spirits rise again; to him, the ship had a good feeling. That changed when they were taken below. The convicts' deck, somewhere deep in the bowels of the ship, was dark and low, so low he had to walk bent double.

They were seated in groups of six on rough benches. As the guards fitted the iron collars and chains that would secure them for the voyage, Will was reminded of Jenkin Smith's terrible crossing to the Americas and his enslavement in Jamaica. His spirits, so briefly high, plunged into mawkish misery as he remembered the stories Jenkin had told of the depravities of his voyage. He wondered bleakly, how many of his companions would die on their voyage. He and John Vertue had been separated and he could not see his friend when he looked for him, though it was so dark, he could only see clearly the two rows behind him where Evans and Doggett sat.

He knew no one in his row, but felt lucky, at least, to be on the outer end. The man next to him said his name was Hart and, when Will asked, he revealed that he was a common thief. He had a roughly shaven head, scabs and scars all over his face, broken and rotting teeth, and the breath of a dying dog. Will closed his eyes and wondered how many minutes, hours or days it would be before they started their journey.

*

Watchman Bennett and his gang of thugs hurried down the narrow ways from Newgate prison towards the docks at Blackfriars. There was an urgency about their step and, as they neared the quayside, Bennett broke into a run.

The dock was crowded with stevedores and lumpers. A small group of sailors stood smoking their pipes and talking at the open door of a quayside alehouse. At the dock, a ketch and two smaller barques rose and fell gently on the swell of the river.

"A ship Virginia bound! Which of those?" cried Bennett, pointing to a large vessel tied up some way along the dock and two others moored in the middle of the river. The sailors exchanged glances. The whole group eyed Bennett and his henchmen suspiciously.

"Come my fine friends," said Bennett as he strode towards the group. "It's a simple question. Which of these," he indicated the ships with a sweep of his arm, "is to cross over to the American colony?"

"What's it worth to know?" asked one of the group, a huge man with long hair tied in a neat queue that ran down his back.

"Not getting a beating from my handy boys is what it's worth, seaman," growled Bennett.

"In that case, Watchman," said the sailor as he turned back to his mates, "you may go and fuck yourself."

Seething with impotent rage, but fearing that time was short, Bennett turned on his heel and marched to the dockside. There were three sailors aboard one of the smaller boats, a lighter.

"Which vessel is bound for Virginia?" Bennett yelled at them.

"The one astern," the nearest man called back, pointing out into the river.

"Take me out now and I'll give you a half guinea."

Bennett and two of his gang climbed down into the lighter and within minutes the oarsmen were pulling for the moorings. Coming alongside the ship, Bennett stood up, taking a moment to gain a sense of balance in the swell of the river, and then called out.

"Hey there! Ahoy! Anyone aboard!"

There was no response from the ship. One of the lighter crew grabbed the scramble ropes on the side of the ship as they came alongside.

"You'll need to go up, captain," he said with a grin.

Bennett winced and grunted, but heaved himself up onto the gunwale and gingerly stuck out his leg to get a foothold on the rope netting. The lighter bobbed up and down. One moment his left foot was on solid wood the next it was suspended in clear air. Hand over hand he pulled his heavy bulk, cursing and swearing, up the rope ladder. At last, he reached the top and could see the deck. Once more he shouted for attention.

"Hey there!" he called out.

The deck was empty, nothing stirred. Above his head, the sails were tight furled. He called out again and now there was movement. A small man emerged through a low doorway.

"Aye, what is it?" he asked.

"You're bound for Virginia?"

"Aye," acknowledged the man.

"Good, good," said Bennett, smiling now as he clambered over the gunwale. "You have a man aboard, name of Staples, I would see him now and take him ashore."

"Staples?" echoed the man. "Aboard now?"

"Come, dolt, do not dally," hissed Bennett, "this is a matter of urgency. I am on Watchman's business. Take me to Staples."

"There is no one but myself and the captain aboard, sir, I swear," answered the man looking baffled.

"Even better," said Bennett with a chuckle, "then we are in time. They are still on the hulk."

"Who, sir? What hulk?"

"The convicts, man, the prisoners who will shortly be brought to this transport."

"But, sir," said the sailor with a smile as he realised the big man's mistake, "we are the Queen Anne Merchant. We ship no convicts, only dry goods and paying passengers. It's the Marie Elizabeth you want and she slipped her moorings this hour gone."

Chapter 22

In Which Polly Arrives in The New World

We are brought up onto the deck. The sun is so brilliant it makes me blink. Men are shouting orders at us, but I do not listen for I am full of wonder. Land; all around there is land. I was never so pleased to see land. The ship is by a dock in a broad river and rocks gently up and down in its flow. There are buildings; some tall and near the dock, I think maybe warehouses, and others are smaller; offices, perchance, inns or houses. In the distance is a grand place of brick, with a flagpole, where the King's flag flutters in the breeze.

Far off, I see carriages and carts, people standing in groups or alone, all eyes on the ship. On either side, the banks of the river are all dressed in greens, red, oranges, and browns, trees that grow right down to the water's edge in places. I never saw the like. The air smells fresh and clean. Above are the cries of seabirds, from the shore, the distant sound of conversation, from the river the slap and pock of the ship bobbing on the current. Though I know it to be a trick played upon me by my own mind, I am thrilled to feel a sort of freedom after that hole down below.

The woman next to me gives me an elbow in the ribs. The sailors are telling us we must wash, hands and faces, and there are buckets of seawater on the deck for the job. I rub my hands hard and my face too, scraping the thick dirt from my forehead, cheeks, and chin. It feels wonderful. Even when I start to dry and my skin feels stretched and coarse with the salt, I feel better. We may look cleaner, I think, but we still stink.

They give us mop caps and bonnets, old cast-off things. I find one that fits and now I am a pretty bundle of rags, fleas, and lice. The men are brought up on deck as we are led away, still in chains, off the ship. We are brought a short way to a square in front of the grand building. 'Tis queer to be standing on solid ground that feels like it is moving like the ship.

From what I see, I guess this square and all the houses have been cut out of the forest that hovers at the edges of this new-made place. 'Tis dark and threatening this forest and I don't like it. The dock is one side of the square. Around the other sides are a few fine houses of brick and many poorer houses built of wood. I see other buildings crouched behind these places. It ain't London, but it is good to know there are people of my own kind in this wild land.

We are kept shivering in the cold air until the men are brought to join us. They herd us into lines, women at the back, men at the front, all facing the water where the Patuxent Voyager lies tied up. Weeks I was on captain Gillard's vessel and only since we arrived have I heard its name spoken.

I am still chained to Annie Jameson, who is shuffling her feet and murmuring like a croaky bird. I fight to stop myself smiling, it is so good to be off that cursed ship. There are people around; two men on horses, one fellow in a rough-looking cart, other men and a few women further off and they are staring at us. We must make a woeful sight and, on thinking this, my spirits fall again until I see two sailors going between the women and taking off their irons. My God, I am near heaven for those blessed few minutes. They take off the metal and I feel like laughing, though I don't; my neck sores no longer rubbed, my wrists and ankles free, my whole body light enough to fly.

It only lasts a short while, this joy, and now I am back in this new place, watching those watching us. Most of those looking on are men and they are moving close, for a better view. I know why they are here, with their money, flocking like flies to horseshit. There's all sorts; rough-looking types in poor clothing and suspicious looks, merchant men in old-fashioned clothing, some wearing the dark wigs popular under the old king, men in expensive silks and brocade with fine black tricorne hats. They are all sun-browned, not like the pasty faces you see in London. Some of them wear hats with wide brims the like of which I never before saw.

One fellow walks around the square with a scribe's tray around his neck, quill in hand. We met this one before, when the ship was held in the river until we were ready to dock. Soon as I saw him, I knew him for what he is, just like the maggot in London who counted us onto the ship. This one, short and fat, red-cheeked and wearing dirty old buckle shoes, a dusty cocked hat, and small spectacles, came aboard and looked us all over, making notes, scribbling on his ledger, naming those who'd died afore we arrived, checking the *merchandise*. Like we're animals. I'm lost in watching the beggar so that I jump out of my skin when I look round and see a man standing so close, I could touch him.

He's all in brown, this fellow, and carrying a cane with a round, red glass at its top. This one is not so tall, but wide with very broad shoulders, makes him look like he might topple over. His face has ruddy skin, pale brown eyes, no beard, and his sandy hair is clubbed and tied at the back of his head with a black ribbon. No wig. He's wearing one of those wide-brimmed hats and he's looking at me, all cold and unsmiling. They're all the customers, these men, customers at a strange market where people are bought and sold. A lump like a stone drops from my chest into my stomach. How low have I fallen?

He swipes his cane up under his armpit, Mr. Customer, and grabs my face with both hands. Not hard, but firm. He tilts my head back and looks up my nose, God save me, and then brings my head back to stare into my eyes. After he's looked in my ears he uses one hand, all thick fingers and rings, to roll my lips to look at my teeth. I wish I could stop him. I want to hold my head still so's he can't do as he wants, but, somehow, I can't make myself.

"A good specimen," he says in a sort of grunt and then he gives me a little smile, but it ain't a smile I like. He's still staring into my eyes when he calls out. "Thomas!"

Up runs a lad, like an obedient dog, wagging his tail and panting with excitement. He's got to be the son, I think to myself; his attire like his daddy's, perhaps fifteen or sixteen years, hat in his hand. He's young, but he's almost as tall as his Pa and has the same set of the shoulders, red skin, and sandy hair. I watch him running. He's all flat feet and flapping arms, no grace in movement like my Abigail, heavy-footed. I would wager he's one for breaking things and tripping over rugs and stairs. But he's vain too, I can see that as he comes to stop by his dad, straightening his cuffs, brushing down his coat, giving himself airs. I don't like his look any more than his Pa's; they both have a bit of the pig about them.

"Try her, Tom, you know what to do," says the daddy.

The boy changes places with his Pa and grabs me by the tops of my arms, squeezing me. I twist and pull away.

"A spirited one," says the Pa, chuckling like it's a joke. "But you are the master here, Thomas."

170

I can see doubt in the young one's eyes, though his body tries to tell me he's proud and strong and better than me.

"Come on, man! She won't bite and if she does, we'll have her teeth out in a trice."

The Pa's got his fists clenched up like he wants to do it right away. The lad pulls a face and puts his hand on my chin, starts to tilt my head, but I pull away again. This time he's ready and quicker than me. His pudgy hands are on my cheeks and he's holding my head still, though I struggle. He does a quick check on eyes, ears, nose, and mouth like his dad did and then he steps away, wiping his hands on his jerkin. He's smiling now too and I like this one less than I liked his dad.

"Very good, father, yes," says he, trying to be a man. His voice is bright as if he's like to laugh, but his face is scowling. I think this be a sulky one.

"You like her, do you, boy?" says the father. "Well, 'tis not for you to decide, but I may be persuaded to like her also."

He's back in front of me, the Pa, and I don't like the hard look in his eyes. My heart is drumming and I suddenly feel my stomach will empty. Before I can move, he puts his hands on my hips, holds me still for a moment, and then, quick as you like, grabs my bubs, one in each hand. He squeezes so that pains shoot through my chest and I gasp, then pulls me so close I can smell stale tobacco on his breath. I can't look at him, turn my head, try not to howl. It's pain, but it's fury too. How dare he, the bastard? 'Tis a word I have thought to use on men before, my old Pa, Silston, Wharton at Newgate, but I never say it out loud. I ain't that stupid. He lets me go and I breathe hard.

"What's your name, girl?"

I look away from him.

"Polly Pruitt," says I and I know, though I don't want to, I have to add, "sir."

I don't like my voice. It's weak and sounds as if I am like to cry. It's almost a hiccup and I feel ashamed, yet I know 'tis he should feel the shame. He grabs my chin, hard, hurting me again, and twists my head to face him.

"Look at me when you speak, Polly Pruitt. What was your crime?"

"Stealing, sir." I don't want him to see me eyes are wet, but I don't have a choice so I give him my hardest look.

"A thief. Yes, I'm sure of it looking at that face. And what was your trade?"

"Lady's maid, sir, after being a maid-of-all-work."

My belly is in twists and knots and I hurt where he grabbed me, but I ain't going to show him any of that.

"Addis!" he calls out.

The fat cove with the writing table waddles straight to him. That tells me something about this so-called gentleman.

"Yes, Mr. Garland, sir," he puffs, and now I know the bully's name.

"You have inspected this girl?"

"I have, your honour, on board as is our habit, sir."

"And you found …?"

The scribe runs his stubby finger down his lines of names and numbers.

"I found her to be strong and healthy, sir, with good body, clear eyes, and good teeth. The bosun's mate tells me she has been no trouble on the voyage, sir."

"Good, good," says this fellow Garland with a wrench of his face that might be a smile.

"My son has taken a fancy to her. We will bid on her."

The fat cove leers at the sulky boy and winks. Though my chest still hurts, I have to stop myself laughing for the boy gives him a haughty glare, but his face turns blood red and I think his head is likely to explode. They go, all three of them and other men come and go, none of them like this Garland, and I hope he will not win his bid. When it starts, I have never known a market like it, all the shouting and hands waving in the air, and men stamping their feet and I am 'mazed by the speed of it all. I cannot keep up and have no idea if I am bought until I see a big man walking towards me. I ain't seen this one before; he wasn't one of those who came and stared and poked, but he comes right up and grabs my arm. He is big and rough looking, having a beard and hair of light brown with a shine of red in it. A man my aunt Susan would have said was *easy to see the ugly in* and she would not have meant his face, but the ugly of his soul.

"McLeod," he says without looking straight at me.

"Am I bought by you, sir?" says I and he looks at me like I am dog dirt on the sole of his boot, then he laughs, a great bellow of a noise and his great mouth open wide showing bright red, wet lips and, inside, a tongue that flutters like a hovering bird's wing, brown teeth and dark gaps where others are gone. I like this fellow less than I liked the man Garland.

He says no more when his humour has gone, but leads me away towards the water and to another boat and I think, *not again*. This one is small, has only one mast, and is filled with boxes and crates. There are men on board and this McLeod cove takes me to join them,

173

settles me in the bottom of the vessel between boxes. I am not to sit on a seat. There is another, like me, a convict, snug between boxes and he shoots me a frightened look.

"Dan'l," he says, quiet like.

"Polly," says I, trying to sound calm.

I look back to shore, wondering about Annie Jameson and Mother Gantry and the others, wondering, can I see them? But what I see is Garland and his son walking slow towards this very boat.

"All ready, sir," says McLeod.

When his master, Garland, comes aboard he does not look at me, but his son does and with the same eyes as Louis Silston did. It makes my heart shudder.

Chapter 23

In Which Will Sees the Folly of His Ways and John Vertue Shows His True Colours

The convicts had been embarked on the Marie Elizabeth on the morning of September 11th, 1721. Their first time on deck, after eight days of sailing, was a disappointment to Will as the ship, the sea, and sky were enveloped in a shroud of fog. He had felt, stored below decks in aching discomfort, that the one compensation would be to be able to see the sea. However, despite the hidden sea and sky, he was pleased beyond words to be out in the air, fresh and cold and full of the susurrating sounds of the ship cutting through the waves and the flap and snap of the sails and rigging.

The men were kept in chains, yet he and John Vertue, with some judicious shuffling, had found a way to be close enough to talk. It was Will's first sight of him since they came aboard. His neck was as bloodied as Will's and, like Will, he was filthy, but he gave his friend a generous smile and they shook hands like long-lost friends.

They talked of the conditions below deck and their possible fates when they arrived in America. They spoke quietly of their old lives in England, conjuring memories to cheer each other until, all too soon it seemed, they were led back down into the bowels of the vessel. Padlocked again on his bench, Will calculated that he might see the sea and breathe the clean air seven more times before they made landfall in early November. However, according to the sailor who gave him the information, their captain was a "moody villain", so Will could only hope he might someday see the ocean.

As the voyage progressed, Will learned that he had a good stomach for the sea, and he quickly became accustomed to the stink of the convict deck. The one freedom his incarceration gave him was time to ponder his fate and future. With each long, dreadful day, eating foul food, drinking brackish water, always sitting in an agony of aching limbs, Will sank lower and lower. It seemed to him, now he had the time to contemplate what might happen when he arrived in America, that he had been the worst of fools. Not only had he not realised his opportunity, as John had told him, to arrive in Virginia a free man by signing up as a ship's carpenter, but he was now shackled literally and metaphorically by his conviction as a common thief. Of that, he would never be free.

This profound understanding of how badly he had erred was not the worst nor darkest of his thoughts. Now that it was clear that, one day, he would make landfall in the colony, he could see that the task of finding Peg in that new land might prove impossible. He would be tied to a plantation for at least seven years with no hope of being able to search for her. His situation was, he realised in his misery, the very worst it could possibly be. His mind was wracked by self-pity, his body was weakening, his head ached much of every day, it was nigh on impossible to sleep at night and one of his teeth had fallen out when he was chewing on a rank piece of salt pork. He stank and itched and was sore to his bones. He was truly wretched.

*

There came a day at the end of October when the weather was fine and the ship becalmed. The convicts had proven to be a docile cargo, and so, in a mood of generosity, the captain decided to allow the prisoners on deck without their usual shackles. So quiet was the weather that he was persuaded to allow the crew 'easy time' for some music and dancing.

So it was that Will and John found themselves under the shadow of the vast sails, standing around a group of sailors sitting on barrels and coiled ropes, and what a glory it was to stand, though their legs were weak and their balance uncertain. Will clapped along to the hornpipes and jigs as the crewmen danced and sang and, for the first time in weeks, he found himself smiling. As the convicts and sailors clapped and cheered at the end of a particularly rousing reel, John felt his sleeve being tugged. An old convict was standing beside him. The man was as thin as a stick and bent, his face a deathly pallor, yet he moved purposefully close to John and whispered, his voice hardly audible above the music.

"Mr. Vertue, I have a thing to say you need to hear, but not among these ruffians."

He turned and walked slowly towards the bow. John's curiosity was piqued, so he followed. The old fellow found a spot behind the mainmast out of sight of the nearest sailor. All on deck were taken up with the music and dancing and the two men were not noticed.

"John Vertue, if that be what ye be calling yourself these days. I know you, yes I do, and I know what ye did."

The old man cocked his head to one side and gave John a crooked grin and a hard stare. "What do you got to say to that, then?"

"I don't know who you are, father," replied John, glancing around. He forced a smile. "You are mistaken, I believe. I am convicted of simple fraud and am to serve my sentence in the colonies."

"The world knows me as Old Dick Withers and I say, simple fraud, maybe, but there's more, ain't there, John Vertue? Or should I say, Thomas Gulley?"

The old fellow gave a satisfied chortle. Behind them, the music rose in pitch and volume. Now the sailors were giving their audience what they wanted, a popular song of the day, and much cheering and clapping accompanied their fast-paced efforts.

"I think, sir, you are mistaken," John repeated, the shifty smile still playing about his lips.

"I would say, Mr. Vertue, that the captain would pay well for the stories I could tell about you murderin' a young girl. But maybe, I'm a'thinking, you'd be even happier to pay more for them stories yerself."

John's face did not change, but he struck like a snake, grabbing the man and spinning him around in one fluid movement. In one smooth movement, his left hand was clamped tightly over the fellow's lower face, his forefinger and thumb squeezing the nose shut. For one half-starved and weakened by sitting in darkness for days on end there was a surprising and deadly strength in the arm that circled the old man and held him fast.

The music on the main deck flared to a crescendo, with every convict whooping, joining in the singing, and some even trying an unsteady dance. Withers flailed and kicked hard against John's legs and he gave out stifled grunts and moans, but the music was louder still and the singing clamourous. John, aware of the danger of being spotted, pulled his victim close to the mast. For every kick the old convict gave, John Vertue squeezed his nose tighter and pressed his hand deeper into the sagging flesh around the fellow's mouth. John's face was set, his jaw muscles tight, his eyes blank pools of blue, his lips clenched white. Slowly the old man's wriggling and animal grunts subsided and he went limp, but Vertue kept his hold over the man's airways for another minute.

At last, sure the man was dead, John released his hold and slowly lowered the body to the scrubbed and sun-bleached deck. He straightened, brushed himself down, and walked casually back to the crowd. Coming up behind Will, he put a hand on the boy's shoulder, smiled at him, and joined lustily with the singing. It was not until the entertainments were ended that someone noticed the body lying in the shadow of the mainmast.

The dead man was identified as Worley Tanner, a common thief of Southwark. Many questions were asked of the convicts, but no one had seen the old fellow wandering away from the crowd. No one could answer for his physical state. No one knew anything about the old man. After a cursory inspection of the body by the captain, his death was ascribed to "a stopped heart caused by age and infirmity". The body was wrapped in hessian sacking and a few words were said before three sailors lifted the sad parcel and threw it unceremoniously overboard.

After that, the atmosphere on the ship, despite the fine weather and previous high spirits, palled and the crew grew surly. It was yet another unexplained death, the third in two weeks, considered by the sailors to be a bad omen. Even as the music restarted, a rumour began to spread that the old fellow had been carrying the plague. The captain, an experienced man, quickly recognized the beginnings of something that could grow towards mutiny. The music was stopped, the convicts were put back in their shackles and led below.

"Another one under hatches, as the saying goes," said John Vertue sadly as they were herded down the companionway. "A heavy toll, Will, a heavy toll."

Chapter 24

In Which Will Is Purchased by Mr. Sowell and Is Taken to
Burtonwood

Some of them heard a cry, distant and almost inaudible above the constant shush of the ship's movement through the sea, but three or four of the men were adamant, they had heard a shout of "land, ho!" A weary excitement spread among the convicts. They had come to Virginia at last. Yet, over the ensuing hours, their initial enthusiasm slowly died as the Marie Elizabeth lingered at sea until the day and night were gone. It seemed they had been fooled by their own hope and their spirits fell until, on the second day since the cry had been heard, six crewmen came down and began to unshackle them.

"First sight don't mean a thing, boys," one of the sailors explained as he worked on the chains. "Lots of capes and inlets to navigate afore we come to the Rappahannock, as the savages call it."

"What day is it, friend?" Will asked, gently rubbing his sore neck, newly released from its collar.

"'Tis the fourteenth day of November, lad, and we are arrived at Port Royal."

Once they were on deck, the men shivered while they washed their hands and faces, shaved as best they could with the old razors they were given, and combed their rank hair. Will could still feel the lice on his scalp and the fleas that inhabited the inner layers of his ragged clothing, but he felt cleaner. Looking around, he could see a mixture of emotions expressed on the faces of his deck-mates. Many looked confused, some seemed fearful, nervous and yet others were too exhausted and starved to show anything, their faces as blank as the half-reefed sails above their heads. He, Will Staples of Harsham, was filled with excited amazement at what he could see and thought it must show on his face. John Vertue, who had made his way to stand with Will, was slapping down his long top-coat to rid it of the dust and mites that colonized it, grinning broadly.

"Well, John," Will whispered breathlessly, "what d'you think to all this?"

"Why...they have made themselves a fine little town, these colonists, ain't they, lad?"

He indicated the rough square, flanked by buildings, grand and humble where the inhabitants milled and conversed.

"No," hissed Will. "I mean the trees, John, the trees, the colours. I ain't never seen the like of it."

The Virginian autumnal foliage was a revelation to him: the pale greens; the yellows, shouting their brilliance; the oranges, reds, and deep scarlets disporting themselves in a glowing mimicry of a conflagration; the browns and blacks and the evergreens adding punctuation to the story. He was not sure, now that he thought about it, what he had expected, but almost everywhere he looked all he could see was forest or fields; tree-lined shores ranging away down the river, pale meadows in the near-distance, and rainbow-hued hills far away. He was entranced, his spirit lifted for a few brief moments.

A small, fussy man with thick-glassed spectacles came aboard, made a cursory inspection of all the convicts, and, after some scribbling with his quill, handed the captain a document, a bill of receipt for the cargo. Once the clerk was ashore again, the women were led off the ship and across the dock towards the open area of the square. The men followed and, soon, they were all lined up, waiting on the motley band of buyers who began to make their way among them, each man carrying a paper detailing the cargo. Will and John Vertue stood together, watching as the inspection started, amused by the questions they heard being asked about morals and obedience, knowing that all the answers would be lies and fabrications.

A well-dressed, broad-shouldered man carrying a cane and walking with a swagger came to John and began questioning him. The buyer was curt, did not waste words, and had a hard look about him that made Will wished he would move on.

"So, a sharper, eh, Vertue?" he was saying. "Makes a mockery of your name does it not?

"Aye, master," says John, bowing his head and looking shamed. "Fourteen years for fraud, your honour and well deserved, sir. I never thought …"

"Yes, man, I have no interest in your thoughts. But I see you were a footman."

"Yes, sir, ten years in service afore I joined the King's army."

"Well, John Vertue, I could do with a manservant. Perhaps it is time to live up to your name."

For the next hour, Will was pushed, pinched, and eyed by many of the buyers. He removed himself from the humiliation of it all by gazing at the forest that enfolded the town like rainbow-coloured swaddling on a baby, occasionally waking from a reverie to answer questions or listen to a ribald comment from John Vertue. He suddenly felt infinitely tired and had to fight the urge to collapse to the ground and curl up and sleep. So distracted was he, he did not notice an upright, thin man approaching until he stood before him. The fellow's attire spoke of riches; brocade, silks, a fine tricorne hat, and shiny black shoes. He looked down at his merchandise sheet and then directly into Will's eyes.

"William Staples," he said. It was not a question.

Will, who had said nothing for the best part of the last hour, coughed his voice awake and replied in the strongest tones he could muster.

"Yes, master."

"A carpenter, I see."

"Yes, master."

"A good one, Staples?"

"Yes, master, I believe so."

Will was wide-awake now; he had sensed something in this man. He watched the buyer closely, careful not to stare, for he was taken with the man's looks. His eyes reminded Will of Sam Royston's, kind eyes, he thought to himself. They had soft crinkles at their corners and fine lines were streaking away across to his temples and Will said to himself, *this is a man who likes to smile and laugh.*

"Where apprenticed?"

"To Master Samuel Royston of Cheapside, London, sir, a fine master and excellent man of wood from whom I have learned much, sir."

"You speak well, Staples. Tell me, have you done rough work as well as fine carpentry?"

"He's a fine lad, sir," John interrupted. "I can vouch for his character and reliability."

"Let the boy speak," the buyer retorted, his voice soft, but full of authority.

Will told the man how he had started out with his father, felling trees, planking them, repairing farm gates, building new field fences, and then how he had learned the arts of window, door and cabinet making.

"If you are true to your word, this is a good deal for one so young."

"'Tis all true, my lord," replied Will enthusiastically, wanting now to be bought by this tall, ruddy-faced man with the kind eyes, "on my mother's grave, sir."

"Well, William Staples, I am Mr. Sowell of Burtonwood. Perhaps, I will bid on you today."

"Thank you, sir," said Will as Sowell turned away.

Once the buyers, like dogs sniffing out a rabbit warren, had finished their inspections, the bidding started in earnest. Will tried to see which of the convicts he knew were being bought and by which planter, but it was impossible due to the speed and noise of the business. John Vertue went under the hammer and Will saw three men bidding, but within moments the transaction was completed and his friend was led away by the stocky man who needed a house servant. Will's heart shrank at the thought he may never see his friend again, but, as he walked away, John turned and gave him a grin and wink, seemingly satisfied with his lot. Minutes later four planters were bidding on Will, one of them Mr. Sowell. It seemed carpenters were a popular purchase. The other three men were not as well-dressed as Sowell and one of them looked positively poor. He dropped out quickly, but the bidding became fierce until the auctioneer cried: "Sold to Mr. Sowell!"

Relief flooded through Will. For a short moment, he felt a quiet elation, but the flame of that joy quickly guttered and died, replaced by an appalled emptiness at the thought that he was now no more than some wealthy man's possession. He thought of Jenkin Smith's years of slavery and his guts turned over. Mr. Sowell approached him with another man, sending his musings into the ether. As the two men came nearer, he recalled that Smith's master, Mr. Wallace, had been a kind man who had bought his servant's freedom. Perhaps Mr. Sowell was such a man.

"This is Mr. Edwards," he told Will. "He will take you to the skiff while I settle my bill."

Edwards, a very tall, burly man, led Will to the dock where he was quickly stowed, the newly bought goods, aboard the skiff. He took a seat next to a woman called Myrtle Gains, who claimed to be a cook, an older man, James Buckler, who said he was a butcher from Salisbury and an anxious-looking boy of perhaps fifteen who kept his counsel. Two of Sowell's men hovered on the quayside as Edwards took his place in the stern of the vessel behind the convicts. These fellows had pistols at their belts and stood frowning at the convicts until Mr. Sowell arrived and took his place on deck.

The journey upriver from the landing was, for Will, full of wonder and did much to restore his spirits. Their route took them past lands that were, for the first few hours, rolling open fields with, sometimes, a rare sighting of farm buildings, but, always, further away, green, tree-covered hills. The riverbanks would change then to forest that ran down to the water's edge, only to be supplanted within the hour by more fields and even, at one point, a brickworks with a smoking stack. One of the armed men, a thin fellow called Aston whose accent Will did not know and who wanted to do nothing more than talk, explained to the convicts that these were plantations blossoming on ground hacked out of virgin forest. Each plantation, he said, was owned by one man, often an ordinary man who had come to the colony to make his fortune, much like Will's new master, Mr. Sowell.

They passed acres of tamed land over the next two days as well as some remaining forest. Sometimes they would catch sight of buildings and chimneys in the distance, the occasional private landing on the river bank and field workers, all of them black. Will felt an unexpected pang of sorrow as the memory of his friend Jenkin Smith came to him, for he felt he knew something of the suffering of those people.

He studied the trees in the untouched forest and recognized elm, oak, larch, chestnut, and pines of several kinds, but there were many trees he had never seen. On the morning of the third day, Aston announced that they would soon arrive at Mr. Sowell"s landing place where a cart would be waiting to take them to Burtonwood. *When we arrive there, my life in the Virginia colony will begin*, was Will's unspoken thought. He felt a thrill of excitement. Now he could begin his search for Peg.

Chapter 25

In Which Polly Makes Two Friends and Encounters Thomas Garland

The weeks have flown and I am only now beginning to understand how these people live and what this place is like. I know what is expected of me for that was told me plain on the first day by Mr. Garland's man, McLeod, a man with malice in his eyes and always a sour look on his ugly face.

From the first, things were strange. The weather turned hot the first days I was here; autumn ain't supposed to be hot. I was never in a village, only London and the Colliton's grand house in Surrey, but this place, Garland's plantation, is what I suppose a village to be, with all its buildings scattered thither and hither. Strange people too; gangs of black slaves, convict workers like me, many surly and unfriendly, wearing the burden of the guilt of their crimes as they would a flea-ridden, stinking, old coat. And the indentured servants – as I have been taught they are called – are haughtier still than a pompous footman in a great house, and I've known some of them. Much of what I have seen is beyond me and some of it sad and hard, but the birds of the air and their cheery songs make me smile with their colours and music, for I ain't seen none but black and brown things afore. 'Tis the first time in my life I looked at birds and I thank my good Lord for them now.

The very first day they cut off my hair, the only cure, they said, for the lice that marched in armies all over my head, and gave me clean, fresh water to bathe – there is a stream runs between the laundry and the blacksmith's shed. I was so sore, under my arms and in my private places, from all the filth piled up like mud on the shores of the Thames over the long weeks, but I was glad enough to be clean. I had a set of rough clothes given me, not soft and comfortable like I had at the Colliton's house, but clean enough, then I was taken to the laundry, my new daytime home, where Daisy Black, a tall, snappish bean-pole with a look on her face like it was her first day in Newgate, let me know quick that I was like a worm and would be 'til I learned the ropes. I never told her I'd served my time washing when I was maid-of-all-work. She's one of those women, Daisy, who spins a lie about someone and uses it to try and wrap you around her finger, but I've known her type before, and some better at it than her, so I don't listen to her beer-garden jaw, with her foul words and vulgar sayings.

Soon enough I was spending my days in that steamy place and my hands were red and sore. I've known worse and I like the nonsense chatter of the women, some who make me pleased I ain't them and others who make me laugh. At night we walk back to the low building that is our shared rooms, where I have a narrow bed in with seven other convict women. I get on all right with them, especially Maggie Wells and Helpmeet Ross who are in the laundry with me and are the ones who put a smile on my face. The others I get on with fine, 'cepting Daisy who doesn't get on with anyone. 'Tis only a few weeks I've been here at Garland's, but I feel like most of the women have me as a friend they can count on, so it ain't so bad as I feared it might be.

Maggie; she's the one who's always smiling and finds the good in everything and she's a real talker. It's she who's told me all about the estate, as they call it here. She says us convict women don't change jobs; she and Helpmeet's been on laundry duty since the day they arrived. That's all right, I can suffer that, though I must find some way to save my poor hands, some goose grease maybe. I ain't seen it yet, but Maggie says the estate is big, really big, with many buildings and acres of fields of tobacco, animals, and green stuff. All I've seen is our dark, little sleeping house, the track that leads to the laundry, the paddocks I walk by each day – they say Mr. Garland loves his horses – and, on top of the hill, Mr. and Mrs. Garland's house, which is a grand thing all of white wood and big windows.

Helpmeet's the one who sees the bad. She sees the world like it is, if you ask me, and she tells it straight. She says the master can be "a right, cruel bastard" and that that McLeod fellow is one who likes to do the whipping and beating. I don't like McLeod, though, thanks be, I ain't got to see him regularly, for he doesn't come to the women's places much. Helpmeet's told me worse stories than whippings and beatings, stories about the young black women. I don't know about those black people, they are strange to me, but Silston taught me all I need to know about what they might suffer at the hands of Garland and McLeod and I feel sorry for those girls. I ain't surprised to hear about pale brown babies in the blacks' camp.

Me and Maggie and Helpmeet go out the back of the laundry when we have a few minutes away from the labour and heat of the cauldrons. The drying lines are out there and, most days, are hung with linen like flags a'flying, but I like it there, even now that November's here. It's a dusty place after a dry summer, with bushes and trees to be seen when the washing's in and a flat place to sit with your back against the laundry wall so that you can gaze up at the sky, which is often blue and clear, listen to Maggie or Helpmeet chatter away and think about better times. It's out there I met a new friend just the other day. He's an old dog called Joss. Maggie says he's a hunting hound, but he's past his best I'd warrant, though I don't know dogs. He's long of leg, tall of body, docked of tail and wet of mouth; not a handsome fellow, but he took to me like I took to him.

The grass out the back had greened in the last week since the rain came and me and Helpmeet were sitting out, leaning against the wall, when Joss turned up. Helpmeet was smoking her pipe and talking her usual nonsense when he appeared out of a thicket and lumbered over to us.

"Here's trouble," she said with a laugh. She's got a low laugh like a cart on a track. Puts me in mind of all sorts of mischief, it does. "That lazy boy has let him go again."

I hadn't seen Joss's keeper then. I'd heard about him and knew he wasn't a boy, but I kept my thoughts to myself. He's one of the people who lived here before English folk came to this country, so all the women treat him like he's a baby. Joss stopped beside me and dropped his old head. I don't know animals, so his big mouth scared me. I must have been showing my fear, for Helpmeet chided me.

"Oh, he ain't gonna hurt you, girl," she laughed, cart and track again. "He's as stupid as a wooden post. He just wants a pet, dearie. Go on, give him your hand."

I wasn't sure, but didn't want to look a fool in Helpmeet's eyes, so I lifted my hand over his head and felt the back of his bony pate.

"Give him a scratch behind his yers, girl," said Helpmeet between puffs on her pipe, "he loves that."

I tried it and he did love it, even I could tell. As I scratched harder, his head dropped lower. He started leaning on me and slowly sank down until he was lying against me, his long legs out. Made me giggle, he's so soft and stupid, but I loved it. Like an old gent, he gave out a big sigh, rearranged himself so that I could reach both ears, crossed his front paws, and laid his head down on them.

"Aw, the old bugger likes you," said Helpmeet.

Of a sudden, we both saw a shape by the bushes, though we never heard a thing.

"There you go, sneaking up again, damn your Indian hide," Helpmeet spluttered like a kettle on the fire.

"Sorry, old woman," said the dog's keeper and grinned.

Without thinking, I ran my hand through my hair, still missing its old length and thickness, but it's growing back now, almost as black as his. His hair was longer than mine, down on his broad shoulders and his skin was a dark colour, and his eyes, the blackest I ever saw. I guessed he was the same age as me, maybe a mite older. So it was that I met my second new friend on the estate, Archie.

*

It's cold today, though there was no ice on the puddles on the way to the laundry. The air is extra clear and you can see your breath like you're a steaming pot. There's small clouds running like animals up above and I can see all sorts in their shapes. The women have been chattering about Christmas, for 'tis only two weeks away. They all have their own ideas about what celebrations might be allowed and I'd had enough of that clap-trap so I came outside for a minute. Maggie will be awhile so I have a few minutes to myself and I use it to check Polly Pruitt over like I did on the ship. I'm happy with my hair now, long enough to tie and I've got some weight on my bones

192

with the regular meals and all the fruit we get to eat. I ain't got a looking glass, but I feel like I'm pretty again as I can feel my face is full and lost its terrible boniness.

Archie's off with the master and McLeod, hunting game. He must have taken Joss along with the younger hounds, for there's no sign of my old friend. I let the cool fill me up, driving out the stink of the laundry. I'm about to sit down and close my eyes for a piece before Maggie comes to bend my ear when I hear the door opening. I look and there's Master Thomas. I ain't seen the boy since that day at the docks on the Elizabeth River and I am all the better for it. My heart chills and I am about to give him a word when he grabs my arm and pulls me away. He's stronger than I took him for and I try to stop him, but he swings me around, rough like, and drags me towards the bushes. I pull away from him hard and he grunts as he reaches out and holds onto my other arm. With a jerk, he pulls me to him. I see what's coming just in time and turn my head so that his wet kiss lands on my jaw, awkward like. I try pulling and wriggling again, but he tightens his grip.

"Quiet, hussy" he hisses. "Be still."

He pushes hard and I tumble backwards, falling to the ground. I'm trying to roll away, but I'm too slow and he lands on top of me and his knee is up between my legs. Hes that close, I can smell his last meal on his breath and it curdles my stomach. He ain't like Silston; he was sure of himself, knew what he wanted and where to find it. This one's still a boy, his hands are everywhere and his face is red with the blood that's up. I'm lashing my arms, beating his back and shoulders, so he grabs my wrists and pushes my arms back over my head. Now he is still and so I stop moving, thinking to cry out for help or if that will put me in deeper waters. He's staring at me like he hates me worse than anything, like I'm an animal that's killed his favourite dog. Then I see he's an animal himself, an animal in a boy's body. I don't like what I see in those eyes.

"Get off me!" I say it low and cold, like I have power over him, though I know I don't.

Of a sudden, he goes slack, gives out a small whimper, like a child, falls full on me. His face alongside mine so that I feel his hot skin on my cheek and his breath puffing in my ear. His cheeks are soft, with no whiskers.

"I will have you, Polly Pruitt," he whispers, then rocks backwards and stands up. Maggie is standing at the door; we both see her at the same moment. The boy gives her a look like she's something dead and rotting. He flaps his hands over his coat, dusting himself off, he ain't in any hurry. Then he walks away, without another word. I'm sitting up now and Maggie comes to me, giving a hand to help me rise. She studies my face.

"You all right, young 'un?" says she.

I am not going to show her, nor myself, that I am a'feared or knocked out of true by that young blackguard.

"I'm all right, Maggie, bless you."

"Did he hit you?"

"No, no, he tried…"

I curse myself for my weakness, for I feel my throat close up and my eyes wetting, but I swallow hard and straighten my back. Abigail, when she was in her rages about her Pa, always said a straight back makes you strong. Maggie dusts me down, blouse and skirt.

"He's a handful, that Thomas," says she. "They say he cheeks his tutor and skips classes. Likes his pipe and riding his pony too much. Old Skipper in the cooper's shop says he's been to a couple of cockfights too. But he'll come good, you see if he don't. Old man Garland will see to that."

I'm not saying anything yet, not trusting my voice. She hates a silence, does Maggie, so she goes on.

"You won't want to hear this, but you might give him what he wants, girl. It ain't so bad and many a girl in this colony has done herself some good and married rich by giving in to worse than him."

"Maggie," says I, "such a thing will never happen as long as I have breath in me."

I can feel my face has gone tight, like I'm angry with her, though I am sure she knows it ain't her.

"Well now Polly, maybe ..."

"No, Maggie, I don't want to hear no more," says I, hard like.

I sit down, shut my eyes and lean back against the wall, thinking I wish I smoked, for a pipe might be a good thing now and tobacco is a thing this place has plenty of. Maggie disappears back inside, leaving me my thoughts. I have wiped the boy's spit off my jaw, and, though I can feel a few bruises from the fall and his hands on my wrists, I am still Polly Pruitt and I will be strong as my Abigail was in showing her parents she would not be sold to Silston. I tell myself that Thomas Garland is an infantile idiot and I will not allow him to frighten me. Abigail's death has made me hard. I am not the silly, giggling girl that was Abigail's maid. I make a decision and a promise to myself. I will serve out my sentence, but then I will make my way in the world. I will still be young when my freedom is granted; I have plenty of time. I am feeling better when a cold, wet nose touches my hand.

"Joss, I thought you'd gone hunting, old boy." I scratch his neck under the rope collar he always wears. I realise I need to tell what has happened to me, maybe all of it. "Lay down, Joss, my love, I have a story to tell you."

Chapter 26

In Which Will Arrives at The Plantation

The autumn day Will arrived at the landing of the Burtonwood plantation was like a balmy July morning in England. *What a land this is!* he thought, *sunshine and warm air in the middle of November.* A cart, manned by a silent jarvey, waited for them, a horse tethered at its back. Mr. Sowell mounted his steed and, after a brief word with the driver of the cart and a wave to his men, he rode away leaving the three male convicts and Myrtle Gains in the tough care of Edwards and his men.

A small tributary flowed into the river not far from the landing. Everywhere there was evidence that this place had been cut from the forest by heavy labour; there were the stumps of many trees and, apart from the track that Sowell had taken when he left, the ground had been left uneven and humped by all the activity of the fellers and their heavy horses. The convicts were led along the stream to a place where the water was shallow and told to sit on its grassy bank. Here, Edwards and his men shaved off all the convict's hair and then ordered them to strip. Myrtle Gains, loud and blasphemous in her objections was, grudgingly and after some argument, allowed to move away up the stream to preserve what modesty she had left after her time in Newgate and on the voyage. Will, the quiet teenager, and the Salisbury butcher set to enthusiastically, splashing their naked white flesh in the water of the rapidly flowing tributary amid gasps at the cold and hoots and shrieks of enjoyment. Will thought it a wonderful luxury to feel the slip of soap on his skin for the first time in months.

He gave his body, face, and stubbly head, bleeding in several places from the rough shave he had received, an energetic scrub with the hard block, hoping to kill off the lice and fleas. When they were all finished, they were given garments; underclothes, canvas shirts and trousers, hop-sack smocks which were very rough, but clean and fresh-smelling, and a coarse dress for Myrtle. While they dressed, their guards – or "protectors" as Sowell had called them – made a bonfire of the rags the convicts had shed. *Goodbye,* thought Will, *to the last of my English life.* The butcher asked for shoes. When the raucous laughter subsided, Edwards informed them they would have none. Will had noticed already that, apart from Mr. Sowell, the ruddy-faced colonists went barefoot. He wondered; would he be shod in time for winter?

Before they moved on, they were made to sit on the coarse grass and a basket of food was produced; dense, rich bread, dried meats and fresh apples, flagons of small beer, truly a feast for the half-starved wretches of the Maria Elizabeth. Once the feast was finished, the convicts were loaded onto the cart and they set off on their final journey. The cart made its unhurried way along tracks that led from the river into the heart of the plantation. For Will, whose heart had been sunk so low for so long, it was a revelatory experience. There were birds he had never seen or heard before darting from bush to tree, flying low over the fields or soaring in the sky, and he reveled in their songs. Indeed, it seemed to him, in that moment, that he had never heard a bird in all his time in London.

As well as his earlier realisation that there were trees here that he, with all his knowledge of wood, did not know, there were large areas put to the cultivation of crops he had never seen. These fields were bare and barren now, though some were covered in ranks of a strange, thick stubble Aston told him was from a crop they called corn. By next summer, the voluble 'protector' said, this corn would be as high as a man and most of the other fields would be covered in the lush growth of tobacco plants. Beside the track there were bushes and flowers, which Will did not recognize. He felt a kind of quiet, cautious elation.

Within the hour they were approaching a small settlement. The jarvey steered the cart between buildings of various sizes before stopping at a livery stable. Sowell's head man, named Christian Hardbone, was there to meet them. Will was immediately struck by the appearance of this big fellow. His mouth was a narrow line, turned down at the corners, his chin and cheeks bristling, like the cornfields, with stubble. His nose was large, fat at the nostrils. His hair was mostly white, but turned a yellowish-brown round his face by constant pipe smoking and refusal to wash it. It was thin to absent on his pate, but long at the neck, folding in slow curls up around and under his large fleshy ears; you could see he had the habit of combing it off his face and over the back of his skull. His eyes were hazel and deep-set with bushy eyebrows that sat low. His cheeks were baggy and showed deep scour lines from the side of each nostril running down either side of his mouth. Will thought he had the appearance of a man who had known hardship most of his life, but he thought he saw sadness there, too.

Hardbone carried a short sword in a scabbard at his belt and a whip in his hand. The convicts were instructed they were to call him 'sir' or Mr. Hardbone. He told them, with no hint of humour, that they would discover that his family name was well-given and well-suited.

He walked them towards the nearest buildings while Aston, his hand on his pistol butt, followed behind. There were many buildings, many more than in Will's old home at Harsham. He could hardly believe that it all belonged to one man. The Master's house was impressive. Built on a rise, it had two brick-built storeys and a roof the size of a small field that was covered in tiles of wood, a thing Will had never seen. There were many windows and a wide and high front door, with a fine brass lion-head knocker, under a wooden portico supported by two fat wooden columns, all painted white and shining in the Virginia sun. Hardbone told them with pride that Mr. Sowell had his own brickworks. It seemed to Will that, in the overseer's mind, Mr. Sowell's success was Hardbone's triumph too.

As they followed the overseer, they saw many other buildings, most set a discrete distance behind the great house. Hardbone told them, with the same pride, that there were "well-lighted houses" for indentured servants, men and women both. He said that, later, he would take them to the huts for the convict servants, again, one for men and one for women, but first he wanted to show them the slave huts. These, he told them, were not divided to separate men and women. The slaves, Hardbone said with a sneer, lived like the animals they were, men and women together, outside of marriage.

He explained that the estate had everything a community might need from blacksmith to butcher, orchards to kitchen garden, animals for meat and wool to wheat and oat fields. There was even a quarry, Hardbone boasted. It was a little empire unto its own self, its emperor, Mr. Sowell.

Will was so engrossed and surprised by the talk he did not notice until they were almost upon the slave huts. This accommodation was poor indeed. They were ram-shackle shanties, with twisted and buckled roofs, doors that hung askew, porches that, on some were half-collapsed. Hardbone said that most of the black people were out working in the fields or on the farm, but a young woman of elegant stature wearing a smock dress stood in the doorway of her hut watching as they passed. Her dark-skinned face was set in a stare that gave away nothing of her mind, but her large eyes tracked their every step. On her hip, she held a tiny child whose nose streamed with snot. It, too, observed the motley group of white people with a leery, knowing eye and expressionless face. Its skin was strangely pale compared to its mother's and Will wondered if these people darkened as they grew older, like a tree's bark changed as it aged. Hardbone gave a guttural chuckle and pointed out that Virginia law decreed that every child born to a slave became a slave themselves, thus expanding the Master's property and making him richer.

Finally, they were brought to a long, single-storey wooden building with no windows and a lone chimney; the male convict's new home. The sun was setting fast and darkness was coming. Will was overcome by a sudden exhaustion that fell upon him like a great weight on his shoulders and he longed for nothing more than to lie down and sleep, but Hardbone was not done with them yet.

"Now, listen close, you sorry scum; Mr. Sowell's business is tobacco if you didn't know, and tobacco is what we live and die by here at Burtonwood. Oh, I know you'm all have smoked the leaf and think you know what tobacco is, but I stand here to tell you that you know not the first thing. But you will be taught. Yonder see the great barn?"

They all turned to follow where he was pointing. There, in the distant dimness, set against a small copse of trees, was a building equally as large as the main house.

"The tobacco house," Hardbone continued, "is the most important house on the estate. There we take the crop after harvest and treat it and dry it and stack it and bundle it and store it until it be ready for transport back to blessed old England so that the likes of you miserable curs can smoke it in your pipes. That is Mr. Sowell's business and everything we do here is to ensure its success, you hear me?"

He stood there a moment giving the tired group the evil eye, staring down each man in turn, passing a silent message of warning.

"When you've served your time, be it seven or fourteen year, you'll be free men …"

"And woman," muttered Myrtle, quiet, but firm.

"Free men," repeated Hardbone, ignoring her, "and you will have your Freeman's package to help you set up here in Virginia or you can work your passage back to England if you so choose, but…but, you worthless idle bastards, until then you are the property of Mr. Archibald Sowell. From your scabby heads to your filthy toes, our Master owns you and you will remember that and you will work as you have never worked before. Any one of you tries to run, you'll be hunted down like animals and brought back in chains. Any one of you steals from Mr. Sowell or tries to cheat him in any way…well, we have gallows here in Virginia too, boys, just remember that. Now, you men, this is your new home. Get yourselves in there with

Forboys here and he'll show you your place of sleep. You, woman, come with me."

Forboys, a gangly youth of around eighteen years, had been idling at the door of the hut when they arrived. Now, grinning like an idiot, he led the three men into the windowless dark of the convicts' quarters and showed them their palliasses laid out on the packed mud floor. The room smelled of earth, rotting wood and cobwebs burdened with the dust of a score of years and something else, something organic, not bad, even faintly comforting.

"Hot as hell in summer, boys, cold as a fuckin' witch's tit in winter, but home sweet home, eh?" He giggled. He was enjoying his short time in authority. "Now, get some rest, lads, the hard work starts tomorrow."

Will lay down gratefully on his mattress and looked up at the rough roof beams of his new home. His mind was a swirling fog of new sights, new sounds, new people, everything unknown and different. He shut his eyes and, within seconds, he felt the warm arms of sleep begin to envelope him. Images from the day swirled willy-nilly past his inner eye and, as he sank deeper, a cold dismay settled in his gut when he remembered Ashton's words, on the river, about how huge the plantation was and how many other estates there were in Virginia. The last bitter thought that surfaced and then sank into the darkness as sleep took him was: *I am here, where I planned to be, but I wonder now how I will ever find my Peg.*

Chapter 27

In Which Will Learns More About His New World and Joins a Manhunt

Morning leaped out of bed like a child on her birthday; an effervescence of colour, an effulgence of light, an ebullience of bird song. After a breakfast of fresh bread, salty butter, a slab of ham, and a mug of small beer – better food than Will had known since his days with Sam Royston – Will was taken, along with a small gang of men, to his first job on the plantation; clearing the virgin forest of all trees, scrub, brush and roots. Two men, Arthur Edwards, who Will already knew, and Henry Horrocks led the work party.

Beside Edwards's massive bulk Horrocks looked small, though he was wiry and tough. Unlike his giant companion, he was a voluble man with a ready grin, rotted teeth, and stinking breath. He talked while he worked, while he rested, and while the gang made their way to and from their work. He was full of stories and gossip and ready to tell the world, it seemed, his whole history. Watching them work and direct the other men, it became clear to Will that these two were both skilled and seasoned woodsmen. So, it was from Horrocks that Will learned that both men were over ten years into their fourteen-year sentences, though it came out that the story-teller had to serve an additional three years because he had got one of the servant women pregnant and the extra sentence was to pay off the county for raising the child, who had been taken away at birth. He swore that, once he was a free man, he and the woman would get the child back.

They were hard-driving men, the gang's two chiefs, but they were fair and quickly saw that Will had skills that they could put to good use. Edwards, for all his normal quietness, was the one who asked questions, wanting to hear about Will's training. When the men left off their work to rest and devour the cider, bread, and cheese they had brought with them, Horrocks continued to satiate his seemingly endless need to hear his own voice and began telling the history of Mr. Sowell.

"Biggest land-owner this side of the Elizabeth, boys," he said, grinning as if the brag was about himself. "Been buying up land ever since he landed on these shores. Second son of a merchant gent from Bristol, come over with some seed money, they say. Started off renting land, he did, but he husbanded it well, borrowed to build his brickworks, first one in these parts, mind, and made money on his bricks and tobacco. Then, by God, he buys up the land he's renting and he's not stopped since, no. They do say he's going in with the Blackwell family in the building of an ironworks, down near Yorktown."

"'E's a good man, Mr. Sowell," growled Edwards, breaking into Horrocks' diatribe, "even-'anded, decent. Won't hear a word agin 'im, I won't."

"Yeah, you boys just be glad you didn't get bought by some of the other bastards run land here. More'n one of them loves a good whipping and some even lays on their selves, so they say."

"But Mr. Sowell's cut from different cloth; God-fearing man who don't like to use to the whip, if he don't have to," said Edwards giving Horrocks a warning look.

They laboured until the sun was setting, cutting out undergrowth, taking down trees, and dragging out stumps behind two of Mr. Sowell's big, shaggy-hooved working horses. As they trudged back to their quarters, exhausted and ready for a meal before they could collapse onto their pallets, Will was full of grudging admiration for his new master. Here was a man determined to build an empire of tobacco, clawing money out of the land. They would be marching back out tomorrow at dawn to continue the clearance work, but Will knew now, come the new season, that land would be burgeoning with Mr. Sowell's cash crop.

*

Will may have been exhausted at the end of his first day of work, but by the third day, his body was complaining bitterly at the vicious questions being asked of it by Edwards and Horrocks. He had never known such hard labour and his strength had been sapped over the months in Newgate and on board ship. To make matters worse, on that third morning, it started to rain; a heavy, cold downpour that quickly turned the ground where he was hacking out roots into a quagmire.

The forest around him disappeared in the cloak of rain and a pungent smell of wet pine needles and rot filled the air. Will was soaked through in minutes and, skinny as he was, quickly became freezing cold and started shivering despite the heavy work. He laboured on, longing for the first break of the day and a chance to find some shelter, wondering distractedly if he would survive a whole day when a cry was heard in the distance. He could not make out the words, but it had all the hallmarks of a chase, a hue and cry.

"Runaway, I'd say," muttered Edwards, who had been helping him attach a chain to a pine stump nearby.

Almost as he spoke, Will heard the word shouted, 'runaway, runaway!' as well as the baying of hounds. Edwards gave him a long look, his face a strange mixture of excitement and sorrow. Later, Will would discover why; the gentle giant knew what would be coming if the runaway was caught.

"Up, lads," he grunted, "up and away."

The men began running, as best they could, across the slippery land they had cleared. Soon, they were joined by the others, led by Horrocks. They quickly crossed the clearing and broke into the surrounding forest. Will was already panting, but the muscle aches and tiredness fell away in the excitement of the chase. His heart pounded as he pumped his arms and skidded across the soaked ground. He was well at the back of the crowd, stumbling and crashing through brush and scrub, his feet, not yet hardened, being pricked, scratched, and bruised as he sought an easy way through the undergrowth. He prayed the chase might end before he was crippled by injury.

At last, he could see the other hunters; Hardbone leading perhaps four or five men. Catching sight of the work party, the overseer waved them away to the right, yelling instructions so that his men and the work party formed a wedge breaking through the forest. Way out in front of the men, three dogs, long-legged, loping hounds, were leaping easily over the brush, dodging between trees. Two more dogs, huge animals with long ears like little saddlebags, were straining against long leashes held by two of Hardbone's men. As they moved forward the dogs sniffed the ground, their massive heads swaying to and fro as they went. Still, the rain came down.

All the men were shouting as they went, the hounds were barking, one of the snuffling dogs was baying; Will understood now the meaning of hue and cry. The noise echoed around the woodland, throwing up ground birds of sorts Will had never seen, scaring a small herd of deer that broke away to the left. His face was streaming with rain and he had to wipe his eyes clear every few seconds. Edwards was taking massive strides, his muscular legs bursting through the undergrowth as he charged forward. Will, almost as tall, but lighter, jumped over low bushes, though he was obliged to break through the heavier scrub. He realised he was smiling, for this chase felt like sport of a macabre kind; the joy of the chase, the exhilaration, and excitement of the hunt. Then a shout went up. It was Hardbone.

"We have him, lads," he roared.

He was pointing as he barreled forward. Will squinted through the rain falling in sheets in the clearings between trees and pouring in tiny waterfalls off every leaf. His eyes were bleary, but then he saw him; a black man, bounding ahead. He was dressed only in a shirt and canvas trousers. He was thin and tall, his head shaved close. He held his arms wide for balance as he leaped over briar and bush, dodging around trees, every now and again bending forward to avoid low branches. The excitement drained from Will; the exhilaration died. His legs turned heavy and the aches and complaints of his tired body ran through to his core. The hard truth had crashed into his mind, the understanding that they were chasing a living man and now he feared for what would happen should they catch him. He slowed, dropped behind the rest of the chasers, gulping breath, more than half of him urging the black man to get away; he had no quarrel with the poor fellow.

He saw the lead hound run close and jump at the man, knocking him forward. He staggered, regained his balance, made to move on, but then another hound was on him and Will was sickened to see it bite into his arm. The runaway howled and fell sideways and that was the end. Men and dogs were on him, though he was hidden from Will's eyes. He felt a great sadness well up in his heart as Horrock's now seemingly prophetic words of whippings returned to him.

Chapter 28

In Which We Meet Augustin De La Fontaine and Learn the Short
History of The Escaped Slave

They whipped the slave at dawn. Hope drained out of Will when all of Mr. Sowell's workers and slaves, rank upon rank of them, were made to stand and watch that terrible punishment. He took some small comfort, at first, when he thought he could tell that Hardbone got no pleasure from the laying on of the whip, but that did not stop the overseer swinging hard. Will stopped watching, discreetly dropping his head when the blood and tiny pieces of loosened flesh started to fly, but he could still smell the poor man's piss and shit. When it was done, Hardbone turned slowly to the crowd and addressed a handsome woman amongst the slaves:

"Ruth, come and take your boy."

The slave's mother came forward with three other black women and took the wretch away to deal with his wounds and everyone went to work. Mr. Sowell did not attend the punishment; Will found himself wondering what that said about his master.

Back in the woods with Horrocks and Edwards, Will's gang of workers laid in again against the trees and brush, but, depressed and angry, Will found it harder. Winter was on its way and the remarkable warm weather of mid-November was fading into memory. There were light moments, like when he saw a bird or animal new to him; a tiny brilliant blue bird with a red breast, a comical animal he was told was called a raccoon, a handsome red bird with a hard-looking beak and a fine little crest on its head, but there was not much time to admire those small beauties. Each day it rained harder than the day before, but Edwards and Horrocks kept their team of clearers at work for as long as they could. Those were days of soaking clothes, steaming bodies – horses and men – mud to their ankles, filth up their arms to their shoulders.

"You wait for summer, lad," said Horrocks to Will one day, a glint of perverse pleasure in his eyes. "You think this is miserable? Wait for the roasting you'll get from the sun come summer. It's unbearable some days, you'll be dripping with sweat instead of rain."

He chuckled malevolently as he wiped the rain from his face.

"Yeah, but the master lets us rest in the shade at midday on the worst of 'em," added Edwards, always quick to come to Sowell's defence.

In time, it became impossible to work the forest clearance and, at last, Will found himself indoors starting as apprentice to the estate carpenter, a burly middle-aged Frenchman named Augustin de la Fontaine affectionately known as Auggie. He had a generous nose and above it, shining out of a ruddy face, a pair of small twinkling eyes. Though the winter work was mainly reparative, the carpenter came to see what a talent Will had and it took no time for the two men, so different yet united by their mutual love of wood, to become friends.

As the temperatures dropped, Will was grateful to be under Auggie's gentle tutelage and in his workshop where the carpenter kept a fire in his stout iron stove. From the day Will started with him, it was obvious that Auggie, like Aston and Horrocks, loved to talk. Soon Will was in possession of a hoard of new knowledge all, of course, as seen through Auggie's eyes.

Will had never met a Frenchman before and expected the man's accent to be exotic. Instead, his new master was more the West Countryman than Frenchman. Auggie's family were Huguenots who, having been persecuted for their religion in France, migrated to England's west country when he was five years old. His accent, he told Will with a chuckle, was a bastard mix of French and Bristol. In common with many Huguenots, his family were weavers, but Auggie never took to the trade. He had the heart for wood, he said proudly. Years later, when his parents were gone and he had fallen on hard times, he met an agent in a tavern who sweet-talked him into signing up as an indentured servant. These men made good money for each servant they shipped to the colony and Auggie had been a fool, he said, to fall for the fellow's trickery, but, after three years with Mr. Sowell, he professed to being happy. He told Will with pride that he would be a free man in little more than a year.

"I'll be getting me certificate of freedom, Billy; a little bit o' land, me ten bushels of corn, me thirty shilling, a trusty musket, and maybe some tools, if I'm lucky."

He planned to set up his own carpentry shop and offered Will the chance to join him, once his sentence was served. That seemed so far in the future Will did not let himself think about it. The same was true of Peg. He thought about her less often now and had given up making plans for escaping with her. He had always made plans, even as a child: planned to read a whole section of the bible on his own by the time he was ten; planned to be a master carpenter; planned to make his fortune in London; planned to find his Peg when she was lost in Newgate; planned a way to come to the New World. Now his optimism was exhausted and cold logic was coming to dominate him.

Will's life with Auggie was hard, but no harder than it had been with Sam. Work started each day at sunrise, after a breakfast of corn or oat porridge and a cup of fresh, clean water, and continued until sunset. If the day's labours went well, he would be given a few minutes rest before dark, to admire the rainbow colours of the evening skies. Tobacco was king on the plantation and was, Auggie said, a backbreaking crop to raise for the slaves and convicts that worked the fields and the tobacco barn. The likes of Will were only called to the fields to help with the harvests; everyone, it seemed, would be working the fields sun-up to midnight every day in late May to bring in the barley, and again for a few days in June to cut the rye. Then in August he and his fellow workers would all be the toiling subjects of king tobacco when the leaves were brought in to dry. After that, once the corn was in, Will would be free to be a carpenter full-time again.

From the outset, the best thing about Will's new life was being well-fed every day. There was too much corn for his English stomach, but he relished every other foodstuff, especially the fresh greens that, every Sunday after Mr. Sowell gave the service, Will happily worked to cultivate in the fields close to the main house.

"Our master's a cunning cove, lad," Auggie told him. "Came over in the old Queen's time and took him a wife. There're two daughters now, plain little things, but good enough. The wife died in her labours with the third one, a boy. The good Lord took that one too, but Mr. Sowell would not be stopped by nothing. He's a sharp one. Most planters have pitiful small places and struggle to get by, tobacco being the hard taskmaster it is. Most don't even own enough candles to light their shacks and have only one servant and two or three slaves. But Mr. Sowell has that grand house on top the hill so's he can see all what he owns as he steps out each morning."

*

Winter arrived with the blessing of a mild December and a Christmas made merry by Mr. Sowell and his daughters for all his people, save the slaves. January came in bone cold. Working outside was a purgatory without gloves and with feet clothed only in rags. In February it snowed, a white ermine blanket two feet deep with drifts reaching ten feet and when the wind blew, beautiful plumes and arcs of spindrift.

One bitter night, lying sleepless and shivering on his pallet, Will sank into a deep melancholy that afflicted him for days. At the heart of it was the nagging understanding, now that he knew more about the colony, that he might never find Peg. Indeed, as he descended into the depths of despond, he came to accept that his fine plans and dreams were no more than that; wisps of fantasy, childish ideas with no basis in the real world. He would never, he realised, find Peg.

As winter's end approached, the great thaw began. The streams swelled to gushing brown rivers and run-off from the land created new rills pouring down gullies, carving ever deeper into the yielding earth. The sun had real warmth again and Will's spirits rose. As the first green shoots started to show, it felt that life was beginning again for him. On a March evening, as they sat smoking their pipes at

Auggie's stove, he told his master he was beginning to feel like a free man.

"You're a good lad, Billy," Auggie replied. "But always remember this, only a small number here have their freedom. We are, most of us, either indentured, slaves, or common felons like you; none of us free men, all of us bound. You got bought, Billy, never forget that. The master paid good money for you, as if he were buying a pig or a cow and you belong to Mr. Sowell, his to do with as he pleases for the next seven years. Until you finish your time, you are his possession and it will go well with you to always remember that."

*

In late March, Will made an unexpected friend. Repairs were needed on the roof shingles of three of the slaves' low houses. Auggie, too busy with work for the master, set Will to the task, 'giving' him a slave to help him. From his first day, Will had been fascinated by the slaves, reminders, as they were, of Jenkin Smith and his sad history. Twenty-six Africans were living in the slave hamlet, and perhaps Will would never have learned to see their lives from their own perspective if the runaway slave who had been whipped, Jeremiah, known as Jem, had not been assigned as his unwilling labourer.

On their first day on the roof, Will could get nothing from him but grunts, though he found his helper to be a quick and eager student. The next morning, he tried a different approach. He told Jem, as honestly and sincerely as he could, that he thought it wrong he had been lashed.

"You were brave," he said quietly. "I know I could not have endured as you did."

Jem did not respond, only kept up his angry hammering on the new shingles they had carried up to the roof.

"I want you to know," Will continued, feeling awkward and heavy limbed, "when my poor Ma died, my dad told me to get used to misery for that was what life had in store for me. He was a drinker, my Pa, always beating, hitting, cussing and I knew I must not become like him. I told myself I would escape that hard life, become my own man and find me a better life."

"That ain't nothin' t'me, suh," growled Jem, not looking at Will. His pent-up fury, contained by his hunched, tense shoulders, expressed itself on his face in ways that Will could never hope to comprehend.

"Please, don't call me sir. Look, you think I know nothing, but I know what you've been through; captured in Africee, the sea crossing and…"

"You truly doan know nothin', suh." Jem's voice was deeply resonant, surprisingly so in one so tall and thin.

"Well might you say so, but I had a friend for a time in London, a man of your colour who was taken slave and knew terrible times afore he was bought his freedom."

That got Jem's attention. He stopped his hammering, looked directly at Will for the first time and his face cleared.

"Black man got his freedom?

"Yes, 'black man got his freedom' and a fine man he is too."

"Yeah, well, I doan know no Africee. I's born right yer."

"Oh, I thought…"

"Yeah, you thought, well, you'se wrong. My ma, Ruth her name, she's born here too. Was my Gran'mammy was taken and brought to Ouidah, had my Ma in huh belly already, put on a ship there. Gran'mammy tell me all 'bout it."

"All right, all right, now I know, but I was telling you, I went to London to be my own man. My old master in Harsham, he told me, 'you can have a better life than this.' 'Will', says he, 'you got the skills, you got the fire in your belly'. And I swear, if you want it, I will teach *you* those skills."

A slight, wary smile graced Jem's lips and he nodded. After a moment he spoke his first civil words.

"So, this be your better life, Will Staples?" Will smiled, then, at the use of his name.

So it began. Grudgingly, in fits and starts, Jem condescended to converse with his new white master; about carpentry at first and the tools of the trade and he listened closely as Will described techniques and skills. By the next day, Jem was content to let Will tell his own history and he obliged, in turn, by relating his story. The two young men figured, as Will had guessed, they were about the same age. Will found he admired and liked the slave and quickly started calling him by his name, while Jem began to call him by his. In Jem's case, this was punishable with a whipping, so, both of them quickly realised they would have to be careful.

The days passed in growing mutual enjoyment of the task and each other's company and, as Jem became more practiced, the work went along smoothly, so that all the repairs were completed in good time. As the last cedar shingles were cut, shaped, and hung, the two young men decided upon a course that would see them finding time and excuses to meet as often as they could so that they might continue to learn from each other.

Chapter 29

In Which Louis Silston Does Business in Jamaica and
Meets Thomas Garland

Louis Silston had not been idle in the months since William Staples
escaped his clutches at the port of London. He may have had a quick
and violent temper, but he prided himself on his ability to quickly
master it and build on the bitterness that its waning always left
behind. He was a man to bear a grudge. He had discovered that
William Staple's ship would have docked at Port Royal in Virginia in
November. His father had advised sending word of his search for
Staples to the factor at the port, but Louis had his own thoughts on
the matter. Not for him remote revenge.

A long winter had passed, but he had not forgotten his promise to
his father. So it was, in the early spring of 1721, that he found himself
staying, in Jamaica, at the residence of his father's agent, Angus
McFarlane, with arrangements already made to sail on to Virginia as
soon as his education in the sugar cane business was finished. Once
he was with Reynolds Garland, he would be free to pursue his
obsession with the two people he held accountable for his loss of the
Colliton dowry.

It was already hotter than most summer days in England. Louis
never enjoyed that miserable season in his home country, preferring
the cooler days of spring and autumn and even the bitter cold of
winter to the sweating days of summer. Because of this, despite his
self-satisfied pleasure at doing his father's business in Jamaica, he was
not enjoying himself as he had hoped he might, for there was no

escape from the heat, even at night. He comforted himself that he would only have to bear the oven-like temperatures for another thirteen days before he would be free to take ship for the cooler, northern climes of Virginia. One evening, he was sitting on the wide veranda of McFarlane's house, smoking a pipe of good tobacco, drinking Canary sack, and discussing with his host the impending arrival of the next shipment of slaves from the west coast of Africa.

"I'm sure, sir, you will wish to accompany me to the market to partake of the auction?" McFarlane asked.

"Of course, I wouldn't miss it for the world," replied Louis with genuine enthusiasm.

Though he had, many a time, seen his father's ships in the London docks, he had yet to witness a slave auction. The prospect excited him.

"You'll meet all the owners and agents from hereabouts. And you'll be interested to hear that I had some unexpected news today about someone who will surely be there. It seems your partner's son, Thomas Garland, is on the island."

"Why, that is extraordinary news. I have not seen the lad since he was a snotty brat."

"Extraordinary indeed, sir," replied McFarlane. His face, which boasted the swollen nose and fine, red reticulations of a man too fond of his sack and Madeira, lit up and he chuckled. "I have it from my source that the lad is staying with a Major Bostock, an owner in the west of the island. I'm told the boy's only a sprat, sixteen, maybe; here to learn our ways with the slaves, and, to my friend's opinion, to toughen him up."

"Maybe so, maybe so, that would be so like Garland," replied Louis tapping his chin with his forefinger, "though I had nothing about this from Reynolds when I made my arrangements with him. Interesting. Let us arrange a meeting with the boy."

"I own, sir, that will happen anyway, for I am sure the lad will be with Bostock at the auction."

Four days later, McFarlane and Louis met Thomas Garland, with Major Bostock, in a tavern near the slave market. All morning, trade had been brisk and hundreds of pounds had changed hands, as ranks of African men, women, and children were paraded and then led away by their new owners. Louis had found the whole thing exhilarating.

Bostock was, like McFarlane, an old infantryman who had forged a new life for himself in Jamaica. Unlike McFarlane, he was a plantation owner, not a mere agent, but they hit it off immediately. While the two older men swapped stories of army life and island gossip, Louis plied Thomas with small beer and bragged of his life in London. From the start, it was clear to Louis that the boy was smitten with him. In the eyes of the young Garland, Louis was distinguished; a handsome young rake, wealthy, the son of a lord, Thomas' father's financial sponsor and business partner, but he also had a burnished aura of excitement and risk. Louis played up unashamedly to this image with bawdy and racy tales of the life of a young buck in London.

Thomas hung on the older man's every word as Louis wove a fabric of stories encompassing business deals, gambling, drinking parties, hunts on the great estates in the verdant, tamed lands around the city, and finally the women who were paraded by their wealthy families as prospective wives. Thomas had never had the imagination to consider life off the plantation, let alone in a great city like London, so now it seemed to him that his humdrum existence was narrow and confined compared to the world of business and excitement that Louis inhabited. He had hated every minute of his time in Jamaica, being horribly homesick and despising the overbearing and bombastic Bostock. He had ached for home since the day he had arrived, but now he had a new dream; he longed to see London and live the life of an independent young man of means.

At first, Louis enjoyed having a young acolyte who looked at him with such unadorned admiration. He also learned something from the young cub; tales of rebel slaves who had escaped and set up their own colony in a mountain stronghold in the interior of the island; McFarlane had mentioned nothing of this. Once Louis had learned the full extent of the escaped slaves' kingdom and how little the Governor had done to quell the rebellion, he became truly angry. It was a quiet outrage that would sit with him for days to come.

Louis's mood soured later when it became apparent that the young Garland could not hold his liquor; by early evening the lad was very drunk and had turned into a fawning discontent, half-coherently complaining of his life, his father's controlling nature, and his older sisters' arrogant disdain for him. By the time the party broke up, Louis had decided that he would not be spending any more time with his partner's son and was thanking the gods of happenstance that the boy was based so far from his father's estate.

"The fellow is a whining dolt. I hardly credit he could have come from my friend Reynold's loins," Silston complained to McFarlane as they rode back to the plantation.

"Maybe the boy takes after his mother," McFarlane speculated.

"Perhaps. In any case, I hope to spend not a minute more of my time in the boy's company during my stay here."

"I think you have no worry on that score, sir. He is kept well busy and Bostock tells me he leaves for Virginia on an earlier ship than yourself."

"Thank God for small mercies," said Silston. "Now, let us forget the odious Garland minor and turn our minds to business for tomorrow."

Chapter 30

In Which We Discover More About the New Life of Polly Pruitt

'Tis fine now that May has come. The spring has been cold and wet, but now the sun is warming everything, and the crop fields are filled with wheat and corn. I don't see the tobacco fields because my world is here, close to the main house, but I've been told there's acres and acres of the big bushy plants in their never-ending rows. 'Tis the convicts and the black people who labour in those places. I have settled now and London seems a dream, nothing but a memory of the past. I don't mind the laundry, though my hands are always sore and my back lets me know how it hates all the bending over boilers and rinsing pans, but the food is better than anything I had in Newgate and on the ship and my cot in the dormitory is tol'able comfy.

One day, out back of the laundry, when Helpmeet shut her flapping mouth, I heard this buzzing and chirping. Helpmeet said it had started two weeks before with a few little chirrups, said I'd missed it because I wasn't expecting it, but, that day, 'twas loud and strange to my ears. Helpmeet said it was insects – bugs, she called them – that had lain buried in the ground and were just now digging themselves out. I didn't believe it. I thought she was making the fool of me 'til she took me to a tree and there was one of the fat creatures. So ugly it was, it turned my stomach. Another strange thing in this strange land.

Now there is talk of a summer party and it keeps me awake when the others in our bedchamber natter on when we should all be a'sleeping, but they are excited, for Daisy went to last year's party at a nearby plantation; 'tis a celebration of the coming of summer and the prospering of the fields. Last year, our master Garland and his family took ten of his people, they say. No slaves, but two convicts went with the trusted indentured servants. Rumour is the party will be here this year, so people are taking bets on who will be invited.

It's been like that all day, all the women prating on about their precious party. Means nothing to me, for I will not be going, that is for sure. So, I sneak out back on my own at the end of the day, sit on the ground and enjoy the silence and heat. I have learned to love sitting here watching the sun go down, its glorious work done for another day. I love how its dying each day thickens the air and turns it golden before it hazes and turns dim and the sky is clothed, like a new bride, with rags and ribbons of many colours. And here comes Archie with old Joss. He sits with me, quite close and I don't mind it, for I think him a friend now. We watch the sun setting knowing we only have minutes afore we have to be in our places for the meal.

"It is so lovely," says I and I'm smiling, happy "'Tis so warm and clear."

He chuckles. He's got a lovely laugh, has Archie.

"You enjoy'um now, girl, 'cos perty soon it'll be so hot them birds'll give up their singin'. Too hot an' sticky to sit yer, an' if you did, them liddle flyin' biters'ud make you pay."

He talks like that, does Archie, kind of queer, but his voice is deep and a little like music; I like to hear it. He was born here, one of those the English call Indians. He told me early, he comes from a tribe with a name that's rum to me, Algonquin, but he's been here for around seventeen years. His face is marked by pox, not so much that it spoils his face, which is broad with the brownest eyes and blackest hair I ever saw. The pox killed his Ma and Pa when he was a little one, and he don't know his true age, but I reckon he's got no more than a year or two on me.

His own people called him Achachak, but he says folks here are too lazy to wrap their lips and tongues around such a sound and so they named him Archie. His name means 'spirit', so he says, and I like that his name has a meaning, unlike Polly. It ain't a bad name but 'tis only a sound for all I know. He speaks good English, though it comes out his mouth with the weirdest sounds, nobody in London sounded like Archie. He has a big heart, is what I believe, and he is good with animals, especially Joss, who he loves. That's why he's top groom and cares for the hunting dogs. Works for a fellow called Ben Gudgeon who was an ostler back in Hampshire afore he signed his indenture papers, and when old Ben works off his time here, by rights, Archie should be head man in the stables and kennels.

In my soul, I know Archie is a good man, maybe the first I have met. He has told me his biggest secret. In all these years, he has kept his own tongue alive by reciting his tribe's old stories to himself at night. He remembers all the skills of his people that he learned from an old man called Machk who was captured with him after his parents died. The old fellow's name means bear and I imagine a tall, hairy cove with sharp nails and teeth. Archie thinks he was ten or eleven when Machk died, but he's proud of how much he learned of his people's ways.

So, we sit here and enjoy the last of the sun. He tells me there is news of master Thomas's return. I never told him about what that boy did to me; didn't want to tell anyone, didn't want to talk about it.

And when the little wastrel was sent away by his father, I knew I didn't have to think on him for a long time. The women talk often of how his dad wants to toughen him up. None of them like him; they say he's a spoiled brat with a chip on his shoulder, and they all know he treats women as if we were animals to be husbanded. And there's another thing about him I don't care for.

"John Vertue likes him," says I, and I can't help the sourness in my voice.

"Yeah, well, John Vertue has to like him, don't he," says Archie with a grin.

I like a lot about Archie, but I think I like his smile the best. 'Tis a good, honest smile.

"They say John Vertue has become Mrs. Garland's favourite."

I don't like the fellow, I don't. He comes in the laundry sometimes, pretending he has business there and he makes my skin crawl. There is something about him.

"John Vertue is not a man to be trusted," says Archie. "Like the bear; you see'um in the distance and he's all shiny and black, looks good, looks fine, but you come too close and you're a dead man."

It's getting dark now and we should be going, but, of a sudden, I see something that makes me jump. A light, a tiny light is weaving up and down in the air near the new planted trees.

"Look, Archie, look!"

Archie looks where I'm pointing and laughs, saying something in his own language that sounds like wow-wah-tow-su.

"What is it?"

"Lightning bug, they call it. Some say firefly."

He always calls the white people 'they' and I understand why; I hope and pray I aint a 'they' to him.

"Another bug, like those clicking things," says I"

"This one's early. You'll see more soon, when it's hot. Stars in the woods, Machk used to call'um. And they don't make no noise like the others."

"'Tis a marvel." I can't take my eyes off it as it wavers and darts.

Then comes a shout from inside, "Polly!"

"Have to go," says Archie with a grin.

He squeezes my hand and is gone.

Chapter 31

In Which Polly Confides in Archie, Thomas Returns Home and Engineers A Fateful Meeting with Polly

News of the summer party had gradually filtered out from the big house and now everyone knew that it was to be held the next week. The guests from the neighbouring plantation would be arriving in just six days' time. Preparations were well under way with John Vertue, under the watchful eye of Mrs. Garland, taking the lead. Everyone assumed that Vertue would be attending the party, as would Hector McLeod, but there was no word yet of which other plantation people might be invited.

Polly, with no expectation of being among those privileged invitees, had put the whole matter of the party out of her mind and avoided the gossip about it when she could. Today, the news that occupied her mind was that Thomas Garland had returned from Jamaica. Tucking him away into her deep subconscious had been easy when he was far away in the Caribbean, but knowing he was back immediately set her on edge.

She knew how the gossip politics of the plantation worked; it was not so different here from how rumour had spread in the Colliton's house. Many people must know about the attack on her; Maggie had been there and Polly knew that Maggie would not have kept it to herself, yet none of the other women had mentioned it to her. At first, there had been looks and whispers behind her back, but these had only served to harden her resolve not to speak of the attack to anyone.

Today, hearing the news from Helpmeet that he was back, all Polly's repressed anger had bubbled up within her. She needed to speak to a friend. She knew that Joss had a love for her that amounted to more than just the accumulated pieces of bacon she smuggled out to him and that he would patiently listen to anything she cared to divulge to him, but this time old Joss simply would not do. Sitting with Archie in the slanting early evening sunshine at the edge of the copse opposite the back door of the laundry, she unburdened herself. She was surprised and disheartened when he hardly reacted.

"You ain't surprised?" she said, her feelings bruised by her friend's muted response.

"I ain't," Archie muttered. He took her fingers in his warm, calloused hand. She looked into his dark eyes and saw there his response. They were moist and blazed with anger.

"It's their way." She could hear his suppressed rage in those few quiet words.

"They take what they wants; they take what ain't theirs."

He lifted Polly's hand to his cheek and she felt her stomach knot as her fingertips touched his skin.

"I's your man, Polly girl," he whispered. "I'll do anything to protect you."

*

In the early evening, Thomas Garland was lounging in the back parlour, smoking his clay pipe, sipping sack, and regaling John Vertue with tales of his time in Jamaica. To hear Thomas tell it, he had been the hero of every part of his story. The lad had arrived home mid-morning and, after a loving reception from his mother, had spent some time with his father before being excused to see his beloved pony and go for a ride. Now he was enjoying the chance to tell his story to one who, unlike his father, could not object to exaggeration and window dressing.

His account ranged from the cane fields to the cane processing plant, to the slave accommodations, to Bostock's irritating little habits and pomposity, to the slave market and to meeting his father's business partner, Louis Silston, whom Thomas seemed to regard as a sort of demi-god. The part of the story that most fascinated John, though, was the story of the negro rebellions and the maroon alliances that controlled the hilly innards of the Jamaica colony.

"You mean, master Thomas, these blacks have the run of the hills?"

"Aye, that's it exactly. The Governor has little power to bring them to heel, so says Major Bostock."

"Well, sir," said John his long, pale face colouring, "that is a flagrant breaking of the natural laws of the world. These Africans are not people as we are, that's what I say, sir. No better than animals. Maybe I shouldn't speak out, master Thomas, but to my mind, the Governor should ask the King for help from the army to bring the renegades to justice. Hang the lot of them, I say, man, woman and child. Make an example just like they did with the old pirates."

"Vertue," said Thomas, looking at the footman with a quizzical grin, "I have never heard you so eloquent or so fired up."

"Well, it ain't natural is it, sir? Something ought to be done. And, hear me now, master Thomas, God forbid it should ever happen here, eh?"

"True enough, Vertue, and I would stay to debate with you, but there is someone I need to see. Clear these things away while I am gone."

He picked up his horsewhip and walked out into the burgeoning night.

*

Outside is a darkness so warm it is like the inside of a proving oven. In our dirt-floor hut, we women are changing for sleep. As I walked back earlier from sitting outside the laundry with Helpmeet and Archie, fireflies rose and fell under the trees and those strange, invisible bugs clicked like mad clocks.

I am in the shadows far from the only candle listening to the women's bawdy chatter. The door opens with a hard shushing noise and Lindy yelps loud as she clutches her nightdress to her naked body. She is in full view of Thomas Garland who is standing, swaying, in the doorway glowering at her and cursing her to silence. Even from here, I know he is drunk. Someone behind me calls out her own curse.

"Shut up, woman," the lad hisses. "Polly Pruitt? Where are you girl? Make yourself known."

I let him wait. Poor Lindy is slowly wrapping the nightdress around herself.

"Tell me where she is, woman."

She's staring at him and it's like the good Lord has taken her tongue. Then she looks around the room as if silently begging me to save her.

"Now, you idiot!" growls Thomas.

He doesn't shout. Like every other man, woman, and child who works this plantation, I know him to be scared of McLeod. He knows, too, that he should not be in the women's quarters after dark. He masters his temper and speaks again, more softly now.

"Miss Pruitt, I know you are here."

It is time to save Lindy. I am clothed only in my nightdress, but I walk out of the shadows towards the door.

"Outside," says he.

I see a gleam in his eye and can tell he's fighting to hold back a boyish grin of triumph. I should be a'feared, but instead I am angry, so I stop and stare at him. He doesn't move and I find I am tilting my head to the side and raising my eyebrows, provoking him, God preserve me.

"Please," he pleads.

I move to the threshold and stop again.

"What do you want?" My voice comes out like a dead thing, falling into the darkness outside and now I feel a prick of fear.

"What do you want, *master*?" says he.

"Master," says I trying to sound insolent. He lets it pass.

"Come outside, please," he whispers.

I suspect he's hatched some plan while he's been away and things ain't going the way he imagined.

"I don't want to, master."

"Come outside," he repeats more boldly.

233

"Master Thomas…"

"Oh, for God's sake, girl, just do as you're told and step outside."

He turns sideways, grabs my arm and yanks me out. I see he has a horsewhip in his left hand. He's turned me as I stumble out and I see the women come to the door to watch. None of them says a word; they all know better. He hooks his fingers around my wrist and pulls me away from the doorway. My heart's bumping and I want to scream.

"Back inside and shut the door," he snaps.

He pulls me to the far end of the building and pushes me up to its back wall. We are part hidden by a bush and its shadow.

"Polly," says he, staring into my eyes. "I've waited a long time for this. Now hear this and listen carefully. I am your master and you're a servant, a convict."

He stops; seems like he's holding his breath. I reckon he's practiced his speech and now it ain't going right. His face goes red and I watch him struggling for the right words. This is bad because it's making him mad with frustration.

"I think you should go back…" I start to say, but it's too late.

He grunts like an animal and lunges for me, dropping the whip and grabbing my arms. He pulls me to him, but I'm ready. I put up my hands and press them into his chest. He can't get me any closer.

"You willful…" he hisses. "You will obey me!"

Out of the darkness comes a figure and my heart almost explodes, thinking it must be Mcleod. I see Archie's face as a quick flash as he ploughs into Thomas and knocks him backwards. The lad staggers, but stays on his feet. He bends and picks up his horsewhip and lashes out, catching Archie's arm as he raises it to save his face from the blow. Thomas strikes out again. Archie's too quick for him. He steps sideways and catches the whip, stopping it dead. He pulls it from Thomas's hand and throws it into the bush.

"Go home, master," he mutters. "There ain't nothin' for you here."

"Why you bastard Indian cur."

Thomas's face is suddenly ugly, twisted in rage. Drops of spit are on his lips and chin. "I'll have you hanged. I'll have you skinned alive and then hanged, damn you to Hell!"

He turns on his heel and strides away. My heart's pounding is slowing, but now I feel a cold dead weight inside me.

"Oh, Archie," says I. "What have you done?"

"Told you I'd protect you," says he, trying to sound like nothing's happened, but his face is dark and I know what he's thinking.

Chapter 32

In Which Louis Silston Makes His Voyage to Virginia and Mr. Garland Throws a Summer Party

The brig, Richmond Lady, set sail from Port Royal, Jamaica on an early morning tide. She was loaded with a cargo of sugar cane, bound for the Virginia colony, and was carrying one passenger. It would take more than ten days of sailing to reach their destination, giving that passenger plenty of time to plan his approach to finding the culprits he held accountable for the death of his Abigail.

Louis Silston's small cabin was adjacent to that of the captain, a bluff, florid-faced Irishman named Donal Kenny. Unimpressed by Kenny at their first meeting, Silston planned to keep himself to himself for much of the journey, enjoying the air on deck when the weather allowed and lying abed in his cabin when it rained. However, when he had first boarded, the genial, hospitable captain had invited Louis to join him in his snug, low-ceilinged cabin for dinner each evening. It was here that Louis learned that his companion was an excellent storyteller and, despite his lowly station, good company. Also, it transpired that Kenny had in a stock of good Madeira wine.

On the fifth night of the voyage, the talk over dinner turned to the subject that Louis had found occupied many of the planters and officials on the island; the runaway slaves and the constant threat of a major uprising.

"Let me tell you, sir," said Silston, leaning back in his chair, a glass of wine in his hand, "I think it a scandal that these rebel slaves are allowed to live, untouched, in the mountains. Why is it that the island authorities tolerate the presence of these bands of marauding blackamoors? Why does the Governor not chase them from the hills and cleanse the island of this humiliating scourge?"

"Well, you know, Mr. Silston, I'm not a Jamaicee man meself," replied the captain.

"No, sir, but you ply your trade between the colony there and Virginia, so you spend more time on that island than I ever will."

"Quite so, quite so." The captain was visibly puffed up by this sudden regard as an expert in Jamaican life.

"Well, to attempt to give answer to your question, sir, I would say that the planters have been beset these last thirty years, truly beset. They saw off the Spanish, as you know, only to have Port Royal leveled by the 'quake in ninety-two and then the fire in oh-three. Much work has gone into building up Kingston since then and some say the old port will be gone in not many years.

"Then there were the rebellions, sir, several of them under King Charles and his mealy-mouthed Catholic brother, and though they were quashed, each uprising sent many escaped slaves into the hills of the divide. 'Tis wild land there, sir, from what I hear. And they say the niggers are well organized, with their own townships, as you may know. The militia has made attempts, but the maroons hold out. 'Tis challenging country up there for battle and the blacks are canny fighters, so they say."

"Yet each planter has good control of his own slaves," said Silston. "I saw no hesitation to use force. These black fellows understand a good flogging, it seems to me."

"Aye, sir," murmured the captain, "I hear there are men and women in the stocks or flogged on plantations every week."

With some small measure of disgust, it occurred to Louis for the first time that perhaps the Irishman was a secret supporter of the slave rebels because, from his tone, the captain appeared offended by these punitive measures.

"But it teaches them their place, Kenny, don't you see? It is a necessity in the same way it is a necessity to beat a recalcitrant dog. If each planter had an iron grip on his slaves, why, then there would be no rebellions. If the authorities took a more war-like line then the island might root out the canker of the maroons. My father's agent told me he fears for our Jamaica investments every time he hears news of fresh outrages."

Captain Kenny poured his guest another glass of wine and diplomatically steered the conversation to the young man's doings in London, a subject he had learned Louis never tired of exploring. His initial enthusiasm for the company of his passenger had waned since the start of the voyage. The young Englishman was too belligerent, too arrogant, and too opinionated to be tolerable for any length of time, but he only had to bear Silston's company for a few more days before they made landfall in Virginia.

*

At the back of the master's house is a shady grove of trees. While me and Daisy carry platters of cold meats and cheeses from the dairy to the tables the men have set up in their shadow, she tells me how these trees were spared at the building of the house because Mrs. Garland wanted them for their summer shade; a place where the lady, her son, and daughters might escape the summer oven of the house and enjoy any breeze that nature might send. It looks well here, with the trestle tables and benches and the family's grand dining table that's been carried out under the biggest tree. Daisy says we will be expecting a good baker's dozen from our neighbour plantation.

The rough grass has been scythed low and the dry-as-dust ground is spread with canvases usually used for baling tobacco. A rich smell comes from them as the sun heats them up. It is mighty hot again today; the sun shows no mercy and we are labouring in the heat, some of us carrying foods and utensils, some bringing out barrels of small beer and cider while Mrs. Garland's maid, Emily, fusses over the table settings, claiming to know the workings of her mistress's mind. The master's jolly carpenter, Erasmus Muller, is helping. Daisy says he's a Prussian though I know not what that means. He has a strange sound to his voice, like coughing and spitting. That blackguard McLeod is here, though he's doing little enough work. It pleases me greatly that John Vertue is missing, though he be a favourite of Mrs. Garland. Word is he's been sent on an errand to Port Royal.

I never thought to be here today and I have had to bear the spike and prick of the women's tongues these last days, since Daisy told me I was coming, but they know, in the laundry, why I am there. 'Tis Thomas Garland, ain't it? And there he is now, standing in the shade watching everything I do. Must have pleaded with his old dad, so I reckon.

We are finishing our work when a shout goes up and we see a carriage and some carts trundling up the hill to the big house. The master's horses, which are in the meadows in front of the house, are running and bucking in excitement at the clatter of so many wagons arriving at the same time. As they come close, we get sight of our neighbouring plantation's master with two young girls in the front carriage before they disappear around the side of the house.

McCleod says his peace about how we must behave and we follow him, spreading out to stand and watch the back of the house. It don't take long, and there are the master's guests, folk like us, being led by Garland's cooper, called Owens, to join us. We all stand staring at each other, them new ones and us already here waiting and no one says a thing; 'tis enough to make a body squirm. I think this may go on all afternoon when Mrs. Garland comes out the kitchen door and we all start to shift a little to see all the high-and-mighties. She is wearing a dress of pale green silks loaded with bright green glass beads and gold brocade. I get a twist in my gut for it is so like Abigail'' beautiful green dress I loved so well. The mistress'll suffer though, for I think 't'will be killing hot this day.

She is a short, proud-breasted woman with her mouse-brown hair up on the top of her head. Her face is red already with the heat, but she's giving all of us a fine smile. Then here is the master and Thomas – who slipped away when the carriages came – standing in the doorway behind her, bringing out the guests. At last, they are all here, the Garland daughters too, and are seated at the great table.

"Welcome all!" shouts Garland, raising his hands over his head. "And an especial welcome to our dear friends of Burtonwood."

The mistress laughs and claps her hands, looking around at all of us and we take the message in her eyes and clap too. Then it's all the guests slapping their hands together and one of our people gives a whoop and some of the women laugh.

"Indeed, indeed," says the master. "Let the festivities begin!"

That's it then; all that staring at each other like silly gulls is forgotten and everyone starts talking together as we take up our bowls and load them with victuals. We fill our mugs with beer or cider, whichever we want, and sit ourselves on our canvasses, us lot on two and the Burtonwood folk on two others. I think 't'will be a long while afore we're talking with each other, so shy are we all.

It don't take long for the food to disappear and, as soon as the first people lay down their bowls, a fiddle starts up from a small group sitting on rough-made chairs at the back wall of the house. Soon another fiddle joins and a woman starts to sing, a bouncing, dance tune. Another cove joins with his whistle and yet another begins tapping out a rhythm on a small drum. We give a cheer when the first two stand and start to dance. It don't take long afore they're joined by more dancers. Muller, the carpenter, is prancing with Daisy, a huge grin on his face, his fat arms up above his head. He's a big man, tall, with a bulging belly. His face is wet with sweat, which flies in every direction as he capers. We are all watching him, cheering him, clapping in time to the music.

I did not think to enjoy this day, yet I am happy, full of good food and a sip of cider and watching the fun. I should know that such things cannot last and, quick as a wink, here is that lunk Thomas coming to me and asking for a dance. All those still sitting are looking at me and, though I would spit in his stupid face if I could, I know what I must do. I stand and he reaches to take my hand. There is a sly look on his face, like he is saying, *see, I got you now, don't I, miss?*

He whirls me around for the next three dances. His mother has trained the boy well. I have seen him clumsy and awkward, but here, on this beaten earth, he is graceful. I grit my teeth, his hand on mine and his other around my waist, just waiting for him to tire.

As soon as we stood up, other people started to join in, even McLeod, who took Emily's hand, and now a crowd is frolicking and romping. I think the musicians are pleased because every tune they play is fast. Of a sudden, Muller staggers sideways, colliding with a small fellow who shouts in complaint. Muller's face is a maze of confusion and pain and he clutches at his chest with his big hand. Daisy steps away as he stumbles into people, knocking them about and then he crashes to the ground.

Garland and his chief guest, who Thomas told me is called Sowell, are out of their seats in the instant. Mrs. Garland whispers to her husband and then whisks her daughters away, waving to Thomas to join them in the house. I am free, but the party is ended anyway. In minutes it comes clear that the poor carpenter is dead, felled like a great tree. 'Tis his heart, so says Mr. Sowell. McCleod sees us all standing, gawping like Bedlamites, and has us clearing away while the two men talk. I hear Garland say, quite clear:

"This is a setback, Sowell. I need a carpenter to finish the work remaking my paddocks for my horses. I have two new mounts arriving in just two weeks. I know this to be an impertinence, but…"

He is a cold man, thinking only of his need when poor Muller lies dead.

"No, sir," says Sowell, "'tis fine. Auggie!" he calls and an old fellow walks to join them, but I hear no more as McCleod shoos us away with our arms full of plates, bowls, and cups.

Chapter 33

In Which Will Is Given a New Job, Makes a Discovery and Meets
John Vertue Again

On his return from the party, as they sat smoking their pipes late into
the evening, Auggie regaled Will with tales of the excellent food and
drink provided by the Garland's and of the dancing. Will's face
glowed with excitement at the vivid descriptions of the Garland's
impressive house – "not as grand as master Sowell's, mind" – the
host and hostess's fine clothes, the pretty girl young master Garland
had hogged for himself during the dancing and the wonder of the
food and festivities.

"I ain't a dancing man, Billy, not so much anyway since the bones
got so old, but even I was on me feet. 'Twas all going well until that
fat German falls on his face, dead as a nail."

The next day Will had been due to continue working on the
tobacco harvest with everyone else, as he had been for the last three
days, but, instead, Auggie told him, Mr. Sowell had loaned him to the
Garland estate.

"The Prussian's boy is only a mite, so they say, and Mr. Garland
needs his paddocks fenced and secured in time for his new horses."

And so, the day after the party, another sweltering hot August day,
Jack Bisden, Mr. Sowell's blacksmith, took Will to the neighbouring
plantation. He had his bag full of tools in the bed of the cart behind
him and a headful of quietly disgusted wonder that, at short notice,
he could be treated like a draught animal and lent by his master to
another man. On arrival, he was greeted by Hector McLeod, who

explained, in blunt, vulgar terms, that his master put much store in his thoroughbred horses, which was why the paddock fences needed to be repaired, strengthened, and extended.

The man had thick forearms and thighs better suited to a large domesticated animal, a bull or heavy horse, and he had a neck, thick at the base, that tapered into his skull like a Grecian column supporting a massive portico, but, instead of intricate carvings, it was decorated with fine curly hairs that glistened with sweat. His glance was not of frank malice or evil, rather it utterly lacked any humanity. It spoke of an emptiness, eerie and threatening even when he smiled. This was a man, Will knew, who needed a wide berth at all times.

It did not take the young carpenter long, in conference with Muller's young apprentice, a lad of thirteen called Tolly, to realise that the boy knew little and had been training for only eleven weeks before Muller was taken to meet his Maker. Recognising that the lad would be next to useless to him, Will set him to splitting and planing posts, while he started work in the paddocks close to Garland's house. After only two day's labour under the unforgiving summer sun, he needed to change his clothes, already rank from the hot, filthy work he had been doing in Sowell's tobacco fields. At the end of the day, when he was washing, Muller's lad came to him.

"I put some clean clothes out for ye, sir," Tolly told him. "Will I take the dirties to the laundry for ye?"

"No, Tolly, I can fend for myself. Just tell me where to go and I'll take them in the morning."

*

As soon as he walked in the door, he saw her. It was a shock that stopped him dead. Months ago he had relinquished all hope of ever finding Peg and, now here she was, her arms elbow-deep in a huge tub of water, talking to the woman next to her. Dumbfounded, he stood like the village idiot, his jaw slack, mouth partly open, not moving, not speaking, just staring at her. A thin woman spotted him and walked to take his bundle.

"Be you Mr. Sowell's man?" she asked as she threw his clothes into a huge basket. Still, he could not speak. "Look, ladies," she continued. "Our guest's a dumb mute!"

She let out a roar of laughter that caused all the women to turn from their steaming vats and drums to gawp at Will's sorry countenance. Polly turned too, but showed no hint of recognition. At last, finding his voice from somewhere deep in the ashes that had been his hopes of ever finding Peg, he spoke, though his heart fluttered in his chest like a flag in the breeze.

"Peg," he said, "'tis me, Will, Will Staples from London…"

Her face creased up and she cocked her head to the side.

"Do you not know me, Peg?"

"I know you, master Staples, yes, are you a phantom? How are you here?"

"Why's he calling you Peg?" asked the thin woman.

"Well, Helpmeet, maybe he has known too many girls and confuses me with another," says Polly, laughing now. "Will Staples. Why, I never thought to see you again." She walked towards him. "Have you grown taller? And where is your fine yellow hair?"

"Aye, aye, 'tis Polly's beau, methinks, though he don't know her right name," said a voice from among the women in the dimness of the large room. Another round of laughter followed and Polly looked around, chuckling and raising her eyebrows.

"No love of mine," she said. "Just a lad I knew for a few days when I was in London, that's how master Staples here knows me."

"Oh, and what did you do with him, to put such a look of love in his eyes? Though I daresay, he don't look so pleased now you told him *you* don't love *him*."

Another burst of raucous laughter.

"Nothing, Maggie, nothing you'd be interested in, anyway. But my true name is Polly Pruitt, though he knew me as Peg, and this lad was kind to me and a friend to me when I was lost in London."

At that moment, as the women's voices combined in a chorus of sarcastic shouts and hoots, as Polly laughed with them and Will stood, unmoving with eyes only for her, a harsh voice stopped the fun and games.

"Too much talk in here and not enough work." It was Hector McLeod.

The women instantly returned to their work. Polly moved back to her workstation and Will turned. McLeod was standing in the doorway. Outside, the day that been so bright had darkened ominously.

"Come on, Sowell's man," the Scotsman growled, "there's wood and nails waiting for you, or are you too much of a ladies' sop for man's work?"

Another type of man would have made the imprecation into a joke, but McLeod never used words to amuse. He had not used Will's name since the day he had arrived on the estate. McLeod's face was set as dark and heavy as the black clouds gathering in the sky behind him. Without a word, Will walked past him and out towards the paddocks, his mind galloping like a runaway horse. He had found what he had looked for and all the McLeods in the world would not stop him from rescuing the girl he now knew as Polly.

*

Will was energised, his passion rehabilitated, sparked up like a new-lit bonfire. What had become his life on the plantation, the work with wood, helping with the crops, learning from Auggie, all of that became a ghost life the moment he saw Polly.

That night, Will lay on Muller's cot, staring into the darkness and listening to the havoc of the storm that had closed in on the plantation during the evening. As the elements seethed and roared, so did his mind. The rain pelted the roof like the drummers of an approaching army and the wind lashed the low shack like an overseer's whip, but all he heard were questions, so many questions. Why did she call herself Peg when he met her in London? Was her friend's name really Lizzie? Were they truly dressmakers seeking Polly's old aunt? Were they running from something? What could be so bad they had to flee from it? How many secrets did the names Peg and Lizzie hide?

He would have loved to have the time to sit with her, declare his love and ask all his questions, but now, for the first time in months, his mind turned again to escape and he found himself thinking of his friend Jem. If he could persuade him to join them, his gut told him that three might stand a better chance than if he fled with Polly alone.

247

He already knew where he would go. According to Auggie, the lands to the east of the plantation were all laid down to cultivation, except for the towns of Jamestown, Yorktown, and, of course, Richmond, where the Governor, Colonel Spottswood, held court. That way lay the militia and capture. To the west, Auggie said, was a range of mountains they called the Blue Ridge and west of that again, new territories, virgin land. This was where he would take Polly, far from the law of the colony, far from the eyes of those who might know their real or imagined sins.

Will's mind was so busy that night, he thought he would never sleep, but he must have, for the cockerel's crowing woke him and, within a half-hour, he was back in the paddocks. He had been working for two hours when he heard an almost forgotten voice.

"Well now, if it isn't young Will Staples."

He knew it was John Vertue before he turned and his heart soared. He broke into a spontaneous laugh and grabbed John's hand, pumping it up and down. The man he had known so well in Newgate looked the same and yet not the same. There was the sharp face, thick hair, and bright eyes, but he was clean-shaven and wore his glossy hair neatly clubbed, and he was dressed in good quality clothes, the uniform of a footman.

"I saw you from the house, Will, and I could not believe it. I asked the mistress and she told me you are here to do Muller's work." He gave a sly grin and continued before Will could draw breath to speak.

"Ah, my friend, good fortune has me by the hand. My master is a fine man, late of the Dragoons, an army man like yours truly, and he gives me his confidence. I am a made man. The only cloud in my sky is that animal, McLeod. You'll have met the bastard. I am the favourite of Mrs. Garland and the Scotchman hates that. He finds jobs aplenty to keep me from her side and seeks to poison the well of her patronage whene're he can."

It was as if John had stored an encyclopedia's worth of tales, for he hardly drew breath, elaborating his loathing for McLeod, describing how he had conspired to keep him from attending the summer party.

"But he is a mere shadow on my life. By God, I love this place, Will! The order, the beauty, and finery of the house, the way the estate turns as the sun turns. A man like me can do well in this place; 'tis only those thieving blacks that cast a shadow. I understand why he has them, but many a time I do wish the master could get rid of them all.

"They are a blight, Will. Why only the other day master Thomas told me how the slaves in Jamaica revolted, fled their plantations, and set up in the mountains. Their own filthy little kingdom, Will, can you believe it?"

Will was shocked by the outrage his old friend felt about the Jamaican rebellions. His face was as dark as the previous night's thunderstorm as he repeated what he had heard from Thomas. Will was taken aback by the force of his loathing and his vile language when describing the slaves. Another time he might have taken John up on it, but he was bursting with news of Polly.

"John, John, I am truly pleased for your good fortune, pleased you are so happy here, but, my good friend, I have news of my own."

John laid his hand on Will's shoulder and shook his head.

"Listen to me, all prittle-prattle preaching when I have heard not a word of your life. Of course, young Will, you know I wish all your fortunes to be good. I am remiss, come, tell me your news."

"John, I have found my Peg." Will's voice cracked with emotion.

"You've found her? By the good Christ, Will, I am as pleased for you as a whore who's found herself a rich benefactor."

"Yes, I have found her and, you may yet call me a liar, for she is here, on this plantation. But, again, she is not, for her name is no longer Peg. She is Polly …"

"Polly?" John interjected with a laugh. "Not the pretty girl in the laundry?"

"That is the very one, sir," replied Will, glowing with pride, "and now I must find a way to see her as soon as may be and tell her what is in my heart."

He was about to go on when a familiar sharp voice sliced like a sabre between the friends.

"I own, this man of Mr. Sowell's is a'lazin' again."

Neither had seen McLeod riding up the cart track towards the house. John had his back to the Scotsman, so gave Will a wink before he turned.

"And what the devil are you doing out here, Vertue? Don't tell me you two ingrates know each other."

"Shipped here together," replied John, omitting a 'sir' or 'm'lord'. He held himself erect and stared at McLeod. *My good Lord* thought Will, *I do admire this man's fortitude.*

"I might have known," grunted McLeod softly. He muttered then, something for his ears only, before speaking up.

"Well, John Vertue the not-so-virtuous, you should be inside hanging on your mistress's skirts, so be gone and, I warn you, man, I will be watching you. Mrs. Garland may be fooled by your false charms, but I know you for the blackguard you are."

If Will could have spoken then, he would have told his friend he would swear the overseer could not speak a word of English that was not loaded with hate or sarcasm or anger, but it seemed that John knew well not to cross the ugly-minded Scotsman. Without any acknowledgement, he walked away, heading back to the house.

"And you, sluggard," said McLeod giving Will the evil eye, "back to work with you."

Chapter 34

In Which Louis Silston Arrives at The Garland Plantation

Louis Silston met the port Factor, Abel Addis, at the dockside as they were boarding the ketch that would take them up the river to the Garland plantation. Addis had been summoned by Garland on colony business. He was brother-in-law to the Governor's assistant, one George Peters, and, as such, had access to the back door of the Governor's office. Garland, ever maneuvering for position in the colony's hierarchy, needed favours.

Fresh from his voyage from the Caribbean, Louis had not lost his ardour for telling stories of the London life and his time in Jamaica. The two men had little in common, but Addis was politic enough to realise Silston was a man with a position in society and an ego that needed stroking, thus he listened with forbearance to the younger man's stories. It was during their first evening together that Louis raised the matter that lurked at the back of his mind most of the time.

"Mr. Addis."

"Mr. Silston."

"I am searching for a man, a convict who would have made landfall here in the colony sometime in early November of last year, name of Staples, William Staples. I have been sore afflicted by frustration these several months in not being able to locate this fellow. I know you have intimate knowledge of the scum who are shipped here and I want your help in finding him."

"May I ask, sir," said Addis, his tone bright for he sensed the asking of a favour in the offing, "what this man is to you?"

"You may, sir," Silston replied. "In summer of last year, Miss Abigail Colliton, a young woman betrothed to me, was murdered in London. This fellow Staples is known to have been with her on the day she died. My father has put up a reward of five pounds for word of the cur, and there will be a bonus of twenty pounds for any man who captures him."

*

Late in the morning of Will's third day working in the paddocks, a wagon carrying two men trundled up the bumpy carriageway of the big house. Will looked up from his work, but their disembarkation hardly stirred his curiosity; his only thought that day was to see Polly again. He had been agonising about how to get to the laundry without McLeod seeing him.

In the main house, Mrs. Garland, dressed in her finest silks, had been excitedly expecting her guests. She stood behind Vertue as he opened the door. A zephyr escaped the house carrying the aromas of new baked bread, old leather, tallow candles, heavy tobacco, and human sweat.

The lady of the house led her guests to the parlour, a spacious, well-lit room. It was densely furnished – as if no opportunity to show off the Garland's wealth could be denied – with quality heirlooms from her family. There she introduced her three daughters, all equally finely attired. The eldest, Angelina, was eighteen years old and Mrs. Garland took her time to make sure that Louis Silston should appreciate the girl's feminine qualities, her household abilities, her knowledge of Latin and smattering of Greek and generally excellent demeanour.

"Angelina was only a child the last time you saw her, Louis," she laughed.

She and her husband had discussed the opportunity that Louis's presence on the plantation would present and were agreed that a marriage would only strengthen their financial and business bond with the Silston dynasty.

Now she sent her footman, Vertue, to find her husband and Thomas, while the party in the parlour sampled fresh, cool lemonade and, at Louis's request, strong coffee. Cakes were served and the light-filled room reverberated to the demur laughter of the three girls. Silston, tired after his long voyage, was content to bask in the over-weaning attention of his business partner's wife and daughters. He knew exactly what was going through Mrs. Garland's mind and it amused him to play along, despite the unfortunate plainness of Angelina.

At last, Garland walked in, smiling broadly. Louis rose to meet his old friend and the two embraced amid shouts of pleasure and remembrance.

"Reynolds! It has been so long, but, by God, it's good to be here. By my word, 'tis wonderful to see you and your fine family again!"

The two were standing by the door patting each other's backs and grinning like schoolboys as Mrs. Garland made her excuses to take her daughters and leave the men to "their business". Addis, ever the diplomatic servant, sat quietly to one side, nursing a glass of lemonade.

"I see you have yourself a white footman, Reynolds, only the best for you, eh?" said Louis. "But why not a black? McFarlane and all the Jamaicee planters have blacks for their house servants."

"Oh, you know Mrs. G," replied Garland, "knows what she likes, likes what she knows. And she can't abide the negars, won't have 'em in the house. All the servants, kitchen, house and all, even in the bloody laundry, all English or Scotch. She'd rather a white murderess wash her smalls than a negar woman."

Just then Thomas appeared in the doorway. Garland grabbed him by the arm and pulled him forward.

"Ah, here we are! Louis, you know Thomas already I think."

"Indeed, I do, sir. I had the fortune to make your son's acquaintance in Jamaica, as you must know."

The warmth of Louis's smile, genuine in his pleasure at reuniting with his old friend, cooled slightly, though none in the room noticed. He inclined his head in the slightest acknowledgement of the boy, but, as Thomas enthusiastically moved forward to shake hands, Louis had already turned away. His face flushing bright red, Thomas walked to the back of the room and hovered there, looking diffident and out of place.

"Now you have been reacquainted with the family," said Garland bursting with energetic enthusiasm, "let me introduce you to Achilles!"

He left the room and returned, moments later, with a small monkey on a leash, sitting on his shoulder.

"Got him from a sailor at the slave market a year ago. Named the bugger Achilles, after the hero of Troy."

What he did not say was that the animal was a bad-tempered, irascible little bundle of spite and that it gave him great pleasure and no small amount of malicious joy to be the only one who could handle the creature. His wife, whose own beloved pet was a pugnacious little spaniel called Hal, hated it with a passion and their daughters avoided it whenever they could.

It was widely known across the estate that, when the monkey first arrived, Thomas had tried to handle it with the same lazy bravado exhibited by his father. In these encounters, the animal had always bitten him until eventually, sullen and sulking, he had given up. There had been a sad inevitability about his trying to dominate the monkey. He had been lucky only to be left with scars rather than succumbing to some exotic infection.

Achilles was more than a mere pet. From the start, Garland had been fascinated by the monkey's facility in learning tricks and tasks. Indeed, he would regularly tell guests that Achilles was more intelligent than many of his servants.

"I tell you, Louis," he was saying now, "the slaves on this estate are more animal than this little manikin. They are like more to cattle, whereas Achilles is closer to being human than any black man can ever be. But come, let us talk!"

*

Around the middle of the afternoon, when the heat of the day had become truly oppressive and the sky had started to cloud again, Hector McLeod arrived at the house. John Vertue ushered him into the back parlour where Garland, Thomas, and their guests were taking tea and sweetmeats. The plantation owner bade his man be seated.

"A cup of tea for you, McLeod?" he asked.

"I think not, thank ye, Mr. Garland," the overseer replied.

Garland waved John Vertue away and then made his introductions.

"Addis you know," he drawled, "and this is my business partner from England, Mr. Louis Silston, son of Sir Crisp Silston of Middlesex."

After the initial pleasantries and the usual exchange of the names of men of power known to those in the room, Thomas stood. Silston's snub still burned in his breast. In his boyish way, he had expected Silston to be as pleased to see him as he was to meet the Englishman again, but Louis's cool manner had embarrassed and disappointed him. The arrival of McLeod gave him the excuse to make an exit and go to lick his wounds.

"Do you need me, father?

"No, I do not, sir, if you have somewhere better to be." If he was irked by the interruption, Reynolds Garland did not show it.

"I thought to see Lightning Girl, father."

"Ah, my son prefers his pony's company to ours, gentlemen."

As the appreciative chuckles died away, Garland looked at his now-blushing son with a face that showed only the slightest twitch of irritation around the eyes. His voice gave nothing away.

"Fine, fine, off you go, sir. We will meet again for dinner."

"Thank you, father," said Thomas and with a curt bow, he made his exit. Garland watched his son depart.

"Still waiting for that boy to grow up, but now to business. Addis, you won't know that Sowell had a runaway last autumn, caught easily I hear and flogged, but it is a problem we all face. Barnes, over east, had two runaways in the last six months and I hear of more in the colony every month. As you know, I have no truck with such disloyalty. I hanged my last runaway; a loss of income and the loss of a strong pair of hands for me, yet necessary to deter others from similar acts of rebellion. These blackamoors need to be kept down, as I am sure you will agree, but the Governor seems weak on this subject."

Addis nodded but did not reply.

"Thomas and Louis have told us of the Jamaica slave uprisings and the nuisance that renegade maroon bands cause. Even though 'tis some twenty years since a rising there, the land suffers under the indignity of these bands of outlaw negars."

Garland stood and pulled his short jacket down. He faced the other men as if addressing an audience at a political gathering.

"In my view, we need to petition our Governor for more action from the militia. Indeed, my first recommendation would be to strengthen the militia and arm it properly. McLeod here was a sergeant gunner in the old Queen's army and knows a thing or two about discipline and training. I'll warrant there are plenty others in the colony whose experience could similarly be called upon. So, sir, perhaps you can tell us of the mood in the Governor's office on the subject of runaways while we enjoy Mrs. Tollard's excellent cake"

Addis knew better that to rise to such tasty bait. His was a delicate position; he had to be careful to remain diplomatic about the goings on in Richmond. With great tact, he steered the conversation away from Garland's question and the talk of slave rebellions slowed to a natural death. Later, when Garland left with McLeod to speak on some estate matter, Louis Silston walked to his host's drinks cabinet and helped himself to a glass of sherry wine.

"For you, Addis?"

"No, thank you kindly, but more tea would be welcome," said the factor with a polite nod.

Louis rang for the maid and sat down, leaning in towards Addis.

"To remind you, sir, of that of which we spoke on our journey, I have business here other than plantation matters and rebellious slaves."

"I well remember, sir," said Addis.

There was a knock at the door and the maid entered.

"Take these things away," said Silston waving at the cold teapot and cups, "and bring more tea for Mr. Addis."

As the girl started to load the crockery on the tray, she had brought with her, he continued.

"William Staples and Polly Pruitt, these are the two names you must take back to your ledgers. And remember, a reward for word on either of them and a reward for their capture."

"I will not forget, Mr. Silston. William Staples and Polly Pruitt."

*

The afternoon was wearing on when John Vertue, bearing a jug of lemonade and an empty glass, crossed the paddock to where Will was working. The heat of the day had become stifling and Will was flagging.

"The high-and-mighties left this, Will and I thought a working man might like a cool drink," he said, grinning as he filled the glass.

Will drank the cane-sugar sweetened drink as if his life depended on it. He was covered in sweat and his rough prickly clothes were sticking to his body like an itchy second skin. John refilled the glass and spoke as the young man sipped more slowly on the refreshing drink.

"So, have you thought more about how you will see Polly Pruitt since we last spoke?"

Will smiled broadly and nodded. "Aye, sir, I have that. I will away early from my work and wait by the door at the back of the laundry until I hear the women leave. Then will I call my Polly out and I will tell her all."

"And risk McLeod's ire?"

"I will be like the hawk hovering silently, seeking out vermin, fear not," replied Will.

"Well, young Will, I wish you well of the telling and hope the maiden looks upon you fondly."

Chapter 35

In Which Will Tells Polly of His Feelings and Jem Hears a Tale of Rebellion

He must have come here from his work, 'cos the day is ended and I'm about to go out back, hoping to see Archie or Joss, when the door opens and there he is, all smiles.

"Polly, please, come out, I must talk with you," says he and there's a choir of vulgarity and catcalls from the women.

"It's her beau back again," I hear Helpmeet laughing.

He's backing away and waving me out and I think it's easier to deal with him away from the laughter and teasing, so I go out and he closes the door behind me. He leads me 'tween the lines of washing.

"What're *you* doing here?" I ask him, not unfriendly like, but I can't be warm for he has me confused. He ain't a bad one, I'm thinking, but I can't get it out of my head how he's got here, so I'm going to wait on him to tell me.

He doesn't speak at first, just looks at me, all doe-eyed like I remember from London. I ain't much to look at, of that I'm sure; my hands all red and wet with sudsy watery, my hair damp with sweat and steam and I know my face will be red too. I think I must look a fright.

"I need to tell you something, Polly," says he. His voice is low, unsure. "I…I came here the same way as you. I stole a book and was condemned to the transportation, but I stole it deliberate, for I could think of nothing but you from the moment I saw you and 'twas the only way to try to find you after I discovered you had been transported."

Well, you could of blown me over with a puff. I could hardly believe my ears. It can't be true, he must be lying, is my thought. I hardly know what to say.

"What are you…?" I start to say, but he cuts me off.

"Please, Polly, I have waited long to tell you this. Making myself a thief was the only way to find you."

Then he tells his story, fast, like he's excited, and has to get it all out as quick as a flash. I can see he's filled up now, filled with some sort of fire, for he's walking to and fro, looking at me the while. Searching for me, beggary, stealing a book, condemned to hang, let off and brought here; 'tis all too much, I can hardly credit it. At last, like he's a clock that's needing winding, he stops.

"But why?" I ask.

"Because…because I love you, Polly."

Well, that does it; that shuts me up, good and proper. We are surrounded by that Bedlam of bug's clicks and whirrings, but neither of us moves or says a thing. And he's gone all red-faced like he's a kid caught in the act of some silly prank.

"Oh, Will," says I, but before I can go on, he's taken my hand and he's staring me in the eye again, hard and determined, like.

"I want us to escape together, Polly, run away…"

I can tell he's going to go on, but there's another voice now.

"Is this'n botherin' you, Poll?"

It's Archie. How he came up on us so close without us hearing him I'll never know. Old Joss is standing hard against Archie's leg giving poor Will the leery eye. Will looks afraid, taking Archie for one of Garland's hard men, so I speak up quick to calm the waters.

"No, no, Archie," says I, "this is my friend from London, Will Staples."

Poor Will. Just the sound of that word, friend, puts a smile on his face and makes him bold again.

"Polly," he says, "I've come to take you away. Westward is where we should go, out of this servitude, away to freedom."

Archie steps closer. I see his face is showing anger. Me and him speak up at the same time.

"Will, that…that would be crazy," I say.

"She ain't goin'. It'd mean a death sentence from Garland," says Archie.

I don't know what Will would have said next 'cos the laundry door opens and Maggie leans out and saves us from this strange nonsense.

"I thought I might find you still 'ere, boy," she says to Will with a wink and a grin. "They'm all looking for you. Seems your master needs you."

*

The storm had brought down a bough from one of the trees that stood at the back of Sowell's tobacco barn, breaking through the roof and drenching stock bales that were stored at that end of the building. Bisden, the blacksmith, sent to bring Will back, took him directly to assess the damage with Auggie. Seeing a chance to spend time with Jem, Will had suggested the slave help him. He had found he enjoyed passing on his knowledge of wood and carpentry and, in working together, had come to like the young slave.

"That black boy did a good job with me on those slave huts. It'll go much quicker with him up there with me."

Mr. Sowell, fearing further losses if the storm returned, grudgingly released Jem from the tobacco harvest. So it was, at first light the next morning, Will found himself on the barn roof with his erstwhile roof-mending companion.

The tobacco barn was the tallest building on the estate, so the compensation for being stranded up there all day under the unforgiving sun was that, provided they kept their voices low, no one could hear their conversation. They spent the morning removing the ruined structures and laboriously setting the new rafters Auggie and Will had made during the winter. For the rest of the day, they hammered cedar tiles knowing it would take most of the rest of the next day to finish the task. Once that was done, they had been told to fell the trees nearest the barn as Mr. Sowell had decided their beauty and shade was not compensation enough for the risk of further damage to his precious crop. Only when all the work had been completed would Will be returned to the Garland plantation. Already he was consumed by rabid impatience.

He had been struggling for some time with a paradox that plagued him. Since meeting him, Will had tried to see the world of Burtonwood through Jem's eyes and, when he did that, what he saw was not good. There was an order on the estate, Mr. Sowell at the top, the God of his kingdom, with his family below him. Beneath the family came Christian Hardbone, himself above the indentured servants. All these were above Will and the other convict servants and workers, regarded by all above them as very lowly. Yet lower still were the slaves, regarded by most as hardly human and looked upon by some, like Horrocks, as lower than the animals.

Will was used to hierarchies, but he knew this to be wrong. His mother had told him that all were born equal in the eyes of God, yet as he grew and matured, he had seen that this was not true. And while he acknowledged Mr. Sowell as his master and he respected and liked Auggie, it seemed to him that the servants, convicts, and slaves all worked as hard as each other to make the plantation yield the products that Mr. Sowell required. So, why were they not all equal? Worse, and this brought memories of his friend, Jenkin Smith, how could men steal people from their homes and families, trade them for money and keep them prisoners for their whole lives because they had skins of a different colour? The plantation was a magnificent tree, strong and green with a mighty canopy and, doubtless, great roots, but at its heart, it was eaten up by the rot and mould of injustice.

The two friends spoke quietly as they worked. Will recounted his experiences at the Garland property, lingering, at first, on his reunion with John Vertue. Jem was set alight by the story of the Jamaican rebellions and the free slaves. He hammered Will with questions as he hammered nails, questions Will was ill-equipped to answer because all he knew was the bare bones of what John Vertue had told him. Also, it was his meeting with Polly that he wanted most to relate.

"What'll ye do?" Jem asked.

"I told you, Jem, the work ain't finished at Garland's. Soon as this roof's done and those trees are down, I will go to see Polly again and persuade her to run with me. You know, I never thought on her feelings for me, all that time. I was a fool to think she would come round to my ways, quick like. But the more I think on it, the more I am convinced that, if I can get her away to freedom, then she will thank me and she may grow to love me."

"If you be a'going, Will, then pr'aps it be time fer me too. Tell me again 'bout the rebellion."

Will watched his friend's face as he told John Vertue's story again. He saw there a fire of passion, saw that their old talks of escape were growing in Jem's mind into something else.

"You wouldn't think to raise a rebellion here, would you, Jem?"

"Why not?" Jem's tone was blunt, surly even as if he suspected Will of reneging on the promise of them fleeing to freedom. "Why not when we have nothin' here but sorrow, a life of pain and the same for our children and our children's children? Freedom, that ain't somethin' special, shouldn't be anyhow. Freedom a thing all men should have, savin' those that done wrong and is payin' for it. Ain't something you take from a man done no wrong. To do that is a sin 'gainst any man's god."

Will felt a shiver of apprehension at these words. He had thought to escape with Jem, but if he was already at Garland's place when he and Polly made a run for it, that could not be. If Jem incited all the slaves to run, that would raise a hue and cry the like of which had never seen before in Virginia.

Chapter 36

In Which Jem Incites Rebellion and John Vertue Gets His Chance

In the deep of the night, Jem brought his mother, Ruth, and the most able-bodied and fittest of Sowell's slaves to the woods and lit a small fire. Being out at night was against the rules of the plantation, lighting a fire felt like asking for awful retribution, but, though there was fear, the small, pleasing spectacle of the dancing flames under the black blanket of the night sky seemed to hypnotize the crowd. Their faces glowed with the oranges, yellows, and reds of reflected firelight as they listened, rapt, to the young man as he related his sketchy version of the story of the rebellious blacks of a faraway colony. The glory of the tale had grown in the re-telling.

In the endless dark nights after his whipping, Jem had talked to his grandmother in the tongue of her native Africa, one of only two things she had been allowed to bring with her from her home. The other had been Jem's mother, Ruth, who had travelled safe in Gran'mammy's belly. Early in his life, she had taught him her language. Jem was clever, quick, and canny. He had learned English better than any of the other slaves, but he had held on to his grandmother's tongue as a talisman kept close to the heart. In those long nights as his back slowly healed he told his mother, *I will escape, they will not hold me, I will be a free man.*

Now he spoke in English, the language of Sowell's plantation. The speech he made was quietly eloquent and electrifying. The time had come, he told the men and women who sat with him around the illegal fire in the humming summer night. The time had come for their own rebellion. At first, there was only stunned silence, then murmurings of dissent and fear, but Jem was passionate, appealing, ardently convincing. He was articulate in his arguments, well-prepared to parry counter-argument. Word by word, minute by minute, he felt the tide turn in his favour, as more and more of his people became convinced.

"Y'all *know* ya'll be slaves for the rest o' yo' lives. What can you lose? You dead already; good as dead anyway. You know that yo' children'll be slaves and their children too. The whites don't make no money outta tobacco without our labour, so there ain't no hope that any of us will ever taste freedom, 'less we take it. S'our time! If them African men and women in Jamaicee can throw off dey bonds, why cain't we? Why cain't we work together to gain our freedom? Enough of us run, s'gonna light a fire of rebellion across the colony. If we do this right, we'll be just like them maroons, maybe even have our own country."

The passion of his voice hung in the air when he stopped talking as murmurs of agreement circulated the group.

"You 'gree with this, Ruth?" asked one man, the oldest in the group.

"No hope fer Gran'mammy, James, she had her time" she replied, holding herself erect, "but I still young. I be going with ma boy. They take away all my other chillun, you know dis. Nuttin' fo' me to stay fo'."

"Yeh, but master, he treat us well," muttered James. "Could be a whole mess worse."

"Worse?" retorted Jem hotly. "Whipping our backs to meat? Putting us in the stocks for crimes children might commit? Punishin' for talking back, not carrying enough of a load, takin' too much water on a hot day? No, James, he ain't kind, he just know how to tend his animals so they gives him the best."

Murmurs and grunts of assent rippled through the group.

"But how we gonna get 'way?" asked a tall, bony girl.

"We gonna do like those maroons I tol' you about, Millie. We gonna all go together, in a band; look out for each other."

"Easier trail to follow," muttered James, never taking his eyes from his large, scarred hands as he rubbed them together.

"They follow my trail pretty easy an' I was one man alone," retorted Jem with a snort. He paused, calming himself, knowing he must not allow his unvented rage to get the better of him.

"An' I was dumb, I ran from the field, ran in the day, thinking the rain'd cover my tracks. Should'a gone at night just as early as may be, when Hardbone was sleepin', so's there was a whole night to put miles 'tween me and here. Tha's what we'll do. An' we won't jes run anywhere. We'll have a plan, we'll find a way to distract them, confuse them, and we'll head west. I talked about it with Will…"

"Yo' friend," growled James in disgust.

"Yeah," replied Jem, gritting his teeth. "My friend, 'cos I found out not all the whites is bad. Will tol' me about the west. There's new land there over the mountains, no whites. We can follow the sun, don't need no maps, jes need to keep going, jes need to really want it."

"All sounds good, Jem, boy," said James, "but how you gonna get this mob off the plantation? How you gonna 'distract'."

There was a sneer in that final word. Jem's eyes glittered in the dying firelight; his determined face set hard.

269

"I doan know what he got planned," interjected Millie, "but me and Ezekiel, we's in, ain't we brudder."

The boy sitting beside her stared hard at James and nodded once.

"Yeh, well, that doan change nuttin'," grumbled James. "Still doan know how Jem here gonna 'distract'."

"Fire gonna help, James. Let me tell you how."

*

The rain had returned. The view from the Garland house was obscured by the thick curtain of water that assaulted the earth. Louis Silston was confined indoors, much to his disgust as he had been looking forward to continuing the tour of the plantation that had been begun two days earlier. His host had ridden out early with McLeod on a visit to a neighbour, a small planter whose land Garland had been after for some time. Polly was at work in the laundry and Archie, having fed the hunting dogs, was mucking out his master's horses. John Vertue was kicking his heels in the kitchen, sitting in a rough-made armchair, smoking his pipe, and listening to the tittle-tattle of the women.

Agnes Smallwood, the maid-of-all-work, was talking to Mrs. Tollard, the cook, and John's ears pricked up as she started to relate something she had overheard in the parlour.

"They was talking 'bout summat 'appened back in London," she was saying.

"Who was, girl?" asked Mrs. Tollard as she kneaded a large ball of dough with strong meaty hands.

"That Mr. Silston and the man who came over from the port. I took them tea when the master was out with McLeod."

"So, what was said about London?" grunted the cook.

"Well, Mr. Silston says his intended was murdered."

"Never!"

"Yep, tha's what 'e said, struck down, 'e said, by a villain's blade."

"Well, that's a right tragedy," Mrs. Tollard intoned as she continued to bully her ball of dough.

"An' 'e's been looking for some folk ever since. Got a reward out for them." The girl hesitated then, seeming doubtful as to whether or not she should continue.

"Well, girl, don't leave it there, tell us what he said; who's he been looking for?" snapped the cook.

"Well, I wasn't sure I should say, like. I been stewing on it."

"Agnes Smallwood, if you don't tell me who he's looking for, I will make you polish copper-ware until you're an old maid!"

Agnes sighed and shrugged her narrow shoulders.

"He said there was this girl was with his intended when she was killed. Said 'er name is Polly Pruitt. An' I been worrying since 'e said it cos ain't that the name of that girl in the laundry?"

"By God, girl," growled Mrs. Tollard, lifting her eyes from the bread dough and wiping her hands on her voluminous apron. "It is. And there's a reward you say?"

"Five pound to know where she is," replied Agnes, warming to her story now the name was out.

"But, didn't you say nothing, girl?"

"Wasn't my place."

271

They both looked around as the kitchen door slammed shut. The armchair where John Vertue had been sitting was empty. Only the slightest wisp of pipe smoke remained in the air above it.

Chapter 37

In Which Polly Is Imprisoned and Will Sees That Desperate Measures Are Called For

As soon as he heard the word 'reward', John swung into action, his mercenary instincts taking over. Ever one to seize a chance, he rushed from the kitchen, walked quickly to the parlour, knocked boldly, and entered before Silston had time to respond. Louis stared at the man as if he had been slapped in the face.

"Sir, beg pardon for this interruption," John said, a half-smile on his lips.

"Well may you beg my pardon, man. I hope you have good reason for this impertinence," Louis replied tartly.

"Yes, Mr. Silston, it is for your sake I come, sir." He bowed his head in supplication and continued. "I have just heard you seek word of a girl called Polly Pruitt."

Like a harvest moon revealed as a skein of cloud clears away, Louis's scowl was replaced by a pink flush of excitement.

"Yes, indeed, man! Do you have news?" he said as he rose to his feet.

"Aye, sir, I do, but afore we get to that. The reward, sir; am I right in thinking there might be, how should I say this, some money to change hands for the right information."

"Yes, yes, man, get on with it." Silston was facing John, hands on his hips, legs apart, boots planted firmly on the floor.

"Excuse me asking, sir," said John, grinning, "but, how much, sir, the reward, like?"

"Five pounds, man. Now get on with it."

"And the money, sir, would I be, as you said, impertinent to ask to see the colour of it?"

"Christ's blood, man, you think I would renege?"

"Not saying that, Mr. Silston, just …"

"On my mother's life, you will get your money," growled Silston from between clenched teeth. "Now, out with it!"

"She's here, sir, on the plantation; works in the laundry not two hundred paces from this spot," said John.

If Silston was surprised by this revelation he did not show it. He blinked once.

"Show me," he said simply.

They hurriedly donned capes and hats and walked out into the rain, which had eased a little but was still drenching. They marched together to the laundry. By the time they arrived, they were saturated, but, each excited for their own very different reasons, neither man noticed. Vertue opened the door. The room was its usual miasma of steam, noise, and the stink of dirty clothes and wet fabrics. All the women turned as one. Vertue pointed at Polly.

"There, sir."

*

I ain't surprised. Oh, my heart is pounding and I feel sick, but I ain't surprised, no. Ever since I heard Silston was here, I've been expecting this. He's staring at me, like to shrivel me where I stand and now he's barging past little Mercy while the others get out of his way. He grabs me by the arm and my heart is frozen and I can hardly breathe.

"Polly Pruitt?" he barks.

When I look at him, I do not see a full man, but a shade filled to the brim with anger and spite and the look in his eye now is all triumph, but, yet, I see he is unsure. How could he not know me? Then the thought springs up, why should he? I was just another wench to a man like him, a girl with something he wanted. There must be plenty of other girls he's taken on the stairs of other great houses. I try and make my voice strong, pretend I ain't afeared of him.

"Yes," says I.

"Yes, *sir*," that lousy Vertue hisses. Silston ignores the cove.

"Maid to Abigail Colliton?"

Hearing that name spoken aloud in this foreign place knocks what breath is left out of me.

"Maid to Abigail Colliton?" he says again, shouting it and shaking me.

"Yes, sir," says I, straightening my back and keeping my eyes on his.

Then he slaps me, hard as he can and my head flies aside like a ball batted away. There is a ringing in my ears and I see sparks like from a new fire. Still, he's shouting so loud I can hear him clear.

"You will tell me all you know of that lady's death, you bloody slut and you will tell me all you know of the cur who helped you, Will Staples!"

I see John Vertue's face change then and he steps up and he says, quiet like:

"There's a jail, Mr. Silston, sir. Maybe she should cool her heels in there a while. The master should know about this."

So that's where he drags me, his fingers biting like a dog's jaws into my arm, shaking me all the while and I see all the women, Helpmeet and Maggie, staring with mouths open as he shoves me out the door.

*

I am sitting in darkness on the hard-packed mud floor of this room. No window, nowhere but the cracks and gaps in the woodwork for fresh air to get in. They dragged me here through the rain, so my hair and clothes are wet. My face stings, likewise my pride, and my head throbs from that bastard's blow. I saw the fury in his eyes and, by God, it surprised me. I never thought him that taken with Abigail, so maybe 'tis the loss of the money she brought. Well, he may be angry, but now so am I. I feel it rise in me like floodwater. I must needs scream to let it out, but daren't.

I see he thinks me guilty in my Abigail's death. If only he could feel the love for her I felt, he would know that no such thing could be true. But if he knew of my love, then, sure, his anger would burn the more brightly. Yes, I feel a bruise of guilt still in my mistress's murder, though I did nothing wrong. I am the one wronged. Archie and Joss and Helpmeet and Maggie had me happy and forgetting all the bad that's gone before, all the wrong I suffered. Had me almost forgetting the pain of losing Abigail, but now that monster's given me that poisoned gift back again.

Him and that sly man, Vertue, dragged me here, shouting threats and demanding to know what had happened on the day of the hanging. I kept my words to myself on that, save to tell him the same as I told the judge, innocent of murder. That got me another good hard slap. Well, damn him and his false distress. The man is a liar and a bully.

"You will abide here," says he, "to think on your guilt and your heinous lies, you fucking bitch."

Nice words from a lord, I say. They shut the door then and I heard the lock go on and some loud words that I could not make out. And now I lie here on this dirt floor and wait 'the master's' judgement. Well, may he rot in hell, is what I say.

*

Archie was returning from the stables when he saw the two men hauling Polly to the estate's jail. Checking that he was not seen, he followed surreptitiously and heard the threats and the name of Will Staples. He watched as John Vertue was sent to bring the padlock from the house and listened to Silston's accusations of complicity in murder as well as Polly's simple denial. He also saw Silston hit her and curse her and it was all he could do not to spring out and put his hands around the damned Englishman's throat. He watched as Polly became saturated in the downpour and saw her thrown bodily into the jail. Finally, he was witness to the moment John Vertue attached the padlock to the door.

He wished he could stay with Polly, break her out that very moment. The quiet, practical man inside him knew, though, that he needed to find out what he could about what was happening to her, so he followed the two men when they walked back to the house.

"This Will Staples," he heard Vertue say. "Is there a reward for him too?"

"There is," Silston answered bluntly, looking at Vertue as they walked. "Do you know something?"

"Aye, sir, and will tell you now if we can come to the same agreement. Ten pounds for the two, sir?"

Silston sighed. He was becoming used to the grasping footman. "Ten pounds for the two. Now … tell me."

After the men had disappeared indoors, Archie turned back. He had heard, from the carpenter's apprentice, that Will was due to return to the plantation that same afternoon, a fact he thought it quite possible Vertue did not yet know. An idea was blossoming in his mind like a dangerous plant. He returned to the little wooden lock-up to tell Polly.

Chapter 38

In Which Will and Archie Find Common Ground

Garland and McLeod arrived back in the mid-afternoon. The rain had stopped shortly before midday and now the fields and trees steamed in the brilliant sun and the horses chased each other around their paddocks in joyous abandon at the ending of the storm.

The master and his overseer were met at the front door by Louis, who had a strange tale to tell. Garland was all for going immediately to the gaol and punishing Polly for her refusal to give up Will. He bragged that he would beat the truth out of her, but McLeod, unusually diplomatic, argued that they knew who this Staples was and that he would be returning from the Sowell estate later in the day.

Silston, eager to move to a conclusion as soon as possible, suggested he should ride out to meet Will, but this time it was Garland who cautioned against the idea. An encounter on the road could go awry; Staples could escape.

"Also, my dear friend, we don't want him turning tail and running back to Burtonwood. Once he is here, he is under my control and Sowell will have no recourse. No, sir, we will wait for his arrival, when he will be all yours."

Silston could see the sense in this, though he still seethed with righteous rage. Over the months he had convinced himself that Staples had had a hand in Abigail's murder and he wanted to be the first man to confront him. The logic of Garland's quietly made argument could not be gainsaid, however, and, grudgingly, he acceded to the plan. While McLeod went to find the iron 'necklace' and chains, Garland dismissed Vertue before pouring his guest a generous helping of sack.

*

Will and Jack Bisden, en route to the Garland estate, had shed the canvas sheet they had pulled over their heads during the downpour. At its peak, the wind-blown rain had been so heavy that Bisden had halted the pony to wait out the squall before moving on.

The air had cooled dramatically during the rainstorm, but, as soon as it stopped and the sun emerged, they warmed up rapidly. They talked quietly of affairs on the Sowell estate, as the blacksmith steered the trap along the rutted, now water-logged, lane. In the past, Will had found Bisden a reticent man on most matters, but when it came to their master's affairs he was very ready to talk, it seemed. They had been on the Garland plantation for some time, making their way past cornfields and meadows filled with rows of cabbages and other vegetables. When they were only a mile short of the village of buildings that constituted the heart of the estate, a young man with coal-black hair that hung loose to his shoulders walked out in front of the cart from the bushes by the side of the lane.

Joss wandered to his master's side, as Archie raised a hand to stop the cart. Will's face hardened at the sight of the stable boy and his ugly old dog. He harboured no love for this so-called friend of Polly's and was suspicious immediately of Archie's motives for this unlooked-for meeting.

"Whoa there," called Archie moving forward to take hold of the horse's bridle. "Need to take the carpenter off here."

"Why's that," asked Will, standing up in the rig.

"Got a problem just over there," said Archie pointing vaguely behind him. The big dog stared malevolently at Will and Bisden. "Needs a man good with timber."

"That can wait, I think," said Will sitting back down. "Better I get to McLeod's place and report."

"Come from McLeod," said Archie, "he sent me. Got a laundry girl stuck in a well. You know her, I think; Miss Polly."

Will's heart started to beat a little faster. He did not trust this blank-faced Indian, but he could not ignore the news that Polly might be in danger. He lifted his pack of tools from the rig and jumped down.

"S'all right, Bisden," he said, slapping the side of the cart, "you get on back. Thank'ee for the ride."

The two young men worked in silence as they helped Bisden unharness the horse and turn the cart. They watched him for a minute longer as he steered the pony back along the sodden track.

"All right," said Will gruffly, "what's this about?

*

Silston waited impatiently in the house until the sun was tilting towards the horizon when, at last, Garland agreed to send McLeod to check the road for signs of the Sowell's carpenter. He returned with news that infuriated Silston. The overseer had found signs that showed that the pony and trap had been halted and turned. There were tracks in the muddy verge showing that two people had trudged off into the underbrush.

281

"This is unpardonable!" Silston fumed, pacing the parlour. "I knew I should have gone; I knew it! Christ's blood, Reynolds, we could have had him. We could have had these two bloody-handed felons strung up by now!"

"Calm, Louis, please, calm," Reynolds Garland purred. "They cannot get far and they will, I warrant, be back for the girl. From what that woman from the laundry tells us, this Staples was sweet on the girl. It is impossible to believe that he will leave her to languish. It's clear he has had help; one of my own people, I must think. We will put a guard on the gaol and apprehend them when they come for her. And do not mistake me; they will pay dear."

"That is all well and good, Reynolds," Silston replied heatedly, "but we could have had him if we had ridden out …"

McLeod, who had been standing by the door, listening to the exchange, interrupted.

"If I might, sirs. We know the carpenter had help from someone and he must be one of ours, as you say Mr. Garland, 'cause who else would know the girl was locked up? Wouldn't be the women in the laundry. They're mouthy, but have no gumption to my mind, so…I asked around and that good fer nothing Indian dog boy ain't been seen all afternoon. I believe it's him as stopped Mr. Sowell's cart.

"With your permission, sir, I'd like to ride out and track 'em. I know where they left the lane and they'll leave a trail through the brush. If you'll sanction it, sir, I'll have them back here before the night is out."

The three men argued the case for a few minutes, but McLeod, who would be well-armed and on a horse as opposed to those he was hunting, who would be on foot, eventually convinced Silston and Garland to let him go. When they agreed, he gave a slow sly grin.

"Thank you, sirs. It will be my pleasure to bring 'em back and," here he chuckled, a deep rumble, "I'll try me best to keep 'em alive."

Chapter 39

In Which McLeod Goes Hunting

When Archie told Will what had happened to Polly, it was all he could do to hold the young carpenter back from running that instant to try and save her. Instead, using soft words and gentle urgings to calm him, he led Will by circuitous paths through the undergrowth and then between towering rows of corn plants, until they came to a clearing amongst a copse of trees. Here, he persuaded Will to sit with him and discuss what had happened and agree on what their options might be for rescuing Polly. Very soon, Will began to see that he might have misjudged Archie.

Slowly, as the sun was beginning to set, a grudging trust for Archie grew in Will, because he saw that, in one thing at least, they were of one mind; whatever the danger, they must save Polly. Once they had agreed on a course of action, Archie stood up and offered Will his hand and then insisted on introducing Will to Joss. Will had seen the creature before and, having no love for dogs of any kind, thought it a great gangling beast. He had observed the dropped haunches, the grey beard of age around the loose jaw, and the way the animal eyed him with human-like suspicion. For his part, he had disliked the animal from the start, but Archie persuaded him to offer Joss his hand and it was not long before the dog was licking him and letting him scratch his back and neck.

"This is good," muttered Archie, "'cos, f'anythin' happens to me, you gotta take care o' Joss. Miss Polly, she loves that old fool."

While they waited for night, the ticking and humming of the insect chorus and the bizarre buzzing and warbling of frogs and toads replaced the birds' constant chatter, Archie spoke quietly of Mr. Garland. Will learned that the people of the estate knew their master to be 'a devil', cruel and quick-tempered. There was a tale of a servant, whipped by Garland himself. It seemed that this servant knew a thing or two of the law and appealed to the county court, claiming unfair punishment. The magistrate decided against the plantation owner and gave the fellow his freedom. Garland had to pay the man's liberty fee. Archie said that it was the talk of the county, but the servant disappeared not long after, never heard from again.

"I say," Archie murmured darkly, "if'n you knew where t'dig, you'd find the bugger's bones, right enough."

Will's heart shrank within him when he heard that it had been John Vertue who had given him up and claimed the reward. At first, it was hard to believe, but Archie assured him he had heard it himself.

"An' 'twas that bugger gave up Polly, too."

"My good Lord," whispered Will. "I am undone. John Vertue was my friend. Without that man, I might not have survived Newgate. John Vertue was my teacher and, in hard times, my protector. John Vertue helped me become a man. And now you tell me he's a Judas, claiming his thirty pieces of silver for my head and Polly's. Why? What makes a man betray his friend?"

"I ain't told you all," said Archie. "This Silston, he told Vertue Poll had been maid to a rich woman. Says she was to marry with him. Says Polly 'n you plotted the lady's murder."

"Christ's tears, that ain't right!" gasped Will.

"Ssh! Keep it low, boy, keep it low. You think on it now; maybe John Vertue heard tell of murder and thought you ain't the man he supposed you to be."

"Oh, my Lord, this is terrible. Yes, I was at Tyburn Tree and I saw poor Lizzie get herself stabbed, but I never knew she was a lady and Polly was her maid. Why would a lady and her maid take on false names and dally with the likes of me and my old master?"

"Cain't answer that, but it don't matter now. We jes gotta get Polly out."

The talk turned, then, to the gaol and its security. Archie was sure Garland would mount a guard, probably McLeod and one or two of his henchmen, but, come what may, they had to try to rescue Polly. Both of them knew events had overtaken them; there was no going back now to how they had been living. Already, they were outcasts and they both knew Garland was not a man of mercy. Polly and Will were at risk of a terrible fate. It was with this knowledge branded into his mind that Will decided to entrust his whole plan to Archie. Even as he spoke, he realised how desperate it must sound, fleeing west, crossing the mountains to virgin land to set up and live as free people.

Archie did not seem surprised by Will's revelation. He nodded and looked at his companion for a moment, his face giving nothing away.

"I'll help," he said at length. "Don't have no choice, do we? An' I ain't leaving Poll. I'll come. I know the old ways; I can lead you."

Before Will could respond, Joss, who had been lying at his master's feet, rose to his feet and growled. A chill ran down Will's spine. They had been careless, talking too loud in their excitement

286

and apprehension. Joss was standing rigid, staring into the darkness. Archie was already on his feet as Will slowly stood up. Seeing a short knife in Archie's hand, he wondered, distractedly, where it had been hidden. At that moment, a large dark shape loomed out of the darkness.

"Well, boys," snarled a familiar voice, "I thought to find you out here."

There was a little light from a shy early moon so that, even in the gloom, they could see McLeod's face clearly. He was grinning and had his hands crossed on his saddle. His horse stood stock still, as if, like the two young men, awaiting the overseer's judgment.

"Time to come home, Indian," he said, "and we'll bring your friend with us."

"And why might we be a'coming with the likes of you," Archie retorted, sticking out his chin.

McLeod laughed, loud in the quiet of the night, making his horse start and take a small step back. He egged it forward again and patted the butt of a horse pistol that hung in its sheath from his saddle.

"Little Beth here's a good persuader, boys. She's barked loud and brought down many a better man than you two curs."

As McLeod spoke, Archie was edging forward, each step a small shuffle, but he was getting closer to McLeod. Will did not feel any fear. The emotion that flowed through him like a wild wind was excitement, as if all his life had been leading to this moment, there in the woods on a summer night in the Virginia colony. He stood tall and took a step forward.

"Back there, carpenter," growled McLeod, sitting up in the saddle.

His right hand moved across the saddle and he wrapped his fingers around the butt of his pistol. Will stopped and ducked instinctively at the threat of the pistol. Joss was crouched and his teeth were bared, his whole body trembling as he growled softly. For a few seconds, the tableau remained frozen, like a period painting of a highway robbery. Then, with a howl, Archie leaped forward. Trying for one smooth movement, McLeod drew his pistol and swung it across the saddle to level it at Archie, but his mount shied. McLeod cursed as his gun jerked off its aim. At that moment, Joss jumped forward and sank his teeth into the horse's front leg. The animal whinnied and its back legs buckled. It brayed in pain and lunged sideways, trying to loose the teeth from its flesh. McLeod was thrown off balance, slumping heavily to the side as Archie reached up towards him.

The horse reared, lifting Joss onto the tips of his hind legs. Then, in an uncannily acrobatic shrug, it shook its leg, threw the dog across the clearing, and, landing heavily on its front feet, bucked and threw McLeod from the saddle. The pistol was pitched from the overseer's grasp and flew away into the brush. As if in a dream, Archie and Will watched as McLeod crashed to the ground. The overseer made a small, strangely high-pitched noise as he landed head first. Archie immediately took the horse by the bridle and began humming to it, calming it. Will, who had not moved in the few seconds in which all of this had happened, went down on one knee at McLeod's side. He hesitated, his breath coming in heaving gasps even though he had done nothing. He put his hand heavily on McLeod's arm. The man's eyes were open, but he was not moving. Will gently shook his arm.

When the Scotsman did not respond, Will glanced searchingly at Archie, who had the horse calm already and was watching Will closely. Behind him, Joss was staggering to his feet and Will, to his own surprise, felt a small jolt of pleasure that the brave animal was still alive.

"Breathin'?" asked Archie in a low, neutral voice.

Will leaned over the body and stared into the open eyes. They were wide and still bright, staring up at the crescent moon, but they did not blink. There was, he saw, something wrong with the way the man's head was lying. He lowered himself so that he was kneeling close to the body and put his ear to the man's mouth. There was no sound, no sense of breath on his face. He laid his head on the overseer's chest and listened, blocking out the noise of insects from the trees. There was nothing; McLeod's neck was snapped. The Scotsman was dead.

Chapter 40

In Which the Burtonwood Uprising Begins

The rule was, once the sun had set, which at this time of summer was around eight o'clock, all the slaves, convicts, and indentured servants should be in their allocated buildings and settling down for the evening. Most would be asleep before nine, as the day started well before sunrise.

Jem, tense, excited, fearful, but aggressively determined, waited a long hour after sunset. Once he was satisfied that all was quiet, he crept from his shack and, keeping to the deep shadows, walked slowly to the buildings he had targeted in his planning. The scrub-grass-covered bare land between buildings and fields shimmered in the icy light of the nascent moon. He carried a sack over his shoulder. If he were to be caught, he would have no good explanation for its contents, so he moved silently over the warm ground like a neurotic cat. He passed the buildings housing the female and male convicts and heard no sound from either. The cicadas were still chirruping, but otherwise, a blanket of peace lay across the estate. With each slow stride, he told himself he was one step closer to freedom.

As he rounded the dormitory for the male indentured servants there was a sound. He stopped by the door of the building and listened. Footsteps. He was standing in the shivering light of the young moon, so he slid back around the corner of the building into darkness. The footsteps, he could tell, were coming towards him. Jem's mouth was suddenly dry, but he held firm and hoped; it was all he could do. A figure, shadowy and vague came into view. Jem pulled back further into the gloom. Someone coughed inside the building, a hacking, chest-wrenching cough. Jem's scalp tingled and he held his breath. The footsteps came closer. The coughing stopped and a voice was heard from inside the building, the words unclear. Nearer still came the footsteps. Another higher, louder voice came from inside, complaining at the coughing only to be answered by an oath.

"Quiet in there!" came a shout from the shadowy man outside. Jem started.

The man was standing at the door only feet from where Jem was hidden. The man banged on the door.

"Settle down."

"You can bugger off, Edwards," came an angry voice from inside.

Hardbone's man chuckled, seemingly content that he had done his job. Jem, still not breathing, watched as Edward's huge bulk moved past. If he had reached out, he could have touched the man on the shoulder, but Edwards did not look to his left. Jem watched as he meandered away and disappeared into the gloom. Sweating and his heart racing, Jem softly lowered his bag of kindling and sat slowly down. He needed to recover his balance and give Edwards time to get back to his room behind the stables. How long he waited he would never know, but it felt like half a lifetime. He knew his mother and the others would be waiting, fretting, especially James the doubter, but he could not afford to take any chances.

At last, he went on, creeping on bare feet from shadow to shadow until he came to the first of his targets. He had chosen buildings he knew would not be occupied not because he necessarily cared to spare any white lives, but for reasons of stealth. He worked fast, so that, less than twenty minutes later, he was on his way back to the slave shacks where seventeen nervous people were waiting for him. Sitting around that small friendly fire after he had fervently preached the gospel of escape and freedom to his fellow slaves Jem had explained how the speedy greed of flames in a dry season could help them. Now the kindling was set, all was ready.

As soon as he arrived at his mother's hut, they hugged each other close. He turned to his grandmother who was sitting in silence on a box. The old woman's rheumy eyes were glittering with unspoken emotion. She stood and embraced her grandson quickly and then pushed him away, looking into his eyes for a long moment.

"G'wan, boy," she murmured, her voice low and hoarse.

Jem kissed his little half-sister and half-brother in their beds. With a single look back and a wordless goodbye, he and Ruth left the shack forever. Minutes later, Jem was leading the men and women who had pledged to follow him off the estate, heading westward, following the trail he had planned. He set his face to the future, banishing all thought of hounds baying, teeth buried in his leg, the whip lacerating his back.

For over seven hours they made as much speed as was possible while Jem's grandmother sat and stared at the wall of her rude home. At length, she rose, pausing only to look briefly at her grandchildren sleeping on their small pallets. Creeping from the room, she moved softly through the night to the smithy, lit a tinder-dry branch from the fire that Bisden kept constantly burning, and walked, ghost-like, from building to building lighting the piles of kindling Jem had set.

In minutes there were seven separate fires, all burning simultaneously, all in wooden buildings, all out of control; the bakery, the winter wood store, Augustin Fontaine's workshop, the laundry, the cooper's workshop, the weaver's building, and Bisden's smithy. Despite the recent rains, the wooden buildings were quick to burn so that soon the conflagrations were so great that people were woken from their sleep by the crackling and unearthly groaning of the burning timbers.

Each building became a pulsating, shape-shifting hand of flames reaching up, grasping into the night air, fingers of fire clutching at the sparks and smoke that streamed up into the blackness as if trying to drag them all back down into the heart of the conflagration.

Jem's grandmother had been back in her narrow bed but minutes when there came a hammering on her door.

"Fire! All hands! Fire!"

She woke the children and together they went to help, just as Jem had instructed them. Men and women, in panic and confusion, were being marshaled by Sowell and Hardbone and were racing backwards and forwards with heavy wooden pails of water. Now the trees and bushes at the heart of Burtonwood were an amphitheatre of reflected red light, as sparks and smoke drove through the dome of light up into the blackness beyond. There was so much smoke and so many people running to and fro it was impossible to tell how many and which buildings were alight. Sowell, wearing a heavy brocade dressing gown over his nightshirt, shouted orders and tried to bring some sense to the effort to quell the fires, but it was pandemonium.

It was Hardbone who noticed how few slaves were helping. Shouting angrily at the man who had roused Jem's mother, he sent the fellow back. Within minutes the runner had returned and the cry went up: insurrection! rebellion! The slaves were gone. All the able-bodied black men and women were nowhere to be found; only the aged and children remained. Sowell and Hardbone stood together as sparks and smoke billowed around them.

"Get you to Garland's with all speed!" roared Sowell. "Raise him and his men and start the hunt. I will stay and hope to quell the burning before it spreads further, but I will need all our people to stop it spreading. Tell Garland to send to the sheriff to raise a posse!"

By the time Hardbone set off northeastwards for the Garland estate, the Burtonwood Insurrectionists, as they would come to be known, were close to thirty miles to the west and making good time.

Chapter 41

In Which Polly's Fate Is Decided

Archie was first to recover from the shock of McLeod's death. He tied the horse and retrieved the horse pistol. Together, the young men covered McLeod's body with loose brush and duff. Holding the horse's bridle, Archie led the animal, with Joss at his side and Will following, through the fields and byways of the plantation. The horse was hobbling, but seemed content to be led by its familiar groom. Joss was favouring his left side, but otherwise seemed unharmed. They did not speak of it, but they knew that it would be murder they were wanted for now.

When they reached the outskirts of the plantation village, Archie tethered the horse and whispered something in its ear. The animal remained calm and quiet as they walked away. They moved forward warily, creeping between the buildings; the tannery, the blacksmith's forge, the carpentry shop where Will had slept and worked. At last, from the corner of the bakery they could make out the shape of the little jailhouse and behind it, looming like a ship at sea, the pale form of the big house.

They took up a position amongst some bushes and gazed on the jail. Three men had been posted outside the building. Two were sitting on the ground with their backs to the wall of the jail; the third was sitting a way off leaning against a fence post, facing the building. This last had a musket on his lap. The two men by the jail wall looked to be asleep, their chins lolling on their chests, but the other, the man with the gun, was in shadow and it was impossible to tell whether or not he was alert.

Archie put his finger to his lips and motioned for Will to wait for him before slinking off into the darkness. He was gone what seemed an age to Will, but when he returned it was with the whispered news that there was another man at the back of the jail. This was more than either of them expected. Perhaps, thought Will, it had to do with McLeod's failure to return. They had planned for Archie to distract the guards, while Will used his tools to break through the wooden planks at the back of the prison. With a man stationed at the back, this was no longer possible. The two sat back on their haunches in silence, pondering their next move. They must do something, but what?

*

I am awake and nervous. I feel I might have come to my end. I cannot see any hope nor good coming from Silston being here. After what he did…I had put all that behind me and had thought never to see him again. In truth, I never gave him another thought after I came to Virginia and now, he is here with all the terrible memories on his damnable coat tails. But these are bad thoughts and I will have no sleep all night if I cannot find a wind to blow them away. I make myself think of what happened to bring me into the darkness of this small room.

I recall Will Staples telling me he loves me, the fool, and I do not know if I should laugh or cry. Why, I hardly thought of him these last months. I cannot believe his story; stealing a book to get himself caught and sent here. The boy must be a Bedlamite or more stupid than I first took him to be. And yet, he is in my mind and, like an old bloodstain on a petticoat, I cannot shift him. I have long thought all men to be perverted by their manhood, driven by evil humours to be bad, but Archie is not like that and now I see this Will Staples is not that either. I remember his kindness in London when he took Abigail and me to see the shops and the great Cathedral he loved so much and, if I weren't so full of trembling, I might smile at how he showed us all those carvings he loved. How he bored poor Abigail.

Archie. I think of Archie and old Joss. I think on the crazy plan he whispered through these wood walls. Going to find Will. Surely, they will come back for me? But, if they do, will they succeed? I heard men, talking a while back, guards is my guess, men with arms ready to stop Archie if he comes, and now, I tremble again at the thought that those boys will be shot down for trying to rescue me; I could not bear it, I could not. My mouth has gone all dry and my heart is a'flutter. It is too dark, too hot, and too damp in here. If only there was a window so I could see the moon, or I could get just one breath of cool air, a swig of cold water; anything to still my heart and right my mind.

This is no good, I tell myself. This is desperate and my old aunt Susan did not hold with desperate. *Pull yourself together*, girl, she'd be a'saying now, and she'd be right the funny old stick. Breathe now, I say to myself, breathe deep and close your eyes. This is Silston's doing and you promised that blackguard would never make you frightened again. You mustn't let him win, Polly, you must not.

*

It was the very heart of night. McLeod lay dead not two miles away, the night was fast disappearing and they were no nearer to rescuing Polly. A horrible sequence of images kept replaying itself in Will's head, over and over: Garland's men finding McLeod's body; he and Archie being caught trying to rescue Polly; the two of them being accused of the murder of the overseer; Polly being accused of being an accomplice; all three being dragged to the magistrates' court; a crowd baying for blood in the court's public seats; the hanging of all three accompanied by the cheering and jeering of the crowd. He had heard enough of the cruelty of Mr. Garland, though, to suspect that this prophecy would be proved false. Once in Garland's hands, the most likely outcome for all three of them was that they would be summarily strung up from one of the plantation's biggest trees. Will, numbed by his experiences, did not fear death as he had when the judge had passed sentence on him in London, but he could not countenance the same fate for Polly.

"T'will be morning soon. We must act," he whispered into Archie's ear.

"Aye."

His young accomplice moved round and Will saw he had his knife in his hand.

"I'll go round back, deal with that one, then we get the horse and use McLeod's gun."

Will was not sure this was the right tactic, but, before he could object, Archie had slunk away. Minutes that were hours went by. Everything was still and quiet but for the sweet song of a mockingbird somewhere in the darkness. Will hefted his pack onto his shoulder. He was not afraid so wondered, purposelessly, why his heart was beating faster? He heard a new sound then, seeming to come from far away. He stood up, being careful to stay in the shadows, and now he could see the first streaks of grey in the sky in the east. Time was running out.

He squinted into the distance and held his breath. It was hoof beats he could hear and, suddenly, shouting, a voice far off, but getting closer by the minute. The man with the musket twitched awake and came up onto his knee. The other two guards stirred and turned to look towards the distant sounds. The shouting was getting louder and, bursting out of the shadows like an actor late for his cue, a horseman galloped up the lane to the front of Garland's house. He was yelling at the top of his voice and Will recognized Hardbone, his heavy tones, and the set of his body, as he leaped from his mount and hammered on the door. A thought sprang into his mind; Jem. He has done it! He has run!

All at once, there was mayhem. The three guards were running to the house and the fourth, saved from Archie's blade, emerged from the back of the jail, racing to catch his comrades. This was his chance. He ran to the jail door, bent and tense, opening his bag as he went and pulling out a short crowbar. He felt rather than saw Archie appear at his elbow. He slipped the crowbar under the belt of the padlock fastener and eased it out slowly, feeling the three screws give with the growl of metal wrenched from wood. He pulled the bar away and the door swung open. Polly was standing looking pale, unsurprised, and determined. She gave them a quick desperate smile. Archie barged past Will and grabbed Polly's hand, pulling her out of the prison and running with her towards where he had left the horse.

Will, in a moment of inspiration, pulled the door closed, picked up the screws at his feet, swung the fastening bar over, and pushed the screws back into their holes as hard as he could. He stood back and looked at his work. He smiled grimly for, in the half-light, it looked as if the door was undamaged. He put the crowbar back in the bag and ran. Archie and Polly were already out of sight, but he knew where they were going. He found them at the horse, Archie heaving Polly up into the saddle.

Behind them all was noise. Archie motioned Will to give Polly his bag, which he did, and then he helped the young carpenter up onto the animal. Will had never been on a horse and immediately felt more at sea than he had at any time on the Marie Elizabeth. He was so high off the ground he felt he must slip off and crash to the ground, but somehow, he kept his seat behind the saddle where Polly sat. Archie ran, leading the horse away at a trot and Joss followed. A thought occurred to Will then: *We are all the Indian's obedient servants now.*

Through the back ways of the estate they went, the horse hobbling and Archie running at its head. After some minutes, when they had made the main track, he mounted the horse, squeezing tight behind Will whose body was forced into Polly's. Despite their parlous circumstances, he was overcome by overwhelming happiness to be so close to her.

They continued along the road with Joss trotting beside them, and, for a while, Will's hopes slowly rose, but soon he experienced a sudden sense of alarm. They were going the wrong way! Worse, the track was muddy and rutted and they were leaving tracks plain for all to see. He wanted to turn to speak to Archie, but there was no space. He was becoming desperate when Archie pulled the horse to a stop and gingerly dismounted, taking care to place his feet on a clump of thick grass at the side of the track. He put his finger to his lips, silencing the others, shoved McLeod's pistol in his belt, and released the overseer's saddlebags. He put them carefully on the ground and helped Polly down so that her feet landed on the bags.

"No tracks," he whispered to Will before leading Polly away into the undergrowth.

Of course, thought Will, no footprints! He slid down off his unnaturally high perch, making sure his feet landed on the bags. Stepping into the scrub, he joined Polly, who was standing with Joss. Her face was white, but there was a resolve there. Archie stepped past Will onto the saddlebags. He pulled the horse close to him, whispered something into its ear, then slapped it hard on its rump and it cantered off along the lane. He picked up the bags and slung them over his shoulder. Being careful to keep his feet on scrubby grass, he motioned the others to move and then followed them into the brush and on towards an area of woodland ahead. They were turning west.

Chapter 42

In Which the Search Party Sets Out

Gabriel Reed was an Iroquois who had been working on the Garland estate for some five years. There had been some falling out between Gabriel and his family, but no one seemed to know what lay behind the Indian's exile from his tribe. Garland, caring little for men's pasts, had been willing to take on 'the renegade', as he had been known for some time after he arrived on the plantation.

It had been Mrs. Garland who named him Gabriel – no one could be bothered to pronounce his Iroquois name; Gabriel, for her favourite archangel, and Reed, after an eccentric tutor from her childhood. The Iroquois had settled in quickly although he showed little aptitude for English and spoke in a stilted kind of pidgin. Gabriel Reed had many attributes that were of use on the estate, but his main skill was as a tracker. He had led every hunt for escaped slaves and convicts over the past few years, all of them successful. It was he who had found the slave who Garland had hanged some months ago.

The Iroquois was a stunningly handsome man. Some on the plantation had mooted, in private, of course, that Mrs. Garland had been moved by more than a passing interest in naming the renegade, but Reed himself had always stood aloof from the comings and goings of the estate and did not much mix with the slaves, convicts or even the indentured servants. He especially did not interact with Archie whom he considered to be of an inferior race. After all,

Algonquin people, when captured in battle, had long been the slaves of the Iroquois.

Now he stood holding the reins of his horse and squinting into the sun, as it sank towards a horizon of treetops. Birds and insects clucked, cawed, and chirruped in the dense forest, while Hardbone and five of Garland's most loyal men stood beside their horses, waiting, saying nothing, breathing deeply from their exertions, several with their hands on the pistols they all wore at their belts.

They had wasted precious time at Garland's searching for McLeod, whom Garland was insistent should lead the chase, but, when the Scotsman failed to materialise, it was Hardbone who was detailed to take charge. It had taken almost two hours for Reed to find the trail left by the Burtonwood Insurrectionists, but once discovered it was easy to follow, for it was hard for a group of eighteen people to move through the countryside without leaving an obvious trail. Now, with much of the day behind them, the posse had been following the trail for hours in the pounding August heat. At length, turning slightly so that Hardbone was just in his peripheral vision, Reed spoke. His voice was low and sonorous.

"Come this way, maybe hours."

"Hours ahead of us, this way?" asked Hardbone, unnecessarily.

"Ahead," repeated Reed, pronouncing the word 'a-haid'. He turned back to the west and set off again.

"It seems we are not to rest, my friends," said Hardbone with a half shrug of apology to his little posse.

Reed plunged on, beating his way through the low underbrush with the heavy stick he carried and leading his horse behind him.

Hardbone and his men followed cursing the dense undergrowth that slowed them.

"You think we'll catch 'em today?" Hardbone called out, squeezing the words out between gasps of breath.

"We catch'um," growled the Indian.

"Yeah, well, you catch'um, red man," murmured Hardbone to himself, "and we'll take the black devils back to Hell."

*

Archibald Sowell, with a retinue of five riders, all trusted indentured servants, had arrived at Garland's house in the late morning. His neighbour's plantation was still buzzing with expectation and excitement at the news of the break out of the Burtonwood slaves, but he ignored the questions of the people who, having seen him riding in, had flowed out of the fields like the tide in a shallow estuary and now walked along beside his horse as he approached the house.

Garland's house servant led him into the parlour. Seated around the room were Garland, his guest, Louis Silston and Mrs. Garland. Thomas Garland was standing in the shadow of a corner, glaring at the company. While John Vertue took his place at the back of the room, Sowell accepted the offer of a glass of cool water from Mrs. Garland and then, at Garland's bidding, began his story. It was a tale of woe, with many buildings lost, most burned to the ground, though no one had died or been badly injured in the fight to put out the fires.

Eager to hear about the search for his slaves, Sowell kept his tale short. Garland then explained that he had sent Hardbone with some of his best men and the Indian Gabriel Reed to track the slaves.

Garland was insistent that the search party would succeed, for, he said, Reed had never let him down; every runaway had been apprehended.

Thomas Garland had been hanging around the house all morning carrying a face of thunder. Despite begging his father, he had not been allowed to go with the search party and his humiliation had been made worse by his father's refusal being so public, as almost all of Garland's people had gathered whilst the posse had packed food, weapons, powder, and shot and prepared their horses. His father was explaining to Sowell why it was Hardbone who had led the search party when Thomas grumpily interrupted.

"I hope, sir, you will punish McLeod soundly when he returns from his carousing. I suspect he has had another of his nights with the bottle."

"You can be sure, Thomas that..."

As if their words had summoned the Fates, at that moment there came a hammering on the front door. Vertue hurried out, but was back in seconds. McLeod's body had been found.

"He must have come upon the Africans, poor devil," said Silston gloomily.

"Was he much mutilated?" Garland wanted to know.

"No, sir. Seems his neck was broken."

"And his horse?"

"Gone, sir."

"So, they took his mount," growled Garland. His face was creased with rage. "Well, they have his pistol, too, is my guess, for McLeod never rode without it."

"They are armed then," said Sowell sounding despondent.

"'T'will do them no good," Garland asserted, as he gathered himself. "Reed and Hardbone will find them. My men are all well-armed, Sowell, and, even if it means you losing a few slaves, they will get them. Come, let us take some refreshment and try to break Thomas out of his black mood."

An hour later, as the party continued to discuss the slave insurrection and Garland renewed his argument for a larger, better-armed militia, there came another interruption.

John Vertue left the room to open the front door to one of the sentries who had been posted to guard Polly's jail. What he heard from the man made his heart pound. His mind running on like a mad machine, he led the guard into the sitting room.

"Pardon the intrusion Mr. Garland, sir," Vertue intoned, "Billings here has some more bad news."

Billings gave Vertue a swift, hard look; he did not need the footman making his situation worse with his portentous words.

"Beggin' pardon, your honour," the man started. He hesitated under the ferocity of his master's stare.

"Yes, man, what is it?"

"I dunno how, m'lord, but…"

"Yes, yes, spit it out, man."

"Well, sir, must have been the excitement an all, sir…"

"For God's sake man, tell me!"

"Well, m'lord, old Mary comes out with some vittles for Polly, I mean the prisoner, sir, and well…she's gone, sir."

"And, sir, again excuse my boldness," said John, leaning to whisper in Garland's ear, "but it seems Mr. Sowell's carpenter has disappeared and so has the Indian groom."

Chapter 43

In Which We Hear of The Hunt for The Burtonwood
Insurrectionists

It had surprised Jem, a man who had harboured a simmering hatred
of the whites since childhood, how much he liked Will Staples. After
they had become close, Will had told Jem of his first apprenticeship
amongst the 'green fields of England', a place Jem could hardly
imagine. Will said that, when he had informed Walter Riddlecote that
he intended to seek his fortune in London, the old man had agreed to
release him and told him, "you are a free man, Will, and every man
should take his freedom into his own hands and do something fine
with it". It was a lesson that went deep with Jem.

When they had been working together, Will had talked about
escaping with his girl over the Blue Ridge, a mountainous range that
separated the English colony from the land known as the
'backcountry', where Indians and, further west, the French were
rumoured to roam. Will had heard from the tinker, Jasper Spender,
that the Blue Ridge was wild territory, densely forested, vertiginous in
places, and, most importantly, out of the reach of the colony's law.
For Jem, with pictures in his imagination of free slaves living in the
high heartlands of Jamaica, there was hope in those mountains.

Today was the second after their flight from the plantation. Until
now everything had gone well. They had made good time, managing
to skirt plantations and farms by always staying in woodland, or by
travelling as far as possible by night. Jem's confidence had been
buoyed by having his mother beside him and had grown with each

step away from Sowell's place, but his growing sense that they would succeed had not dimmed his vigilance. Now, as their third night came on, they all stood or crouched in silence in a wood of maple, hickory, and willow, trying to blot out the symphony of crackles and clicks of the evening insects as they strained their hearing to make out the distant sounds that Millie had thought she had heard. For several moments no one moved or spoke. Then, far away, they heard the snort of a horse.

"Aw, sweet Jesus, here they come," moaned James softly.

"Ssh," Jem put his finger on his lips, glancing at Ruth. He could see she was frightened, but she forced a smile, a small, weak thing summoned from somewhere deep beneath her fear.

Jem's eyes were wide and his heart clattered against his ribs, but he knew what was needed. He had been crouching, one hand resting on the thick bed of mouldering leaves of the woodland floor. Now he stood and turned away from the group, raising his hand as he did so and waving them on behind him as he made off through the trees. They had no idea where they were. They had no map, no compass, only the sun during the day to keep them on their westward path, but now, through the trees, they could see clouds shredded by unknown winds and coloured lilac, pink and orange by the setting sun. They ran through the forest towards that fading light.

Their way was often impeded by long-dead goliaths that lay gently mouldering into new food for a thousand species. It was not easy work traversing that crowded land; it was clutching and tripping, clawing and scratching, intimidating. On they ran, dodging around trees, ploughing through the undergrowth, pushing aside low-hanging boughs. Each man and woman on their own track, spread out, though Millie and Ezekiel stuck close to Jem and Ruth. They ran in terror, knowing their pursuers were behind them. They ran for their lives, for they knew the penalty they must pay if they were caught.

Suddenly, the crack of a musket. Late evening birds roosting for the night flew up amid squawks and trills. Several of Jem's people ducked instinctively as they ran. Ruth stumbled and fell heavily into the brush with a scream. Jem and Ezekiel stopped to help her up.

"Come on, ma," hissed Jem, "gotta get up!"

The others held up, stopped by Ruth's cry. Jem was aghast; her leg was a mess of blood. Though he had pulled her to her feet, she could hardly stand and was shivering all over, bent double and unsteady. There was a six-inch-long splinter of wood protruding from her calf. James and another man came lumbering over. A dog barked; not far away.

"Got to get her out of here," muttered Jem. He reached down for the shard of wood.

"No," hissed James. "You pull that, she bleed out, boy."

Jem ignored James, but left the splinter, instead slipping his shoulder under Ruth's armpit, heaving her up. She let out a small moan.

"Cain't do it, Jem," she whispered.

The dog barked again, closer now.

"You can, ma. I got you, come on."

He tried to move forward, but he was impeded by the thick under-brush and Ruth's writhing. She was in terrible pain.

"Please, ma," he pleaded. "I cain't go without you."

Two more barks echoed through the woods. They heard a muffled shout.

"Jem!" James's voice was low and urgent. He was already walking away.

Jem looked back. There, not a hundred feet away in a small clearing was a huge hunting hound, moving inexorably towards them.

"Leave me, Jem," Ruth gasped through clenched teeth.

"Not gonna do it, ma; we all stick together," he replied, dragging her forward.

She cried out and let her whole weight fall onto Jem's shoulder. He bent under her weight.

"Cain't do it," she whispered again.

"Jem!"

He looked up to see James' wide eyes, whites glowing, staring at him.

"They comin'."

"Get you to freedom," Ruth gasped in Jem's ear. "I done, boy, but doan let me die knowing you dead too."

"No, ma," he cried, tears streaming.

"Go. Set me down, now."

With a gut-wrenched sigh and a choked back gasp of frustrated horror, Jem lowered his mother gently to the ground. He bent down and stroked her cheek. Ruth looked up at him and tried to smile. James was already running, leaping over undergrowth, catching up with the others when Jem started out. His face was wet with tears, his throat fit to choke and his chest was tight. He did not look back.

The hound loped up to Ruth and lowered its head to sniff her. It lifted its head, staring in the direction Jem had gone, then brought its snout, all wet nose and dribbling chops, back to the woman again before letting out two great huffing barks. Ruth startled at each yelp and cowered. From the trees to the south came a voice.

"Okay, Luther, okay, boy."

Moments later a man appeared leading a pale horse. He had a long musket over his shoulder and a wild turkey was dangling by its neck from his saddle, swaying to and fro, as the horse, its head lowered, ambled forward. The dog turned to look towards its master and gave another bark. As he approached, the man, a tall broad-chested fellow with loose hair that fell over his shoulders, caught sight of Ruth lying behind his hound. He grinned and lowered his gun, pointing it at Ruth.

"Well, we wuz after birds, Luther, but we got us a nigra."

Chapter 44

In Which the Search for Polly Begins

The instant Louis Silston heard that Polly had escaped and that Will Staples and the Indian lad had helped her, his mind span into a gyre of incandescent rage and frustration. He was a man for whom a grudge was no mere passing whim, but a career, not to be taken lightly and never to be forsworn. If he had quietly analysed his feelings and the role played in Abigail's death by the two young people he had been relentlessly obsessing about and pursuing for over a year, he might have admitted to himself that it would be better to move on; seek another suitable bride and forget Abigail Colliton and the opportunities she had represented, but this escape was a personal slight. His ambition for one of the largest dowries to be had in England had been frustrated and now he had been cheated out of a double hanging.

There was a dark inevitability, then, to Silston's fury on hearing of the escape. He raged and ranted around the parlour, striding here and there, bumping into furniture, banging his fist on tables. He was oblivious as Mrs. Garland left in silent objection at her guest's vulgar choice of language in front of a lady and continued to curse the gods of ill luck until Garland managed to calm him enough so that the men could start to make plans.

Sowell announced, with regret, that he must return to his own plantation to oversee the reclamation of whatever could be salvaged from the wreckage of his buildings and initiate the immediate clearance of the devastation in advance of the rebuilding of what had been destroyed in the fires. Before he left, he insisted that three of his riders should chase after Hardbone's posse in search of his slaves. The case for their capture was even more pressing now that there was a possibility that it had been they who had killed McLeod. However, he offered his other two men to join Silston in the search for Garland's girl and his carpenter. It was at this moment that John Vertue made his move.

"May I speak, sir," he asked Garland.

"If you make it quick, Vertue, and if you make it good," Garland retorted, coldly.

"I know Will Staples, sir. I spent much time with him; I know how he thinks. We were locked up together for weeks in Newgate. The boy was green when he came in, sir, and I took him under my wing. He looked up to me. And again, on the voyage to the colony, sir, chained side by side for weeks." The lie slipped out like a silk kerchief from a well-lined pocket. "Gave me time to really get to know him. He told me all, Mr. Garland, all about his hopes of finding this slut of a girl…"

"So," Garland snarled, eyeing John intently, "you knew he was going to snatch her away?"

"No, sir, never, your honour. Had I known that, I would have told you as soon as I saw him here on the plantation. And…I never knew Mr. Silston was looking for them."

"So, you don't know everything, do you, Vertue?"

"No, sir, that's true, but, as I say, I know how the lad thinks, I know his skills and I know what he knows."

"And you know the reward?" Garland's tone was scathingly sarcastic.

"Aye, sir, I'll not lie. I'd like a piece of that fifty pound, and I'd like my freedom, but I also want to help, Mr. Garland, honestly I do."

"I doubt you've ever said an *honest* word in your miserable life, Vertue."

Mr. Sowell interjected then.

"But we do need men, with so many gone after the slaves, Reynolds and, though I share your suspicions of this fellow, there seems little doubt he knows the carpenter better than anyone else."

"If the beggar is not lying."

"We have to trust to something, Reynolds," Silston said hotly.

Garland strode back and forth, absent-mindedly tapping his hand on his thigh. At last, he said:

"Well, they will be going for the coast, I am sure of it. Like so many of their kind, they'll be looking to stow aboard a ship bound for England, back to their gutters and hovels. I suppose we could send Vertue to alert the port authorities, Addis and his like."

Silston and Vertue responded at the same instant.

"No, sir," Silston barked, "I shall be going!"

"I'm thinking they'll go different, your honour," Vertue said. "Will Staples sees nothing back in England for him, sir. My bet is they are making for virgin territory. I know that boy, sir, he won't risk getting caught in England again, he knows he'd get the rope this time."

"Making for the backcountry?"

"Aye, sir, same as the slaves."

"So, your belief is they will cross the Piedmont towards the Blue Ridge?"

"I do believe so, sir."

"Well, if you're right, once over the mountains they will be in Indian territory and, if the Iroquois or the French don't get them, then they will have escaped us for good."

"Yes, sir."

Silston listened to these exchanges with growing impatience. His colour had risen and he was literally fidgeting with frustration at the delay.

"Reynolds," he said loudly, "we have already agreed Sowell's damnable slaves must be prevented from getting to the Ridge. It is the same case with these runaways; Staples and the girl must be apprehended before they attain the Ridge, sir, or they will be lost to us and I for one will be damned if I don't see those two strung up from a good strong bough!"

So, it was agreed and, after hurriedly making their preparations, saddling up and mounting, Silston, Vertue, and Sowell's two men had set out in pursuit of the three fugitives.

*

Gabriel Reed moved away from the main group as they settled their horses and made ready to rest for the night. By late morning, Silston's group had caught up with the posse. The four had made exceptional time following the posse's clear trail.

Since then, for perhaps three good hours, instead of having to lead their horses through dense forest, they had been able to ride across broken, scrubby ground. On encountering more woodland, the party had kept up their chase into the early night, trudging on foot over root and duff, until, at last, they had surrendered to the darkness and stopped to make camp. Reed was sure they were close behind the slaves and may have them the next day if the ground allowed them to ride again. At that moment, he was inspecting the track to the west of the makeshift camp. The escapees had left a good trail for the pursuers to follow; flattened brush, broken branches, footprints in mud by waterholes. As the others readied the area for their camp, John Vertue sidled up to Louis Silston.

"Mr. Silston, sir, if I may?"

"Yes, Vertue, what is it?"

"Our job is to bring back the three miscreants for Mr. Garland, not the slaves for Mr. Sowell."

"I am well aware of that," said Silston sharply.

"Yes, sir. Begging your pardon, but I was thinking, it could hold us up being mixed in with this lot, you see, sir. We'd be better to go out on our own. I know Will Staples and he will be taking them to the Blue Ridge with all speed, sir. He is obsessed with that girl. My bet is, if we make best use of our horses, we'll come upon them soon enough."

Silston nodded and stroked his chin.

"Vertue, you make a good point. We could be mired with the main group for some time in chasing down the slaves. Hardbone!" he cried, walking towards Sowell's man. "Mayhap t'would be an idea to split the group. Reed is Mr. Garland's man and Mr. Garland's main goal is to re-capture the girl and her two accomplices. I suggest Vertue here, myself and Reed, with one other of Mr. Garland's men, perhaps Sherwood there, make our own way to discover the tracks of the smaller party. I'm sure, Hardbone, you are eminently able to chase down the negroes without our aid, or do you fear a pack of unarmed slaves?"

Christian Hardbone raised himself to his full height and shook his head.

"Well now, your honour," he replied, "that's as maybe, but you'll remember that Mr. Garland was very clear that these slaves must be brought to heel the soonest, lest word of their escape incites more uprisings. I counsel staying in one group, that way we conserve our strength of numbers and we have more eyes on the task."

"You'll do as I say," Silston snarled, glaring at Hardbone. "You'd do well…"

He was interrupted by a shout from Reed.

"Man comin'!"

Approaching through the trees, his dog trotting a few steps ahead of him, was a tall man leading a horse. There was something draped over his saddle. It looked like a body.

"Hey, there!" The fellow's voice was rich and deep. "I got somethin' here you boys might be lookin' for."

As he came closer they could see the body stir. A head rose up. A face appeared, eyes wide with fear. Ruth, bouncing up and down with each step the horse took, saw the group of rough, tired-looking men all staring at her.

"Oh, Lord," she whispered.

Chapter 45

In Which Jem's Reckoning Comes

When he heard there would be no reward for returning the slave woman, the hunter, one Richard Lionel Boone, a small planter, had left in disgust within half an hour of arriving in the camp. Before he left, Boone told the posse that the other slaves could not be more than two hours ahead of them and this had fired up Hardbone and Reed enough to help them to the easy decision to break camp immediately and carry on through the night.

Ruth's leg was in bad shape and she could not walk. None of the men would have a slave sharing a saddle with them and they agreed they could not leave her. For minutes the debate billowed back and forth.

"Why are we arguing about this?" Silston had wanted to know. "She is guilty of a capital crime and should pay the capital price. We have good rope and there are plenty of trees."

"I agree with Mr. Silston," said John Vertue, looking around at the others. "We need to get on and this one will only slow us down."

Some of the men looked away, but one or two others muttered their agreement. Gabriel Reed stood off from the main group, his face impassive. Hardbone scowled and stepped forward.

"Mr. Silston, sir, I say this ain't right. This one belongs to Mr. Sowell and my responsibility is to get his goods back to Burtonwood in one piece. It'll be for him to decide punishment then."

"I think this has gone further than that, Hardbone," said Silston quietly. "This is not a simple runaway. This has been an uprising, a rebellion and we know from what happened in Jamaica that you can't give these animals any mercy, for they will take and take until they have their own country here. Is that what you want, Hardbone?"

"No, sir, but…"

"And look at that leg, man. It's as like she'll be dead by morning anyway. Now, stand aside or you'll be explaining yourself to the magistrate."

Under Silston's orders, a rope was brought and Ruth was led, staggering in pain, to stand under the low branches of a young beech tree. She was sobbing and pleading for her life, as Vertue tied a knot and slipped the makeshift noose around her neck.

"Please, mister," she wailed. "No, please, no, not this, suh."

She reached out to Vertue, placing her hands on his arms. He gave her a look of pure disgust and shook her hands off. He took the end of the rope and threw it high, missing the branch he aimed for. Two more tries and the rope was in place. Ruth's sobbing was the only sound in the clearing. Most of the men stood watching in silence. Two were looking away into the woods.

"You two, take a hold, help Vertue," said Silston. "Haul her up!"

They pulled, the three men, while Silston, Hardbone, Reed, and the others watched. Ruth screamed once and then, her body weight crushing her windpipe against the rope, was silent. Her hands grasped wildly, ferociously at the rope around her neck, as her legs pumped, running to eternity. Her eyes bulged and her mouth gaped. Her bowels and bladder emptied as she continued to thrash against her terrible fate, but, by then, no one was watching. Someone had quenched the fire and the men were saddling up and following Reed, not one of them looking back.

The Iroquois led them unerringly through the trees, always keeping west as if by some internal compass, picking up on clues and signs even in the darkness. It was hot work, walking their horses in file through the stifling woodlands. By early morning, when a mournful grey light revealed a cloud-strewn sky, they had emerged out of the woodland into a more open land of bushes, small trees, and scrub. They mounted their tired horses. The land ahead was rough, but the riding was easy. At last, they came to a narrow valley, cleared of trees and laid to crops. To the north, far away, they could see buildings.

They spurred their horses for one last rush, cantering in a tight-knit body across the open ground, now weaving between fields, now galloping down tracks, now flattening a path through a crop, until, at a cry from Reed, they saw, not a half a mile distant and illuminated by the rising sun as clearly as if on a great stage, a group of figures moving across the open land towards woodland that swathed the opposite side of the valley.

"We have them," shouted Hardbone. "On, men!"

The final dash was easy for the riders, even though their steeds were exhausted. They rode up to the forest into which the slaves had disappeared. No one needed instructions what to do. Dismounting and leaving the horses in the care of one of their number, the posse proceeded on foot.

*

Jem led his people up a steep, wooded hill. The night had not dispelled the tyrannical heat of the previous day so that, even now, under a white early morning sun, the forest was an oven, a sweltering trap. They had only known of their pursuers when they reached the cover of the trees, where they had stopped to survey the land. The sun was rising directly behind them and looking back into it, low as it was in the sky, it had been hard to make out detail, but Jem had caught sight of something; a plume of dust. He had known at once what it was; riders galloping across the dry land.

He had led his people into the woods, encouraging them, willing them to make good speed. They had meant to rest at the beginning of the previous evening, but, with Ruth's injury and in the belief that the posse was close behind, they had not stopped all night.

It had been their practice, since their escape, to rest in the evenings before moving on, using the darkest hours of the night for cover. Now they had been travelling for almost twenty-four hours with only moments of rest here and there and no time to look for food or water. They were exhausted. As they climbed, crashing through undergrowth and dodging around trees, each man and woman listened for the dread sound of a gunshot or a shout. The going was hard and, as the slope steepened, they toiled to try and keep up any speed. Behind they heard a dog bark.

As Jem broke out of the trees into a small clearing drenched in sunlight, there came a cry from behind. He turned and saw Millie helping young Ezekiel up from where he had fallen. The boy, no more than sixteen, looked shocked, his eyes wide.

"Hit his head," gasped Millie between breaths, as Jem approached them.

"C'mon, boy," he breathed into Ezekiel's ear. "Gotta keep going, come on!"

The youngster shook his head and rubbed his cropped hair.

"M'all right," he said, trying to smile.

Jem took his hand and pulled him forward, meaning to lead him across the puddle of light ahead of them. As they moved off, they heard a shout.

"There! Just ahead, there!!"

It was faint, but much closer than any of them cared to think about. They ran. Jem waved to the others who had stopped in the clearing.

"Keep going, just run!"

There was a shot. Birds squawked and rose out of the trees. Ezekiel was stumbling along, much of his weight on Jem's arm. It was clear the boy was dazed. Jem glanced at him as Millie passed them. There was a smear of blood at his hairline. Another shout went up behind them.

"Over here, Mr. Hardbone!"

"Come on, Zeke, you can make it," Jem muttered.

Another shot rang out. Splinters flew out as the ball separated bark from trunk on a tree nearby. More shouts from behind. The riders must be more rested than his people, thought Jem, for they were gaining fast. They were back in pine woodland again, the trees widely spaced, the ground steeply inclined. There was little undergrowth and nothing to impeded their flight over the thick duff of long-dead pine needles, but Jem was keenly aware that that made it easier for the chasers too. The slaves were running in a group, always casting glances at each other, making sure they stuck close.

Another shot and a grunt from out in front. A tall, thin man, David, fell to the forest floor with a heavy thud. Blood bloomed a dreadful flower of crimson, across the back of his shirt. Grief gripped Jem's heart and squeezed it. He had lost two of his people. This was not meant to happen. But they were making better speed now on level ground. The men chasing them were all shouting now, but there were no more shots. Jem felt Ezekiel's weight ease. The boy freed himself from Jem's grip and ran unaided.

"Good now," he gasped.

They ran together, Millie a few steps ahead of them, as the posse, spread between the tall pines, continued to gain on the escapees. Behind them another dog barked. Suddenly, a thickset man, perhaps fifty yards ahead of Jem, broke away from the group and ran south.

"Scatter," he yelled.

Jem recognised James's voice.

"No," he shouted, panting for breath. "Stay together!"

But it was hopeless. Terror had seized them and the group fragmented, as individuals fanned out to right and left. Jem's heart felt like it was breaking from a toxic mix of grief, exhaustion, despair, and disappointment. His lungs had red-hot wires pressing down inside them and his legs were starting to fail. Yet still, he ran on. Millie, Jem, and Ezekiel reached a summit and plunged over together. The other side was even steeper than the ascent and they skidded and stumbled, trying to stay on their feet as they rocketed down the hill, sliding on the dry, packed pine needles, slipping down onto their backsides, bumping straight back up again. Immediately ahead of them, a huge rock rose up out of the earth like a totem. It was covered in growth; ferns, moss, low bushes. It was greater in size than a post coach. The three skidded and staggered around the side of it. At the bottom of the descent, they could see a rill, a narrow stream that ran southwards disappearing into dense bushes. Jem led them on.

"Into the water," he gasped. "This way."

He turned and ran splashing through the shallow water into the overhanging bushes. He slowed them to a walk, showing them how to drag their feet through the water so as not to make much sound. Keeping their heads down, they walked like this, swilling their feet and ankles through the fast-running brook, for a long time. They heard another shot and then another, followed by some prolonged barking. Undeterred, Jem led them on. By now his feet and lower legs were freezing and he was starting to shiver. He realised that his exhaustion was likely to get the better of him if he did not stop soon. He stopped the other two.

"Can you go on?" he whispered.

Both of them had drawn faces and were lathered in sweat. Ezekiel's eyes were hooded and he leaned forward heavily, his hands on his knees. Millie's normally beautiful dark skin had a sheen of grey like she might vomit at any moment.

"Bit longer," she gasped.

"Good, stay low."

On they went, going horribly slow when it felt like they should be flying. Time dawdled to an agonizing crawl as they continued on, shrouded in the thicket of bushes and low trees. At last, they came to a large willow, its feet dabbling in the stream and Millie laid a hand on Jem's shoulder.

"Gotta stop," she said. Her eyes welled with tears.

"Right," said Jem.

His heart ached, but he knew he had to accept that they were done. He crouched down until his backside was in the water. The other two did the same, their eyes locked on his face and he realised, with a sudden shock of hopelessness, they were seeking strength and hope from him, but there was nothing he could do for them or for himself. He was played out and, so, they waited.

Chapter 46

In Which Polly, Will and Archie Are Put to The Test

I am furious with stupid Will Staples, yet I am flying with happiness
at my freedom; freedom from Garland and his foul son, freedom
from toil in the laundry, freedom from every day the same, freedom
from the kind of people who believed I could be a thief. But I am
angry that Will Staples has dragged my friend, Archie into this crazy
escapade, risked him, put him in danger. Yet, I am so happy he is
here, with his comfortable face, his wonderful knowledge of these
woodlands, and his loyal old Joss. There is a war inside me 'tween
despair and delight.

There was a brief rain in the night though it cooled us not, hidden,
as we were, in the swelter of low trees. We have been walking mostly
at night to escape prying eyes, though sometimes we had to move by
day when ways and tracks have been too difficult to follow in
darkness. But we have been lucky and the land has been kind to us
giving us milk from the teat, eggs from the coop, and fresh vegetables
and fruit from the fields. We have never taken anything other than
these natural gifts of God, never stolen from a farmhouse, and fresh
water has been in abundance on all the land we have crossed. Archie
is a miracle on roots and berries and has guided our hands to find the
nourishments we have needed when the farms and their orchards
have become sparse.

Now, we have entered an emptier land. Long it is since we saw a
plantation the likes of Garland's place. For the last two days, we have
only passed smaller tobacco patches owned by poorer planters and a

few farms. These, too, were poor places; Archie says these folk only have a few animals and some corn and barley. The further west we have come, the fewer farms we have seen; each one cut out of the forest. This last day, we have seen only one place, and that in the early morning. Since then, all else has been trees and what Will calls underbrush. He still tries to teach me of his trees, points out huge monsters with a smile, tells me what I can smell is sassafras and sumac, strange words. I do smell something and I admit I am beginning to see why he loves them.

Early in our flight, we found tracks and, when we saw no people, we risked using them and made good time, but, today, with the disappearance of farms and plantations, the roads and tracks have petered out and now we march through forest. Our last track dwindled to a narrow path this morning and even that now is gone.

We were making ready to go this very morn and I, having slept little and wakened with a thorn of bad thoughts in my head, asked, angry like, the question that's been brewing these past few days.

"So, Will Staples," says I, giving him the eye and my hands on my hips. "We have come far and still no plan. Still no idea of how we will live."

We had argued, soft and low, but hissing and spitting at each other on the first night of our flight. Archie had sat like the mute girl who used to sell posies beside me when I was a girl at the morning market at Poultry Street. Oh, I was full of rage, as much with Silston as with Will, but he it was I blamed for putting me and Archie into harm's way.

"I'd've been better for never meeting you, Will Staples," was what I told him back then, though it shames me now to think of it.

And now I was angry again, for I had bottled all my feelings for too long, but I would not have another spat of shouting like that first night when Archie had to break us apart and move us on – though we were tired to death – for fear we woke the district. So, I am keeping my voice low, my face as sweet as I can make it.

"We will build a place for ourselves," he says in answer.

"A place?" I ask.

"Aye, a house and…"

And I cannot abide it, though I promised myself, and I break in on him and face him with my anger.

"Fool!" says I, keeping my voice low. "Better to have run to the coast and stowed away on a ship bound for home, than to be wandering the wilderness for the rest of our days!"

"Polly, my dear…"

"I am not your 'dear', Will Staples." I cannot help myself. It just spills out.

"Polly," says he and he closes his eyes and puts his hands in prayer before him. "Auggie told me about the ones who run for England. Most of them get caught soon enough and find themselves back here with twice the sentence or else hanging from Tyburn Tree. And even if we were not caught, could you get work again as a maid, without letters of favour? Could you ever go by Polly Pruitt again, wanted for a reward, as you would be? It would be a life of beggary for us, Polly."

He has me mute with these truths I cannot bear to acknowledge. Had I but thought, I would have come to the same end myself. I stay still, but I know my face speaks loud my displeasure.

"That man Silston would have come even if I had been still in Newgate, Polly, you know that. The fellow has the devil of a hatred for you. If we had made for home, he might have even found us there. And Archie here and Joss, we could not take them. No, Polly, please…"

He is right in this, I know, and it makes me crazy for him to be proved so. I feel my face is red and I might be making a fool of myself.

"'Tis so unfair. I stole nothing," I say. "It's men, always men who spoil and put good things at hazard."

"Oh, you did steal, Polly," he says with a smile, all lopsided. "You stole my heart and with it my life."

"I never asked for your heart, Will Staples." I wait then, but he says nothing more. "So, if not London, then where? Over your precious Ridge?"

"Yes, Polly, over the Ridge."

All the while, Archie has sat listening, saying nothing, but this is him now, making himself heard. He stands up and walks toward me, Joss ambling along at his side.

"'Tis true, Poll. I heard the land is good there and empty." He comes up close to me, giving me a small smile. "There a man or a woman can be free."

"Doing what?" I ask him and I hear my own voice is quieter now.

"Farming," says Will.

"Hunting," says Archie.

"I am a good carpenter, Polly," says Will. "I have my tools and I know my wood. I can make us a home, a good home, and we can grow what we need, hunt for meat, as Archie says. We'll be free,

Polly, free to do what we want with no master, no law to tell if we are wrong or right. Auggie says that over the Ridge it is open land, ready for the taking by anyone willing to stake a claim. It is a dream, Polly, our dream and I will make it happen, I promise you."

I look him in the eye and my heart tells me I only see good there; this is a good man, maybe stupid, but good. I do not love him like he wants, but I think to myself, in that moment, maybe I can like him in time.

"All right, Will," I say to him, as soft as I spoke to Archie. "Let us go and find your dream."

So, we have another morning of dodging roots and breaking through bushes and briar. We stop to rest and it's Will who lifts our hearts with a tale. He speaks of his friend, Jem, and we listen close. Who would have thought the fool to be so good with stories? To my thinking, 'tis queer he has such a liking for a black fellow, but I have known none of them, only seen them about the plantation. He has a love, he says, for his friend's intelligence and his pride in his father and grandfathers in Africee and for his strength, though he be skinny, so Will says, and for his determination for freedom. All this talk brings him to another black man, one Jenkin Smith, who he knew awhile in London, and this fellow, too, had stories to tell, which we, lucky listeners, hear now.

We are in a bowl in the forest floor, where I lie hugging old Joss. I have the side of my face against his warm fur and breathe his comforting doggy smell. Archie is below me, sitting in the middle of the hollow and Will is lying on the opposite slope. I can read the cove's mind, for his face tells me he'd like to be in Joss' place.

This is our first daytime rest since we fled. We've been too a'feared before today to stop in the light, but I am exhausted. When first we entered wild country, the going was hard. It was there we discovered Will's love of telling his stories. And he showed me the trees, talking like they were his friends; beeches, elm, ash, and chestnut he says we have in England, though I knew them not, only the good old planes of London do I know. And he showed me hickory, sourwood, hemlock, sassafras, and red oak, trees he has learned since he came to these shores. Some of those woodlands were thick as stitches on a maid's dress and cutting through them was a trial.

Then yesterday in the gloaming, the forest changed, turning to what Will calls hummocks and hillocks, roving up and down like a sea of waves and all covered in roots like badly made lace or those purple lines on the back of aunt Susan's hands. Will says these are pinewoods. I don't care what they are called, just glad of the big spaces 'tween the trees. Under our feet are pine needles and the crisp dead leaves of the few maples, sycamores, and willows that live with their piney brethren. Oh, how well I know my trees now! Where 'ere we go, we are always followed by the songs of birds, the hum and buzz of those damnable bugs, and the heat. What I would give for a good wash.

I close my eyes and I feel on my eyelids the soft kiss of sleep coming. My mind brings me to springtime and memories of the grumbling, funny women of the laundry, the easy, warm weather, and the food; whatever you say about the blackguard, Garland, I ain't ate that well since the Colliton's. But this just puts me in mind of what I have lost and my warm feeling goes cold. The die is cast, my life is upside down again and I feel that old anger rising in me, for, since I was in Garland's jail, a cold, coiled rope has rested in my belly.

We have crossed a line and Will and Archie are to blame, though I know, in truth, it is Silston at the heart of all this. From the moment I saw his face in the laundry I knew I was finished; the hate, disgust, and malice in his eyes was terrible. My thoughts might rage, but, truly, I can't find Archie and Will at fault for what they've done for, though I would not tell them, it has been an excitement and an adventure to be running, despite the privations. Oh, I must quiet my mind, it troubles me so, going back and forth. I give Joss a squeeze.

"You'll look after me won't you, Jossie. Such a good dog," I whisper in his smelly old ear.

*

The four men were coming through the trees on moccasined feet like a silent tide. They were hunters used to the forest, versed in its secrets, absolutely in tune with their surroundings. They moved slowly. They had seen the three travellers and their dog from some distance. Now they floated, ghosts in the forest, the running front of the flood tide, their feet feeling for a silent footfall with each step, their eyes on the three in the hollow, their breathing soft and contained.

Clad only in loincloths of duffel pulled front and back through a belt of leather, they had their hair shaved from the front half of their heads. Two had it pulled up into a tight knot at the crown of their heads, the other two had theirs in simple ponytails. All of them had colourful feathers of blue jay and cardinal adorning their hair. The oldest bore an ugly scar from the corner of his mouth to his ear lobe. In his belt was a tomahawk decorated with faded paintwork and an eagle's tail feather and in his hand he held a bow and six arrows.

One of the young men wielded a heavy cudgel and wore a long knife at his belt, a third carried an English wood chopper, and the last, the tallest and broadest of the band, their leader, held an old musket across his chest whilst a powder bag flapped from his wampum-decorated belt. This last man had broad stripes of charcoal and red pigment painted across his face from temple to temple. His dark eyes, lit with the fire of ambush, shone out from the depths of the black stripe.

*

In a sudden movement that made Polly jump awake, Joss raised his hoary old head. A moment later he sat up, then scrambled to his feet. He was trembling all over and his tail hung between his legs. Instantly, all three were alert, Polly sitting up, Archie in a crouch, and Will standing, but bent low. Joss growled a low grumbling sound. He took three steps to the top of the declivity.

"What…?" Polly started in a whisper. She was silenced by a look from Archie.

The seconds ticked by. Archie stood up, hurriedly primed the pistol, and craned his neck, scanning the dense trees. Will did the same, straining to see in the dim light of the forest. Polly remained sitting on the ground, looking to where Joss was watching. A figure broke clear of the trees, not more than fifty yards away. Joss barked, a huge sound in the silence of the forest. Another man emerged maybe fifteen feet to the side of the first. A second later, all four Iroquois were in the open, walking slowly towards the three in the hollow. Their faces were stone. Joss barked again. Archie moved past Polly, handed Will his knife, and leveled McLeod's pistol at the man with the painted face.

Chapter 47

In Which Archie Must Prove Himself

Louis Silston's backside was aching. The saddle sores appeared to be scabbing over, though that did not stop them troubling him every time he shifted in the saddle, it was his thighs that were agony. He had always thought himself an excellent horseman and he had surely proved himself in the dragoons, so now he wondered at how just sitting for hours could cause so much pain. Nothing, it seemed, had prepared him for days in the saddle sweating under a Virginia August sun. He made himself sit up straight to take the stiffness out of his back and concentrated on what lay ahead.

In front, Reed led the way whilst Vertue and Sherwood rode behind him. After the search party had caught or killed all the slaves, these four had split from Hardbone's posse, sending them back with what remained of Sowell's slave population, and forged onwards after the girl Pruitt, Will Staples, and the heathen. He had to admit, reluctantly, that their own heathen, Reed, had led them well. Each day, the Iroquois had found signs of the escapee's progress through wood and brush and, often, evidence of where they had set camp for the night. Some of their journey had involved laboriously leading their mounts through dense forestry, but equally, and this was where the agonies in his bruised body originated, most days, they had trekked along narrow tracks in more open woodland and across farms and plantations, pushing the horses to their limits.

This morning they were on an easy stretch, a lane running between small fields of summer crops. It was the first farm they had encountered in some time. In the distance, perhaps half a mile away, Silston could see a building that he took to be the farmhouse. On a rise to the north of the house, several cows grazed somnolently on parched grass. Before they reached the dwelling, they came across two men, one a sturdy fellow almost six feet tall and the other a scrawny specimen with a leery mien. Both were dressed in poor, much-patched clothing and had dirty faces and unkempt hair. They were heaving bales of hay onto a low wagon. A thin, ill-looking pony had been left in harness while they worked. As the riders approached, Silston saw the taller man look at his workmate, and words were exchanged. The smaller, ugly fellow moved behind the cart and picked up a musket that looked so old that Silston thought it had to be from the time of the second King Charles. Neither of the men spoke. Reed brought his horse to a stop some feet short of the men, so Silston rode around him.

"Good morrow," he started, looking down from his saddle with undisguised disdain, "we seek three runaways; murderers and thieves escaped from the plantation of Mr. Reynolds Garland."

"Do ye now?" muttered the smaller man. He seemed reluctant to offer any more, so Silston continued, standing in the stirrups to take the weight off his aching buttocks, in doing so, raising himself even higher above the two farmers.

"Have you seen them? Heard any word of them?"

"Doan see none in these parts," the ugly fellow said after a long silence. "Doan hear nought neither, cain't, when us doan see none."

The big man guffawed at this and swung round to look at his friend as if to congratulate him on his sparkling wit. Silston, already too hot, sweat trickling down his back under his coat and with thighs screaming at him to dismount and lie down, had no time for imbeciles and obstructionists.

"Don't you play with me, you fool," he growled.

The musket was swung upwards to point at him. Reed did not move, but Vertue and Sherwood both edged their mounts closer to Silston. Sherwood had a horse pistol in its holster and he laid his hand on it now.

"And doan you come with yer tame savage a'lording it on my land," muttered the farmer, scowling.

The fuse of Silston's temper was already lit; now, the farmer's resistance was fanning its flame. As he sank back in his saddle and put his own hand on his pistol butt a voice came from close behind.

"Now there, sir, I think maybe we have a misunderstanding." It was John Vertue. Silston looked quickly round at him, giving the servant a scathing look. Undaunted, he continued.

"We are tired men, sir, and have travelled far in search of these renegades and would beg of you only any word you may have of them. We ask nothing more, sir, and then we'll be on our way."

"Well," grumbled the farmer. Perhaps recognizing the odds were against him and having been offered the gift of Vertue's face-saving speech, he took the olive branch and lowered his gun.

"As I did say, we hain't seen none in these parts, not afore yerselves, fer months."

"And you know the penalty for aiding criminals?" Silston asked, unable to let go of his anger.

"Aye, sir," said the farmer, now sounding suddenly weary. He laid his musket back from where he had lifted it. "I swear, we seen none."

After they had refilled their bottles from the farmer's well and ridden on, Silston slowed enough that Vertue could draw level with him.

"If you ever speak over me again or take my part without my leave, Vertue, I swear, I will have you whipped," he snarled.

By late afternoon they had made good progress through deciduous woodlands, more broken land, and, for the last quarter-hour, through pine forest. Reed brought them to a halt and dismounted. He studied the ground for several minutes, walking forwards and back where they had just ridden, stopping, dropping onto one knee, staring at the ground, feeling with his large hands.

"Mebbe half a day and a night and we have 'em," he said as he remounted.

"Excellent!" Silston exclaimed, his face exultant. "Let us finish this."

*

Joss is barking and barking and everything happens too fast. Archie walks to the lip of the hollow and I hear myself gasp, for I see the gun, knives, and axes coming on and I fear for his life. He raises a hand above his head, the pistol held tight in his other hand. I cannot move, I am stone, though my heart races and my head bangs with terror at the sight of the savages. All of a sudden, the hot air has become heavy and pressing. I keep my eyes fixed on them, as they come towards us. Joss stands against my leg, a small comfort, and he is crouched, his head up, still barking. His whole body jerks with each bark and, oh, how I wish him quiet. There are too many for us and I fear the worst.

One of them, the one with the chopper in his hand, is coming from the side. His face is blank as if he has no mind. His mouth is like a dark slash in his face. He raises the axe. My heart slaps against my chest like a smith's hammer. I try to move, but to no avail. Then Will is moving. He has Archie's knife, pointing it ahead of him, and he comes, fast, to my side.

Archie says something, but my ears are full of sound, like a wind, like the breath of God and I cannot understand his words. The Indian is near, oh Lord Jesu, he is so close. His eyes are wide, the whites shining out of his face like a threat of death. Archie calls again. His voice is strong, but, an amazement to me, he sounds calm. I do not look. My eyes are only for this fellow with the chopper, coming on. Suddenly, Joss can bear it no more and leaps forward and now the scream in me blows out like the devil's own blast. The one with the axe tries to step to the side, but the Joss is too fast. He digs his teeth in the cove's leg, just above the ankle, and he lets out a grunt of pain. He swings his axe at my Joss, but loses his balance, missing by a hair's breadth.

God forgive me, but I scream again. I can't help myself, I ain't thinking. I lunge forward, hoping to do what I do not know. Will cries out. The man staggers and swings at Joss again. *No, no!* I'm yelling. Will is by my side and I hear Archie's voice again, this time louder. He is shouting at Joss to cease. 'Tis too late. The axe swipes and Joss is laid low. I'm howling like an animal, all the anger and pain flowing out through my mouth in curses and screams. I push the killer square in the chest with both my hands. He falls backwards and lands on his arse-end with a heavy thump. His face says, *how could a woman do this?*

I fall to the ground beside Joss and cradle his poor head and, though I am quiet now, my cheeks are wet with tears. I think I am to die. The savage is back on his feet, holding his hatchet at his side, watching this stupid English woman crying over a dog and when I look to him, I see he is young, not much more than a boy. Will is standing by me, holding his knife and I think, if that one comes swinging his axe, we are done. But still, he does not move, for Archie is speaking again, quiet like and they are listening. He's moved to be closer to me and Will and I see he is not five feet from the big one with the stripes on his face. This fellow, the leader it seems, has stopped, his musket in his hands. The other two have moved to flank the big one, who is talking now, but I understand not a word.

The one on musket-man's right is old, scarred, and ugly, but it is his eyes that grip me; they are wicked eyes, they have seen much death, I know in my guts. I am already trembling and the look of this evil cove has my stomach again in knots. I wipe my face and stroke Joss's poor head. And then a thing happens that takes away my breath. The fellow with the hatchet nods at me, a look in his eye, and my heart almost stops. What does it mean? It is almost a smile like he knows me and I am suddenly a girl again and father is there and that nasty boy who robbed me of my little bit of silver at the May Fair and Silston is there. I hardly understand what it means and can only watch as he moves slowly to stand by the other three.

Archie has finished his speech and for a few moments, there is silence. Then the ugly one speaks. A surprise, his voice is soft and low, like the tolling of the vespers bell. He looks at musket-man while he speaks. Again, the silence and I feel I cannot bear the waiting. If they mean us harm, why can they not go to their work? Musket-man nods his head and speaks again and Archie, my good Lord, I can hardly believe it, Archie smiles. The tall fellow does not smile, but something passes between him and Archie, and the dread that had made the hot air so thick, moments ago, has gone. It seems we are not to die today; words have taken the place of battle.

Will kneels by me and lays his hand on my shoulder. He puts his mouth close to my ear.

"I'm sorry for old Joss, Polly, I'm so sorry."

I see he knows how much I love this stupid dog and his unlooked-for kindness brings me to tears again and I hear a sob come up from deep in my guts. I turn and let him hold me to his chest while I cry. Archie's speaking again, words I don't understand flowing like a gentle stream over me, and then, bobbing in the flow, two words of ours, 'Grand Agreement'. I pull away from Will, wipe my face and look to Archie; he is surrounded by the savages. The young ones are stone-faced as Archie talks on and they stand very close to him, yet, I sense, he has no fear. Musket-man puts out his hand and touches Archie on the shoulder. It feels like a moment of friendship, but the older man scowls and shakes his head. He has his hand on the painted axe at his belt. Will sits beside me.

I wonder, as I look at the strangeness around me, the forest, the foreign sky above, the painted men with their bodies bared and arms threatening, my two friends, now loose-limbed and seeming free from fear, am I in a dream? Am I to die or will I go on in this dream, this strangeness that has become my life? Archie's speechmaking goes on a long while, him standing with the four Indians, the younger two

341

watching their leader, and the old one, as if waiting for a sign. All the time, I sit with Will and Joss. I can feel poor Will wishing he could hold me again, but I am in sadness on account of Joss and have no wish to feel his touch again.

At last, Archie nods at the four men and then the savages turn to the trees. In moments, they are gone. Archie comes to us, sits by me, and puts a hand on Joss. Then he does a strange thing; my good friend lays his head on the dog's chest and closes his eyes.

"He lives," says he as he straightens up.

I cannot say how glad I am that this stupid old hound is not dead like I thought. Even then, as if he has heard his master's call, Joss stirs and opens one eye. There is a knot in my throat and I feel like to cry again, but Archie laughs and we all join in, with relief that we all live is my guess and then we hear what came to pass with the savages. Archie tells us his people call them Haudenosaunee, these Indians; says the English call them Iroquois. They were a hunting party who happened in the forest at the same time as us; a coincidence, nothing more. It was not us they were hunting.

He admits things were going badly after Joss bit the boy and I pushed the young heathen to the ground. Had to do some quick talking, he says. It seems his language ain't the same as those Iroquois and it was hard for him to make himself understood. It was the ugly one, the old fellow, who helped in the end, as he had some words in Archie's language, but even then, things looked bad. All Archie could think to do then was to remind them of the treaty with the English. Gave them the evil eye, he says and told them killing us would bring the redcoats down on their people. He says he knew not if that treaty would hold any fear for the savages, but we could thank our God, he said, that the old one with the scar knew of it, otherwise, things might have gone worse for us. Will says he knew not that the English had an agreement with the savages. He asks Archie how he knew of it and he tells us he'd heard Garland talking to McLeod about in the stable one day. On such luck do our lives hang.

Archie says he had hoped to discover something of our pursuers, but these young coves had no knowledge of us nor the men chasing us. We sit awhile and take stock, but we have dallied long. Archie gets old Joss on his feet and looks him over close. Says he thinks t'was the chopper's flat side that hit him. Had it been the sharp edge, our Joss'd be gone. 'Tis a relief when Archie says it is time to leave.

Chapter 48

In Which Will, Polly and Archie See the Blue Ridge

Throughout their journey, the nature of the forests they crossed had changed, by turns, from well-spaced and regimented pines, as if planted by a greedy tree farmer, to more open, mixed deciduous woodland of redbud, serviceberry, ash, oak, and locust trees, with mighty tulip trees towering above their smaller neighbours. Other woods were murky, low jungles tangled with underbrush, near enough impenetrable, boggy underfoot – as if even the angry, August sun had never penetrated the ranks of twisted trees – or sometimes dim cedar woodland, blue trees creating charcoal shade. The cedar forest was easily passed, as the lower limbs of towering trees had died and were fragile and easily snapped off, giving out a cloud of powdery dust that got into the eyes, into the ears and mouth, and up the nose. Even when they came to clearings of scrub grass and bush, they were assailed by the baking pollen- and dust-burdened air.

One morning they came to a place of water; an iridescent mirror the surface of hidden black depths. As they approached, Joss bounded forward sending up a scurry of water birds, small ducks, and waders clattering off the surface, shattering the mirror and disappearing into the reeds beyond. Above was a blanket of pure blue, the first large piece of the sky they had seen in a while. In this watery clearing, the air was heavy with humidity and the temperature extreme, yet Will felt exhilarated – this truly was unspoiled country. No hand of man had changed or plundered it. They must be getting close to the land of freedom they so hungrily sought.

The place did not hold the same appeal for Polly, as it was infested with biting flies and midges and soon welts were rising on their bare arms and ankles.

"Let us get away," she said, batting away a storm of midges, "'tis like they will bite us to death and I am so hot my own skin feels like a coat I am wont to peel off to cool myself."

Soon after, they came to a river, the first large body of running water they had come across, and were astonished to see a canoe tied up at the bank. There was no other sign of habitation or human incursion into that wild place except for the little vessel. Archie was for stealing the boat, as, even though the river's sluggish flow was from west to east, paddling it would be an easier way of making progress than continuing through the dense forests.

"I think that a bad idea, Archie," Will said. He was now quite used to calling his companion by name. "Auggie told me that runaways who steal get hanged."

Archie exploded with laughter at that. "They gonna hang us anyway, Will, for the murdering of McLeod."

At last, they agreed it best to leave the canoe, but Archie could not help a long look at it as they followed the riverbank westward.

*

I don't sleep right in these damn woods. I dream of running, always running, covered in sweat and no breath to speak or shout or scream and the bare trees reaching up like arms breaking out of graves, scrabbling at the sky and always the high, keening words: "help us, save us". Now, every morning I wake from this night lunacy, thankful to be alive still, yet afraid of what the day will bring.

I cannot tell how long we have been running, so hard it is to keep track of the days; days of the hard labour of trudging and nights of dreams, and little sleep for fear that our pursuers are close behind. Yet, Archie thinks we must be at the gates of the Blue Ridge and I can tell that Will, for the first time in many a long while, is filled with a quiet hopefulness. For myself, I am no longer delighted by our adventuring. I am fair baked and weak in limb and leg for all that and most heartily sick of the filth, the heat, and the trees.

We settle for the night, each of us wrapped in our own thoughts and hopes. We do not talk; we have little to say to each other and we have nothing left to eat. Since we left the orchards, chicken houses, and fields of food behind us, we have eaten only berries, roots, and mushrooms that Archie has found for us. He caught a strange squirrel all in a grey coat, but that is the only meat we have shared for days. Even Will says it is only Archie's wit now has kept us alive.

I am so tired; I collapse to the warm ground without a word of 'goodnight' and sleep comes soon. At first, Archie had us take turns of wakefulness during the night to keep watch, and I made them let me take my turn, though both felt it wrong I should. But tonight, as the darkness of the forest enfolds us, we are too done in to think of pursuit and danger, but only the blessed relief of sleep.

I am stirred by a sound. I am quick awake, my scalp all a'prickle, my body tense, yet I keep still, too afraid and muzzed by sleep to do anything. I am on my back. When I move my head, I see that Will is awake too and his hand is on his pack and I know he is feeling for his oak staff. It is hard to know how close the sound is, but even I, a paper-skull about these wild places, sense it is not far. Is it breathing I can hear? Will has a hammer now, gripped in his hand. I worm my way onto my side and look around. A twig snaps and there is a soft rustle. I cannot see Archie as he is hidden on the other side of Will, but my hope is he is awake too. He is, he must be. Please, let him be there, awake and ready, for I hear the sound again and it rattles the bones of my fear. I don't want to move, that a'feared I am, but I raise me up, just a little to see him and, yes, there he is. He's rolled on his stomach and has a hand on Joss's muzzle, keeping him quiet and still. Will stirs, looks at him. Archie puts a finger to his lips as he slowly raises himself up.

Another sound in the bushes. Like Archie, Will is on his knees, ready to spring. A silence and then one more noise, like a heavy breath or sigh. I see Will's fingers around the hammer haft, knuckles squeezed tight and white. My body is tense. I raise my head higher and look around me, trying to see into the undergrowth. God, it is so damnably dark. I am like a sharpened blade now, ready to cut through the night and flee, run and run if need be. All weariness is gone as my heart flutters, ready. Another rustle. Whatever it is, it is coming closer. Even though my eyes have settled to the gloom, I can see no more than a few feet. Then suddenly, appearing from the darkness like a puff of smoke, close to the ground, something pale and ghostly ambles forward.

A face? A scrabbling sound and then eyes, bright eyes rimmed in black, grey snout with whiskers like a cat. All fear leaves me and I sink like a stone in the sea, for I know this 'enemy', I have seen him out the back of the laundry. Archie laughs and I enjoy watching him, his face, so gentle when he's happy, his eyes, even in the dark, sparkling. Will grunts and stands up as Joss joins the celebration with one good bark and the raccoon turns tail and disappears into the night. I clap my hands for the show. We are all laughing now, but soon, we settle again, and, in minutes, I am asleep.

I wake to a morning cool for once. No one speaks about the fears of last night and the shared laughter over a raccoon. We are too hungry. My belly is grinding on nothing and pains me, a reminder of the dark days on the ship, but I have faith that Archie will find us berries or nuts or roots to chew on in good time. We move on and find that the ground here is less rugged and testing. Still, we are surrounded by trees, as we have been since we climbed this long hill, but they have thinned and the light of the morning sun streams down in shafts that penetrate to the forest floor, where it forms pools of brilliance.

We make our way in single file, Archie with Joss in the lead, then me and Will last. We see, through the trees, glimpses of the land ahead as we come down from the hill into a valley stretching out beyond to more trees and scrub. At last, we arrive, partway down the mount, at a wide, barren clearing. The ground here is all boulders and stone, unwelcoming to trees. To one side is a large rock, as big as a small London house. Archie and Will help me up and we climb to the top, leaving Joss below. It is like God has opened his hand to show his most precious secrets. The view takes my breath and my voice with it, for it is the like I never saw before. I have never been so high, never seen so much set out all below me. I feel I am as close to God as he will allow. Trees are matchsticks, bushes only green fluff. On the far side of the valley, the land rises up towards high peaks, all dressed in the thick green of tree growth. We see how far up we are, yet the mountains before us are far higher.

"It's the Ridge," says Will.

"Yeah, it's the Ridge," Archie agrees with him.

Since the cool start, the day has warmed, and yet there are thin streamers of mist clinging like pale, ragged flags to many of the trees at the summits. Excitement builds in my breast; perhaps our adventure is almost over and I realise a feeling I have not admitted to myself, for all my weariness, for all my harsh words when we started out, I am pleased, yes, pleased we are here. Deep in my heart, there is a delight at my freedom, at this venturing. Then my mind goes, like a tongue to a gap where a tooth once lived, to the problem that has filled my thoughts these last few days.

Will I, a woman alone with two men in the wilderness, have to choose between them? Does one of these two have to be a husband to me? Once I loved Abigail and would have happily lived with her for my life, but these two men; can I countenance taking one as a husband? I have a liking for Archie, a softness inside me for his lean looks and quiet ways, full of confidence. Is it a liking that binds man to woman, I think? And what of Will, could I bind myself to him? It is a whirl, a trap, and an ache in the head.

I have proved myself stronger than I ever thought possible when I set out with Abigail to run from her parents, so do I need to be a wife to one of these two, can we not be three equals, going forward to a new life of freedom together?

I look again at the view before us, to empty my head, and see that the valley between our hill and the mountains is small, like a pocket in a hairy, green coat. It is littered with tree stumps and the bodies of felled giants and, in the roughly cleared spaces between, are crops. It is not military ranks of tobacco; I can see that. At the far side, nestling against the trees that run up to the Ridge, are some buildings. They squat on the edge of the valley, like a family of bulky beetles, probably poisonous, waiting for us to show ourselves.

The edges of the valley are steep and treacherous-looking, too hard for us to go around, so little have we eaten. Archie says we could wait for night and cross the valley in darkness, but, in any case, our path must bring us past the house and there is a chance that we may be caught. And can we afford to wait the best part of a day? Those who chase us may be a day away or only hours. For sure, they will have horses and will not shrink from crossing the open ground and, if we are to stay ahead, neither must we. So, we argue it; Will is for avoiding the house somehow, though he says not how and is a'feared to wait for night, Archie is sure we should not wait, but worries what might lie in wait for us at the house. Why I shall never know, perhaps it is my adventuring excitement returned anew, but I feel these will be people who will help us and say it so.

"So, then, we go now," says Archie without eyeing us. "When we get down, best if you talk, Will."

"That I will and methinks we should give false names," Will answers.

So, we begin our trek down the slope towards the valley. Will's face is dark with worry, but he holds his peace while Archie and Joss lead us down. The trees, holding with gnarled exposed roots to the thin soil, cloak us until we reach the foot of the hill. There is many a pine here, rough-barked individuals with sparse heads, so underfoot is slippery with needles. At last, we reach the floor of the valley and, after a few minutes wending our way through the patchwork of forest that remains, we break into the morning sun. Immediately, the cooler protection of the forest is gone and I begin to sweat. Or is it fear? For, now that we are exposed, my good feelings about these people have disappeared.

*

They came upon a depression in a clearing. Silston was delighted, hardly able to contain his excitement when Reed read the signs of the confrontation with the hunting party and was convinced that the escapees were no more than half a day ahead, for, though the riders had been slowed by the density of the forests, they had continued to make good time and had ridden at every opportunity.

They followed the trail with all haste and came upon the river and the canoe.

"Coulda took the boat," Reed grunted. "Woulda been hard to follow."

"But they didn't," crowed Silston. "Can you see where they went, Reed?"

"This way," said the Iroquois, unsurprised that the Englishman could not see the obvious tracks left by the three they were following.

On they went, making up minutes every time they mounted their horses. Hardly a word was spoken now as they trudged on. They beat their way through heavy underbrush, led their steeds down steep inclines and up again towards hilltops. At last, Reed brought them to a stop at a small clearing.

"We get 'em tomorrow," he said quietly.

The heavily built man standing outside the door of the cabin turned and called out. He had dark brown eyes set in a weather-beaten face, lined with toil and age. Those obsidian globes looked as cold as a harsh winter's day. A thin-faced woman, wearing a formless dress over her stick-like body and a large bonnet tied tightly under her chin, appeared in the doorway drying her hands on a cloth. Behind the homesteaders, off to the side of the house under the burgeoning shade of the trees, were two graves.

"There," grunted the man with a nod in the direction of the visitors.

They stood outside the house, a ramshackle affair, low to the ground, built of thick logs, brutally lopped branches, and mud. It was roofed with sods that had grown up into a tiny meadow of grasses. The two stared out across fields of vegetables, wheat, oats, and corn at the three strangers and their dog approaching along the track that the constant back and forth of the farm's two working horses had made through their fields.

A younger man, tall and muscular, was standing amongst rows of green vegetables away in front of the house, leaning on his hoe. He had the same dark eyes as the older man, but his face was leaner and sharper, less lined, though equally weather-beaten. It had been he who had first spotted the strangers as they broke the cover of the woodlands to the east. It was a rare thing in these parts to see any human other than the occasional itinerant Iroquois band, or bear hunter. The farmers could see now that their visitors were two men and a woman. All three looked ragged, dirty, and tired. Even in their reduced state, it was clear none of them had seen many more than twenty-five years. Their hound walked with a stiffness that belied its age.

"One's a native," said the younger man, swinging round to speak, so that his words flew back to the couple by the rude house. "Got a gun."

"Yes, son, I see it," replied the older man, the expression on his face tightening.

"But no horse," said the woman quietly, as if to herself.

"Need to get ready, Sara," said the older man, his eyes narrowing. "Go you inside and see that we are prepared."

"Are they trouble, Garrett?" she asked before turning inside.

"If they are, you know how we will deal with it, wife."

On they came, the young Indian with the dog leading, followed by the woman, then the white man, never straying from the path, each staring ahead, never speaking. Many minutes it took for them to come close enough for their faces to be seen clearly. They may have been dirty, but they looked determined, closed, giving nothing away. The Indian's hand rested on the butt of the pistol in his belt.

*

I can tell they have seen us from afar and are waiting for us, standing as still as if they are growing where they stand, like the trees behind us. For some minutes the woman disappeared inside the house, but now she is out again, her eyes on us. I get a sick feeling in my stomach. 'Tis a sort of cold expectation of something wrong, something that will upset our plans, yet we have to confront these three, for they stand between us and the Ridge. All my hope of help and understanding has been born into the air with the morning dew.

We walk through their fields, and grasshoppers, flies, and all manner of bugs fly up with each step. As we come closer, I smell pigs. Their stink wafts on the summer breeze that flows from the west down the wooded mountain slopes and I find my mouth wet with spit for the taste of bacon. There is the house, looking small and low and tumbledown. Next to it, a way off, are two sheds, even more rickety-looking than the house. As if he is reading my mind, Will mutters;

"No great house builders these."

Somewhere, I hear a cow making that sad sound of theirs, though I cannot see it. I can see their faces now, the three statues, and they are blank, unwelcoming. I tell myself there is no reason for fear, other than their ungodly stillness, yet I feel with my whole being that we are walking into danger and wish I had not been the voice to make us come in the light. Archie, who has been leading us at a proper trot, slows down. He has his hand on the pistol. Under different circumstances, I would smile at the joke because these people cannot know that we have no shot nor powder for the weapon. Archie likes to keep it because he says it makes folks wary. Maybe he is right.

At last, there is movement. The one closest to us, the younger fellow, moves forward a pace and swings his hoe over his shoulder.

"Strangers," he calls and his voice is loud but hollow.

It is an odd greeting. I cannot shed the feeling we are making a big mistake. The woman in the doorway folds her arms across her chest. I can clearly see her face now and her mouth is a thin straight line, her eyes narrowed. Archie stops. Joss slumps to the ground beside him. I walk to Archie's left, Will to his right.

"Good day to you, neighbour," says Will, and I find I like his voice. He has made it strong, but it is soft too, like a friend would speak. "Might there be a cup of water for thirsty travellers?"

The young cove stands silent for a moment then turns to the man and woman outside the house.

"Let them come on, Zachariah," says the older fellow with a nod. "There be water enough for all."

Chapter 49

In Which the Three Travellers Enjoy a Day of Rest

It was too mean and hot in their small home to seat so many for a
meal, the older man claimed, so, while Polly, Archie, and Will washed
in the stream that emerged from a spring at the foot of the hills
behind the homestead, the three settlers worked together to bring
food and utensils outside. It was bliss for the three travellers to feel
that some of the thick dirt and grime of their journey was gone, even
though they could not disrobe to wash more than their exposed, sun-
burned skin

It was a feast that was set before them: cold pork in thick slices,
pickled greens and fresh vegetables, bread and cornmeal, and as many
cups of cold, fresh water straight from the stream as they could drink.
It was the patriarch who did the talking while they ate. He had already
introduced himself, his wife, and his son as Garrett, Sara, and
Zachariah Harding.

"We are Friends of the Truth, that some call Quakers, and have
come to this land to serve our God in peace for we were sore pressed
by the 'good' Christians of the high Church of England of our
hometown."

They had made the pilgrimage, like many of their brethren, into
the wilderness of American colonies from the small market town of
Wimborne in Dorset seeking a simple life and the religious freedom
afforded by their remoteness. It had taken eight years to carve their
"small patch of heaven", as Garrett called it, from the wild and they
had lost his bachelor brother, Walter, and their daughter Maud, in the

doing of it. This led to the sad and somewhat ambiguous benefit that the family had extra bedding that Archie, Polly, and Will could bed down on for the night and they were welcome to stay, Harding said.

"We have no weapons, save the love of Christ, our guide and protector, and we will do what we can to help you. You can be easy with us for we have no muskets or pistols or swords, only our farm tools, this mean kitchen paraphernalia you see before you and gutting and skinning knives. Our way is the way of peace and love, so, please, eat and be easy and later you can rest."

Will's belly was slowly filling and he felt himself mellowing. The warmth of the air under the shade of the trees behind the house, where the picnic had been laid out, the food and delicious cold water, the joy of seeing Polly eating well and looking relaxed – he thought he could almost see her travel-hardened edges softening – was slowly evaporating his fear and mistrust. He had worked with Sam Royston on a small job for a Quaker family in Westminster and had found them to be peaceful, thoughtful, and generous hosts, opening their home to himself and Sam and engaging them in hearty conversation about all manner of things. Like that London family, the Harding's, though taciturn and unsmiling, seemed genuinely caring and helpful and their food was delicious. He had not tasted such good cold pork for years. Indeed, he took pleasure in telling Sara Harding so and relating the tale of the London Quaker family.

At length, the Harding's reticent son took his leave, complaining there was little time to finish his hoeing before night. Polly was sitting against the trunk of a healthy young tree and, finished with the food and talk, her eyes were closing. Will too was half asleep, so it was Archie who stood up with Zachariah.

"We thank you for your good food and kindness," said Archie, using his best English. "Now we'll be getting on."

Will woke from his doze to Polly's heartfelt objections.

"No, Archie," she protested. Like Will, her fear that their pursuers might be close behind had faded in the comfort of being relatively clean, full, and warm. "Please, we have come so far. Can we not spend one night of proper rest?"

Archie stared at Polly, telling her with his eyes that they should go. Before the debate even started, Garrett spoke up to reiterate what Zachariah had said about the short time before nightfall:

"And, believe me, you will not want to attempt the Ridge in the dark, so steep and treacherous is it."

There were beds for a night's stay and a hearty breakfast for them before they set off, he said, but now, he needed to attend a broken fence, so he would leave them to debate the issue. Will felt conflicted about going on straight away. He too, despite his lethargy and newfound ease, understood Archie's anxiety about going on and keeping as wide a gap as possible between themselves and Garland's men or the militia or whoever it was that was after them, but one look at Polly's face melted his heart. There was no telling that their pursuers had not already given up and he knew he could not sit by and watch while his host worked, so he picked up his bag of tools and followed Mr. Harding.

Archie gave Polly another look, but she was unmoved. Polly helped Sara to clear the remains of the picnic and then removed herself with Joss back to her seat under the shade tree while Archie talked quietly to Sara Harding about the woodlands that spread up the hills behind the house to the Blue Ridge, eking out information about the paths and barriers to the crest.

Not far from where Polly sat on the hard-baked ground was Sara's small flower garden, planted with seeds she had carried religiously from England. She watched a parade of bees and hovering flies, labouring from flower to flower, heavy with their burdens of pollen, their legs laden with yellow swags. Though she was sore and exhausted, she realised that for the first time since those spring days in the laundry, she was happy. For once the sun's heat felt benign, she had eaten well and the Hardings were fine people, a family they could trust, folk who would help them.

Late in the afternoon, when the day had passed the zenith of its heat and the sky was turning from startling blue to greys, pastel pinks, and orange, Garrett returned with Will and Zachariah, their work completed. Over fresh glasses of cold water, he gently probed Will for information about their journey. Getting little of any solid value, he turned the talk to Will's skill as a carpenter and was rewarded by the tale of Will's flight from Harsham and apprenticeship in London. Then it was Polly's turn, though she gave little away, talking mainly of her time learning silk ribbon weaving from her aunt Susan and working the streets of Cheapside as a costermonger. While they drank and talked, Will noticed how Zachariah looked at Polly. He did not stare, but he appropriated greedy glances when he could. A belligerent jealousy blossomed in Will's heart, but he quashed it, reckoning that they would be off in the morning and would leave the young Quaker behind.

Sometime later, Sara disappeared inside. Polly moved to get up and help her, but Garrett put up his hand and asked her to "hold hard".

"Let my goodwife go to her task, young Polly," he said quietly.

"But I may be of some help, you have been so kind…" she said, moving towards the front of the house and doorway.

"No, madam," said Garrett sharply. Then, softening his tone, he continued. "Please, I beg you, let Sara be. She knows what needs to be done and I can assure you, it will take longer to teach you her ways than the time you might save her with your help."

Will glanced at Archie who was sitting at the edge of the group, staring out at the distant hills away to the east. They exchanged a look that said, 'what is going on here?'

"Maybe we should just be going on," said Archie, rising to his feet.

"No, no, I beg you, please, do not take it a'wrong. We mean not to be rude, but my wife has her ways. Why even Zachariah and myself are not welcome in her kitchen!" He laughed, a rumbling guffaw that gave the lie to his usually gruff exterior. "Please, enjoy the warmth of the sun and stay. Your path up the mountains tomorrow will be steep and hard, better to rest while you can."

Polly smiled at Archie and signaled for him to sit. Grudgingly he settled back down and the talk returned to England. For all the talk and good humour though, for all Garrett's kind words, Will felt a creeping back of the doubts and fear he had experienced on approaching the Harding's house. What was in that house that Sara was doing that was so private? What was she preparing?

360

The evening was deep by the time Sara returned from her secret task. Together, they shared a spartan meal and, after darkness had hidden the valley from their eyes, the Hardings, with Will and Polly's help, prepared for the night by bringing out quilts and blankets to make three rough beds on the floor. Zachariah and Will would sleep on these makeshift pallets in the main room while Polly, at Sara's insistence, would sleep in Zachariah's bed at the back of the house. Archie, meanwhile, had begged leave to remain outside with Joss, watching the eastern horizon. The bedding was laid on the dusty floor and, as a dense quiet descended, they all settled down to sleep.

*

I hear someone moving and open my eyes. I have slept deep and well, the luxury of good sleep I have not known for so long. I push myself up onto an elbow. I can hear someone dressing quietly in the room next door, Sara and Mr. Harding's room. I yawn and stretch and lift myself heavily off the pallet. My whole being tells me to go back to sleep, but we leave soon and there is much to do.

I find Sara in her tiny kitchen and we work together in silence to prepare cornbread with curls of freshly churned butter, thinly sliced cold bacon, and eggs. Archie wanders to my side and asks did I sleep and I admit I did as he smiles and agrees he did too. Now Will is up and stretching in the low doorway, his long arms touching the low roof. I thought us to be the first awake, but here is Zachariah coming inside with a large jug of water from the stream. And, last, here comes Mr. Harding, wearing that serious face of his. Sara leads us outside into the bright sun of a new dawn and, as yesterday, we sit on the dusty ground and break our fast.

We fall eagerly to the task of devouring the simple food and it is delicious. Our hosts even have vitals for old Joss which he wolfs without thanks. I, for one, find myself even more hungry than I was when we arrived here and wonder how that can be, I ate so well last evening. While Mr. Harding and Zachariah talk of the work for the day, Sara excuses herself and disappears into the house. I see Will watching her go, Archie too, and I am thinking I see suspicion on Will's knitted brow. It makes me wonder, what is there to do inside that cannot wait until we have all eaten? She is back as we finish eating and hurries us along with the clearing away, but Archie does not help. He is shading his eyes, staring into the distance beneath the rising sun.

"What is it?" I ask and feel my poor heart, so often put upon these last months, start up its fearsome rattle.

"Somethin', Poll, can't see yet…"

I look too and feel Will by my side and know he will be straining his eyes to find what it is that bothers Archie. Then:

"Riders," he says quietly.

"I don't see anything," I whisper.

"They're there," says Archie.

Behind us there is movement

"Inside, quickly," Mr. Harding growls. It is a new voice from him, one I ain't heard and it scares me.

We sweep up the cups, plates and cutlery and hurry inside. I go to the window, a hole in the wall they cover at night with a shutter of planked wood. Now I can see them, distant smudges on the horizon.

Even as I watch, the dark shapes sharpen like a shadow in the midday sun. They are riders and they are coming on at a steady pace, cantering and making good ground. A voice from behind makes me jump.

"You seem a'feared," Mr. Harding is saying to Archie.

He is giving Archie the very knife of a glare and that old fear grips me again. Is this a man to trust? Is it too late for such questions? I look round to see Archie glancing at Will. A moment passes as he struggles with what to say and I almost speak up for him, but then:

"You too, Mr. Hardin', sir."

"But you are truly a'feared, son, is that not so?"

Archie pauses, looks at the floor and I want to scream, for the riders are out of the trees now.

"Aye, I am," he says at last.

"And you guess these riders to be not friendly?"

"I do, sir," says Archie.

"There is no time to run," says the old man. "They would be on us in minutes. Come, let us get you away. Bring your hound else he give you away."

We have all been careful since yesterday to not talk of our crime of running. The Hardings have not asked, bless them for that, and we have only offered stories of happy, distant times. If we are to be betrayed, this will be the time. They must know we are runaways and they could give us up, yet, looking to Mr. Harding, his good, strong face and determined eyes, I feel now that they will not. We have no choice; we have to trust to their Christian goodness. He and Zachariah are moving the small heavy-looking table. Will takes my question from my mind with his words.

"Where will we hide? They will be armed and they will search."

Sara is hurrying the bedding into her room.

"Help me, Polly," says she, and I jump to her side.

We bundle the sheets and old blankets in a rough-made box, "winter storage" she whispers to me as we work. This work of terror, come on all a'sudden, has my guts churning anew. Maybe we should have run, but the rising ground between the house and tree line has few trees and we would surely be spotted. They have horses and would gallop over the open land and we would be caught. No, we have no choice and my whole body is a'tremble with…what is it? Not just fear, for that is there surely, but the excitement again, the adventure again. We are so close and now, are we to be caught?

"They're coming," says Will who is at the window. "I can see Silston and John Vertue."

John Vertue, come to claim his Judas money. One night after the savages attacked us, we were talking. Most evenings we were too baked to speak, but that night we talked and Will told us of his friendship with that man, Vertue. I could not countenance before he spoke, how any man could call such an earwig friend, but when I had heard his tale, I think I understood. I could tell a part of Will wanted to believe his treachery was not true, yet here he was, riding in with that blackguard, Silston.

Zachariah is pulling back the old and faded Araby rug that lies across the floor. Beneath it, I see another planked shutter, this one with two slots cut for its lifting. When it is removed, we stand looking down into darkness.

"Our winter store," whispers Mr. Harding. "Dark, I am afraid, but down with you, now. We will not betray you; you have my word."

364

Archie is the first to move. He has done the same calculations as I and knows this is our only chance. Down he goes, carrying Joss over his shoulder, down the rough ladder.

"You will not be alone," says Mr. Harding and I think it is our good Lord he means. "There is no time now to explain, but please, whatever happens, at all times stay quiet. Now, down with you."

I am already half down into the darkness when I hear Will's voice above.

"Sir, this is perhaps beneath me and I do not mean to insult you, for I do believe you mean us no harm, but I must ask; will you act for us or should we run, even now?"

"Only the good Christ knows what is best, son," says Mr. Harding, "but we will do our best to help Him."

Chapter 50

In Which the Riders Come

There is only the light from the opening above and now it is gone as
the hatch is shut on us with an ominous clunk. Coming down the
ladder, this seems a small room, but there are shadows and such dark
it is impossible to guess its real size. Who can say how far the place
spreads in any direction? Who can say what is down here? Mr.
Harding's words still ring in my ears and I hope our God is with us
down here.

Light shines through the gaps between the planks of the hatch,
making lines of brightness on our faces, which are still turned
upwards. I hear the footfalls of the Hardings and, with a quick slide,
the rug is pulled over, all light is gone. It is cool and, as Mr. Harding
said, darker than the darkest night, as dark as blindness. We stand
silent, close to each other, we have not moved. From above, the
sound of the heavy table being moved on to the rug and I pray this
will deceive Silston. I feel a hand touching mine, breath on the side of
my face. It is Archie, his voice, the slightest whisper.

"Sit."

I feel both of them go down as I lower myself to the floor, beaten
earth, cold, good for storing. I can see nothing, but guess there are
pickles and salted meat, bottled vegetables and fruits and the like. The
air is stale, but not horrid. I am leaning against someone's shoulder,
Archie's, I think. It is mighty still and only silence from above. I
cannot but help myself thinking of the grave. Aunt Susan's and
Laura's graves must be like this; closed, shuttered from the living and

sun-warmed world. I feel my eyes wet and I squeeze them tight as if my companions might see them. Oh, my dear sister, Laura, my protector. Who will protect me now?

After the warmth of the morning up in the world, I begin to shiver. Archie, if it is him, is cold too, for he pushes closer to me and I feel the warmth of his flesh through his clothes. This small thing heartens me and I wonder; is Will squashed close to Archie too? I remember Joss and pray he does not give us away with a bark.

It is still silent above and I must guess the Hardings have gone outside to greet the riders. We can only have been down here a few minutes yet I feel I know this place already and there is something awry; a strange breathy noise, like a tiny breeze. Joss gives a little growl. How can the air move down here, sealed away from the world? My skin turns to gooseflesh and the hairs on my neck stand up like obedient soldiers. It is breathing; the sound is someone breathing. Someone else.

I am thrown to the winds of confusion and dread, rigid in my blindness, shivering like a child awaiting punishment for some small crime. My mind is a battlefield of crazed thoughts. I grip Archie's hand and he squeezes me back. But there is no time to think. From above come the sounds we fear. Heavy treads on the boards and the sound of conversation, muffled, yet clear to those who know the owners of those voices. I recognize Silston and John Vertue. And then another whispered voice, in the night of this cellar.

"Will?"

And then, in his turn, Will's voice.

"Jem?"

Gabriel Reed had lost the tracks of the three escapees on the dried-up trail across from the wooded glade on the hill opposite the homestead, but he was sure they had come to the house. While Silston, Vertue, and Sherwood, spoke with the farmer, he inspected the mess of footprints, slight as they were, in front of the house. There was no telling who or how many had made them, so, giving up, he joined the others as they were ushered into the house. The rugged-faced young man stayed outside when they entered, hanging around the open door. The woman was emerging from a back room with a crude jug and some wooden bowls and cups. She poured the water and it was handed round to the riders.

"And your horses, sir?" Sara enquired.

"We saw your brook, madam, we will water them later," said Silston shortly. "So, Mr. Harding, returning to our question regarding the criminals; you were about to say…?"

Garrett Harding, who did not hold with lying, chose his words carefully.

"The three people you speak of were here, sir, I own, but they have left us now."

"To go where, sir?" asked Silston, his tone as sharp as a wood axe. He had asserted his leadership as soon as they had arrived at the homestead's door. He did not like the Indian, suspicious of his foreignness, and he did not trust Vertue. Garland's man, Sherwood, seemed to be a simpleton. He felt surrounded by idiots and villains.

"That I could not say, erm, Mr. Silston…is it?"

Silston continued, ignoring the question. "And why can you not tell us?"

Again, Garrett sought words that would not condemn him to being a liar, yet would give nothing away.

"Because they spoke little of their plans, sir."

"I have to tell you, Harding," said Silston, "we have wasted a day searching the woods for the escaped slaves I mentioned to you. I will waste no more time, these are desperate criminals, convicts all."

"Oh, I thought you said one was a native?"

"Ah yes, sir, I see you have been listening," was Silston's condescending reply, given with an unctuous smile. "Anyway, my point is that we have lost time and must apprehend these runaways before they reach the path to the Blue Ridge."

"Well, sir," said Garrett without a smile, "behind us you see the foothills of the Ridge. I would hazard that your criminals are close to their goal, if you think that is where they are going. All I can say is that they left us, going into the dark, and I know not their plans, nor their intended direction."

"Thank you for the water, madam," said John Vertue, filling the silence that ensued after Garrett's reply.

"This lad, Will Staples, Mr. Harding," Vertue continued. He looked at his leader. "If Mr. Silston will allow?"

Silston nodded and drained his cup.

"He is a fine lad in appearance and behaviour, sir, but I know him of old. I am not proud to tell you that I was in Newgate Prison, sir and it was there I met Staples. I thought him a naïve boy with no knowledge of the world, yet, and let me tell you, sir, I was with him all our time in Newgate and on the ship that brought us to these shores, I slowly saw his devious and evil ways. Why I saw him take a man's eye out in Newgate and all for one wrong word.

"Oh, he can turn a good story, sir, he can tell a good tale, he can appear as innocent as the day is long, sir, but he is a bad one, take my word for it, bad through and through. T'was long before I came to see the depths of his depravity, I am sorry to tell you, Mr. Harding. Whatever tale he spun for you, sir, you can probably believe the opposite to be the truth. So, sir, if you know anything, you'd best tell us."

Garrett Harding hesitated before replying. He looked taken aback, discomfited, but he nodded and made his reply.

"I am sure you know the fellow best, sir, but what you say changes nothing, for, as I have said, neither he nor his companions let us know their ideas for the future nor exactly where they intended to go."

"Well, sir," said Silston briskly, setting down his cup on the heavy table that stood on a large rug, "we will search the property, by your leave."

Once again, Garrett Harding paused before making his response.

"I would consider it your shame, sir, rather than mine that you do not believe me, but, if that is your will, by all means search."

Chapter 51

In Which A Discovery Is Made and There Is a Reckoning

Time had no meaning in the darkness of the winter store. All were shivering, trying to stop their teeth chattering and there was a paradoxical sense of despair mixed with suppressed, almost hysterical hope, but Will had taken heart from discovering that Jem had been hiding in the cellar since their arrival yesterday. He realised his poor friend must be freezing cold. Jem, who had also been buoyed by hearing Will's voice, sidled closer and whispered in his ear. On hearing his news, Will passed on the word, in a low hiss, into Archie's ear.

"There are three friends here."

As the slow realisation spread amongst them that they outnumbered those above who would do them harm, the six huddled close together. Darkness was a great leveler. It removed or negated feelings of difference and hierarchy and allowed their shared peril to become a unifying factor. It also had the practical effect of bringing their bodies into close enough contact that they began to warm each other. They listened to the search party doing its work above; heavy footsteps, shouts, bangings, and clatterings. If the searchers' success was measured by how much noise they made, then, Will thought, they surely would be named champions in their art.

At last, the sounds from above gradually died away. Distant voices could be heard and the six understood, without discussion, that the search had moved to the rough quarters the Hardings had built for their animals. Trusting that all the posse were engaged in the search, the fugitives exchanged stories. Jem, in subdued whispers, related his tale, starting by naming his companions, Millie and Ezekiel. He admitted no knowledge of what befell the others who ran with him, but told of the fires his mother had set, the flight, the pursuit, the terrible moment when the posse came for them, his band scattering, and the hours he, Millie, and Ezekiel crouched in a stream up to their waists under thick, low trees and bushes, shivering until the hue and cry died to nothing.

The Quakers, he whispered, did not hold with slavery and took the three of them in when they arrived, exhausted and starving. They fed them and gave them rest and, the moment Will and his companions were spotted, they hurried the three of them down into the darkness. Will then started his story, but stopped at the sound of voices approaching the house. They were coming back. He leaned forward in the darkness.

"They are not looking for you, Jem. If they find us, get you into the shadows!"

There was heated debate above, some shouting, Silston's voice, making threats. Then, ominously, a long silence save for the drone of a low voice, one Will did not know. After a pause, they heard Garrett Harding make a mumbled reply, though they could not catch the words. A foot began to thump hard on the floor above, someone was seeking the sound of hollowness. Jem's voice came out of the darkness, a harsh whisper.

"We are greater in number than they. We will fight."

He felt hands reaching out and touching him, squeezing his arms and hands in reply. They heard the sound of a piece of furniture being shifted, then a muffled, dragging sound. Like water escaping under pressure from a crack, streams of light hissed through the gaps in the hatch. Archie whispered defiantly:

"Let 'em take us. Hold back…"

But he was interrupted as, suddenly, brilliant light flooded in.

*

It was Gabriel Reed who had asked about a winter store. He had quietly noted to himself the Herculean work the family had done to clear their land, raise their crops, and husband their animals. He had also noted the organized way they had laid out their land and buildings, but it was not until they were back inside the house that the idea came to him of a cellar.

Silston, the crazy white man who loved the sound of his own voice, was raging at the family, cursing and telling them he knew they were not telling him everything. Reed waited patiently for the tirade to abate, then he turned his eyes on the older man and asked him about his winter store. When the man faltered and mumbled a poor excuse for a reply, he knew he was right; it had to be below their feet. He stamped his heel over the floor, but his efforts were hampered by the rug. Even so, he was sure he had heard the hollow sound of a basement. In seconds they had moved the table and the rug. When they lifted off the hatch, they saw a rude ladder leading down into the dark and, on the edge of the pool of light that spilled down, a pair of feet.

"There," said Reed bluntly, pointing downwards.

Silston's face broke into a triumphant grin. He drew the pistol from his belt and pointed it down the hole.

"Come up now or we start firing!" he crowed.

Blinking in the brilliance of the light, Will, Archie and Polly slowly climbed the ladder. Silston was standing back from the hole, covering them with his pistol. John Vertue also had his gun raised, whilst Sherwood had the Hardings herded into a corner, his pistol pointing at them.

"So, you blackguard," growled Silston, glancing at Garrett, "you had them all along."

Will stared at Vertue, his eyes asking the obvious question. Why? John shrugged and, was that the slightest of smiles? But, no, his face was impassive. The room was crowded, now that the three were up. Silston waved his gun at them, indicating the open door.

"Outside," he barked, before turning his attention to the Quaker family.

"You too. We have hanged one runaway already, methinks there will be more of that work to do today."

*

The three runaways were forced from the house at gunpoint. After the cold of the cellar, it was startlingly hot in the August sun and it took minutes for their eyes to adapt to the brightness. The posse herded their captives, pressing them with their pistols and hard words until they were standing with their backs to the fields and their faces to their aggressors. Louis Silston was in the mood for a sermon. He had waited long for his revenge and he was going to savour every minute of it, taking centre stage as he laid out his grievances and expectations for the "day's amusements", as he put it.

When the trap door had opened, Will had been pierced by a needle of fear as sharp as anything he had ever experienced in his life. Yet, now, half-listening as Polly's nemesis droned on, the fear melted away to be replaced by a strange hypnotic numbness. His mind was hazy and he found himself thinking back on what he had been through to find Polly, all the suffering and hardship, and for what? To be hanged here, at the border of freedom? To lose Polly? It felt like a bad joke life was playing on him as if the whole of the last two years had been a grand, elaborate confidence trick.

A harsh laugh brought him back to reality. Silston's face was a picture of mirthful smugness. He was berating Garrett Harding for harbouring "the criminals".

"You chose a path of lawlessness, my friend," he said, clearly enjoying himself. "You chose to comfort criminals and fugitives, feeding them, giving them succour, and then hiding them. When you were challenged by a rightful representative of the law of this colony, my good self, you lied, sir. You could have trodden the righteous path and given up these convicts and outlaws, but you chose the devil's way and now you face the noose."

"God will be my judge, sir," said Garrett quietly. His face, as ever, was impassive. "However, I would entreat you recognize that my wife and son were not complicit in hiding these poor people."

"Poor people?" Silston exploded. "You are a naïf, sir, and a fool and must suffer the consequences."

In a moment, the soft dew of Will's stupefaction evaporated in the unforgiving sun of Silston's aggressive and hateful words. It was as if he had awoken from a hundred years of sleep. A ferocious sense of injustice boiled within him, tightening the sinews in his neck and shoulders, tensing every muscle in his body, a stark, naked emotion. He was overtaken by raw fury at the unfairness of life. But he did not move. He mastered the rage and started calculating odds. Could six take on four? The four were armed and fired up by their anger or greed or desire for violence or whatever it was that made them do what they were planning to do. And would the Hardings fight? What might it take for the peace-loving family not to turn the other cheek? As quickly as it had bloomed, his rage withered. He felt suddenly so weak he thought he might fall down. Where was his courage? Where was the righteous anger that had sparked his attack on the murderer, Makepeace, in Newgate?

"You pretend Christian values, Harding," Silston was saying, "yet you break God's laws as well the Colony's. No Christian you, sir. No, a devil-worshipper, I would hazard."

Zachariah, who until now had remained absolutely still, took a step forward, his chin jutting out in defiance. Silston swung his pistol barrel up to point it at his chest.

"Not a step further, villain or I'll drop you where you stand!" Garrett reached out and pulled his son back. "Well, sir, your son does not seem to me to be meek. I believe you people to be all as guilty as each other. Enough of talk. Reed, get the ropes from the horses, it is time."

"Mr. Silston?"

It was Polly's voice. Will had almost forgotten she was standing next to him. He turned to look at her and saw that Archie was also watching her.

"Ah, the pretty Miss Pruitt. No doubt you are going to claim your innocence?"

"Mayhap, sir, but I would ask you what it is you think we have done, sir? I mean, if we are to die, should we not first be told of the accusations against us? Should we not be tried?"

"You mean apart from the cold-blooded murder of Mr. Garland's overseer, breaking the bonds of your conviction and sentence and, I have no doubt, helping foment a rebellion of the blackamoors? Oh, you know full-well what you did, whore. You and your miserable consort here killed my Abigail."

The toll of months of repressed anger, anger that had been lovingly coddled and nurtured in his breast, was apparent as his face turned red, his eyes closed to slits and his mouth hardened into a thin line.

"No, sir," said Polly, her voice gentle, but firm. "No, sir, that is wrong. As God is my witness…"

"As God is her witness, gentlemen!" His pent-up feelings burst forth as a mocking laugh, loud and boorish. "What lies now?"

"Sir, this is the truth. On that day thieves were being chased by the crowd and myself, Will and mistress Abigail got in their way. One pushed a pocket-watch into my hand, the other stabbed my poor mistress…"

"And yet, no one could be found to speak at your trial to corroborate your story. Ah yes, I see you blanch, but I know what I know, girl. My man spoke with the clerk of the court and the Newgate jailer…"

"Every word Polly speaks is true," Will snarled through gritted teeth.

"So says another thief, who, by his own admission at the Bailey, stole a precious text, worth ten shillings. Yes, sir, we know all about you, too." He turned to Vertue. "And these wretches expect us to believe them?"

There were tears in Polly's eyes. She rubbed her hand roughly across her face and stood up straight.

"She would never have married you," she said hoarsely. "She hated you. She knew what you did to Clarice Farquarson, she knew you for what…"

"Silence!" roared Silston, panting, his gun hand trembling. "Not another word."

Undaunted, Polly continued. "I can see you will never believe what we say, but I would like Mr. and Mrs. Harding to know, we are not guilty of Abigail's murder, nor am I a thief." She took a breath and, fighting back her tears, she looked directly into Sara's eyes and said, "thank you, mam."

"I believe you, child," said Sara with a rare smile, "and God shall be your kindly judge, as he will be ours."

"Excellent, excellent, she believes!" mocked Silston.

"Sir, with respect," said John Vertue, his voice taut and high-pitched, "can we just get on? Reed has the ropes and I for one would like to see an end to this business."

Silston gave Vertue a sly grin and nodded.

"Wanting to get your hands on that reward, eh, Vertue? Can't wait to string 'em up, eh?"

Chapter 52

In Which We Witness the Beginning of The End

The Indian is leading one of the horses to a tall tree behind the house. I think I am shocked so by what is happening that my mind has left this world, for I am wondering what the name for this tree is and wishing Will could tell me. Vertue, I notice, is standing beside his master with his pistol at the ready and he has a grin on his face. He is enjoying this. How could Will think this devil a friend? The one called Reed has dropped two ropes on the ground and is throwing the third over a low branch. I am like a statue; my body is rigid; I feel I am in a dream as I watch him tying a noose. Even if I tried to move, I do not think I could.

The three with guns herd us, with the Hardings, towards the tree until we are close. We stand together, miserable. The Iroquois's work is done. He moves the horse so that it is under the branch. I want to scream at the evil of this, but I know there will be no justice gained by howling like a dog if justice is to be gained at all.

"I think we will start with the lying murderess," says Silston jerking his pistol towards me.

There is, of a sudden, a freeze in my guts and I feel my face go cold and I am swaying like a tree in the breeze. I am trembling all over, but fear is the lesser thing for I am filled with righteous fury. Vertue has grabbed my arm, his grip hard and strong and, though my legs are weak as water, he is dragging me towards the rope.

"Sir, you know this is not right," I say.

My voice sounds not like me, it is husky, but I hear a power in it, the power of right. It is as if I had not spoken, for Silston and his men ignore me. Vertue pushes hard against my arm as he bears down, causing me to slump to the side as I stagger forward. He is pointing his pistol at Will.

"You will be cursed by God for this, Silston!"

I am shouting at him, though in my mind I am paying out my innocence in humble statements, as if to a judge. Vertue has me stumbling, tugging roughly, shaking me when I try to resist. He brings me up to the horse. How strange the mind of a human: now, clear as clear, I am at the hanging with Will and Abigail, seeing those men on the cart with nooses around their necks. Did I really see that? I cannot recall. I see my Abigail, smiling at me. I am brushing her beautiful hair, she lays her hand on mine, as she never did in life. We kiss, as we never did.

"I will not beg," I shout again. "As God is my witness, I am innocent of Abigail's murder. I would never…"

I cannot finish, for Reed is lifting the noose to slip it over my head. I will not go without a fight. I will make them pay. I kick him in the legs and he grunts, but hardly moves. I whip around and lash out with my free hand at Vertue. He ducks away, always keeping his grip on my arm, where the bruises are already deep. I spit at Vertue, but miss his face. The Indian hits me in the back of the head, a slap not a punch, but it brings stars to my eyes. I swing with my leg raised and I catch him again, this time on his thigh. He grabs my foot before it can drop and pushes me back into Vertue who grabs me with both hands. He has dropped his pistol; I see it at my feet. I try to kick it, but Vertue pulls my arms back so that I am a trussed chicken. Reed is behind me and he punches me in the back, low, and a crushing pain shoots through my guts to my belly. I sag in Vertue's hands, but still, I wriggle.

"I am innocent!" I yell.

Vertue pushes me up against the tree and I feel Reed move beside him. I feel his fingers on me as he ties my hands behind me. I am yanked back, sudden like, and there is the noose over my head before I know it. I hear Silston bellowing.

"Stay or we fire!"

I come to myself and look over at the house. The Hardings have been brought to stand with Will and Archie and all are transfixed, under the gaze of Silston and Sherwood's pistols. I think Will has moved out of the line, but he is still now.

"Archie!" I scream. There is the scream, at last, that scream of terror and it is for Archie.

Tears are streaming down my cheeks. Reed tightens the noose and steps away.

"Take me first!" I hear Will cry out.

"Or me, take me!" echoed Archie.

Silston laughs. "Two martyrs for you, Polly Pruitt." Oh, how I hate that sneering voice. I hate it and I hate him, hate him, hate him.

"No, my fine young friends," says he. "As part of your sentence, you shall watch, as your pretty accomplice dies. I have seen how you both covet the girl. You can watch as she pisses herself while she slowly strangles. Her death will be a small death inside you before your own."

The two men have the measure of me now and even though I lash out with my feet, it is quick work to manhandle me into the saddle.

Everything I see from up here is changed. Archie and Will, the Hardings, their house, the fields, the trees and mountains in the distance, all is there, yet it is different; brighter, sharper, clearer like I suppose I might see through looking-glasses. Even the colours are stronger and I feel I can hear every tiny creak of the horse's leathers, every distant bird. I am numb. I do not want to cry. I don't want Silston to get pleasure from my sorrow, but it is all so unfair I cannot help myself.

"No, no." I hear my voice, a tiny breath, a breeze in the trees.

Reed has the free end of the rope and walks behind me. I cannot see him, but my neck feels him pulling on the rope until he is satisfied that it is tight enough. All is ready. The horse is jittery and steps back and then forward again and like a Bedlamite I pray that he may stay still in case I fall off. I almost laugh then at my lunacy for they will drop me in moments anyway. I look across the short distance to those who were my friends in this life and silently wish them goodbye. They stand, miserable and horrified. Then, it is as if a curtain has been drawn; everything in my mind is changing. The strength I felt, the anger, is flying away. My breath comes fast, faster, and faster so that I think I might faint. Do not let him see my fear. Panting, quicker, faster, shorter.

"Time for the last dance, darling," says Vertue.

Oh, God, oh, please God, no, no, no…

*

Vertue's cruel words broke something inside Will; the casual violence of his once friend's pronouncement was too much and the white heat

382

of his rage at this final betrayal smashed through his wall of self-protection. He let out an animal roar and leaped forward. An outburst of wronged hatred and anger, it was not planned and anything could have happened. As it was, many things did happen, very quickly and in ways none could have expected.

Sherwood had his pistol on the Hardings, but was only half-watching them, regularly turning his head in fascination at the proceedings. Silston was looking at Vertue. As Will ran to cross the five long steps that separated the captives from the captors, Silston swung his pistol and fired; a brilliant flash from the pistol's pan; a sharp crack of the report. Will's head jerked sideways and his body spun around, as if on a puppeteer's string. He crashed to the ground, rolling once onto his side, there to lie still. Archie was already running. Vertue saw him coming and turned his pistol. Polly screamed. Vertue pulled the trigger, but his pistol misfired. There was no flash from his pan. Archie was on him.

Zachariah was on the move. Sherwood had taken an instinctive step towards Will as he had started moving, but, when he was felled, he turned his pistol back towards the Hardings. He was too late. Zachariah ploughed into him, forcing the pistol up into Sherwood's face where it exploded in another violent flash. Sherwood screamed, as the powder in the pistol's pan detonated into his eyes. Silston dropped his pistol and dragged his sword from its scabbard. In that same instant, with shouts, screams and wild barking, three figures and a dog burst from the house. Jem was brandishing a stout piece of firewood; Ezekiel had a kitchen knife in his hand and Millie was holding a skillet high above her head.

At the first shot, the horse on which Polly had been trying to stay absolutely still, started, lunged forward, and then backwards. When Sherwood's pistol went off, the animal reared and Polly slid sickeningly backwards with a despairing groan. The horse trotted away, leaving Polly dangling from the bough. Garrett Harding had been watching her, marvelling at her courage and now he ran towards her, his arms pounding up and down. As he moved, Silston moved too. He stepped back, trying to block the older man's way, but Garrett was a big man and knocked Silston aside before the sword could come into play.

Polly was pedalling the air, twisting in a slow circle. Her face was already turning puce. Garrett ran up to her and threw his arms around her, raising her up as high as he could manage, taking her full weight. She gasped air into her starved lungs and began to cough violently. Joss was at Garret's feet, barking crazily and pouncing to and fro.

Archie was getting the worst of it with Vertue. The bigger man had rolled on top of him and was trying to release a dagger from his belt. His pistol lay useless behind them. Three paces away, Will lay absolutely still. Silston had regained his balance and was looking wildly around.

"Reed! Do something!"

The Iroquois had been standing back, watching, his knife in his hand. Now he charged towards Archie and Vertue. The horse that had borne Polly whinnied and stepped sideways in front of Reed, blocking him as Joss leaped towards the Iroquois, baring his teeth and growling. Millie ran past Sara Harding, who was standing motionless, watching in horror with her hands to her face. The girl did not hesitate. She ran up to Sherwood, who was staggering and moaning, his hands clawing at his eyes. She hit him hard on the back of the head with the pan and he fell, a pole-axed ox.

"The rope," shouted Garrett, "someone cut the rope."

Zachariah was running to intercept Reed. The Indian saw him the moment before he reached Archie and Vertue where they grappled on the ground. He turned to face the young man and both men came to a stop. Reed crouched, his left arm out his right hand holding the knife towards Zachariah. Joss stood with his head low, barking loudly at the scout. Jem ran up to stand with Zachariah and together they advanced on Reed.

On the ground, Vertue had his hand on his knife hilt and was pulling it from his belt. He bore down with all his weight on Archie, his right arm across the younger man's throat. Vertue had his knife in his hand and was slowly twisting it round in his grip. Archie's right hand was at Vertue's neck, squeezing while, with his left, he pounded into Vertue's side. The bigger man's face had turned red and his breathing was hoarse and loud, but now he was ready for the final strike. He raised his knife, meaning to plunge it into Archie's eye. The Indian loosed his grip on Vertue's neck and grabbed his wrist to stay the blow.

Ezekiel had run to the horse, which stood a few feet away from Garrett and Polly. He led it quickly to Garrett's side, clambered into the saddle, and slashed at the rope, once, twice, three times before the blade cut through to release Polly's body into Garrett's arms.

Reed, not liking how the odds had changed, was backing away from Jem and Zachariah. With each step he took backwards, Joss advanced on him. Silston seemed to have been in a daze, a spectator for the last few seconds. Now he came to himself and strode towards Archie and Vertue struggling on the ground. His sudden movement caught Joss's attention. The hound loped forward, snarling at Silston, but Louis saw him coming and lashed out with a vicious kick that caught the dog full square on his face. Turning to the pair on the ground, Silston raised his sword above his head, ready to strike at Archie's face.

"Fucking savage!"

There came the loud report of a pistol and Silston staggered two steps backwards. His sword arm went limp, the weapon fell to the ground. He looked in shock at his chest, where a bloom of red was spreading rapidly. His hand strayed towards the stain. For a moment he was immobile before his legs buckled and he fell forwards onto his face, landing with a thud in a small cloud of dust. Behind Archie and Vertue, Jem stood holding Vertue's pistol. On the second try, it had fired.

Surprised by the explosion just behind his head, John Vertue had flinched and Archie, feeling his aggressor's momentary hesitation, bucked, kicked, and reared, knocking the bigger man off balance. Millie had run to his side, and, as Vertue lurched sideways, she hit him with the frying pan, a forceful blow that struck both his jaw and clavicle, shattering the narrow bone. Archie squirmed to his feet as Vertue struggled onto his front and came onto all fours.

Archie lunged forward, grabbed Vertue's knife hand, and swung it upwards, as he stepped in close and bit hard into the big man's ear. Vertue screamed. His empty hand flew to his head, shielding his ear from further insult. Blood trickled between his fingers. Archie twisted round, still holding Vertue's knife hand in an adrenalin-fuelled grip.

With his free hand, he grasped the big man's little finger and yanked it viciously, until he heard it snap. The knife fell into his hand and he grasped it, two fingers on the haft and two fingers wrapped around the blade. He had no time to change his grip; instead, he swiveled around and thrust the shortened blade into Vertue's neck. The other groaned and staggered sideways. The blade had sliced into Archie's fingers, but he was able to change his grip enough to stab again and then again, this time with the full length of the blade. Now blood spurted from Vertue's neck in a horrifying arc. He gasped and wrapped his fingers around the wound, but his vital fluid would not be stayed. He fell to his knees.

He raised his eyes and looked at Archie. His face was twisted in shock. He supported his weight on his knees and one hand while the other squeezed uselessly at his neck. His mouth moved, but no words came, then he fell onto his face where he lay still, as his blood soaked into the desert-dry, summer ground.

When Jem had picked up Vertue's pistol, Zachariah had continued to advance on Reed. Knowing a lost fight when he saw it, the Iroquois turned and ran like a hare to the horse that had wandered to stand in front of the Harding's rough byre. The two younger men raced after him, Jem yelling in frustration and fury. Launching himself into the saddle, Reed kicked hard and galloped away. The still morning had been rent for a few furious, frenzied minutes by screams, grunts, curses, and gun-shots, but now there was silence, broken only by the rapidly receding drum beat of Reed's horse's hooves. Will, Silston, Vertue, Joss, and Sherwood all lay still.

It was Polly who moved first. With her right hand on her neck, softly massaging, she walked slowly to where Will lay and gently lowered herself beside him. There was a dark brown patch of drying blood beneath his head.

"Oh, Will," she murmured.

Chapter 53

In Which the Fragments of Tragedy Are Pieced Roughly Together

In the immediate aftermath of the small, violent, and very short battle, people broke off, in shock and horror, into small groups. The three Hardings huddled around Sherwood and Jem, Millie and Ezekiel waited by the sycamore. Archie moved first to Joss, who was already struggling back to his feet.

"Hard head you got, old feller," he muttered before shuffling to stand close to Polly where she sat with Will.

"What we do now?" Ezekiel wanted to know.

They had only been at the Hardings for two nights before Polly, Will, and Archie had shown up, regaining their strength, eating well, and sleeping as they could. There had been no other plan, in the first days of Jem's obsession with escape, than simply running to the west. It had been Will who had the vision in his head of what their life would be once they had traversed the Blue Ridge. Now it was clear that, even in this remote place, a posse could track them down.

"We go on," Jem replied, keeping his voice low. He was badly shaken by Will's fall and, like all the others, waited in hope that his friend would recover. It would seem a travesty to him to not go on with Will over the Blue Ridge to that faraway heaven his friend had first described to him up on the tobacco barn roof.

"Wid dem?" Millie had wanted to know. She did not have to specify whom she meant.

"Yes, mam, wid them; they our best hope. Now we lost all our others, we need numbers, Millie. When Will is up an' fine again, we gonna climb them…"

"You think he gonna be fine?" Ezekiel interrupted.

"He tough, gonna pull through, like I did from the whippin'"

There was a soft murmur of voices from the house. The three of them looked across. Garrett was talking quietly to his family, Zachariah nodding, and Sara, in her habitual pose, standing straight, her arms crossed.

"Doan know 'f I wanna stay wid dem."

"Zeke, what you gonna do? Strike out on you own? Up dem mount'ns when you doan know where you goin'? You gonna be dead 'fore you know it. An' you, Millie, you staying or you goin'?"

"I wid you, Jem," the young woman said.

Millie had always been a quiet, subservient girl, often afraid of willful ghosts that seemed to haunt her and spirits of the forest she believed to be offended by the sacrilegious felling of so many trees by the planters, but her critical part in the battle seemed to have imbued her with new strength and resolution. Her voice, usually soft, sounded out strong and confident.

"You brung us this far, Jem. I happy to go wid you."

"That settled then," said Jem not without some measure of pride and pleasure, for Millie was a comely woman.

*

Will is breathing and I thank God. I am all a'tremble and I feel a horrible weakness in my limbs. I settle lower to the ground and make myself be strong. Around me I feel people moving, talking in low tones. They will do what they must do, but I cannot take my eyes from this poor boy's face. It is covered in a smear of dust thickened by sweat. His hair too is a field of dust and dirt and matted on the side with the black of his blood. I lift his head and my stomach twists and I think I am to be sick, for there is blood dripping still, but I swallow hard and gasp in great breaths. There is so much blood.

"Oh, Will," says I.

The sound I make is strange, rasping, hoarse and I understand it is the rope that has done this and there is a catch in my voice like I am to cry. His eyes are closed and his breaths come in ragged little gasps, yet I feel in my heart he can hear me.

"You've been shot, my poor dear," I say in a little whisper, bending to his face. "That bugger Silston shot you, Will."

I don't like bad words, but I cannot help myself. One little word is a single drop of poison in the ocean of badness that has almost drowned us all.

"The good Lord has spared you, Will. If you open your eyes, you shall see that you have saved me."

Archie and Sara have walked to my side and I feel his hand on my shoulder. He says nothing; just him being there is a comfort to me. I hear voices, movements, but I cannot take my eyes from Will. He will open his eyes at any moment, I know.

"Tell us another of your stories, Will," I whisper. "Tell us about your poor ma and how you learned to love the trees in that wood by your house. Tell us again about kind Sam Royston and his goodwife Betsy and that French fellow, Auggie; how the old cove's tales of this wild place gave you the courage to plan our escape. Will, please, my dear," I say, stroking his face.

I could not love this fellow, once proud and tall, his yellow hair, his strong face, but I have come to like him well enough and trust him. I wish for him to wake so that I can tell him all these things. What would I say to him? I would say I have had much time to think since the night we ran from Garland's. It was not my choice to be here today, not what I wanted for my life. I bend close to his ear.

"I had a hard start in life and maybe you did too, Will Staples. I was saved by the Collitons, they took me in and I became maid to Abigail. Will, I never lived so fine. We was all treated well in that house. I had good clothes, ate good food, even had a glass of Madeira or French wine on holidays. I shared a bed, but it was warm and we even had our own little fireplace in winter. And Abigail was kind to me.

"I loved that girl, Will. Yes, she was a caution betimes, fiery and willful her mother called her and she was like to drive me to Bedlam on occasion, but she had spirit, the best-hearted girl who truly made me her friend. She was the only person, apart from my poor sister Laura, the only person I had ever loved and I miss her, Will. Sometimes my heart aches for her and the love I held close to my breast. And I miss that life and curse the name and soul of Louis Silston, for that devil was the cause of Abigail's sorrow. I would do anything to get that life back, but that is all gone.

"I have thought about what you said and you were right, Will; no point in running back to London. Even if I wasn't caught, there would be little chance of work as a maid without letters. Maybe with a woman of the middling sort, but that would be poor fare and a drudge, for sure. No sparkle, no fun like life was with my Abigail. But, Will, though I never thought to, I have come to like you. You are a good man and I have met few enough of them in my life. Most have been villains beneath their smiles. I know you think you love me and you are brave too, you and Archie both. I don't love you, Will, but I will say this, I ain't never been a farmer, but I will get on with it. I'll try and maybe we can make it work if the militia don't come for us and the Indians don't kill us in our beds."

Someone touches my shoulder and I look up at Sara. She is bending over me and I see the others standing behind her, all of them. Even old Joss is there. She gives me a strange little smile.

"He's gone, Polly," she says, very soft.

I shake my head, no, and look at his face, wait for his breath, wait now, wait, just wait, Polly says I to myself, wait and that breath will come.

*

Tobias Sherwood had not been killed by Millie's blow to his head. Sara and Millie tended to him under the shade of the sycamore tree where they had dragged him. When he regained consciousness, he had first been confused and disorientated and then, on remembering that he was blind, emotional, and angry. He had thrashed around, crying out whilst holding his hand to his face.

"Oh, Lord above, I never thought…" he shouted. "Dear Christ, what have I done to deserve this darkness?"

"Shush," Sara had whispered in his ear. "Be still now, man. Let yourself lie in God's hands, let Him care for you, as we are caring for you."

In time the two women calmed him and he allowed them to bathe his eyes and clean his face. Once he was still, he realised that, perhaps, all was not lost. Gradually the darkness was lightening to grey. He could see shapes and movements with his left eye, although in his right eye was only blackness. While the women worked on him, the men stood around, dazed, quietly talking of what needed doing and what must come next.

"What of this fellow?" Archie asked Garrett, indicating Sherwood with the women under the sycamore tree.

"'Tis a conundrum," replied Garrett distractedly. He turned to gaze into the distance.

"We cain't let 'im go. No sayin' who he may bring back."

"That is true, that is true. Well, I must needs speak with Sara, but he could stay here, work his keep. There is always more to be done and we are fortunate in having enough to feed him if he will countenance staying."

The conversation was left there and Garrett, Zachariah, Jem, Ezekiel, and Archie worked the rest of the morning with picks and long-handled shovels to dig two graves in the hard-packed, dry summer soil. They chose a patch of ground behind the byre, partially shaded by the crude structure, out of the general way of things and far from the two family graves.

It was slow, hot work. They had to loosen the soil with the pickaxes and scoop out small portions of dusty loam. Before long, their clothes were soaked in sweat and they had to stop many times for water. As they dug, Garrett argued that they should make crosses to mark the graves as a sign of respect, but Archie and Jem resisted this suggestion. To them, anything that marked out the place where their aggressors lay was asking for trouble. What, they asked, if more pursuers came? How would graves, on a relatively new farm, at the outer border of the colony be explained? After much debate Garrett was persuaded, though it felt ungodly to him, that it was in his and his family's best interest to leave the graves unmarked and let the ground lie fallow, turning to grass and weeds.

Over by the hanging tree, Silston's, Vertue's, and Will's blood, already brown and dried up, stained the innocent ground of the farm. The gravediggers scraped it up and threw it into one of the graves before moving the bodies into their final resting places. Because they feared the arrival of yet more pursuers, Garland's men or the militia, they had had no time to clean up the corpses so the marks of violent death were still horribly obvious. Slowly they filled in the graves, packing the earth once they were half full, by treading it down before finishing the job. Zachariah used a rake to flatten the last of the earth and spread the excess soil around.

The men stood then at the heads of the graves and gazed out eastwards across the Harding's holding. A heat haze had gathered in the far distance where the shallow hills tumbled down, tree-clad, to the valley below. The air above the fields rippled like silk in a breeze. High in the sky, a large bird of prey circled on outspread wings.

"Will we say some words?" asked Jem.

"We Quakers don't normally hold with that sort of thing," said Garrett softly, "but you may say something if the spirit is in you to do so."

Jem stood silent for some moments shaking his head slowly from side to side. Finally, he said: "Wouldn't know what to say."

"We'll leave them to their peace then," said Garrett.

They then began the hardest pilgrimage of the day; the slow walk to the family graves where they had laid Will's body in waiting. Here they dug the third grave, each taking a turn to loosen the soil and dig until it was time. Polly had washed his face and rinsed the blood from Will's wound and hair. Though his face was a grey-white, he looked at peace, as if he had dropped off to sleep after a good day's work. With great care, Archie, Jem, and Zachariah lifted the corpse and lowered it gently into the grave.

When all was ready, Polly, Sara, and Millie joined them and they all stood together, ranged around the grave, silent, steadfast, and sad. No one said anything, no one had the heart, but, at last, Polly bent, dug her hand into the mound of soil, and threw a handful onto Will's feet.

"Goodbye, friend," she whispered.

Chapter 54

In Which The Travellers Start the Final Journey

They fed Sherwood and left him tied up in the byre. Earlier, Garrett Harding had spent some time with the man, under the sycamore tree, quietly and patiently discussing his future. He was a convict servant of Garland's, committed to the transports some nine years earlier with a fourteen-year sentence for stealing chickens to feed his starving family. He claimed he had been well regarded as a useful field hand on the Garland estate, having worked all his life as a farm labourer. He also claimed that he had only been selected as a member of the posse because he was a good horseman and known for his strength and resilience.

When they fell to discussing their plans it was agreed by all except Millie that Sherwood should stay with the Hardings and be offered the chance to live and work with them rather than return to Garland's estate. Millie was adamant that the man could not be trusted and would bring ruin on the Hardings and another posse, maybe even the militia, onto the escapee's trail. Polly, sick of all the violence and horror, suggested that Millie might like to be the man's executioner herself and, after a heated argument, Millie reluctantly agreed that even she, with her fear of capture and the brutal reprisals that would mean, did not want the man's blood on her hands. It was dark by the time Garrett and Zachariah returned to the cowshed to put their proposals to Sherwood. When they came back it was with the news that Garland's man seemed not to want to be Garland's man anymore, but wanted to think about their offer overnight.

Though Will was gone, all of the runaways agreed that their best chance of freedom was to see out his vision. From the outset, Jem and Millie were enthusiastic about continuing over the mountains; they had nothing to lose by forging on into the new territory and, potentially, everything to gain. Ezekiel was happy to cede his vote to Jem, so that was three in favour of crossing the Blue Ridge. Only Archie and Polly seemed uncertain. Polly, still in shock from what had passed that day, seemed confused and asked Garrett to tell them all he knew of the place over the mountains.

The land on the other side was called, by the Indians, Shenandoah, he told them. The Hardings had heard that the Governor had sent a party in 1716 through one of the gaps high in the Blue Ridge, to explore and they found a fine valley, wide and long, with good soil. He said the place was found to be well watered by rivers and streams, but had been deemed, at the time, too remote for settlement and too close to French territory. This was as much as Garrett knew for sure, but Archie appeared buoyed by the information of the valley's apparent riches. Before they retired for the night, it was agreed that the five of them would continue on, taking two of the posse's horses and leaving Sherwood's with the Hardings.

The next morning, Sara was all business and calm. She prepared a good breakfast for all, set out, again, on the ground outside the house, and Sherwood was brought to join them. His vision was still poor, though he could see well enough to walk unaided from the byre, and, far from being disgruntled or angry with Zachariah for causing his blindness, he happily agreed to take the Hardings up on their offer.

When the meal was done, everyone helped to load up the two horses with supplies from the Harding's stores: fresh food and dried meats; corn, rye and wheat seed and beans and peas for planting; two or three rudimentary tools, including the Harding's second-best axe; a cock and two hens, tied and bundled and all the powder and shot they had gleaned from the saddle bags of the posse.

"If'n it's all right wid you," Jem said to Polly, "I'd like tuh take on Will's tools. That boy taught me some and I'd regard it mighty well if'n I can have 'em."

Polly glanced at Archie who nodded.

"I think Will would have liked that, Jem," she said, putting her hand on his arm.

Archie bemoaned the fact that the search party had brought no muskets with them, which would have been better for hunting, but the pistols would be good protection. Despite the soreness of her throat, it was Polly who said their goodbyes.

"You have been true Christians," she told the Hardings, "and we thank you for all you have done. I feel ashamed we brought this trouble on you…no, let me say it," she added quickly as Garrett tried to interrupt. "You could not have done more for us and I trust in my heart and in the eyes of God that Mr. Sherwood here will thank you for the home are giving him and that he will not betray you." Here she threw a meaningful glance at Sherwood. "I know his life with you will be better in every way than service under Garland."

With that and after much shaking of hands and wishes of good luck and God's blessings, Archie, with Joss beside him, Polly, Jem, Millie and Ezekiel set off. They led the horses up the shallow slope, through the sparse trees behind the house towards the denser forestry ahead that marked the start of their long climb. For Polly, it was the saddest moment since Abigail's death, leaving Will behind. He had been the architect of their escape and he had, she knew now, truly loved her. She walked close to Archie, who was leading one of the horses. Jem followed with the other and Millie and Ezekiel.

"Don't believe we'd ever see that missus Harding shed a tear, though we wait a hunnerd years," Archie said with a smile. "Strong woman. You too, Polly, not many stronger'n you."

Polly nodded an acknowledgement. She did not feel strong. Her neck was badly bruised and the rope burns were livid red. Her voice, which she was trying to protect by not speaking unless she had to, sounded like it belonged to someone else, some much older, rougher person. She had only slept fitfully and wondered if she was capable of a full day's trek, but she smiled at Archie, took his hand, and gave it a squeeze.

*

I walked with Jem today, while the two young slaves chattered to Archie. He's a deep one that man and I am surprised at how good is his English. He told me how Will taught him woodwork and how proud he is to be the keeper of his friend's bag of tools. We laughed together too something I never thought to do with one of these dark people, so unsure of them was I when I first came to this country. And then he told me about his mother. He told us her name, Ruth, and right proud of her he was. I thought, from his troubled face, she must be dead and asked if he often thought of her and that was when his eyes filled and his face fell for it seems she was with him when they all escaped, but was injured and had to be left behind. Poor man has no idea what has happened to her; so, he says to me that he thinks of her many times every day, and each time it gives him pain. Had to wipe away a tear, I did, for I could see the fellow was broken-hearted.

It is late afternoon now and the sky, what I see of it between the branches, is turning from bright blue to grey. The going has been slow, for the woodland is thick with undergrowth that makes us work hard to find a path. The horses are tired and hungry, I daresay, though there is little here for them, and we humans are becoming forlorn with tiredness and our own need for sustenance. Archie suggests we must find a place to stop for the night before it gets too dark to see our way and all agree heartily.

Within an hour we find a place, a small clearing with some scrub grass that will please the horses. I managed to walk most of the morning, but these last hours I have been riding as Archie was adamant that I needed the rest to recover myself. I was pleased for his kindness, but now I am only glad to get out of the saddle. Our night place is a pretty glade with some saplings and enough ground for us to spread ourselves for sleep. The two bedrolls we had from the Hardings, beds they insisted we bring for Millie and me, are laid on the ground. With axe and knife Ezekiel and Jem knock down the low bushes to make enough flat ground for the three men to lie, while Archie, ever watchful, scouts the area around our clearing. Such a good man and a comfort.

The light is going fast. We tie the horses and unsaddle them, then sit, making a circle on the ground, and share out apples, cold pork – we will keep the dried meats for another day – cold boiled eggs, and cornbread from Sara's oven. We still have fresh water left in the stoppered jug that Garrett gave us. It is a feast. There is not much talk, as we chew our way through the provisions. Near the end of our meal, when the sun has gone and the sky we can see through the trees is all blazing reds, oranges, and flowery pinks, Joss, who's been playing dead, sits bolt up and snuffles at the air. Archie is up too and he touches his ear. I believe he is telling us he has heard something.

We all strain to hear, eyes wide, fear on some of our faces, but my ears are filled only with the usual chorus of insect life and the soft sound of one of the horses, as it moves around slowly on its tether. I swallow my last mouthful and hold my breath. Then, I hear it, the sounds of movement through the scrub. Something is coming towards us, blundering noisily without care or fear. I am on my feet and dizzy from rising too fast. I put out my hand to Jem beside me and hold his shoulder. He looks at me concerned, but I shake my head, trying to tell him, without words, that I will be all right. Archie looks around our circle. We are all standing. He waves us back under the trees. The sounds are getting louder. It surely must be more than one man, I think. We retreat slowly, quietly to the trees away from where the sound comes, Archie leading Joss, his pistol in his hand. Jem leaves my side and pulls another pistol silently from its saddle holster.

The noises are very loud now, crashings and crackings of branch and bush. They are close, whoever they are. We all peer into the trees, but the light will be gone like a snuffed candle in moments. I see nothing. I feel like shouting; this cannot be happening again. I can only just see the far side of the clearing, now that the sun is so low and the trees screen its weak light. I find I am leaning forward, straining to see when, out of the gloom comes a shape, black as the Harding's cellar. It is enormous. Joss barks once, loud like a gunshot. The horses are scaring, stamping, and turning on their tethers, desperate to see what has come, frightened out of their wits. Even in the dark, I can see the whites of their bulging eyes.

I pray that Archie and Jem will discharge their weapons, without waiting to see what this monster is, for monster it must be. I have never seen anything so great in size, so dark. I can sense its power from across the glade. Out of the corner of my eye, I see Millie pressing backwards into the trees. Archie and Jem are holding their ground, but I can see terror in Ezekiel's face. Jem raises his gun.

"Wait!" Archie says in a harsh hiss. Jem lowers the weapon. One of the horses whinnies in fright.

"Bear," says Archie and as he speaks, the blackness halts and we all hear the deep rumble of a growl.

"Not sure these guns'll bring him down," says he softly. "Gotta try an' scare him."

I marvel that he walks forward towards the beast. This surely is madness. His gun hangs at his side. Jem and Ezekiel are still pointing their weapons at the bear.

"Don't shoot," says Archie.

He creeps forward as if sensing the urgency of our fear. Joss is at his side, growling and snarling. The bear has stopped near the bedrolls we laid out earlier. Archie has stopped too. My heart and head are both pounding and I feel faint. Archie says something I can't hear. The beast does not respond. It is so black that I cannot make out its features, but I can see the grey of its snout. Archie speaks again. With a monstrous roar, the bear rears up on its hind legs. Its front paws are enormous, bigger than a man's head. Its voice shakes the trees, rumbles through the very ground on which we stand, echoes about the forest. Joss barks, again and again, his noise small next to the bear's roars.

"Don't shoot!" cries Archie again. "Wing him and he could go crazy."

He does not move. Still, the bear is standing like a human, taller by several heads than the man who stands before him. We all wait, our breaths stopped in our chests, our hearts playing a drummer's chorus. I know I must lie down soon or I will collapse. As if he can bear it no more, Joss jumps forward, right under the bear, and barks like a hound from Hell, over and over. There's spit flying from the stupid old dog's mouth and his head bobs with each bark. With a grunt, the bear drops on all fours, turns and, as if it had never been there, is gone, gone back the way it came, folding itself into the darkness beyond. It feels like a Cheapside market magician's trick. Archie lets out a long low breath and grabs Joss, giving him a shake and a hefty pat and laughing out loud.

"You done it, old feller," he shouts and then turns back to look at us through the deepening gloom.

"I'm a'thinkin' that was Machk, my old friend, come to wish us well in Shenandoah," he says with a boyish grin. It is the first time I have seen him smile for many a long, weary day, but I think to myself; *if there are any ghosts with us here, it surely must be Will.*

Chapter 55

In Which the End Comes With a New Beginning

I was scared they would be coming for us, not being able to get Silston's terrible hateful face out of my mind and feeling the bruising of my neck and voice, and I was worried that monster bear would be back for a meal on one of us, so I wanted us to take turns to watch. The others agreed with me, though Archie was sure that his old Machk would not be back to bother us, and so, all night we watched. I do believe, when he wasn't watching, only Archie slept soundly that night. I could hardly get comfortable, though I had been sleeping on hard ground for days, and Ezekiel was the same, so we was all wrung out by morning and Archie was like a kid, so sure was he that our journey into freedom is blessed now by his Machk. I never thought my dear Archie a heathen before today, but maybe he is.

The killing heat of summer has broken, for this morning is fresh and cool. I feel a shiver, but I am pleased if we are not to roast again. I know not what season we are in; I lost my place in time so long ago, but Archie says August is ending now and we should be grateful the dry weather is holding. We break our fast and pack quickly, eager to get on. I think, perhaps, I am more convinced by Archie's words that no one will come 'til they start to worry about Silston not returning, but that damn bear has upset my mind and still I feel the fear of another posse. And so, we set off on the second day of our journey over the mountains.

Our way is hard, more of the same, beating our way through like we have for so long. Then, our luck changes, and Archie, spying a thinning of the trees, leads us to a rough path that winds its way through great columns of pine and fir that put me in mind of St Paul's cathedral and that reminds me of Will and brings me a few tears again. Roots wriggle across the track like the snakes Archie warned me about when I first met him, yet our progress is faster than before. Our way leads us on all day. 'Tis too wide for animals to have made it, so says Archie; he thinks it be made by those Haudenosaunee people. I know he tells us this to make us feel content and I do not feel scared, though they frightened me when we met them, I see that Millie and Zeke are not happy when they hear of our meeting with the hunting party and their savage looks.

So, our journey goes on and we rest again for the night. When we rise in the morning it is to find ourselves in fog. Archie is excited and reminds me that we saw this mist on the mountain heads from the other side of the Harding's valley. We must be nearing the 'tops', says he. It is damp and chilly and I find myself shivering until we get into the work of climbing again. It is impossible to know how time is going, for we cannot see where the lady sun is in her heaven. We do know, that even now, the still mist hangs around us like smoke, making our skin, hair, and clothes wet and cold. We talk little as we walk, but when we rest Archie always sits by me, close and comfortable, and we cast our futures in the air before us, excited about the freedoms we will be winning when we reach the other side.

*

It is raining. I welcome it, though it makes me uncomfortable, for I have not been dry since the fog came and the coarse fibre of my

406

clothes rubs, but the rain is cooling and freshens the air. It brings the smell of pine to me this early morning, a smell I knew not before Will. Somehow it brings me a clear head, like breathing an apothecary's vapour medicament for raising the spirit. With Archie now our leader and even Jem happy to follow, these woods feel good to me, welcoming and friendly. We still had our path until late yesterday, though 'twas narrower and winding then, and 'twas a pleasure to walk through the fresh wet forest.

We were still in fog in the morning today, but we knew we had reached the top, for since then we have been walking downhill, though our path has gone. Twice before, the mountain has fooled us into thinking we would see Shenandoah soon, but both times it was merely a trick. Now we are sure we are over the head of the mountain as we go down and down on slippery, wet, sloping ground, forcing us to lead our horses with care. Yesterday was the first time I walked all day and bore my proper load. I am renewed, ready for freedom and I think of Will often; his bag of precious tools is tied onto a saddle and I wish he was here to carry them himself.

The slope is not so steep here and our progress is easier. Millie walks in front of me with Zeke behind us. He is a good boy, I think, with a laugh that comes easy now we are coming close to Shenandoah. I could see he felt full of pride this morning when Archie asked him to walk last, guarding us. Archie is in front, leading a horse, with Jem bringing the second horse behind him. We stop for a rest and Archie sits with me. We have talked little of our friendship, but, with each day, I find myself more taken with his noble ways, his inner strength, and courage, his love for me, which he shows in his every glance. When we set out again, Zeke is allowed to take a horse and he puffs up like a cockerel, grinning and giggling. Jem leads now with Millie walking beside him. I walk with Archie and we let a small distance separate us from the rest.

"I bin thinking, Poll," says he without looking at me. "I never did think I'd be here, in these woods on the edge of the world. Never knew what I wanted fer my life, but it sure as hell weren't this."

He pauses and chuckles.

"That didn't sound right, Poll. Sorry now. I mean, I ain't unhappy. It's good I'm here with you. We ain't spoke much of our lives, but I know you had a hard start, like me. You tol't me 'bout Miss Abigail and I ain't never lived like you did there in that house; good clothes, good food, warm bed. An' I ain't never had a friend like Miss Abigail was to you."

"I loved her, Archie," I whisper.

"I guess you did, Poll. An' I know you don't have much trust fer men. I feel the same sometimes; they can be villains. But I try to be a good man…"

"Oh, Archie," says I. "I have learned that many men are frauds or violent or both and many men are little boys in men's clothing like poor Will, but few are evil. Silston was evil, I believe that with all my heart"

I take his hand then, for I think I know what he wants to say and I am surprised by the filling of my heart I feel. "You *are* a good man, Archie."

"Yeah, well." He squeezes my hand and glances at me. "I know you ain't never bin a farmer, Poll, and I ain't neither, but we got to make a try, ain't we? An' I think that Will, he was right. I think we can make it, 'cos, you see, I got a fine strong feeling for you, girl, an', if

408

the militia don't come fer us and them Iroquois don't kill us," he laughs, "I think we gonna be free and happy here. I never knowed much 'bout them black folk, but that Jem, he's a good man too, I wager. So, I think we got five good hearts and we got a chance now for freedom. Well, I guess that's all I got to say."

We have stopped walking and are facing each other. He has made his speech and now he looks at me strange. I think he is wondering if he's said too much. I look at his strong face, his high brow, and fine nose, his hair, thick and black as mine. I do not know what to say, for I do have feelings for this man, this good man. I put my hand flat on his chest and he lays his atop mine.

We stand like this for a moment and then he lifts my hand into his, pulls me to him, and puts his arms around me. 'Tis a good feeling, like a tasty food I've been missing for a long time. I put my arms about him and pat him on the back, unsure what to do or say next.

There is a shout and we break away fast, turn to look. Millie is running and I see that the others have stopped. I feel I am blushing for they must have been watching us, but they are turned away. Up ahead, there is a break in the trees, more light, more space. Archie and I hurry forward and join the others. We find ourselves standing on a small outcrop. From this point, we look out over a vast valley to more mountains in the hazy distance, purple and dark green and black. It has stopped raining and the sun is glimmering between thin clouds. Archie stands beside me, close enough that our bodies touch. Below, there is a great river that looks like a ribbon of light, throwing back the shine of the sun and there is a lush, welcoming land only a half a day's march away, the land called Freedom. Shenandoah.

Archie is grinning like he did after the bear. I think he must start to laugh again and he does. Jem takes it up and then the rest of us join them, laughing and hooting. At last, we are still, each of us in our own thoughts, and Jem says:

"Come on, let's get down there and build Will's house."

And Archie lets out a heathen whoop. Millie is giggling and Zeke is laughing again.

"Yes, Jem," says I, "let's go and build Will's house."

Epilogue

The first claim for land in the Shenandoah Valley was staked in 1727, six years after the arrival of Polly, Archie, Jem, Millie, and Ezekiel. No official record exists of the settlement established by the Burtonwood and Garland estate runaways until Archie registered their land in 1738.

A document written by Polly Staples, dated 1794 when she claimed to be ninety-three years old, charts her life story and that of her diverse family. She tells how she and her friends arrived in the Shenandoah Valley in 1721; how she took the surname Staples in honour of a friend who died en route to their new home; how the little party laboured over the first five years to clear and cultivate the land, build homes and establish a community.

Polly's memoire is an enduring testament to a family established from English, West African, and Algonquin origins, which blossomed during the rapid expansion of the Valley population in the 1730s and 40s. Polly died, surrounded by her children, grandchildren, and great-grandchildren, shortly before the dawn of the new century and is buried in the cemetery of the First Baptist Church at Taylor's Fork.

Acknowledgements

The making of this book has involved some wonderful people, each of whom has contributed something critical to its final form. Greatest thanks go to my generous readers, Sally Light, Anna O'Kennedy, Joan Nassim, and Ian Hagues.

Sally is always my first reader, willing to battle through the shoddiest initial draft and give me honest feedback and advice. So, to you, my dearest friend, unending thanks for your love, patience, continual support and encouragement through all my writing adventures and for helping me focus my storytelling efforts on whatever strengths I may have.

To Anna, thanks for your love and for giving Polly her own voice; without your advice, this would not even be half the book it is now. To Joan, thank you for your grammar chops, insightful suggestions, cheerful and well-thought-through advice, and for willing me on to success. To Ian, thanks for being my writing buddy, your sense of humour, and your cool, analytical approach to feedback.

Big thanks also to Wil Harvey, for reading a later draft of the manuscript and giving me your own hilarious brand of feedback and encouragement, and for your artistic eye and input in putting together the final, final cover illustration.

When I sent this work to agents, three suggested I use a writing consultant or workshop to help improve my manuscript. Thus, I found my way to Daniel Goldsmith Associates. I owe a debt of gratitude to Lorena Goldsmith for her guidance and good advice, and especially to editor Angel Belsey who did such a good job of helping me sharpen up the story and characters. My thanks go to both Lorena and Angel for believing in my work and for their kind encouragement.

This novel started with an idea that was seeded when, shortly after moving to the community in which Sally and I now live, I read a wonderful book, The Village Carpenter by Walter Rose (EP Publishing, 1973). Will Staples came into my mind almost fully formed; a young apprentice carpenter, recently made an orphan, wanting to go to London to better himself. I made notes and, in wrangling some ideas, Polly Pruitt emerged from her cocoon like a defiant, self-reliant butterfly.

Sometime later, I read Anthony Vaver's unsparing account, Bound with An Iron Chain: The Untold Story of How the British Transported 50,000 Convicts to Colonial America and I was shocked that I'd never known about the transportation of British convicts to the nascent North American colonies. I knew then that my narrative would take my protagonists to Virginia.

With further research, everything started to fall into place. The sources that provided the best learning and sparked many new ideas for the story include Encyclopedia Virginia (Published by Virginia Humanities In Partnership With Library Of Virginia); Indentured Servitude Unchained: White Slavery In America For Over 250 Years – Rainey & Rainey; Savage Kingdom: Virginia And The Founding Of English America – Benjamin Woolley (HarperCollins Publishers, New York, 2007); White Servitude In The Colony Of Virginia: A Study Of The System Of Indentured Labor In; The American Colonies – James Curtis Ballagh (Hanse Books, 2017).

Finally, early Georgian London came into sharp focus for me on reading the following excellent books and reference texts: London in the Eighteenth Century: A Great and Monstrous Thing – Jerry White (The Bodley Head); Children of the Poor in London 1700-1780 – Dianne E Payne: A thesis submitted in partial fulfillment of the requirements of the University of Hertfordshire for the degree of Doctor of Philosophy, 2008; A Listing of 18th Century Slang by Leon Bienkowski – (compiled from, in the main, Partridge's Dictionary of Slang and Unconventional English, Online, 2000).

Finally, my warmest thanks to anyone not mentioned here, but who kindly gave their time and thoughts to the project that turned into this finished novel.